ARTEMIS
INVADED

TOR BOOKS BY JANE LINDSKOLD

Through Wolf's Eyes

Wolf's Head, Wolf's Heart

The Dragon of Despair

Wolf Captured

Wolf Hunting

Wolf's Blood

The Buried Pyramid

Child of a Rainless Year

Thirteen Orphans

Nine Gates

Five Odd Honors

Artemis Awakening

Artemis Invaded

ARTEMIS INVADED

JANE LINDSKOLD

A TOM DOHERTY ASSOCIATES BOOK
NEW YORK

ARTEMIS INVADED

Copyright © 2015 by Obsidian Tiger, Inc.

All rights reserved.

A Tor Book
Published by Tom Doherty Associates, LLC
175 Fifth Avenue
New York, NY 10010

www.tor-forge.com

Tor® is a registered trademark of Tom Doherty Associates, LLC.

The Library of Congress Cataloging-in-Publication Data is available upon request.

ISBN 978-0-7653-3711-5 (hardcover)
ISBN 978-1-4668-3050-9 (e-book)

Tor books may be purchased for educational, business, or promotional use. For information
on bulk purchases, please contact the Macmillan Corporate and Premium Sales Department
at 1-800-221-7945, extension 5442, or write to specialmarkets@macmillan.com.

First Edition: June 2015

Printed in the United States of America

10 9 8 7 6 5 4 3 2 1

To Jim
Here we go again!

ACKNOWLEDGMENTS

Many, many thanks to . . .

My first readers: Julie Bartel, Sally Gwylan, Jim Moore, and Bobbi Wolf.

The team at Tor, especially my editor, Claire Eddy, and my publicist, Leah Withers.

My agent, Kay McCauley.

Julie Bartel and Rowan Derrick for helping me out with the complexities of social media. Special thanks to Rowan for designing the "What Would Your Profession Be?" quiz.

My husband, Jim Moore, because none of this would happen without his patient and perpetual support.

ARTEMIS
INVADED

I

Forbidden Areas

F orbidden,' you say? That sounds promising."

"Yes, I think it is. Look at this codex, Griffin. Maiden's Tear has been a forbidden area since before the slaughter of the seegnur and death of machines. There were other such prohibited zones, but they were not as absolutely off-limits as Maiden's Tear seems to have been."

Adara the Huntress looked to where two heads—one deep gold, the other a warm, dark brown—were bent with excited concentration over the map spread between them on the polished boards of the long table. Two heads, two men, two friends, both of herself and of each other.

Terrell, the dark-haired man, rubbed a hand against the bristles of the not-quite beard that usually adorned his face, even though he shaved at least twice a day.

"I asked, but couldn't find out much about the place," he continued. "Maiden's Tear was forbidden territory in the days of the seegnur. Since then, it has been shunned by our people." Terrell looked uncomfortable. "You see, Maiden's Tear was where many of the seegnur met their deaths."

"And not one loremaster has explored the area in the five hundred years since?" Griffin Dane asked incredulously. "Not one treasure hunter? I'd think they'd be eager."

"Not one who is admitting it," Terrell replied. "We of Artemis take prohibitions seriously. Some say obedience to the commands of the seegnur is bred into our bones."

Terrell shifted uncomfortably, his brilliant blue eyes looking away from Griffin. Adara knew why. Terrell had trained as a factotum, that ancient profession whose first duty had been to act as guides and advisors to the seegnur when they came to Artemis during those long-ago days when the planet had been the most exclusive and sought-after destination resort in all the empire. All who lived on Artemis knew that those halcyon days had ended some five hundred years ago with the slaughter of the seegnur and death of machines.

What only a few knew, Adara and Terrell among them, was that the catastrophe on Artemis had been the beginning of the end for an interstellar empire so vast that their planet in all its rich variety was by contrast less than the smallest spot on a frog's foot. All technology had not been shut down, as it had been on Artemis, but, even though ships still braved the dark oceans of the void, they were as leaf boats powered by a boy's breath to what had gone before.

Yet the end of the seegnur had not meant the professions created to serve them had become useless. Even today, the factotum's training was both wide and deep. Factotums knew how to set up a comfortable camp, no matter the surroundings; how to marshal mounts and servants; how to treat injuries. Additionally, they could advise their employers as how to best interact with the peoples of the various regions. Factotums were a font of trivia, not all of it useless. This eclectic training had kept the profession of high value, even after the seegnur ceased to visit Artemis.

What had only been rumored about the factotums was that, beneath their superficially normal appearance, the best of the profession were as adapted as any hunter or dive pro, reshaped on some unseen level, the better to serve the seegnur who had created Artemis and all upon it.

Not long before, Terrell had learned that this rumor held truth. Adara knew he still struggled with what he had learned, but his discomfort had not been enough to drive him away. Instead, thirteen days after the catastrophe that had ended with the vanishing of the Old One Who Is Young and the flooding of the complex the Old One had called his Sanctum Sanctorum, Terrell sat across the table from the man who had unsettled his world, planning the next stage in their journey.

Griffin, a tall man, golden-haired with warm brown eyes, his skin regaining the tan it had lost during his enforced residence in the Old One's subterranean complex, now rested a finger on their possible destination.

"If no one has been there, how do we know for certain whatever was there wasn't completely destroyed? It's a long trip to make for nothing."

"The lore says thus," Terrell began, his voice falling into the prescribed cadence. "After the slaughter of the seegnur and the departure of those who had slain them, a small band ventured into Maiden's Tear, for they felt that enough that had been prohibited—from flying craft to weapons that fired lightning—had been seen over the preceding few days to permit some bending of established regulations. When they returned, they reported that they had found no one alive in that place, not man, nor woman, nor child, not Artemesian nor seegnur. Following the rites for burial in such terrain, they had dealt with the corpses, so that these would not breed disease. As they had done so, they experienced great unease. Some heard ghostly voices speaking in the winds, warning them away. As soon as possible, they retreated.

"After, so says the lore, the members of this band admitted to great puzzlement as to why the seegnur had fled from Crystalaire, where they had been attending a wedding, to Maiden's Tear. The band had thought to find a fortification or even a weapons cache. All they had found was a single small structure. Although this structure was of exceedingly hard stone and appeared undamaged, it was not large enough to shelter more than a few adults. A mystery, then, and one not to be profaned by either professions or support. The original prohibition was declaimed again. Those who administered the region swore to maintain it until the seegnur should come again."

Terrell bowed his head briefly. When he next spoke, his voice had lost the cadence of lore. "Anyhow, that's what I heard about Maiden's Tear during my training. The same tale was repeated to me when I questioned the loremasters, both those based locally and those who have been pouring in to Spirit Bay ever since word of what happened here started spreading. It's likely a formal conclave will be held before long. I don't need to have the gift of foresight to know that the end result will be that the Old One's Sanctum Sanctorum—both the landing facility here on shore and the base out beneath Mender's Isle—will be declared off-limits."

Adara nodded. "I have heard similar rumors. Only the fact that the Old One Who Is Young established himself in Spirit Bay before any current resident was born will save the locals from being proscribed."

Griffin grinned. "That and the fact that if the loremasters condemned the residents of Spirit Bay, they would also need to condemn a considerable number of their own order. The Old One was very popular with many of the more liberal-minded loremasters, something they are all too eager to deny now that they cannot ignore the extent to which he violated the proscriptions."

Terrell nodded. "Although no one but ourselves and Bruin—and the Old One—know that you came from beyond the void and bear the seegnur's blood, still your tale of having been held captive by the Old One, especially combined with what was discovered after his Sanctum was flooded, has sorely injured his reputation."

Griffin returned his attention to the map. "So, unless I am willing to give up any chance of contacting my orbiter, I'm going to need to look elsewhere for remnants of the seegnur's technology. This forbidden area—haunted or not—seems my best bet. I know you two have said you would help me, but I don't want you to feel obligated. You've done so much for me already. I could ask the Trainers to suggest a guide . . ."

Adara tossed a cushion across the room that caught Griffin squarely in the face. "Seegnur," she replied with mock formality, "this huntress begs leave to travel with you." She laughed, her amber eyes dancing. "It's no longer about you and your desires, Griffin Dane. Both Terrell and I have our own reasons for wanting to know more about what the seegnur left behind. Since the slaughter of the seegnur and death of machines, the people of Artemis have lived in waiting.

Whether or not any of us asked for it, with your coming, that waiting has ended."

Terrell nodded. "She's right, Griffin. Matters have evolved beyond
hoping we will find some technology you can reactivate. We need to
know exactly what your coming has awakened."

Griffin went to bed that night thinking how lucky he was to have made
friends like Adara and Terrell. Stranded as he was on an isolated world
with no hope of rescue in the foreseeable future, he could have fared
much worse. He might have been buried in the landslide that put his
ruined shuttle permanently out of reach. He might have died in the
lingering winter of the mountain heights. He might have met up with
people inclined to react with fear, rather than with curiosity, toward
those who were different.

Instead, he had been rescued by Adara—slender but strong, quick
thinking if given to odd moments of self-doubt. He grinned to himself. And could he deny her beauty? Amber eyes that caught the light
like flame; long blue-black hair; sharp, fine-boned features. No . . . He
couldn't deny her beauty. He saw it even in the cat's-eyes pupils and
the claws her adapted nature let her form at the tips of her fingertips.
Someday, he hoped, Adara herself would learn to see her adaptations'
beauty, rather than considering only their usefulness.

Griffin was drifting off to sleep, cushioned by the warmth of these
thoughts, when the assassin came for him. Griffin didn't know exactly
what alerted him that something was wrong. Perhaps he heard some
sound his subconscious couldn't account for. Perhaps he felt the change
when the assassin's body momentarily blocked the flow of air from
the open window. Whatever warned him, Griffin opened his eyes in
time to see a darker figure against the darkness looming over his bed,
hand upraised.

Griffin rolled to one side, narrowly escaping the blow that struck
down where his head had been. As he dropped to the floor, he heard
a dull thud against his pillow.

Momentarily, Griffin considered shouting for help, but the thought died in mid-breath. They were staying in one of the outbuildings on the Trainers' property. A cry would surely bring help, but it might also awaken small children or some of the old folks to whom the Trainers gave a home. A yell would also surely alert the dogs—the Trainers had dozens.

Even as he put distance between himself and his attacker, Griffin realized that anyone who could sneak in through a compound over-run with guard dogs was very dangerous indeed. Therefore, instead of calling out, Griffin counterattacked, his body coming to the conclu-sion that this was the best course of action even before his thoughts had taken shape.

Griffin viewed himself as a scholar—a historian and archeologist—but the Danes were a warrior clan. In truth, Griffin had learned to fight hand to hand before he had learned to read. Right now he was seri-ously angry, every bad thing that had happened to him since his shut-tle had crashed boiling up and fusing until it was embodied in the figure seeking him in the darkness.

Surging up from the floor, Griffin struck for what his brother Alexander had humorously called the man's "vulneraballs." Either the man could see in the dark—Griffin had met those on Artemis who could—or he was just lucky, for he turned enough that Griffin's blow caught him on one thigh. When he staggered back a few paces, Griffin swung for his midsection. This time he landed a satisfying blow, and the man began to crumple.

Or so it seemed. Griffin was readying a knockout strike when his would-be assailant dropped, rolled, then rose in a graceful leap that carried him up and out the open window. Griffin listened for a crash or some other indication that the man had hit the ground but, if there was one, it was covered by the sudden baying chorus of howling dogs.

Griffin started to rush for the window, halted, and was making a more cautious approach when Terrell burst in, lit candle in hand, un-clad except for a pair of loose trousers barely secured around his waist.

"What the . . ." he was beginning to say when a slender figure darkened the window.

"What . . ." Adara began, but Griffin cut them both off.

"Someone attacked me. Left by the window. Do you . . ."

It was his turn to be cut off. Adara dropped from sight. Griffin knew that she and her demiurge, the puma Sand Shadow, would be looking for any trace of his attacker.

Terrell sighed and crossed to light the candle near Griffin's bed from his own. "If whoever came after you is to be found, Adara and Sand Shadow will find him. We'd better go tell the Trainers what has the dogs all stirred up."

A short time later, Griffin, Terrell, and Adara gathered in the single room that made up the ground floor of the small building they had been given to use by the Trainers. With them was Elaine Trainer. Her husband, Cedric, was still quieting the dogs.

"No one was hurt," Elaine said, taking the indicated chair, "although a couple of the guard dogs are suspiciously groggy. We're guessing they must have been darted, since they're trained not to take food from anyone who doesn't give specific commands. Whoever hit them had to estimate the dose and we're lucky they didn't make it too strong. The dogs were already coming around when Cedric found them."

"I'm so glad," Griffin said. "We've proven to be unlucky tenants for you."

"We knew you had enemies when we invited you to stay here. We're grateful that you aren't angry that you weren't better protected. We were sure the dogs would keep you safe."

"I don't blame the dogs," Griffin insisted. "I'm only sorry I didn't get the bastard."

"Tell us," Adara said from where she sat on the ledge of an open window, half in and half out, "what happened."

Griffin did, ending, "While you and Sand Shadow were trying to track the fellow, Terrell and I searched my room in case he dropped anything. We found this." He held up a neat cosh, leather sewn around lead shot. "Happens that I recognize it. It looks very much like one that belonged to Julyan."

"Julyan?" Elaine asked, seeing that the name meant something to her three guests.

"Julyan—once called Hunter," Adara said, her voice stiff with suppressed emotion. "He was a senior student with Bruin when I was in the middle of my own training. He left Shepherd's Call some years ago. I heard nothing of him until he resurfaced here in Spirit Bay as an assistant to the Old One Who Is Young, working on the secret base on Mender's Isle."

Griffin mentally filled in what Adara did not say. Julyan had also been Adara's lover and had thoroughly broken her heart. He'd also tried to kill her not long ago, but if Adara didn't care to talk about that . . . Still, he felt fairly certain that Elaine, her thin features as sharp and alert as one of her own greyhounds, guessed that something had been left out.

Griffin continued, "Julyan enforced the Old One's rule on Mender's Isle. He carried this cosh as a means of subduing without killing. I'd thought whoever came into my room meant to kill me, but now I wonder."

Terrell nodded. "Certainly, the Old One could want you dead. You know things about him that would ruin what little reputation he has left. Apparently, though, he may value you more alive."

Adara cut in. "Even if the cosh didn't point to Julyan, there's reason to think he might have been your attacker. His hunter's training would have given him the skills to slip in here unseen, to climb up to your window, even to drug the dogs, since part of our training includes techniques for taking prey alive. When Sand Shadow and I tried to trail your assailant, we had no luck. Julyan would have known how to blur his trail to fool even another hunter. Given the number of dogs here, especially the trained trackers, he certainly would have taken precautions to mask his scent in advance. Sand Shadow is checking outside the compound, but I'm guessing she will have no luck."

Elaine's disappointment showed. "We were going to suggest tracking with one of our hounds, since—excellent as she is in many things— Sand Shadow is not a scent hunter. If this Julyan was trained by Benji

Bear, though, then it's unlikely even one of our best could find him—
not if he took advance precautions."

"Julyan is a ruthless man," Terrell said. "It's best you and Cedric
not attract his attention any more than you must."

Griffin agreed. "We were lucky this time. I think we need to leave
Spirit Bay soon, before anyone else gets drawn into our troubles. Next
time someone might get hurt. We may be in as much danger on the
road, but there, at least, we won't involve the innocent."

"I think we'll be in less danger on the road," Adara said. "In the
wilds, Sand Shadow and I are much more in our element. It will be
far harder for anyone to sneak up on us."

Elaine looked torn between protest and reluctant relief. "But where
will you go? Back to Shepherd's Call? To where your friend Lynn took
those you freed from Mender's Isle?"

Griffin hesitated, wondering how much to tell. Terrell spoke with
absolute confidence. "Best you not know, Elaine. Best for all of us, if
you don't know."

"You failed . . . No matter. Capturing Griffin was a long shot at best."

Julyan wanted to protest, wanted to point out that he'd gotten past
all those damn dogs, gotten right into the room with Griffin, that even
with Griffin waking up unexpectedly as he had, he would have managed. Who could have known that the man was a trained fighter? Griffin had shown no sign of being anything but docile during the twenty
or so days he had resided against his will in the complex beneath
Mender's Isle.

Julyan wanted to say, "I did perfectly what I set out to do. How
could I know a lapdog would turn out to be a mastiff?"

But he didn't. There was a mocking expression in the Old One's cool
grey eyes that forbore protest, which made Julyan feel certain that
his explanations would be dismissed as excuses.

"We're not giving up, are we?"

The Old One gave a thin smile. "We are not, although I think it
wisest if we delay. All the indications are that Griffin and his escort

will soon leave Spirit Bay. I have some idea where they might be headed."

"Where?"

"Crystalaire, or rather, somewhere in the vicinity of Crystalaire."

Julyan searched his memory. The name made him uneasy. In a moment, he remembered why. "That's where many of the seegnur were gathered when the attack came, isn't it? There was a wedding. Those who were not slaughtered outright fled for the hills. They died, just the same."

The Old One nodded. "There is a prohibited area near Crystalaire called Maiden's Tear. Both historians and loremasters have speculated that the seegnur fled there because they believed something in the vicinity would help them against their enemies. No one knows what, but clearly they did not find it—or perhaps they did not have time to find it."

Holding back an instinctive shudder, Julyan asked, "But why do you think Griffin and the others will be going there?"

"Because Griffin Dane is searching for remnants of the seegnur's technology. That is what brought him to my Sanctum at Spirit Bay. He doesn't desire mere relics, such as are in any loremaster's museum, but more or less undamaged machines. As with my former home, there is little evidence that the widespread destructive measures employed elsewhere were used in Maiden's Tear—even though they were used freely in the town of Crystalaire itself. Where the hotel stood—the one in which the wedding was being held—there is nothing but a crater."

"Nasty . . ." Julyan said.

"I still have friends among the loremasters. Fewer, true, but there are those who continue to revere my knowledge. From these, I have learned what maps and archives Terrell the Factotum has consulted. The evidence confirms my conjecture."

Or you conjecture based on that evidence, Julyan thought. *You still long to be thought wiser than any other, despite your recent failure.*

He glanced quickly at the Old One. He didn't believe the Old One Who Is Young could read minds, but a man did not live as long as the

Old One had without learning to read people as easily as some men read print.

Julyan wondered that he could fear a man as much as he did the Old One. The Old One was small and neatly built. There was something fussy in how he had trimmed his pale blond hair every few days, so that the short cut remained similar to those shown in representations of the seegnur. When the Old One had dwelt in his Sanctum, he had affected clothing that evoked the seegnur. Although now he was a fugitive and had adopted attire that would not excite comment, he remained meticulous in matters of grooming.

The Old One looked like the sort of man Julyan—large, strong, in perfect condition—could break with one hand, but Julyan knew from experience that the Old One could throw him across the room.

Yet that is not why I fear him . . . Even when I doubt he knows as much as he claims, I am continually uneasy. I know—few better— how he uses those around him. I am useful to him, so he treats me well, but I have seen him step on others with as little concern as I might step on an ant. Even now, unwelcome where once he was re- vered almost as a king, exiled from his home, I cannot help but feel the Old One remains a power in the land—perhaps in this whole vast world. Certainly his facility beneath Mender's Isle shows that his ambitions are unlimited by more normal concerns.

The Old One's research had led him to conclude that the seegnur's technology had possessed an incorporeal element, that the most sophisticated devices had not been controlled by switches or levers or push pads, but by thought. He had also believed that the adapted might hold in their genes the ability to breed those who could use the seegnur's devices. Implied in this theory was the idea that those systems had not been completely disabled by the attackers, as had always been held by the lore, but that, with the right operators, it could be made to work again. The Old One had set about to create those operators—and had resorted to imprisonment, rape, murder, and other atrocities even without any certainty that he would achieve his goals.

The Old One gave no sign of following Julyan's thoughts, only said mildly, "You will come with me?"

Julyan nodded. "If my reward will be as you promised. I get you Griffin. You give me Adara."

"I promise." The Old One's smile was thin-lipped and cruel. "Griffin has proven solid bait to lure Adara the Huntress in the past. I will get her for you—and deliver her to you better than a captive. With Griffin in my hands, I will have the means of making Adara your willing slave."

Well, this will be a journey through the maze of memories, Adara reflected, as she checked the condition of their saddlebags and related tack.

Molly, the pale red chestnut mare who was Griffin's mount, hung her head over the half-door out into the paddock, supervising Adara's preparations. Beyond her, Tarnish, Adara's own smoky grey roan gelding, and Midnight, Terrell's black gelding, were methodically ripping hay from a rack, as if aware the slow, easy days were coming to an end.

First, Julyan, now . . . I wonder if Terrell realized that the route he has suggested will take us through Ridgewood, where my family lives? I can't remember if I ever told him where I grew up. Probably not, since I have lived with Bruin since I was five and Shepherd's Call is home. That's the problem with traveling into the mountains. Unless you're willing to go by more difficult routes, everything narrows down to a few passes.

I could suggest an alternate route, but that would mean explaining why I don't want to go through Ridgewood . . . And that would mean admitting just how insecure I am when it comes to my family. I'm woman grown now, an official huntress. Surely, I can face . . .

Adara's memories of her early childhood were scattered and diffuse. Her family had farmed and herded sheep. Adara was the second child of five. Initially, she had suffered no more than any younger child with a talented older sibling but, eventually, she had come to realize that the differences between her and the other children were more than age.

I could see in the dark, Adara remembered. *All the other children were afraid of the dark, but I wasn't. What was there to fear? I was as afraid as anyone else of the creatures who came to prey on our flocks, but of the darkness itself? I liked it. It hid me, protected me, allowed me to sneak away . . .*

With her more adult perspective, Adara contemplated the child she had been. *I suppose I was a nuisance. I think I knew it even then. Was that why I was so certain—no matter what my parents said when they sent me to Bruin—that they were getting rid of me? Because I knew I'd been bad?*

"What," asked a voice inside Adara's head, "is 'bad'?"

Adara jumped, startled enough that she nearly dropped the harness she had been inspecting. Thirteen days was not enough time to get used to someone reading your mind. It *was* enough time to learn that ignoring the fact didn't do much good—especially when your new friend was the very planet upon which you lived.

The huntress was still not completely certain what had awakened the planet Artemis from the long sleep that had come with the slaughter of the seegnur and death of machines. She did not think that Artemis was a machine, precisely. Perhaps that was why Artemis had slept when so much else had died.

Or maybe more will awaken. Adara shivered at the unsettling notion.

"Bad..." Adara shaped the words inside her head—at least her relationship with Sand Shadow had been good training for this sort of communication. She'd long ago learned not to talk out loud to herself. "You certainly don't ask easy questions, do you? Bad is the opposite of good. And good is, well... Good is what is optimal for a given situation."

The not-voice sounded puzzled. "So bad is the least preferred choice for a given situation? Therefore, when you think how you-the-child were bad, you were not acting according to what was preferable? Why would you have done that?"

Adara sighed. "It's not quite that simple. The child me was acting according to what I wanted to do—what was preferable for me. But I knew that what I was doing wasn't what my parents would have liked—so, to them,

my good was bad. Since I knew I was behaving in a way that might be fun
for me at that moment, but that might have consequences that wouldn't
be so much fun later, I knew I was being bad, even when what I was doing
seemed good. Does that help?"

"No." The word was accompanied by an image of bubbles rising to
the surface of the water, then slowly popping, one by one. "Yes. Maybe.
What is good. What is bad. These are not precise. What is good for the owl
is bad for the mouse. What is good for the wet is not good for the dry."

"Something like that," Adara agreed. "But a lot more complicated."

"Ah…" And just as suddenly as it had manifested, the sense of another presence faded away.

One of these days, Adara thought, *I'll have to teach her social
conventions like "hello" and "good-bye." Maybe I'll even manage
to explain that it's not polite to probe someone else's mind, especially
when they can't return the favor.*

She remembered some of the dreams she had experienced as Artemis learned to touch her mind. They had been bizarre precisely because they were filtered through a sensibility that didn't find the images
bizarre at all. Adara had talked a little with Griffin and Terrell about
their nascent telepathic link. Once the two men had accepted that their
minds were able to communicate when they were asleep—thus far
they had not managed any contact when awake—then the communication had not been all that different from what Adara shared with
her demiurge, Sand Shadow: images augmented by an occasional word.

Communication with Artemis was easier than communication with
Sand Shadow in that the neural network—as Artemis had initially
identified herself—understood words and used them easily. However,
it was complicated because, compared to Artemis, the way Sand Shadow
thought was positively human. Sand Shadow hadn't needed to have
good and bad explained to her. The puma had understood the concepts in a very basic fashion: bad was what got you hurt; good was
what got you fed. The intricacies of different bads and goods could be
presented as variations on a theme.

Since Artemis did not really understand hurt or hunger or desire
or any of the dozens of impulses, named and nameless, that drove other

living things, Adara was discovering that she must start from a different foundation.

Foundation? Adara laughed softly to herself. *More as if I must mold the bricks to make the foundation before I can even build a foundation. Still, Artemis is rather sweet in her strange way. I'm not going to push her away while she learns to toddle about in the dark.*

⚜

They left Spirit Bay two days after the attack on Griffin. By Artemesian standards, they were a group of eight: three humans, three horses, one mule, and Sand Shadow, the puma.

Initially, Griffin had found this manner of reckoning very odd.

Sand Shadow was certainly an extraordinary individual. Not only could the puma communicate mind to mind with Adara, she had been adapted so that her front paws possessed rudimentary fingers and thumb. The earrings of which the puma was so obviously proud had originally been meant to help her train in finer manipulation of those digits. Sand Shadow might not be as intelligent as a human—but if she wasn't, Griffin wasn't going to be the one to say so.

The three horses—Tarnish, Molly, and Midnight—were not adapted, although they were specially trained and would tolerate a puma as a companion. Sam the Mule was as ornery as any of his kind, but his strength and tenacity made him a valued addition. He was trained to carry a rider, as well as baggage, so could serve as a stand-by mount if any of the other three needed a respite.

Although, Griffin thought, *Sam would have some say as to who his rider would be. If Tarnish or Molly couldn't carry a rider, then I'm guessing Terrell would turn Midnight over to one of us and ride Sam. Sam might be trained to carry a rider—as long as that rider is Terrell.*

Although they had left Spirit Bay somewhat shorter of supplies than they had intended, neither Terrell nor Adara seemed particularly concerned.

"We're past the thin times of spring," Adara explained, "and will be traveling through the low lands for a good number of days before we go into the mountains again."

She gave Griffin an impish smile. "We kept you well enough fed during harder times, seegnur. We might even fatten you up before we reach Crystalaire."

"And there are any number of small villages where we can stop if we find we forgot something vital," Terrell added.

"I noticed those on the map," Griffin commented, shifting his rump in the saddle, earning a critical look from Molly. "I thought that Artemis was supposed to be mostly pristine wilderness. From orbit it still appeared to be so, but this area seems well settled."

"Remember, Griffin," Terrell said. "Five hundred years have passed since the days of which you speak. Although we of Artemis have tried to live as if the seegnur might return any day, when it comes to our survival—well, we've had to make some changes. Even in the days of the seegnur, there were areas given over to the raising of crops and food animals. Most of these were sequestered where they would not interfere with the sports and entertainments that brought the seegnur here. I suspect—heresy though some would have it—that the seegnur used their technology to make sure that picturesque villages in outlying areas were kept supplied."

Griffin nodded. "And without that technology those supplies wouldn't arrive . . . Yes. I can see why things needed to change if the population was to survive. Were many areas abandoned?"

"Some," Terrell agreed. "Especially those that existed mostly to provide a stopping point along the way to some particularly isolated spot. Others lost population. Crystalaire, for example, was a renowned beauty spot, one where the seegnur who came to Artemis to partake in strenuous sport could leave more delicate companions. In those days, Crystalaire supported several very fine hotels and restaurants, as well as a fleet of pleasure boats and like amenities. Today, there is one hotel. Although the views are still magnificent, the reason the area remains settled is because the lake offers excellent fishing. Fish and timber are the basis of the local economy, not the views."

"Not all settlements declined," Adara added. "Shepherd's Call, for example, was smaller in the days of the seegnur. Then it was little more than a stopping point for those who wished to hunt and ski in the mountains—or try the rapids on the river. Today, we support ourselves and supplement what we cannot grow by trading—mostly wool, but also hides and furs."

"Don't forget, Adara," Terrell said. "Another reason that Shepherd's Call has done so well is that it boasts not one but two professionals: your own teacher, Bruin, and Helena the Equestrian, with whom I was studying. People come from great distances to learn from them or—in Helena's case—to arrange for her to train a mount or to buy one of her protégés."

"Like our horses—and Sam," Griffin added, patting Molly on one reddish-gold shoulder "I'm certainly grateful Helena let us take them. Without Molly, I wouldn't be much of a rider."

Adara laughed. "Even with Molly, you aren't much of a rider, but you are improving. While we're traveling, I'd like you to ride Tarnish for a few hours at a time. He's more patient than Midnight. Molly's so well behaved you're not going to expand your skill—and there may come a time when you need to ride without a coach."

These first days of their journey were very pleasant. As Adara had promised, the hunting—even in settled areas—was very good. Often she and Sand Shadow would leave for long stretches, returning with a brace of rabbits or game birds. Sometimes she left the hunting to Sand Shadow, and picked berries or gathered wild greens.

"Is Adara safe out there alone?" Griffin asked Terrell one day when the huntress was later than usual rejoining them. "We do have enemies."

"She's safer out there"—Terrell waved a long arm to indicate the rolling green that surrounded them—"than we are here on the road. We're much easier to find. Still, I have a feeling that even we are safe for now. The Old One and Julyan took a chance at grabbing you in Spirit Bay, where I'm guessing they had a bolt hole or two. My guess is they're watching us, waiting to see where we go and what we learn. You've found some interesting things in the past, seegnur. The Old One will not have forgotten that."

"Watching us?" Griffin looked around nervously, causing Tarnish to snort and crow hop a few paces to remind Griffin of his place.

"Tracking us, rather," Terrell said. "They'll ask about us along the road. By now, I wouldn't be surprised if the Old One has a pretty fair idea where we're headed. There aren't many reasons for us to head this way—not unless he thinks Adara wants to introduce us to her parents."

He chuckled at Griffin's open astonishment. "That's right, you wouldn't know and Adara certainly wouldn't tell you. Her parents are settled on the outskirts of Ridgewood, a town right along our route. In addition to food, they raise sheep, llamas, and alpacas. Adara's mother has some fame as a weaver. These days, I'd say much of the family's income comes from selling exotic wool blends and the products of her loom."

"You sound," Griffin said, aware that a certain stiffness had entered his voice, "as if you did some research."

Adara was the one problem in his relationship with Terrell. Rather, it was Adara the woman—rather than Adara the Huntress, the companion along the road, and the friend—who was the problem. Adara had been the first person Griffin had met after his shuttle had crashed, stranding him on Artemis. She had been his protector and guide. They had shared a tent in the cold reaches of the mountains, nearly died together in an avalanche. All of this would probably have been enough to create a bond—even if his rescuer had been big, burly Bruin, rather than lithe, lovely Adara.

But his rescuer had been Adara. At first, Griffin had thought Adara might have been interested in him as a man, even as he couldn't help but be interested in her as a woman. However, she had not encouraged him. Was this because of Terrell? From a few scattered comments, Griffin suspected the two had been lovers—if only briefly. Certainly, Terrell remained interested. The two men's dreams did not touch as often as they had when Griffin had been a captive and Terrell his lifeline, but there were hints, images, some of them astonishingly erotic.

So now Griffin looked over at Terrell and repeated his statement, inflecting it into a question. "You sound as if you did some research."

Terrell gave a rueful smile. "I won't deny it. There can be few secrets between us, seegnur. Before you plummeted out of the skies, I was doing my best to convince Adara to marry me—or if she wouldn't marry, then to at least consider me as a serious suitor. She wasn't encouraging—but she wasn't sending me away, either. Then you arrived and, well . . . We both know how the world has spun since."

Griffin bit back the question he wanted to ask—although he wasn't sure he wanted the answer. *Are you sleeping with her?* Instead he managed a casual shrug.

"Adara has made clear that she's not interested in courting games."

Terrell nodded. "Julyan resurfacing isn't going to make matters any easier. I'd hoped he'd drowned."

Griffin agreed. He'd gotten to know Julyan fairly well, enough to understand how charming he could be—and how utterly ruthless. The charm made it easy for Griffin to understand why Adara had fallen in love with Julyan, back when they both had been Bruin's students. It was harder for him to understand what emotions Julyan awakened in her now. Did she still love him? Hate him? Feel something else entirely?

He decided to pretend that what Adara felt didn't matter but, looking at the flash of Terrell's white teeth, he knew he hadn't fooled anyone, most especially himself.

Interlude: Not Absolute

Bad, Good
Good, Right
Right, Left
Left, Abandoned
Abandoned, Wild
Wild, Uncontrolled
Uncontrolled
Bad? Good?

2

Ridgewood

When they were a few hours' ride out from Ridgewood, Adara slipped from Tarnish's saddle and handed the reins to Griffin. "Sand Shadow and I will go ahead. I'll find out if there is room for us at my parents' farm and, if not, where we can set up our tents."

She saw Griffin glance at Tarnish, obviously wondering why she didn't continue riding, then, as obviously, answering the question for himself. Adara slipped away without offering confirmation.

So Griffin's figured out I'm nervous, that I'd like to be able to sneak in and check the place out first. What of it? My home is elsewhere now. Wouldn't it be rude of me to assume my parents could take me and my friends in at such short notice? True, once I knew our route, I did write ahead to warn them, but . . .

Sand Shadow flicked Adara an image of the two of them skulking in enemy-filled darkness through the maze of passages beneath Mender's Isle. Even without words, the inference was obvious: "You did that. Surely you have nothing to fear here."

"Are you so certain?" Adara muttered. "The Old One's minions could only kill me. The blows family deal out can cut into the soul."

Sand Shadow huffed in exasperation. During the year and a few months since they had bonded, they had visited Adara's family only once, and that briefly. They had gone for the wedding of Adara's younger brother, Orion, to the daughter of an itinerant river trader who had thought settling down on a farm would be ever so much nicer than living on a boat. Using the puma kitten as an excuse, Adara might not have even attended the wedding, but Bruin had insisted.

The puma's memories of the event were the enjoyable ones of a kitten who had been much fussed over. Adara's were less so. She also had been fussed over—both for having passed her training and for having bonded with Sand Shadow. However, that fuss had reminded her once again how she was set apart from her family. Nikole was married and had little ones of her own. Hektor and Elektra had come in for quite a lot of teasing about when would their weddings be . . . No one had teased her.

I felt myself a stranger. Many of those attending the wedding had never been farther than Spirit Bay; most had never been even that far. Most followed some variation on the work done by their parents and grandparents, back to the days of the seegnur. I was a huntress.

Had lingering memories of the events surrounding Orion's wedding led Adara to that imprudent tumble with Terrell the following midsummer? Had she been seeking proof that she was marriageable, even if she chose not to marry?

She shoved those thoughts away, concentrating on circling back and around the village, on finding cover where any but a hunter would have sworn there was none. In time, she came to her family's holding, out some distance from the village itself. She swarmed up a tree. Those dots on the road would be Terrell, Griffin, and the mounts. They would need to thread through the village, so she still had time, although wending through memories had slowed her feet.

Sending Sand Shadow an image to wait for her—her family's livestock would not be acclimated to the scent of a puma as were the animals who resided near Shepherd's Call—Adara loped down the hillside to the sprawling farmhouse she barely remembered as "home." A sheepdog barked, more in warning than in threat. At the dog's summons, a figure stepped out the back door to see what had roused the creature. For a moment, Adara didn't know him, then he turned slightly and the lines of cheek and jaw were familiar.

"Hey, there, Hektor," she greeted her youngest brother. "You've grown again."

Hektor—now, Adara scrabbled through her memory, seventeen?—knew her right away. "Adara!"

His pleasure at seeing her was so obvious that Adara felt ashamed of her snake pit mind. This was the brother born after she had gone to live with Bruin, yet he treated her arrival as a cause for celebration.

Hektor stuck his head inside the door. "Mom! Dad! Adara's come at last!"

The patter of feet on wooden floorboards, a flooding out, arms and hugs and kisses. Her mother, Neenay Weaver, grabbing her, holding her as if she were still five, and not half a head again taller.

"We'd heard something of what happened in Spirit Bay, even before your letter came. We heard you were involved. Willowee's father brought news, turned his boat right around as soon as rumor reached him at one of the river ports."

Adara's father, Akilles, tall and lean like her, hair dark as her own, though showing silver now. (Had that all come on since the wedding?) Wordless except for the hug he gave her and the brightness of tears in his eyes. Sister Nikole, baby on her hip, a toddler by the hand, grin brightening her face. Little Elektra, budding into womanhood, unsure in her young woman's dignity whether to join in or stand back. Orion, holding his Willowee by the hand.

When the tumult ebbed, Adara asked her mother, "I wrote that I am traveling with two friends. We have three horses and a mule as well. Is there room for us?"

"Plenty." Neenay gave a casual wave of her hand. "You know we built a cottage for Nikole and Stanis when the babies came. None of us could sleep for all the fussing. We just finished a cottage for Orion and Willowee . . ."

Adara noticed for the first time that her brother's wife was rounding out in front.

"Folks in Ridgewood are saying we should rename the area Weaverville," Hektor cut in with a chuckle.

"So there's plenty of room in the main house for you and your friends. We had good moisture last winter, so you can put your animals to pasture. There's space in the stables, too. Your choice."

Elektra said, "Did you bring the kitten?"

Adara smiled. "Cat now and a big one, too. Yes. Sand Shadow is with me, but she's staying out in the hills for now. Her scent frightens livestock who don't know her."

Elektra's eyes asked a question she was too uncertain to ask. Adara answered it.

"Would you like to greet her? She's been wondering if anyone remembers her. She remembers all of you with great fondness."

"Can I? See her, I mean? And do you really know what she remembers?"

Adara felt that alienating uncertainty again, determinedly pushed it away. "I don't know everything she thinks, but we've been practicing. I know enough to know she remembers her visit here and being fussed over. She understands that she'd scare all the hens and cows, so she's fine with staying in the hills, but I'm sure she'd like a visit."

An image from Sand Shadow flickered into her mind: Terrell and Griffin passing through Ridgewood, turning onto the road toward her family's lands.

"I should go down the road and meet my friends," Adara continued.

"Can I come with you?" Elektra asked, glancing between her mother and Adara.

"Can she?" Adara asked.

Neenay smiled. "I think we can handle clearing up from supper without you, Elektra, but mind that you make up for it tomorrow, understand?"

"Yes, ma'am," answered both sisters at once, then giggled as if they weren't ten years apart in age and nearly strangers.

Not surprisingly, Terrell and Griffin were a great hit. True, Nikole did give Adara a long look or two, as if wondering what games her sister was playing with two such handsome fellows, but both men had the gift of making themselves pleasant. Griffin was introduced by the tale they had evolved when they had stayed with the Old One. He was a member of a family who had lived isolated in the mountains somewhere vaguely near Shepherd's Call. They had become friends when Terrell and Adara had escorted him to Spirit Bay because he had desired to meet the Old One.

Questions regarding the upheaval in Spirit Bay—the flooding of the Old One's Sanctum and that revered personage's disappearance—were so based on garbled rumors that answering them was easy enough without going into uncomfortable details. When some element of the conversation became awkward, Terrell showed a factotum's gift for turning the discussion in other directions while appearing to give a complete reply. The full truth would mean explaining too much that must be kept secret, including Griffin's true origin and the existence of the unfortunates who had been born as a result of the Old One's experimentation.

When, toward the end of evening, Neenay Weaver beckoned for Adara to come with her, Griffin was deep in conversation with Akilles, Willowee, and Orion about the manner in which this region was governed. Willowee, who had grown up on one or another of her family's watercraft, proved to have a sophisticated view of the differences of rulership in theory and in practice.

Terrell held the rest spellbound with tales of his travels as he had trained to be a factotum. Watching her littlest sister, Adara wondered if Elektra—like Sashi in Shepherd's Call—was counting through the months until she would be fifteen and of legal age to propose marriage.

"I'm taking Adara out to show her what we've done since she was last here," Neenay called. "We'll shut up the hens while we're out."

Adara suspected that Neenay was taking this opportunity to probe after which—if either—of the young men might be a candidate for future son-in-law. The grin that quirked Hektor's mouth and a knowing look on Nikole's face confirmed her guess. However, when they were safely away, and Neenay had led Adara to the pleasant, well-lit building that was her new workshop, Neenay surprised her.

"Adara, the time has come for me to tell you things I hoped I would never need to raise."

Adara was about to explain that she understood where babies came from and that she knew to take precautions, when Neenay went on.

"I never told you why we fostered you with Benjamin Hunter. However, now that the Old One has been discredited I feel I must. Why don't you sit there?" Neenay gestured to a heap of cushions patch-worked from what must be scraps of her own weaving. "I'm more comfortable behind my loom."

She slid into the chair, and her hands began moving the shuttle and the beater bar through their routine with a practiced rattle and thump.

Adara thought, *Putting a wall between us again, even if the wall is only spun wool. But what is this about the Old One?*

As if reading her daughter's mind, Neenay said, "Would you be surprised if I told you that the Old One tried to play matchmaker for me, some years before you were born?"

Adara made no attempt to hide her astonishment. "You knew the Old One?"

"I did. When I was about Elektra's age, my parents sent me to Spirit Bay to stay with my mother's older sister. Auntie had a shop there—still does—that specialized in exotic dyes as well as weaving. I was among her students. The Old One was one of her customers, for he loved the subtle colors she blended. Indeed, he often brought her oddities—fresh shellfish, peculiar nuts, exotic flowers. They would discuss for as much as a half hour at a time how a certain color might be extracted and the best way to fix it."

Neenay sighed, her gaze distant, her fingers moving as if they had eyes of their own. "Given your recent experiences, I don't expect you to believe me but, for those of us who worked in the shop, those visits were like visits from a king. The girls in particular could get quite silly, for the Old One was—I suppose 'is,' for he doesn't change—very hand-some in his own way. His slim build and measured manner were quite a contrast to the farm boys most of us had grown up with. He was even grander than the rich tradesmen who came to buy my aunt's cloth."

Adara reassured her. "The Old One is not my type, but, yes, I be-lieve you. He can be very compelling."

Neenay's lips shaped a small smile of gratitude. "The Old One was not my type either but, nonetheless, I was flattered to be among the small circle he chose to talk with from time to time. One day, he brought with him a young sailor, a handsome fellow with raven-dark hair and light brown eyes. This Jor asked me to go dancing with him that evening. He was quite flattering in his attentions for the few days he was in town, before his ship sailed again."

Adara felt dread rise, making her heart flutter. As if in answer to her apprehension, Sand Shadow leapt in through the open window and settled at her side.

Burying her hand in the puma's plushy fur, Adara asked, "Do you mind her here? She circled to avoid the flocks."

Neenay shook her head. "She *has* grown, hasn't she? No. I don't mind. Now, let me go on . . . While Jor was off to sea, the Old One came by the shop. He found some pretext to get me alone, then asked me what I thought of his young friend. I said I liked Jor well enough and that seemed to please him.

"The Old One hinted that he would smile upon our making a match, that he might even take an interest in our children—arrange for their education and suchlike. I wasn't at all certain I wanted to wed a sailor—they're gone so often—but Jor was in port often and it was fun to go about with him. He was a free spender, though somehow I gathered that the Old One helped line his pockets.

"I might even have married Jor—my aunt was pleased with my work and hinted that someday I might become her partner. That would make staying in Spirit Bay more inviting. However, fate had strung my loom with other threads. During one of his visits, Jor brought with him his cousin—Akilles was his name. They were much alike in appearance, but as unalike in temper as whirlwind and a hearth fire. Since you are Akilles's daughter, you know which lad I wed.

"Jor eventually married one of the other girls from the shop. The Old One lost interest in me as soon as my preference for Akilles was known, but he remained very interested in Blithe and Jor. Even after I had moved to Ridgewood with Akilles, Blithe and I corresponded. She had her first child about the same time I had Nikole, her second a year later.

"Now I must skip a few years. Jor was lost at sea when you were about two. However, the Old One continued his patronage of Blithe. He was very interested in the children, especially the second, a boy who showed some signs of being adapted. The Old One offered to adopt the boy. Blithe refused. The Old One offered to send the boy to a special school he had founded for adapted children. She refused this also. Then the boy vanished—apparently drowned, although from birth he had swum like a fish.

"Blithe was not stupid and she had a weaver's mind for patterns. When she learned that other children had disappeared, other children in whom the Old One had shown an interest, she grew nervous. She grew more nervous when she learned that no one seemed to know anything about his special school. Soon after Blithe, too, vanished, along with her older child.

"Most people accepted the story that Blithe had moved to be away from the seas that had taken both her husband and her son. I said nothing but, based on her letters, I think she was either killed by the Old One or given a chance to be with her son if she agreed to cut off all contact with the outside world.

"When you, Adara, showed signs of being adapted, I hoped no one would notice. You, however, were a determined little thing. There was no keeping you in if you wanted out—and you would insist on roaming about after dark. The bias against the adapted is not strong in Ridgewood. We are too close to those areas like Spirit Bay and Crystalaire that the seegnur frequented, and the seegnur favored the adapted. But I feared for you. What if the Old One took an interest in you? Would you, too, vanish?

"I confided in Akilles, showed him Blithe's letters. Though it broke our hearts to do so, we decided the best way to protect you was to hide you in plain sight. Bruin trained hunters. Far from being biased against the adapted, he was adapted himself. Moreover, we learned that he protected his students as closely a mother bear does her cubs. If you could be safe anywhere, you would be safe there."

"But," Adara protested, "Bruin was the Old One's own student. He revered him."

"That is what we meant by hiding you in plain sight. In Bruin's care, the Old One would know of you, but he would also know that he could not touch you without risking alienating one of his most prestigious and well-known followers—a man who was known for teaching and protecting the adapted."

"I see." Adara fell silent, feeling reality as she had always known it shifting and reshaping. "You never told me."

Neenay shook her head. "We couldn't, because Bruin *was* the Old One's follower. We had no proof, only suspicions."

"You cut me off," Adara said, not able to rid herself of her lifelong belief.

"Did we?" Neenay smiled sadly, her fingers wrapping around the shuttle. "Did you see matters that way? We felt you cut us off. Since we needed you to bond with Bruin, for him to be your protector, we accepted this, but always with sorrow."

Adara pressed her face into her hands. Her voice muffled, she said, "I . . . I'm glad you told me. I only wish . . . But I see . . . Yes."

Surging to her feet, she crossed the room in what seemed to be one step and found Neenay on her feet, arms open wide.

"Mother!"

"My little girl . . . Welcome home. Welcome home."

Something happened between Adara and her mother, Griffin thought, *something that has cleared the air considerably. I'm glad. Adara was so tense on our way here. It's good to have that gone, now that we're leaving.*

After several days at Adara's family home, during which time they had completed laying in needed provisions and updating their information about the region, the three had set out in the direction of Crystalaire.

"At least the road is a good one," Terrell said as he guided Midnight to point. "Since Crystalaire was regarded as a major resort, not just a stopover, the road was designed to accommodate heavier traffic."

As so often, Griffin found that his expectations for a "good" road and those of the Artemesians differed markedly. True, this road was often wide enough for them to ride three abreast, with Sam ambling behind. However, although the surface was graveled, it was not paved. Deep ruts had been cut by hundreds of years of coach travel. Since axle sizes were standardized—a tradition dating back to the days of the seegnur—the ruts provided tracks though which wheeled traffic rolled.

The road bed, drainage ditches, and rest stops were piously maintained by local governments who collected tolls for the purpose. Griffin thought these groups must surely see the advantages of good roads to modern trade, but every tax and toll collector loudly proclaimed their labors as demonstrations of fidelity to the wishes of the absent seegnur.

Although they could have joined a larger group or hired bodyguards—something they were encouraged to do at several points along the way—they decided against it. The fewer people Griffin interacted with, the better, since he was still inclined to be curiously ignorant about the most routine things. Then there was the problem of Sand Shadow's effect on domestic animals, most of whom were convinced she intended to eat them at the first opportunity.

"Besides," Adara said, "if we joined a caravan, we'd likely end up taking care of them—especially if anyone learned that Terrell is a trained factotum. They probably wouldn't even pay him."

"Also," Griffin added, "since we plan to leave the main road before we reach Crystalaire, the fewer to miss us, the better."

Several days before, they had decided to head directly for Maiden's Tear. As Terrell put it, "Why give anyone the opportunity to formally remind us that the area is restricted, or try to stop us?"

Adara explained that if they were caught a claim of ignorance would be of no help to either Terrell or herself. Both hunters and factotum were indoctrinated as to the restricted areas, especially those in their immediate vicinity, so they would know to avoid them. Griffin might not be penalized, but he would certainly not be permitted to proceed to Maiden's Tear.

No one said, although Griffin was certain they all thought it, that the Old One might have influence in the town and use it to have them detained. Given the length of the Old One's life, it was impossible to know who might be in his debt or how far his influence had spread.

Although Crystalaire was the final destination for many of the travelers, traffic did thin out the higher they went, as merchants stopped along the way to sell their wares in villages or small holdings. They hadn't seen anyone on the road for over a day, when the arrow impaled itself in the road only a few yards in front of Terrell and Midnight.

"Dismount. Step away from the horses and gear," shouted a harsh voice from the cliff above. "Don't try anything or the next arrow won't miss."

"Do as he says," Terrell ordered, dismounting. He muttered something incomprehensible. Griffin had thought he'd heard all the curse words Terrell knew. This one must have been particularly vile. Even Molly pricked up her ears and stamped.

"Now back away from the horses," continued the harsh voice. "Raise your hands. Keep them away from your weapons. I'm coming down with a few men, but we'll have you covered."

As they backed away, hands raised, Terrell spoke, his lips hardly moving. "Let them get down here. Once they're in the middle of us, any archers will be useless. They're not going to want to risk hurting the animals in any case."

Adara's expression was grim. "Sand Shadow was napping. It'll take her a bit to reach us. However, they'll find me harder to disarm than they imagine."

A rattle of gravel heralded the descent of their attackers.

Griffin risked a quick question. "Do we try to take them out?"

"Only on my signal," Terrell said.

Griffin understood. A factotum was trained to deal with such contingencies. Terrell would know best how to judge if this was a fight they could win or whether they needed to let the thieves "win"—only to learn how badly they had lost later.

The bandits emerged in a body from a cleft in the cliff, neatly hidden by a cluster of some small-leafed shrub. Griffin had wondered if they might have been hired by Julyan or the Old One, but discarded the idea once he got a look at them. They were a shabby lot, scarred and battered. They might serve as cannon fodder but, based on the organization he'd seen on Mender's Isle, the Old One would never choose such riffraff for an important job.

He'd come himself before using men like these.

The bandit leader was a lean, wiry man with a vivid white scar from the left side of his forehead, down across his nose, and trailing to an end across his right cheek. He carried a narrow blade, somewhere in length between a short sword and a long dagger. Like many of the men on Artemis, he wore his hair long, but it was dressed in a tight braid, coiled so that it would not provide a convenient handhold in a brawl.

His band—five had descended—was equally unsavory. Two were big, broad, dark of hair and eye—probably brothers. One held a sword, the other a spiked club; both men looked ready to fight. The other two held long knives and weren't nearly as impressive. One had a patch over his right eye. The other limped.

Scarface cast a covetous eye over the three horses and mule. "I think we'll accept the lot. The horses are noticeable, but we can drive them across the mountains and sell them there. Might keep the mule. Useful beasts, mules. Easier to feed than horses, too."

"And us?" Terrell said, sounding very nervous. "You'll let us go?"

"You're more noticeable than the horses," Scarface said, "more talkative, too. Be dicey trying to sell you. We can clear out with the goods and be gone before you can go screaming to the law in Crystalaire."

For a long moment, Scarface's gaze lingered speculatively on Adara, then dropped, seeing something in those amber eyes that made him reconsider whatever he had been contemplating.

"Patch, Dunny," he ordered. "Grab the black and the roan first. Me,

Bruiser, and Smasher will cover these kind donors to the poor, in case they regret their charity."

But a curious thing happened when Patch and Dunny laid hold of the bridles. Neither horse stirred a step, not even when slapped sharply on the rump. Griffin saw Midnight bracing his hind legs as if enjoying this game. Not even when Scarface had Patch and Dunny trade places with Bruiser and Smasher would the horses move an inch.

Scarface looked narrowly at Terrell. "You're being Mister Clever, are you? Have some command to make them stand?" He strode over to Terrell and pressed his knife into the factotum's throat. "Well, uncommand them then, else you'll be wearing a necklace of blood."

Terrell's voice shook very convincingly. "Very well. Don't cut me! Drowsing nursing chair!"

The effect of the nonsense phrase was astonishing. Not only did the horses move—they attacked. Spinning in place, Midnight kicked out and caught Bruiser in the chest so hard that he flew across the road and crashed into the cliff face. Tarnish reared, dragging Smasher, who held his bridle, nearly off his feet. Then he arched his neck and bit the man on his shoulder. Gentle Molly squealed and backed away, but Sam the Mule let loose with every ounce of orneriness in his soul and charged straight at Scarface.

"Now!" Terrell yelled, pulling out his belt knife and running toward Patch.

"I'm for above," Adara replied, vanishing up the cliff trail faster than any human should be able to climb. Screaming from above dispelled any lingering apprehension regarding arrows—and announced that Sand Shadow had rejoined them.

Dunny was angling toward Molly. Griffin drew his knife, wishing that he had a nerve burner. Still, he wasn't about to let his horse be hurt or stolen.

"Drop the knife," he barked. "You're not getting away, so you might as well surrender."

What Dunny might have done next Griffin would never know, for Molly—overcoming her fear when she saw "her" human in danger—reared and brought her forehooves down, smashing the man's head and right shoulder. Then she snorted and backed away, reminding Griffin of a dainty lady who didn't want to admit to a capacity for violence.

Griffin finished the downed man. Saving him would have been near impossible back in the Kyley Dominion. Here on Artemis . . . Impossible.

Over to one side, Sam the Mule was stomping on Scarface with every evidence of satisfaction. The hole Tarnish had bitten in Smasher's shoulder had hit something vital. The bandit was a dead and very bloody mess.

Terrell had finished Patch and was now inspecting Bruiser. Seeing Griffin's inquiring expression, he said curtly, "Broken back," and cut the man's throat.

Adara and Sand Shadow came down the trail. "Three," she said. "All dead now. Judging from the stuff we found, no doubt that they were bandits. My guess is that they were probably moving west when they got a glimpse of us and decided that one more job couldn't hurt. We'd better bury them. Otherwise, the bodies are going to draw attention."

"And we don't want that," Terrell agreed. "Not so close to Maiden's Tear."

Griffin looked at the three horses and Sam the Mule. Despite being dappled with blood, they were all calm now—all but Sam, who looked as if he was hoping for another fight.

"Helena the Equestrian does some very fine training," he said.

Terrell grinned. "Now you know why they don't worry about travelling with a puma."

Interlude: Generation

Germinating spore forms hyphae.
   Hyphae (divided by septa)
      Create mycelium.

Hyphal strings bring nourishment.
　　Fruiting bodies (cup, club, coral, capped, bell, shelf, jelly)
　　　　May emerge.

　　　　And be eaten.

Mother/ Father/ Male/ Female
　　Enfruiting bodies
　　　　Create a child.

　　　　To be eaten?

3

Maiden's Tear

After the encounter with the bandits, Adara decided to confide her mother's story to the others. After all, she might not be so lucky another time, and this was information they all should know. "I hadn't realized until this visit that my mother knew the Old One many years ago—before I was born, even."

"She did?" Griffin asked. "Tell!"

Adara did, concluding, "I didn't tell my mother about what we found beneath Mender's Isle. I doubt that her friend Blithe was among those we rescued. I hadn't thought about it before but, other than Thalia the Stablekeeper, I don't recall any more mature women among those we rescued."

"Me either," Griffin admitted, "nor any mention of such, even when Julyan was offering me my choice of bedmates—and believe me, he could get very detailed about what was on offer when he chose. I think he was trying to learn if I had any kinks he could exploit."

"Griffin, you probably have a better feeling for the Old One than either Adara or I do," Terrell said. "Not only did you live there on Mender's Isle, but your view of him isn't colored by his legend the way ours is. Do you think the Old One killed his captive women once they stopped being useful?"

"It's very possible," Griffin said, looking very unhappy. "He certainly couldn't turn them loose without risking his secret getting out. When you think about it, rumors among the women as to what fate awaited the noncooperative would have provided a powerful incentive to obey. On the other hand, perhaps the Old One let it be thought he did let them go free—the promise of freedom would also serve to control those who remained."

Adara heard her voice tremble when she spoke. Her mother's story had made Blithe very real to her. "But, either way, you think they are probably dead."

Griffin nodded. "The Old One had one use for them—as bearers of potentially adapted children. My understanding is that the children were reared communally—under controlled circumstances. He didn't want them to know their mothers, nor their mothers to know them."

"The Old One probably kept a few like Winnie," Terrell said, his voice rough, "even after they ceased to bear, in the hope that they would recover from the abuse and be able to bear again."

"After all," Adara added, her voice dripping with loathing, "Little Swimmer and Littler Swimmer were proof of Winnie's value as a brood mare. I've blamed my parents unfairly all these years. They did me a kindness when they sent me to Bruin."

"My skin crawls," Terrell said, brushing away imaginary bugs, "when I remember working side by side with the Old One, eating at his table, sleeping under his roof. I feel as if my skin should break out in a rash after exposure to such evil."

"Ah," Griffin replied softly, "but the Old One Who Is Young does not consider himself evil. He considers himself a scientist, a benefactor who seeks to lift the people of Artemis from the primitive morass into which they have been plunged through no fault of their own. He seeks to be their savior."

"And if a few women and children die while he seeks the necessary key," Adara finished, anger replacing the tremor in her voice, "what of it? More probably die each year from banditry in places where law has vanished. Or from natural disasters such as flood and fire. Think how many more would survive if the technology of the seegnur could be made useful again."

"I don't want to twist my mind along such paths," Terrell protested.

"If I do, I'll have to dunk my head in cold water to clear it. What say I tell you a more pleasant tale or two to pass the time?"

"It certainly won't help to discuss the Old One further," Griffin replied. "Maybe we're done with him."

Adara didn't believe this for a moment, but she was willing to play along. "Terrell, tell the story about the farmer and the beans that grew chickens. I bet Griffin hasn't heard that one before."

Julyan Hunter was finding his association with the Old One uniquely trying. He agreed that disguising who they were was crucial, but he found the roles the Old One had suggested exceedingly distasteful.

After you had associated with the Old One for a while, it was easy to forget how young he appeared to be. Indeed, after a time, one forgot his slim build, his boyishly fresh skin, utterly unlined by time, forgot that he never grew a beard. Instead, one only saw those grey eyes, so cool, so calmly appraising, holding within them the calculations of hundreds of years.

Now, although the Old One's hair remained uncommonly short (although longer than it had been and styled differently) and his eyes just as grey, his build just as slim, Julyan bet that not a single one of his former associates would recognize him. Before, the Old One had moved with a contained grace that wordlessly testified that he had long ago mastered his body. Now, not only had the Old One adopted the fidgety manner of a much younger person, he positively fluttered, moving his hands constantly, gazing up coyly through lashes that Julyan had never before noticed were quite long. Where the Old One's habitual expression had been cool and ironical, now he simpered, pursing his lips and giggling girlishly.

Julyan would have been ashamed for his employer were he not more ashamed for himself. If the Old One was playing the boy toy, then Julyan must play the sort of man who would keep such a creature about him. His brown hair had been bleached almost white, so that he looked like an older man struggling to appear younger. With a surprisingly deft hand, the Old One had stained the incipient lines around Julyan's eyes and mouth so they appeared to be deeper. He had replaced the close-fitting hunting leathers Julyan preferred with baggy tunics and trousers that effectively hid Julyan's well-muscled body.

"I suppose," Julyan said, looking in horror at his reflection, "you want me to slouch."

"No need," the Old One said. "That would be helpful, of course but, if you forget, any who see you will assume you are acting the part of the strutting cock."

The reason for this particular set of disguises went beyond concealing the pair from those who might wish to bring them in for questioning. The Old One had added a third member to their group, a boy of about eleven. Although Seamus was actually not a bad-looking boy, with curling brown hair, full lips, and eyes of such a dark blue they almost looked black, his complete lack of affect made him seem plain, even washed out. Seamus was very thin, with long fingers and toes. Although he was shooting up toward adult height, he carried himself so limply that he seemed smaller.

If the Old One posed as Julyan's (or Ryan, as he was now called) current favorite, Seamus was a catamite in training. But the Old One was not dragging Seamus along for any reason so simple. Indeed, he claimed to have gone beyond sexual desire of any sort and, in all the time they had been associated, Julyan had seen nothing to give lie to that claim. Even the most sensual of the women the Old One kept captive had been viewed clinically, her blood line and the adaptations hidden within the only items of interest.

Seamus had been one of the near successes of the Old One's breeding program, possessing a form of telepathy. However, Seamus could not communicate with just anyone. Instead, he single-mindedly fixed his attention on one person only. The first of these had initially been one of the children's caretakers, a man who had come into the Old One's circle from a community that had shunned the adapted. This man's gifts were minor enough—an uncontrolled telekinesis that manifested in poltergeist activity when he was under stress. Noisy and wild though they were, small children did not unbalance this man in the least, so the Old One had used him as a nursery minder while seeking the right mate with which to crossbreed him.

However, when the Old One realized the nature of Seamus's adaptation, even proven telekinesis was not enough to keep the unfortunate man alive. He had been killed so the bond would be broken. Then the Old One let Seamus see no one but him until the boy bonded with him. Success—but only after a fashion—for, whether he had been born that way or whether the shock of his first bond-mate's death had damaged his mind, Seamus never progressed mentally beyond about five years old.

Sometimes, Julyan thought the Old One was actually pleased about this, for a five-year-old was much easier to control, although harder to train. Training was necessary, for their telepathic ability depended completely on Seamus. The Old One claimed no adaptations for himself—other than his unique immortality. Over time, Seamus was taught to respond to certain signals. Only in response to them would he dare touch the Old One's mind. Harsh punishments for early errors now made it impossible for Seamus to probe the Old One's mind beyond accepting messages and sending replies.

When the facility under Mender's Isle had been raided, Seamus had been living with an old man a few hours' brisk walk from Spirit Bay. The Old One had been experimenting with having the boy check in with him at set times, testing the distance over which they could communicate clearly. At this point, the link was solid to a few miles, as far as many hunters could maintain with their demiurges.

If Julyan found the Old One's current persona revolting, Seamus made his skin crawl. When the Old One was near, the boy kept his round, blue-eyed gaze fastened on him with what most probably thought was adoration, but which Julyan knew was raw terror. If the Old One didn't need him, Seamus lapsed into docile passivity.

And I'm supposed to sexually desire either of them? Julyan thought in disgust. *I can't imagine it. Maybe any who see our little "family" will think those two are the couple and I am their guardian.*

When he dared, he dropped hints that this was so, but Julyan wondered if his denials did him more harm than good.

Once they left their hideaway near Spirit Bay, they made a leisurely journey to Crystalaire. Although the town was full—summer being the peak fishing season—a house on the outskirts of town proved to have a nice cottage on the grounds that they could use. Julyan suspected that the Old One owned the entire estate, but he had learned not to ask questions.

"Next we will make a few enquiries, listen for rumors," the Old One said. "Two handsome men and an interesting-looking woman will not have passed without notice."

"And if they weren't seen?"

"Then we will know they went directly to Maiden's Tear," the Old One replied calmly. "You will have ample opportunity to discard the role of Ryan and go forth in secret as Julyan Hunter. For now we stalk our prey, but not interfere. It seems only right to give them an opportunity to replace my Sanctum with a new stronghold of the seegnur's lore."

"What was Maiden's Tear called before?" Griffin asked as they led their mounts up a particularly steep bit of trail—it had ceased to be anything that could be called a "road" days before.

"Before what?" Terrell asked.

"Before the slaughter of the seegnur," Griffin said. "Didn't the name come from that, from some murdered maiden or something? Maybe that bride whose marriage was never to be?"

Terrell shook his head. "As far as I know, the area was called Maiden's Tear before then. The story I heard was that the name had to do with sisters who were separated . . . I don't remember why. I'm not certain the legend ever said. Anyhow, when the pair was separated, one twin wept so copiously that a lake was formed."

"Pretty tale," Adara commented. "Though from the maps Bruin showed me during my training, I'd guess that the fact that the lake is teardrop-shaped probably had something to do with the name as well."

She didn't add that for several nights now her dreams had been filled with the sound of weeping. Doubtless her mind was still adjusting to the information her mother had given her. It was frightening to realize how close to becoming one of those pitiful women they each had been. Adara wondered if Jor had indeed drowned at sea or if he had been among the adapted men whom the Old One had given a "refuge" that was little more than a prison. If so and if he had survived all those years, he had likely drowned.

The memory of the bodies they had pulled from beneath Mender's Isle still haunted Adara. She'd never know how many of those men had been willing collaborators and how many dupes—for the Old One had recruited from among the adapted who had found themselves unwelcome in general society. Since the Old One had kept the women and children isolated from the majority of the men, the Swimmers, who, along with their mother, Winnie, had stayed behind to help explore the submerged facility, had not known much about the men whose bodies they helped drag to the outer world.

So many died, yet the worst of them got away, Adara thought. *Julyan and the Old One escaped. I wouldn't be surprised if the others who escaped were the ones willing to climb to safety on the bodies of their drowning comrades.*

They took the last part of the climb to Maiden's Tear in easy stages, for Griffin felt the air too thin in his lungs. Griffin pushed himself hard, never insisting on riding when Molly needed a break, instead walking alongside her, so by the end of each day's travel, he looked drawn.

"I'll adjust," he said, "faster than you might think. I knew I was coming to a planet where many of the settlements were near or within mountain ranges. Among the preparations I dosed myself with was one to trigger my body to produce extra oxygen if the conditions warranted it."

Griffin spoke of such "doses" routinely, Adara mused, but the capacities of the adapted still surprised him, whether adapted humans like herself or adapted animals like Sand Shadow.

Of course, Adara thought, sharing the image with Sand Shadow, *my eyes and claws are more showy than Griffin's tiny lung bugs.*

In return, Sand Shadow sent an image of her own fingered paws. The puma had recently made a breakthrough in knot tying and was quite pleased about it. One of her goals was to learn how to set snares and make fish traps, for the large game her kind usually hunted was not always available in the places her bond with Adara took her.

When the companions reached Maiden's Tear, they set up camp in a cluster of evergreens, even though the alpine meadow near the lake provided inviting camp spots.

"We'd be more visible," Terrell said. "The prohibition regarding Maiden's Tear is still in effect, but we don't know how strictly it is enforced. We're reaching the time of year when shepherds will be taking their flocks higher for the best grazing. Best if a shepherd going after a strayed lamb doesn't glimpse a cluster of tents. Humans will be much harder to spot, especially if we practice some elementary concealment."

"And the horses and Sam?" Griffin asked. "They're pretty big."

Adara replied, "Sand Shadow scouted out some sheltered vales with excellent grazing and water. One of the good things about this area being restricted is that the grass is thick, belly deep even on Midnight and Sam in some places."

The first night in their new camp, Adara took herself up into a long-needled pine to sleep, this despite the fact that evergreens were far from her favorite sleeping trees, since the bark was prickly and tended to shed. In warmer weather, sticky sap could soil her clothing. Still, sleeping in an evergreen was better than watching the men looking sidewise at each other as bedrolls were spread.

Adara liked both Terrell and Griffin, but evenings were when the awkward question of who slept near/with whom became a forever undiscussed but omnipresent issue. Along the trail, the question had diminished, but now that they were "in residence," Adara noticed each man looking to see where she would bed down, hoping for an excuse to pick a spot nearby.

Making matters worse was that spring was giving way to summer. Traditionally, midsummer and midwinter were times when usual restrictions on sexual dalliance among adults were suspended. Most who had married did not abuse their vows (although couples who were feeling dull had been known to exploit the occasion), but these festivals were very good times for young, unattached people to experiment without incurring a commitment thereafter.

Although that "no commitment" is not always remembered afterwards, Adara thought, settling herself comfortably into place. *Terrell has clearly never forgotten our tryst. How I wish he had! Though I blush to think of it, maybe Julyan felt the same about me. We also first made love in midsummer, though Julyan was certainly more than happy to continue after, whereas I have not teased Terrell.*

She let her mind wander, shutting out Sand Shadow's lewd commentary from where the puma hunted not too far away. Eventually, Adara drifted off. When she did, she dreamed again of tears.

She awoke to find a pale yellow fairy circle surrounding the base of the tree in which she had fallen asleep. Silver grey shelf fungi with pale lavender undersides made a spiral staircase around the trunk of the tree, ending level with where her head rested against the trunk. Adara turned her head and saw, picked out by starlight, a delicate female face sculpted from minute, lacy threads. Unsettled, Adara was trying to still her suddenly wildly beating heart when the planet's voice spoke within her mind.

"Adara? Huntress? This place. You are in. One place. This one place. It makes me...I cannot see, taste, hear, touch, smell..."

The words were less words than a sense of agitation, disorientation, near panic. Adara had felt many emotions from the entity she thought of as Artemis. Curiosity, certainly, puzzlement, often, but panic? What could frighten a world?

"Do you know where I am?"

"You are where if you were not there I would not know it was there. Where I must make mycelium feetholds to stand, else, like water on rocks on shore, I flow around, pass over, perhaps...If you were not there, would I know it is there?"

"What is there?"

"The where you are. The where where killer of many, drinker of blood, is also. Until you went there, I did not know it was there."

"Wait...How much of the world can you 'see'?"

How Artemis perceived the world that was herself was something Adara had wondered about for a long time, but she hadn't been able to figure out a constructive way to ask. Intuition rather than logic had led the huntress to the realization that the thoughts flowing into her dreams were those of the planet upon which she lived, a planetary intelligence that had been put out of commission, along with the rest of Artemis's peculiar technology, by an attack that heralded the destruction of a great interstellar empire.

But although Adara acknowledged that Artemis existed, she didn't understand exactly what was entailed in being a planet with a sense of personal identity—with a soul.

A fresh wave of panic was the only reply to Adara's question. Burying the thought as deeply as she could, lest she frighten Artemis further, Adara considered. *How can a planet without a heart or lungs or glands feel afraid? How can it feel fear without a heart to pump wildly, breath to come short, adrenaline to course like fire through the brain? Is fear separate from the sensations of feeling afraid?*

The answer came instantly, whether from her own soul or a flicker from Artemis, Adara didn't know. *Artemis has been dead and come to life. How could she not feel afraid that something will make her unalive again? Of course it is possible to feel fear without sensation— and who is to say Artemis does not experience sensations of her own?*

Much as she would stalk wary game, the huntress tried to lead Artemis away from her fear. Adara might not have much in the way of what Griffin thought of as education, but she had patience in abundance. "Let's think back to before you were afraid. Yes?"

Adara sculpted a picture in her mind, retracing steps along a trail, walking to where all was still and tranquil. As she shaped the image, Adara felt a thrumming purr join her words and knew that Sand Shadow had joined them and was helping enforce the image with her own calming presence. Adara's relationship with Artemis was not a partnership but a tripartite bond. The planet had touched their minds when woman and puma had been practicing to strengthen the non-verbal communication that was crucial to the demiurge relationship.

Artemis had slipped into the link, spoken to them both, then bound them together, a three who remained three, but could share as if one.

Once they had walked the path toward tranquility, Adara tried again. "To understand what is different about this place where I am, I need to understand what is the usual for you."

Sand Shadow sent a visual image, her own idea of contrast: two snakes, very similar at first glance, yet the one deadly poisonous, the other good, if a bit tough, eating. In response to these clarifications, Artemis sent an image of her own, so vast and vivid that Adara found herself gripping the tree limb lest she fall.

What Artemis shaped for them resembled a spider's web, thin lines joined at points of overlap, sticking one to the other. Initially, the joins were far apart, the junctions separated by such great distances that they were out of sight of each other. Then, more lines filled in, more joins were established. The spider's web became less tenuous, the original lines stronger, the junctions more frequent, new lines filling the space between. There was still a great deal of emptiness, but the sense of connection was there. Through each wider line, each new bit of mesh, information crashed and trembled, overwhelming the huntress with sheer quantity until Artemis took mercy and damped that particular element.

Then, suddenly, in the midst of this vast web, a hole appeared. Or rather, two tiny dots of awareness entered the hole, making awareness of the hole manifest to the web. No longer could the web be sure that it was strong and solid. The belief that the web was all-present vied against the undeniable realization of the hole's existence. Finally, dusty spores erupted forth, swirled through the hole, took tenuous anchor. Sprouted near the dots.

Adara understood. Artemis had been rebuilding her connections throughout the planet that was herself. From the start, Artemis had defined herself as a neural network. The rebuilding of that network was far from complete, but she had believed the process to be methodical and thorough. Only when Adara and Sand Shadow had entered a place in which Artemis had failed to establish connections had Artemis realized such places existed. Somehow, using her link to

Adara and Sand Shadow, Artemis had pushed through and made contact.

"No wonder you're afraid," Adara said imagining herself caressing, patting, hugging, offering physical comfort. "You've just discovered a great big numb spot in your body—and you don't know what other 'numb' areas there might be. Or how large this one might be."

She rose from her perch, dusted tree bark off her back, then swung lightly to the ground. "That last, at least, we can resolve. Can you continue to 'see' me if I move from this place?"

"I will flash/scream/alert/storm if I feel you grow thin."

Adara nodded. "Good. Sand Shadow and I will walk. You will tell us how strongly you feel us. In this way, we can learn the boundaries of this numb spot, this hole within your web."

The process was slow, although it sped up once Artemis understood what was wanted from her. After that Adara and Sand Shadow split up. The mental link supplied by Artemis expanded their usual communication range so that, by dawn, Adara had constructed a tidy little map of the surrounding area with special attention to those parts Artemis could not "see" without considerable effort.

The smell of applewood smoked bacon sizzling over the fire drew Adara back to camp. Sand Shadow, yawning hugely enough to show off every one of her teeth, from fangs to molars, joined them soon after.

"Cook more bacon, please," Adara said to Griffin, who was handling the pan. "We're both starving. We were out all night."

"Not hunting," Terrell said, taking out his knife and slicing some generous pieces. "If you had been, at least Sand Shadow wouldn't be hungry."

"For her the bacon will be mostly for taste," Adara admitted, though the puma's moonstone gold eyes were fastened on the frying pan in a manner that made very clear she expected her share.

"Well," Griffin said, reaching and rubbing the puma behind one round ear, "she shares her venison. We can share our bacon. What had you out all night? Last I saw, you were settled comfortably in that tree."

Adara told them about her odd conversation with Artemis, noting as she did so that the mushroom ring, along with the step fungi on the tree trunk, had faded away. Did this mean that Artemis was having trouble maintaining a "feethold" in this place?

Feeling anxious, Adara drew out the map and talked more quickly, as if words and pictures could make more real a place that felt increasingly tenuous to her.

Griffin listened with increasing amazement as Adara unfolded her tale. His bond with Terrell made it easier for him to believe what Adara said about her and Sand Shadow's link to the planetary intelligence, but belief made the reality no less astonishing.

"These," Adara said, tracing her fingers along the edges of the map she had drawn in the little notebook she carried everywhere, "are the boundaries of the area within which Artemis has difficulty 'seeing.' There are some interesting complexities. For example, she is aware of the mountains that surround this vale, but not of the vale itself. Even when I pressed her to admit that the slope of the mountain all but established the vale, she could not see it without her link to us."

"How about the lake?" Terrell asked, gesturing to where the Maiden's Tear glistened in the morning sunlight. "It's not large for a lake, but it's certainly larger than a pond. I haven't had a chance to go out on it yet, but I'm guessing it's fairly deep as well."

"She can't see it," Adara said. "Nor can she 'see' that little building the seegnur left. Here's what's even stranger. Her normal perceptions don't just involve the surface. They can extend to the depths as well. But her blindness involves both surface and depth."

"We guessed," Griffin said, sliding bacon from the pan onto thick slabs of slightly stale bread, "that the seegnur left a complex here—underwater or underground or both. The extent of Artemis's blindness seems to confirm that."

"But 'blindness,'" Terrell put in, "is a deceptive term. A blind person has the other four senses to compensate. Artemis's blindness extends to all her senses."

"I think," Adara said, "we will eventually find that only a few of her senses match our own. She awoke in dreams. Part of what she wanted from me and Sand Shadow was a means of anchoring herself in the sensory world. I think she's managing to build her own senses now, so that when she found there were things we could sense that she could not, she panicked."

"Is Artemis here now?" Griffin asked, realizing he was looking side to side like an idiot.

"No," Adara replied. "I think we wore her out, although that's another concept that boggles the mind. I'm guessing she's off resting and wondering if she has any other blind spots."

"Now that you've introduced her to the idea of mapping," Terrell asked, "won't she be able to figure out where the blind spots are by checking where the edges of her web don't meet up?"

Adara shook her head. "No. It doesn't work that way. I think the reason I chose blindness to describe what she's going through is that she is truly blind to these places. They don't exist for her, the way a blind person can't comprehend color. A deaf person might feel the vibrations of a sound, but there's no way a blind person can know what color something is. Color isn't there. These places aren't there."

"Not there?"

Adara nodded. "Artemis can sense the edges of bodies of water, even those as big as oceans, although, at this point, I gather that she can't extend her ability to sense over water itself."

"So bodies of water are defined for Artemis, like negative space defines the shape of a sculpture," Griffin said, then clarified when Adara looked confused. "Negative space are those holes that are as important as what's there. But the blind spots aren't even outlined. I can see why she found that creepy."

"Maybe," Terrell offered, "she'll be able to see this place in time. We still don't know precisely what awakened her. We've all been assuming that the awakening was complete. Perhaps there are gaps, places where those nanobots Griffin told us about linger more strongly."

"That's possible," Griffin agreed. "But I can't forget that Maiden's Tear was a forbidden zone. We'd assumed this meant restricted to the human inhabitants, but what if it was restricted even from Artemis? That's an amazing thought."

"So, have you changed your mind about exploring here?" Adara asked. "Perhaps we would do better to go back to Spirit Bay. Some of the furor will have died down. If we operate from Mender's Isle, most people won't even guess we're there."

Griffin shook his head. "I probably should be ashamed to admit it, but rather than scaring me off, what we've learned makes me more eager to explore. It's like that one door in the Sanctum, the one that was so well hidden we nearly didn't find it and, once we did, we never could figure out how to open it."

Terrell chuckled. "Not that repeated failure kept you from trying."

"Well," Adara said, rising from beside the fire and stretching in a manner Griffin found very distracting, "I'll leave searching to the two of you. I need some sleep. Sand Shadow says she will combine keeping watch on the horses and Sam the Mule while getting some rest herself. Look for us in time for dinner."

She waved vaguely and a moment later was climbing gracefully back up into the branches of her chosen tree. Griffin watched until she vanished into the shadows. He discovered Terrell watching too, and they shared an uneasy laugh.

"First," Terrell said, "no searching for anything until camp is secured. Sand Shadow's scent will keep most problems away, but neither bears nor ants respect pumas. After we've cleared up, where do you want to start?"

"That little building is the obvious place," Griffin said, "and for that reason I'm tempted to ignore it. Why create a facility so secret that you hide it even from your planetary intelligence, then mark it with a structure? Still, we can't overlook it, so we might as well start by checking it over."

"Sounds good," Terrell said. He extended the frying pan to Griffin. "Scrape the grease out into that clay pot. It will be good for cooking mush to go with dinner. Then take the pan to the stream. The sand's just right for scrubbing."

Griffin followed orders, thinking how much his life had changed.

He drew in a breath of mountain air so fresh that he could almost believe he was the first person ever to suck it into his lungs. The food had been good, too. He'd never been lazy, but life here on Artemis demanded constant labor.

As he glanced between his friend and the sleeping figure in the tall tree, he found himself wondering, *I keep saying I need to get off this planet and I suppose I do. I hate being trapped, if nothing else. I miss hot water on demand, sleeping without worry that rain will soak me or a snake will crawl into my bedroll. I miss fast travel and faster communication. I miss having a library in the palm of my hand but, greasy pots, latrine duty, and all . . . Really, life here isn't bad at all.*

Interlude: Soundless Song

Hyphal strings play life's song

I feel them grow

But I am deaf

4

Searching

They're up at Maiden's Tear all right," Julyan reported to the Old One some days after they'd settled into the little cottage. "They're scouting, but I don't think they've found much of interest."

"Are you sure the 'scouting' you've seen isn't meant to deceive any watchers?"

Julyan shook his head. "I'd bet my left testicle I'm right. These binoculars you gave me are the best I've ever used. I've been spying from a neighboring peak and I feel as if I'm right next to them. First, they spent a couple days checking over that little white building. I even saw Adara up on the roof. Looked as if she was checking the seams with the blade of her knife. Then they examined every rock and tree within about twenty feet of the building. Now they're hiking the banks of the lake. It's a big lake, so they've been doing that in stages."

"Sounds as if they're fairly confident they're not being observed."

Julyan nodded. "They're not exactly drawing attention to themselves. Adara was up on that roof in the late evening, when any shepherd—not that there are any near—would be gathering in the flocks. Darkness isn't the problem for her it would be for most people."

"How about Terrell and Griffin?"

"They're staying under cover whenever possible, but I can usually find them by noticing how the animals—especially the birds—are reacting. If I can't figure out where someone is—and that's mostly

Adara—I figure she's sleeping. Even when I knew her years ago, she was given to sleeping during the day."

"I have often wondered," the Old One mused, "how many of the behaviors adopted by the adapted are innate and how many are adopted because of the affiliation they feel with aspects of their adaptation? Or, I suppose, similar abilities could lead to similar behaviors. Those of us who cannot see in the dark must be out and about when there is light."

Such idle speculation was typical of the Old One, but Julyan couldn't help but think how odd it was coming from him in his current guise, especially since, even as he spoke, he was carefully stroking a line of smoky purple shadow over his eyelids.

"I don't suppose we'll ever know, sir," Julyan said.

The Old One's smile was thin. "Oh, when you reach my age, you learn to never say never. Opportunities for research tend to arise, especially if you lay the groundwork in advance."

His tone was cool and clinical. Despite the warmth of the summer sun beating down, Julyan realized he was shivering.

✦

Finding the entry into the seegnur's facility proved far more difficult than anyone had anticipated. Indeed, if it had not been for Artemis's curious blind spot, they might have decided that they had been wrong about why the seegnur had forbidden access to Maiden's Tear.

They had begun by searching the small white building Griffin said reminded him of a "temple"—and then had to explain what a temple was, since the people of Artemis did not construct such buildings. Myriad religions had evolved over time, some worshipping the seegnur as creators, some revering speculative beings who had created the seegnur, a few very odd ones denying the historical facts entirely. However, whichever form the religion took, temples were not included, for they were not part of the lore.

The temple was made from a glistening white marble impregnated with tiny flecks of gold. Other than the peaked roof, which served well enough for shedding snow in winter, the structure was not constructed with the mountain climate in mind. One side was completely open except for a few elaborately carved pillars. The foundation was high enough that three steps led up to the entry—this despite the fact that the entire building was about the size of a one-room cottage. Although the exterior was unornamented—other than the undeniable beauty of the stone—the interior was covered with elaborate bas-relief carvings, mostly depicting naked young men on horseback involved in some sort of race or game.

Over several days, Griffin and Terrell took turns studying the carvings, but found nothing significant. Adara examined the structure one evening, wondering if her night-adapted vision might see something the men had missed. However, although she poked and prodded, even going so far as to climb onto the roof to see if anything was hidden there, she found no indication of what purpose the structure served.

The next logical place to search was the lake, for the seegnur often hid their technological facilities beneath the water, thus maintaining the illusion that Artemis was a pristine planet.

Griffin and Terrell spent several days hiking the lakeshore, first one direction, then the next, checking for anything that might be a hidden entrance to a facility. Among the loot they'd taken from the bandits was a collapsible canoe with an oiled hide cover and a frame of bent wood. The craft was too small for Sand Shadow to ride along with Adara, so Adara paddled out alone to see if she could glimpse any structures through the cold, clear depths. Adara also prowled the meadow surrounding the temple, spiraling out in increasingly large circles that assured she would not miss even the smallest indication of the seegnur's long-ago presence. In that way, she made their first significant find.

"Come with me," she said, when Griffin and Terrell limped into camp one evening, "before it gets too dark."

"Woman," Terrell said with mock severity, "this time of year it will be hours before full darkness falls. I want to get my boots off, have a long draft of the cold tea we set to steep last night, then eat whatever it is Sand Shadow is turning on that spit over the fire. Even if you've found the door into whatever sanctum the seegnur left, I don't care. It's waited this long. It can wait a few more hours."

"Duck," Adara said. "Sand Shadow is cooking duck. There are several. And are you sure you can pass my discovery by so easily? Does this awaken your dulled curiosity, factotum?"

She held out her hand, upon which rested an object about the size of her palm. The artifact was rectangular, but with softly rounded corners. It was made from one of the strange synthetic materials sometimes found where the seegnur's workings were exposed, something so strong that even after five hundred years of exposure in a mountain meadow, the lovely blue-grey surface held its polish with barely a scratch.

Griffin, who looked as tired as Terrell claimed to be, immediately perked up. "Let me see it! Where did you find it? Are there more?"

Adara chuckled softly and dropped the thing back into her pocket. "I want you to see where I found it. I can show you now or after duck and tea, as Terrell requests."

"Terrell withdraws his request," Terrell responded. "Show us!"

Pleased, Adara led them to where a very small heap of seegnur artifacts rested amid the meadow grass. Griffin hunkered down, carefully turning over each bit—no matter how insignificant—then returning it precisely where it had been before.

"These are the remnants of fasteners—what the seegnur used instead of buttons or laces," he said. "I've seen the like elsewhere. This looks like a belt buckle. This odd twisty thing might have been part of something larger. This is a comm bracelet—similar patterns are still used in the Kyley system. I wonder if this ring was ornamental or if it had another purpose? Where did you find that thing you showed us?"

"Over here." Adara pointed to an impression in the grass. She handed it to him.

"Part of a clasp," Griffin said, "possibly meant to hold items on a belt."

Adara smiled. "I found two other locations like this. Would you see, seegnur?"

"Definitely!" Griffin leapt to his feet. Terrell sighed in mock exasperation, but his blue eyes were shining with excitement.

Adara led the way to the other locations. Each held a scattering of seegnur artifacts, none very functional, but many quite fascinating. Each scatter looked as if it had been in place for quite a long while.

When darkness forced their retreat, Griffin insisted that they leave everything in place. "We'll sketch, then excavate first thing in the morning."

Adara had her own thoughts about what her finds might be, but she wanted to hear Griffin's speculation first. After all, he had spent much of his life examining things the seegnur had left behind.

"What do you think I found?" she asked as she carved one of the ducks.

"I think," Griffin said, shredding the greens for the salad into such tiny pieces that Terrell removed them from beneath his hands before they were rendered inedible, "those are what's left of the bodies of three of the people who died here. They didn't necessarily die in those specific places—scavengers could have dragged the bodies—but that is where they came to rest."

"The lore says," Terrell reminded, neatly chopping wild carrot and onion, then adding it to the salad bowl, "that residents of Crystalaire buried the dead seegnur."

"They might not have found these bodies," Griffin countered. "I doubt they knew how many seegnur had fled here. Given that they were violating the prohibitions by coming here—and that not long before this area had been a battlefield—I doubt that they spent much time searching for the dead."

"I agree," Adara said, pleased that Griffin had confirmed her own speculations. "Believe it or not, scavengers might not have dragged the bodies very far from where they fell. They would only do so if there was competition."

Terrell added, "I notice that each of Adara's finds was in a relatively sheltered area. Perhaps these seegnur hid in those places, rather than near the temple, but were discovered, slain, and their bodies left to rot."

"We'll look more closely tomorrow," Griffin said. "I believe the so-lution to our puzzle is at hand."

Adara was less certain, but why ruin Griffin's excitement? He had been brave in the face of so much disappointment. Could she blame him for being excited that, perhaps, at last, he was one step closer to re-turning home?

Griffin contentedly settled into the familiar routine of excavation. He found his two apprentices easy to teach. Terrell had done some exca-vation before, since the loremasters (under whom the factotums did much of their early training) were fascinated by the seegnur's culture, especially anything that might give a hint as to the mystery of their beliefs and ethics. From her training in tracking, Adara understood the need not to destroy traces before they could be examined. Neither were in the least squeamish about the occasional fragment of bone.

I could have done much worse. At least, unlike the Old One, their thoughts are not cluttered with notions about what is important and what is not.

One evening, as they rested after a long day that had turned up mostly dirt and rocks and only a few more artifacts, Griffin posed a question.

"Maybe we're approaching this the wrong way. What do we know about the seegnur and how they built here on Artemis?"

Terrell said, "Anything technological was hidden—often under water."

Adara added, "The seegnur were like foxes; they always built with a hidden exit. If what we found in Spirit Bay is anything to go on, that exit could usually be opened with nothing more than a knowledge of how to operate the locks and fail-safes. It wouldn't even take a great deal of muscle."

Griffin nodded. "So why build the temple? Why make Maiden's Tear such a noticeable shape? If this area was intended to be forbidden pretty much from the creation of the planet, then why draw atten-tion to it?"

Terrell intoned in his best imitation of a loremaster, "The ways of the seegnur are mysterious to these humble ones they created."

Griffin threw a pheasant bone at him. "Misdirection. I think they knew that eventually there would be curiosity about this place—about why it was forbidden when there was no obvious reason for it to be so. I bet that whatever was here was something they did not want the locals to even get a sniff of . . ."

"So they created in a fashion that anyone coming here would not look in the right place," Adara cut in excitedly, "the way a mother bird pretends to have a broken wing to lure a predator away from her nest."

"Precisely. So I think we're going after this all wrong. Adara, where's the map you and Sand Shadow made? The one that showed the areas where Artemis is 'blind'?"

Adara reached into her pack and pulled her notebook out, then held the map where firelight would illuminate the details.

Griffin stared at carefully drawn lines, considering, then rejecting, possibilities, sometimes for reasons he wasn't certain of himself. Finally, he pointed to the mountain that more or less dominated the reaches above the meadow and lake.

"You've shaded that mountain very oddly. As I recall, you said that Artemis is aware of the mountain when she traces along the surface of the range. There isn't a gap in the midst of the chain."

Adara nodded. "Yes. She sees it, but we worked out that there is a large portion near the base that simply isn't there for her. This upset her badly because, by comparing this peak to those of similar height, she is aware the mountain must have more slope than it does. However, she could only trace a portion of it. It was as if it was both there and not there at the same time."

"I can understand why that would be upsetting," Griffin said. "The more I think about it, the more I feel sure that Artemis's blind spots are our most reliable clue. The rest—especially the lake and the temple—are misdirection."

"The bodies?" Terrell asked.

"Those weren't planned," Griffin said, "so I don't think they're part of the misdirection. My initial enthusiasm may have been all wrong. They may not be significant."

"So," Adara asked, "do we stop our digging?"

"Let's give digging one more day," Griffin said, "for luck. How about Terrell and I dig while you and Sand Shadow scout the base of the mountain for anything significant? Have you 'heard' from Artemis lately?"

Adara shook her head. "Our link is still more her to us, than ours to her—and she finds it difficult to touch us here. Occasionally, in a dream, there is a whisper. I believe she is busy spinning her net wider, spreading out so that she will at the very least know where her blind spots may be."

If there was ever a time Adara was reminded that Griffin had not been born on Artemis, it was when he said something like "scout the base of the mountain." Clearly, he had no idea how complicated the base of a mountain could be.

Mountains were not neat triangles topped with snow, as they were so often drawn on maps, nor were they simply defined by their elevations, although this way of drawing them came closer to the reality. Real mountains were more like the figures children made when they draped their bedding over their knees and let it cascade into ripples and folds. Those bedclothes ranges did not include the complexities of caves and ridges, of streams that barred passage, of undergrowth and overgrowth that made it impossible to see the underlying rock, but they did come closer.

So it was that Adara did not set out on this very generalized search with a great deal of confidence.

"We will start," she sent to Sand Shadow, shaping her communication into images, although she spoke the words aloud as well—she'd long suspected the puma grasped more spoken words than was obvious, "by restricting ourselves—at least at first—to the portion of the mountain that faces this lake meadow. True, all of the base was blocked from Artemis's sight, but I think this was more to keep her from realizing that something was missing than because all of the area was significant."

Sand Shadow buzzed approval. Not for the first time, Adara was grateful that pumas were the largest purring cats. That one sound made communication so much easier.

"We will begin at the base because, although the seegnur had devices that enabled them to fly, that does not mean that they always would have had such devices with them when they came here. Indeed, flitting in the air would have raised the chance of their being seen by someone on a neighboring part of the mountain."

And not being seen—at least our not being seen—is another good reason to stay low. The plant cover is much thicker. We were fortunate that all three of those places we've been excavating were near some feature that blocks direct view from other mountains. What failed to shelter the seegnur from death at least shelters us from observation.

Although Adara didn't articulate this last, Sand Shadow caught the gist of it. She sent back a cheerfully arrogant image of a shepherd catching a glimpse of the puma's tawny magnificence, then fleeing, driving his flock in front of him.

Probably exactly what would happen, Adara thought, *if a shepherd saw a puma, but humans in violation of the prohibition? That might be another thing entirely.*

As they began their search, Sand Shadow was a bit peevish. Explaining to her why they were searching for nothing Adara could precisely define had been difficult. All the puma had gathered was that the end result of their quest would be Griffin's departure. Since Sand Shadow liked Griffin—she had adopted him as her favorite playmate when they were in Spirit Bay—a search that would end up with her losing her "toy" did not seem worth the effort.

She cooperated because Adara asked her to do so, because Adara had been her friend since she was a small, foundling kitten, the last left of a litter whose mother had been killed and who were being used as a sort of cannibal larder by a male puma who may or may not have been their own father. Sand Shadow had cried out, although whether only with her kitten mew or with her mind as well, neither were sure. Adara had heard. The rest began their private legend.

Despite her reluctant participation in the search, Sand Shadow was the first to find something interesting. An impression awash with sensory detail flooded into Adara's mind. The odor of slowly moving water, of minerals, of algae scum caught in corners. The plink-plink of water dripping into water, the shrill complaint of air sighing through crevices. The tightness of rock around the puma's shoulders, releasing into an open place lit only with what gleams slipped through crevices.

Adara hurried to join her demiurge, found the narrow crevice hidden from view by a facing slab of lichen-streaked stone that had slid down the mountainside to nearly—but not quite—close off the narrow passage that opened like a night-blooming flower into a cavern almost completely filled by the sullen waters of an inky black lake.

Despite the fact that it differed in almost every way, Adara was reminded of another seegnur facility she had located. That one had been hidden behind a deceptively small waterfall. The passage had been narrow, although always large enough, and had eventually opened into wonders. She felt in her gut that this place was what they sought.

She went to fetch her canoe and to tell the men what Sand Shadow had found. It would not do if both she and Sand Shadow vanished, for Adara knew that even though the canoe was too small to hold them both, the puma would explore with her. The great cat was even now padding cautiously along the narrow ridge that bordered the subterranean lake, but if the ridge would not hold her, pumas were strong swimmers.

As Adara expected, Terrell and Griffin both protested. She overrode their protests by the simple expedient of not listening. She let their voices wash over her as she stripped the covering skins from the canoe's frame, for the passage would be too narrow for her to take the vessel through completely assembled.

When Adara had readied her burden, she paused, ticking off points on her fingers. "The canoe will only hold one. You cannot see in the dark as we can. We are not leaving you behind, we are only scouting.

Now, if you would speed our search along, you could help me carry the parts of the canoe to the cave entrance. I will bring back a report and we will plan from there. It could be that this cavern is as much a false lead as the temple and the lake."

But Adara didn't think it would be. She was even more certain a dozen paddle strokes deep into her voyage. Early on, stalactites had hung so close to the water's surface that she had to dodge among them. Later, she had been forced to lie flat and push herself along. Following the edge of the cavern, Sand Shadow reported that the ridge became a ledge of sorts, although one interrupted with gaps that a human could never leap.

(Sand Shadow, of course, could, but then pumas excelled at leaping.)

Then, with a suddenness like nothing in nature, the stalactites ceased to provide a barrier. The air chilled the dampness on Adara's skin, proving that despite the darkness, there were openings through which air, if not light, could enter. Adara straightened and paddled ahead. She knew she shouldn't be able to see—for her adaptation let her see where there was little light, but not where there was none—but somehow she sensed the pebbled shore ahead of her and was backing water even as her canoe ground to a halt.

Sand Shadow leapt beside her, excited and alert. Unlike Adara, she was not accustomed to relying on sight as a primary sense. Her hearing, sense of smell, even the caress of her long whiskers and the prickle of a breeze along her fur oriented her. Adara found herself wondering if her own confidence came from a filtering of the puma's senses through to her own.

However, she had not planned on relying on her ability to see in the dark. After making sure the canoe was secured against drifting away, Adara pulled a candle and a box of expensive sulfur matches from her pack. The light flared, momentarily too much, then just enough to enable Adara to see as clearly as a normal human would at the moment when twilight is fading into full night.

"Ah . . ."

The sound was not so much a word as a sigh of deep satisfaction.

No doubt remained that this was what the seegnur had hidden. Gone was the illusion of a normal cavern. The walls were straight, either coated with or made from the same hard material she had seen in the facility beneath Mender's Isle. What surprised her was the size. Based on what Griffin had told her, one could dock an interplanetary shuttle here. Indeed, molded into the fabric of the ceiling were rails and other devices that vaguely reminded her of those she had seen in the landing facility the Old One had called his Sanctum Sanctorum.

Yet, even more than these technological artifacts, one other thing told Adara that this place was not some remnant left from the days when the seegnur had created Artemis, but was instead a place they had done their best to hide. The walls were blackened with marks she recognized as having been left by the energy weapons carried by the seegnur. Time and scavengers had done for the flesh and bones, but scattered artifacts told of the men and women who had been slaughtered here.

Together, woman and puma used the light of the single candle to prowl about, looking for an open passage. Adara was unsurprised when they did not find one, although she did find something that might be a closed and locked door. If the seegnur had gone to so much trouble to hide this place, they would not have made it easy for some overly curious Artemesian to find her way in. That there would be a way in, she felt certain.

"Come on," she said to Sand Shadow. "Let's get Griffin and Terrell."

If there was one thing worse than canoeing beneath toothy stalactites in pitch darkness, it was being pulled beneath the same. After consultation with Sand Shadow, Adara had decided that the ledge that ringed the cavern was too incomplete and too slippery for human travel.

"It might have been intended for such once," she said, "but those gaps speak of someone deliberately blowing holes. We'll rig a raft. I'll pull you and Terrell across on it."

The hastily constructed raft floated, but it also leaked. Both men arrived on the gravel beach wet and cold. Terrell, with a factotum's foresight, had anticipated this and had insisted that a duffle packed with changes of clothes join Adara in the canoe. The duffle also contained candle lanterns, matches, rope, chalk, and some other provisions.

When the men had dried off and changed their clothing, Adara led them to where she had found a possible door, although before their stay with the Old One in his Sanctum she would have had trouble thinking of a door as something without either hinges or handle. This "door" looked like nothing so much as a few lines traced on the wall. Leaving Terrell and Griffin with all but one of the candles, Adara went to see what else she could find.

By the time she returned with the news that she had located three other places where there might be doors—although all were shut and she couldn't find any way to open them—Griffin had puzzled through how to open the first door.

"At least I think I have," he admitted. "The release system doesn't look terribly different from the door into the crew quarters at the Sanctum. I waited to try the levers until you were here, since it's likely to be dark on the other side."

Adara nodded. "Good idea. Go on."

Griffin did so, shifting this rod, moving that one, but when he pushed down a final time, the clunking sound that indicated hidden locks had been released didn't follow.

"It feels," Griffin said, pressing down again, "as if it is jammed. It's possible the lock was broken—either over time or to prevent entry."

"Possible," Terrell said, but he looked thoughtful. Griffin recognized the expression and waited for Terrell to say more, but all the factotum added was, "Let's try the other doors."

They did. Two were constructed in such a fashion that Griffin was willing to bet that they had never been intended to be opened from this side. The final one was a small access hatch and penetrated only a hand-span deep. Griffin studied the neat array of rings and lines that—if the theories he'd read were correct—represented the most sophisticated of the ancient technologies. Although they looked like nothing much more than a child's drawing, the theory was that each figure held within it complex routines condensed and ready to be activated at the correct command.

Terrell stepped beside Griffin so that his candle could join Griffin's in illuminating the space. "What's this?" he asked, reaching and picking up the only thing that wasn't a flat drawing—a curving piece of some bright material that rested on the edge of the compartment. It was a pretty thing, a shining, glimmering spiral that would have made a very attractive pendant.

"I have no idea," Griffin said, "but I'm sure I've seen the like and not long ago."

Terrell mimed slapping himself on his forehead. "I remember! There was something like this in with the bodies we found—well, with two of them, at least. Different colors, though. This one is golden topaz. The other two were dark green and orange-red."

Adara joined them. "I remember. We thought they might be jewelry of some sort. The other two are pretty, but I like this one best. It's nearly the same color as my eyes."

"Your eyes are darker," Terrell replied in a caressing tone, "and more mysterious."

Griffin wanted to kick him. "Earlier, we dismissed what we found as jewelry, but somehow I doubt someone left a pendant here in an access cabinet."

"The owner might have taken it off so it wouldn't get damaged while he was working on something . . ." Terrell began, then shook his head. "No. I agree. We were wrong. This is something more important, maybe a tool of some sort."

Again, Griffin caught a hint of that thoughtful expression, but he didn't press Terrell to speak, trusting he would when he'd worked through his idea.

"If this is a tool," Adara said, "so are the others. Did either of you bring the artifacts with you?"

Griffin nodded. "I didn't want to leave the really interesting stuff behind. I kept imagining a squirrel or raven carrying it off, deciding they were lunch. I didn't take all the buttons and fasteners, but I'm sure I brought the pendants."

After Griffin extracted the green and orange-red pendants from the bundle he'd carried close to his skin, they examined them by candlelight.

"I hadn't thought about it before, but they have slightly different shapes," Terrell said. "They're all spirals but, look . . . The topaz one is rounded, the green one is triangular, and the orange-red one is squared."

Adara was twirling the golden topaz artifact so that it caught the candlelight. Griffin wondered if she fancied it for herself. He imagined how the ornament would look resting against her tanned skin, just above the twin rounds of her breasts. He decided it would look very good indeed.

Adara's words, however, showed that her thoughts were far from personal adornment. "You two might have trouble seeing the detail in this weak light, but when you look closely, you'll see that the reason these sparkle is that they're made from tiny crystals. They remind me of sweet ice, a candy Bruin would make for Winterfest by soaking a bit of string in a sugar solution. These crystals are much, much smaller and with the candy you could see the string. These seem to have formed around nothing at all."

"Maybe we should go outside and examine them in sunlight," Griffin suggested. "I wonder if there are others. I'd like to take a look."

Adara shrugged. "If you don't mind getting wet and cold, I don't mind towing you. We certainly seem to have come up on a dead end here. We've found the doors, but we can't get them open."

Terrell nodded. "Let's go out. There's something I want to check, too . . . Something I've been wondering about ever since Adara found those three clusters of artifacts."

Once they were outside, Terrell hardly took time to change out of his damp clothing before making a beeline toward the location where they had found a skeleton but had not found one of the pendants.

"I've been bothered all along," he said, to Adara and Griffin, "by why these bodies were separated from the rest. There's something too alike about their situation."

Struggling to button his trousers, Griffin hurried after, his mind swirling through possibilities. "Alike . . . You mean how all of them were near large clusters of stones?"

"Yes! I know we agreed that those people might have taken shelter there, but why then didn't we find evidence of more than one person? You said the scraps we found—buttons and things—indicated one person, maybe two, but probably one."

"Right."

"We also concluded that the reason the bodies weren't found and buried, as were those in the temple, was because they were isolated."

"Right again."

"What," Terrell said, coming to a halt by the cluster of boulders, "if those three people went to those places deliberately? What if they had the means to open a way into the cavern?"

Adara frowned. "Then why did the people wait in the temple? I thought we agreed it was built as misdirection, nothing more."

"Maybe we'll find there is an opening," Terrell said. He had begun to methodically search the surfaces of the clustered rocks. Griffin joined in. Without asking, he sensed what Terrell sought. "However, we only have legend to tell us that the people were hiding in the temple when they were slaughtered. Maybe they were waiting for something else and hid when they saw the enemy coming. Maybe those who came to bury the bodies assumed they had been hiding in the temple and had been forced out into the open by the attackers."

"It would be a reasonable assumption," Adara agreed, "if they didn't suspect there was anything else here."

"I think," Terrell said, "that these rocks hide some sort of mechanism, one that would enable emergency access. I think it took at least three keys to open it. I think we have two of those keys. If we're lucky, we'll find the third and with it . . ."

His voice trailed off as he slid his hand into a crevice between two of the larger rocks. He pulled, and one of the rocks moved as if it had been set on a pivot.

"There!" he said with satisfaction. "There! What did I tell you?"

Hidden in the space between the two rocks was an incision. Set into that was a glittering elongated oval spiral patterned in indigo-violet crystals. Griffin leaned to get a closer look.

"Fascinating. The pendant stretches out like a spring to fill the space. That explains the spiral shape."

"Beautiful," Adara said. "Now I'm torn as to whether I like this one or the topaz one better." She grinned impishly at them. "Shall we go find what the other rocks hide?"

Terrell pushed the rock back into place. "There's a grip here, hidden so that it looks like a flaw in the rock. I felt something click when I pulled the rock out. I think the mechanism—whatever it is—won't work unless the rock is pushed back into place. See? When the rock is pushed in, that little jutting bit will press into the middle of the spiral."

"Makes sense," Griffin said, slogging through the tall grass toward the next site. "If they went to all this trouble to hide whatever it is we've found, then they wouldn't want it left open."

Now that they knew what they were looking for, finding the second and third keyholes proved relatively easy. One took the dark green triangle, the other the orange-red square. However, inserting the keys and locking the mechanisms caused no miracles to happen. They inspected the temple and found it unchanged.

"It's closing in on evening," Griffin said, "but, if Adara is willing, I'd like to go back into the cavern and see if anything has changed on the other shore."

Adara grinned. "Willing? The only question is whether you two come with me or I go on my own. I've checked with Sand Shadow and she says the horses and Sam the Mule are doing well. She's killed a mountain deer and will share part with us. She's even put our haunch in a bag to chill in the pool near our camp, so the bugs won't get at it."

"Then," Griffin said, his heart pounding with excitement. "What's keeping us? Let's go!"

Interlude: Searching

Like swirling water
I trace the edges
Of nothing

5

Lights from the Sky

Adara had never claimed to have as good a sense of smell as Honeychild, not even as good as Sand Shadow, but it was her sense of smell that told her, even before they had slipped behind the rocky shelf that hid the entrance to the cavern, that something had changed. The air now reeked of rotting vegetation, mud, and slime, mingled with a suggestion of dead fish. When they passed through the opening into the cavern, they saw why.

"The water's gone!" Griffin exclaimed, holding his candle high. "Well, mostly gone . . . It's still draining away."

Adara pointed. "And look . . . There's a path. I never even imagined it was there because the stalactites were so close to the surface of the water that I couldn't canoe through that area."

"Whatever the surface is made from," Terrell said, going to where the path began and kneeling to touch the surface, "may look like rock, but it isn't. There isn't a trace of slime or weed or even mud on the surface. The surface is already almost dry."

"Do we trust ourselves to it?" Griffin asked.

Adara shrugged. "There's not enough water left for my canoe and certainly not for the raft. The ledge around the rim is even less inviting, since now you'd fall into that sludge, rather than into cold water. So it's either use the path or climb down and slog."

"I vote 'path,'" Terrell said. "I'd been wondering how the seegnur hoped to get to safety if the only way to the other shore was using small boats—and we saw no evidence that any were kept here."

Griffin nodded, but he seemed uneasy. Adara didn't blame him. The engineering involved in what they had activated had her thinking of the seegnur as she had when she was a small child—godlike creators, makers of worlds—rather than the relatively understandable mortals whose quarters they had examined back at the Sanctum.

"I'll take point," she said, "and warn you if anything seems unstable. I've let Sand Shadow know what we're doing. She's bringing her dinner closer so she'll be within contact range if anything goes wrong."

The men followed without comment, first Griffin, then Terrell. With the indirect lighting from the candles carried by the men, Adara could see easily. Periodically, she looked down to assure herself that nothing remained other than fish that hadn't swum fast enough to get away when the water drained.

Once or twice, the huntress thought she saw human figures outlined in the mud and wondered. The lore contained tales of the armor the attackers had worn. That would survive even after the corpses within had rotted away. She decided not to mention what she had seen until she was sure. Time enough to come back and take a better look later. Griffin was easily distracted and certainly old suits of armor—presumably broken or they would not be down in the muck—offered neither threat nor help.

The path ended where the gravel beach curved up from beneath, showing the artificial barrier that had assured the shore staying in place all these centuries.

"It's like a big swimming pool," Griffin said, "complete with drains. I wonder where all the water went?"

"There's probably a holding basin," Terrell said. "I'm guessing that overflow ultimately ends up in Maiden's Tear, but the seegnur would not have wanted the water to dump directly in there without some sort of intermediate stop. Otherwise the lake waters would become turbulent and muddy without reason. That would be as good as announcing that there was a hidden source of water that had just emptied out."

"Good point," Griffin said. "I never realized just how thorough a factotum's education must be."

"We are educated to think of contingencies," Terrell replied. "All the better to be of service. Now, seegnur, shall we see if that door is open?"

It wasn't but, with Adara's ability to see in the dark, it did not take them long to locate a panel that, when moved aside, revealed a keyhole shaped to hold the topaz key.

"I'm positive this panel wasn't here before," Griffin said as he inserted the glittering pendant into its place. "I looked right at this spot."

"You did," Adara assured him. "We all did. However, until the other three keys were readied, this was meant to remain invisible. This is different from the other escape hatches we have seen. Those were clearly meant to supply a backup in case the technology failed. This seems to have been meant to keep people out unless they knew exactly what to do."

"This complex," Griffin agreed, "seems different. The technology is of an entirely different order. I've seen nothing like these crystalline keys, nor were the surfaces coated to resist water—not even on Mender's Isle where that would have been useful."

Terrell frowned. "So if this setup wasn't meant to provide an escape route, what was it for?"

Adara pressed her finger into the middle of the sparkling spiral. "There's only one way to find out, isn't there?"

The doors slid apart with hardly a sound. A line of pale blue light glowed to life, illuminating the outline of a corridor otherwise in shadow.

It was one thing to hear about such miracles, but another thing entirely to see them happening. Adara stepped back inadvertently, then worried that the men would think her a coward. However, Terrell looked as startled as she felt and Griffin not much better.

"I guess this light confirms that something is undoing the damage done by the nanobots," Griffin said. "We've suspected it, what with the metal spider and Artemis's speaking to you but, when nothing in the Sanctum or on Mender's Isle worked . . ."

Terrell nodded. "Different location, maybe? As the crow flies, Maiden's Tear is actually closer to where you crashed."

"Possibly . . . Perhaps this area didn't take as much damage."

Adara waved them to silence. The blue light wasn't very strong, but it penetrated more deeply than candlelight. Within it, shapes were taking form . . .

"Griffin, Terrell," she said. "On the floor ahead . . . Looks as if there are bodies. Stay behind me."

She strode forward, acting more confident than she felt. Around her, as if reacting to her motion, the quality of the light changed, the blue hue shifting to a warmer, brighter yellow that better illuminated their surroundings. From the outside, other than the damage to the trail around the cavern's rim and some burn marks, the facility had seemed untouched. Light showed otherwise.

Black streaks along the walls, ceiling, and floor showed where the seegnur's weapons had burned, buckling even those seemingly inde-structible building materials. The corridor was wide enough that a horse-drawn cart could have driven along it with room for flanking outriders. Nonetheless, the heap of bodies nearly blocked it.

Without realizing, Adara had been holding her breath, expecting the stench of corruption. Now she realized this was foolishness. These people had died five hundred years ago. All that gave them the sem-blance of men and women was the armor they had worn, armor marked across the back of the necks with a narrow sooty line. A second black mark, this one rounded, punched through the pack that rested between the shoulders of each suit of armor.

"Stars above!" Griffin's voice was tight. "They were shot from be-hind. Probably they were lined up, expecting attack to come through from the door into the cavern. An enemy snuck up behind them. My brother Falkner always says that no matter how carefully you construct any sort of armor, joints are always the most vulnerable point. First shot was to the neck joint, then a finishing shot to the back—that would take out the power supply, weapons."

Terrell knelt down next to the body nearest to him. With infinite gentleness, he turned the helmet as if hoping to see a face within, but what met his gaze was a skull, remnants of mummified skin stretched tight across the bones.

"I don't disagree," he said, "not quite. But I don't think it was the joints that made them vulnerable. I think they were shot by someone they trusted. I can't believe the seegnur wouldn't have had the means to provide protection from their own weapons. What use armor otherwise? No . . . I think these people were murdered."

Griffin nodded. "I see what you're saying but . . ."

He never had a chance to finish. From nowhere and everywhere at once a voice, clear and childish, spoke in strange accents:

"Who are you? Speak rightly or be prepared to die."

That evening, when Julyan came down from his day's spying, he discovered a strange horse tied outside the cottage. Despite lines that spoke of quality and speed, the gelding clearly had been ridden hard. As Julyan mounted the steps, a young woman wearing the badge of a post rider came out of the house, gave him a terse nod, then, without another word, mounted up.

He hurried inside to find the Old One so immersed in a letter that he didn't even acknowledge Julyan's return. It was odd seeing him acting this way. He still wore the colorful fripperies of Maxy, the catamite, but every line of his body was that of the Old One of Spirit Bay, arrogant and in complete control.

Ignoring his employer in turn, Julyan went into the kitchen and worked the pump handle until cold water gushed forth. He'd drunk his fill and splashed the worst of the day's sweat and grit from his face when the Old One came in.

"We're leaving. Tonight. Going back to Spirit Bay. How quickly can you be ready?"

Julyan answered with a question of his own. "Are you sure you want to leave? My report might change your mind."

"I sincerely doubt it, but you will not get moving until you have told me what you think is so important. Speak."

"They've found something significant." Julyan went on to describe what he'd observed that day: how the dull grubbing about in the dirt had changed to more purposeful action, how Adara had vanished for much of the morning. How she had returned for the men. How they had all vanished, returned, vanished again.

Julyan had expected the Old One to be pleased and impressed. Indeed, he had amused himself with imagining what would happen next. His favorite scenario was being told to go down and capture the lot. He'd imagined how Griffin would be shocked, the factotum frightened, and Adara . . . Oh, he'd enjoyed imagining what she'd do once Julyan had her men in his keeping. How far he could make her go to preserve them . . .

Even now the thought made him lick his lips and his trousers uncomfortably tight.

But when Julyan finished his report, the Old One looked only mildly interested. "We knew they'd find something eventually. What you learned is helpful in one way. We know where they are. If they've found something, they won't be leaving quickly. Griffin is extremely methodical and Terrell tends to follow his lead. That means we can depart without worrying they'll become bored and we'll lose their trail."

"You still wish to depart?"

"Didn't I tell you so?" The Old One tucked his letter into an inside pocket of his tunic. "Allies of mine at the college of loremasters in Spirit Bay have asked me to return and look into an interesting matter. A few days ago, something large splashed into Spirit Bay—something large enough to cause waves to crash in the harbor and small boats to be wrecked. Since then, lights have been seen on Mender's Isle."

"Oh . . ." Julyan tried hard not to seem impressed, but knew he had failed. "And how did they find you?"

"I left partial notes with three of the loremasters I felt I could trust but who I knew did not completely trust each other. I knew they would never collaborate unless they felt the matter was urgent."

"Then you anticipated this thing that splashed from the heavens?"

"Not precisely that." The Old One steepled his fingers. "Griffin confided in me several things that I did not make public, nor will I now. However, they led me to believe it was not impossible that eventually something remarkable might happen. When the situation made it prudent for me to relocate, I took steps so that if such events occurred, I would know."

"And we leave tonight?"

"Yes. We will take only what can be carried on one pack horse. I will send for the rest later, if it appears we will remain in Spirit Bay."

"Perhaps," Julyan suggested, "I should stay here and keep an eye on Griffin and the rest. It's possible something remarkable will happen here, too."

The Old One shook his head. "That is always a matter for consideration, but I want you with me. You have skills I do not care to do without, nor do I wish to leave Seamus unsupervised."

Julyan wondered what would happen if he refused, but decided that he did not wish to find out.

"I'll go check on the horses. At least they've had a good rest."

"Yes," the Old One replied. "We are going to be pushing them hard."

✵

"Who are you? Speak rightly or be prepared to die."

Griffin glanced around wildly, seeking the source of the voice which seemed to come from all directions at once. Then his perspective adjusted and he was back where voices often came from nowhere. Judging from the expressions on Adara and Terrell's faces, they were frightened. Without a word they had moved so that each faced an opposite direction, covering all angles of approach.

"Who are you?" repeated the voice, speaking in an accent that was like, but not quite like, the speech of the Artemesians.

Griffin spoke. "Griffin Dane, of Sierra in the Kyley System. These are my companions, Adara the Huntress and Terrell the Factotum, both of Artemis."

"None of you are on my list of authorized visitors."

Despite the precision of the answer, Griffin caught a note of confusion in the voice.

"When was your list last updated?"

A slight pause, then the voice gave a date—a date five hundred years in the past.

"Your list is out of date," Griffin said confidently. "The current date is . . ."

He recited it in three different formats, beginning with the one that most historians agreed had been used by the Old Imperials. "If you doubt me, check the stellar alignment. You can do that, correct?"

He was guessing wildly, but if this place had been created by the seegnur then surely there would have been a means of assessing in-system traffic.

"I can," the voice said, then, "I should . . . I could . . . I cannot! Malfunction detected. Uplink reports repeated failures!"

"Wait then," Griffin said. "Shortly, the sky will darken and you can check manually. You have the capacity?"

"I do . . . Did . . . What has . . . I am remembering . . . What has happened?"

"What do you last remember?"

Terrell murmured, "Griffin, who are you talking to?"

Griffin held a finger to his lips. Terrell obeyed, but his gaze continued to rove nervously over the corridor, resting repeatedly on the heap of ruined battle armor. Adara was superficially calmer but, when Griffin started speaking, she had padded back to the door into the cavern and now leaned against one edge, assuring herself that their exit remained open.

"What I remember . . . I remember you are not authorized!"

"Wait until nightfall if you wish," Griffin suggested. "After you check the stars, I think you will agree with me that it is unlikely that anyone authorized remains. Will you tell me what you remember or shall we wait until you check the stars?"

"I must wait." The voice sounded distinctly unhappy. "I have no choice. I will wait. I must request that you do not attempt to penetrate further into this facility until I have confirmed the current date. Will you comply?"

Griffin looked at the others. "I hate to say this, but I think we'd better do as this person suggests."

Adara shrugged. "We came here because you so desired, seegnur. I will be guided by your wisdom."

Terrell nodded agreement, then motioned to the line of armor. "It's several hours until full dark. I'm not sure I want to wait here with these."

"And I'm hungry," Adara added.

Griffin was astonished by their new calm. Then he understood that they were following his lead, trying to act as if this was all some variation on normal.

He spoke to the air. "Shall we return an hour or two after full dark?"

"You have the access keys . . ." The voice considered. "You may return after full dark. Telescopic sights are active, but orbital relays seem nonfunctional."

"Very good. We have the access keys. Remember that."

Without another word, they left, retrieving the oval key when they passed through the door into the cavern. Griffin was aware that he was holding his shoulders very stiff and straight, awaiting a shot that never came. When they were outside of the cavern, Adara held a finger to her lips, then led them some distance away, beyond, Griffin realized after a moment, the area within which Artemis had been "blind."

"I think we should be able to talk freely here," Adara said, sinking onto the grass and leaning back against a tree. "Sand Shadow is bringing dinner. She warns you that it is not her fault that it will be cold."

"I'm not really hungry," Terrell admitted.

"I am," Adara said, "and you should be. Bruin always said it was foolishness to hunt on an empty stomach."

Terrell nodded. "Bruin is a wise old bear. I'll eat, but I'm still not hungry. I've seen fragments of that sort of armor. Do you know what it takes to punch a hole in it? Let me give you the short version . . . Nothing we have can do it: not arrows, not swords, not spears. Drop a boulder on it and this stuff is as likely to bend as not. Sink it in the sea for five years or ten or a hundred and it comes up needing a wash, that's it. Put it in a fire and it gets sooty, but doesn't burn. Not even forge heat does much damage. Yet something punched holes in that stuff so fast that not one person in that line had time to turn around."

Griffin nodded. "I saw that, too. The boots were aligned pretty much as they would have been if the soldiers fell all at once. "

He didn't add that similar materials were still in use in the Kyley Domain and other systems as well. Much of the Old Imperial technology had been lost, but if the base materials could be found—something that was not always possible—their creation was a problem of fabrication. Entire fortunes had been made by reverse engineering Old Imperial technology.

"So who were you talking to?" Adara asked. "Not a person. Was it a machine? The lore said that the seegnur had machines that could talk, but that such were forbidden on Artemis except in the gravest circumstances."

"Forbidden," Griffin repeated, "just as Maiden's Tear was forbidden. Yes. I think it's possible that we were talking to a machine or perhaps a creation like Artemis herself—a neural network, specific to this one place, rather than meant to embrace the entire planet."

"The maiden," Terrell said suddenly, "who was separated from her sister and wept so copiously that the lake was formed. No wonder the legend never said why they were parted."

"It's as good an answer as any," Griffin said. "Here's what I think happened. When Artemis was invaded, the advanced technology in this facility suffered the same fate as elsewhere. That explains our friend's memory lapse. Eventually, the invaders found the place and wiped out everyone inside. I'm hoping that whatever they found was at least as interesting as the landing facility, because then they won't have destroyed everything. And then I'll have a chance of finding something I can reactivate and use to get in touch with my orbiter."

"We won't know until we look," Adara said, "and we won't know if we can look until we return."

Griffin hesitated, then thought he might as well ask. "Does Artemis have any thoughts on the matter?"

Adara laughed without humor. "Am I a seegnur to command a planet? I tell you, Griffin, Artemis speaks to me when she wills. She does not come at my command. Neither Sand Shadow nor I have heard anything for many days . . . She seems to be avoiding us."

When Griffin asked about Artemis, Adara did not add that both she and Sand Shadow had felt uneasiness prowling their dreams. After all, how could she be certain this came from Artemis and did not simply mirror their own feelings about this very strange hunt in which they were involved? Griffin could not understand how difficult it was to know that one was violating a prohibition. Perhaps Terrell—bonded as he was to Griffin, and as a factotum trained to let another's will override his own—did not feel the sense of wrongness as strongly as Adara did. Hunters were perhaps the most independent of all the professions and, because they needed to be able to make their own decisions, were expected to know right from wrong.

And who is to say this is wrong? Adara thought. *Griffin must be a seegnur of some sort or Terrell would not have bonded to him. If Griffin is a seegnur, the prohibitions do not apply to him. Our first commandment is to obey the seegnur, and our seegnur wishes to explore this place.*

But she still felt uneasy. She wanted to go back to those days when her greatest worry was whether or not to marry Terrell. Or the days when she worried about the mockery of the village maidens. Or about who might notice the odd appearance of her eyes . . .

Might as well wish myself unborn, she thought wryly. *For all we humans imagine otherwise, life moves only in one direction until death puts an ending to all motion.*

Sand Shadow arrived as dusk was darkening the sky. When they had been visiting Adara's family, Griffin had suggested that they alter a small set of saddlebags so that Sand Shadow could use them if she wished to carry larger burdens. The puma still lacked the dexterity to work a buckle, but she was getting very good at knots.

Although she griped about acting as a pack animal, Sand Shadow actually took considerable pleasure in being able to expand her abilities. Of course, her idea of what made a balanced meal was a bit odd, but she had remembered meat and journey cakes. Terrell foraged and found some wild greens growing along a nearby stream and Adara contributed wild strawberries.

After, they all napped or at least pretended to do so. When full dark came, they were all up and ready to go with a rapidity that suggested rest had not been very deep. Letting Sand Shadow—who had departed to check on the horses and Sam the Mule—know what they were about, Adara led the way back into the cavern.

They'd been concerned that the waters would have returned, but the path remained open—although the drying mud reeked as things long sealed beneath the surface began to rot. When they found the huge double doors had closed again, Griffin momentarily panicked, but the topaz oval key worked as before.

This time, when the doors slid apart, there was no pale blue light. Instead, the brighter yellow light rose as if in greeting. When they had advanced a few paces into the corridor, the voice spoke again. Although the manner in which it framed sentences was still odd, there was much more emotion. Perhaps because of Terrell's reminder of the maiden for whom the lake had been named, Adara now heard the voice as that of a girl the same age as her sister Elektra.

"The stars have turned," it said. "I have cross-referenced and the patterns match projections for five hundred years into the future. All my friends are gone. I am filled with bodies far gone into death."

"What do you last remember?" Griffin asked gently.

"I remember . . ." There was a pause, then, "You have the keys."

"All four," Griffin reassured her.

"The keys authorize unauthorized entry, especially in extreme circumstances," said the voice.

"These are extreme circumstances," Griffin replied. "I say that other than complete destruction, the circumstances don't get much more extreme."

"I am shamed. I remember almost nothing. Last I remember, there was much excitement. We expected visitors. There was to be a tour of inspection and we would reveal new developments. Everything was readied. Wise O'Rahilly was gravely excited. So were the rest of the staff. Then we all felt the thunder that was not thunder. I alone felt the fire that was the rain. After that, a swirl of color, a thousand small battles fought, each lost in an instant. I died. Perhaps I only slept? I was gone out until I began to dream. The opening of the emergency access door awoke me."

Terrell chanted softly. "So speaks the lore. The attackers broke through the heavens with a thunder so loud that the ears of many who heard it bled. Rain fell. Where it touched, the hidden devices of the seegnur were rendered useless. Then came death, swift and ruthless, and with it the end of the seegnur's time upon Artemis. So it shall be until the seegnur come again and the rain falls cool, bringing life again to all that was not flesh and blood. So says the lore."

Adara bent her head in respect. "So says the lore. Now, seegnur, what do you command?"

Griffin nodded, acknowledging that from this point he must lead. He had to tread carefully. At this moment, the entity to whom they spoke was confused. Apparently, it had been taken out in the earliest stages of the attack on Artemis. It had only been reactivated for a few hours. He didn't know how similar it was in construction to Artemis but, from what Adara and Sand Shadow had gathered, it seemed as if the planetary neural network had been damaged as well as disabled. The same could be true of this entity.

"What shall we call you?" he asked.

"I was called Leto," the voice said.

"Leto, you have told us what you remember of the attack. Thank you. I think you can also help us understand better what happened here after you went to sleep. We need to understand so we can put this facility into order."

"Operations have been derailed. Full level of damage has not yet been assessed."

Leto sounded distressed. Griffin was not surprised. All the evidence indicated that Leto had been created to coordinate activity within an

area so encapsulated from the rest of the planet that Artemis had not
even been aware it existed.

"Let us begin with these bodies," Griffin said, indicating the crumpled suits of armor. "What can you tell me of them?"

"I can tell nothing. They do not belong to this facility. The style
of the armor is wrong. Although it bears similarities to various types
I hold in my memory, it is not any of our models."

"Well, that's interesting," Terrell said. "The lore has always held
that the seegnur did not recognize their attackers."

Adara spoke in the cadence reserved for reciting from the lore. "And
the seegnur cried out in dismay, 'Who are these who seek our lives?' "

Griffin was fascinated. Since Artemis had been lost to history soon
after the battle which had taken place on her surface, he knew little
of what had taken place. He restrained an urge to ask for more details
and returned his attention to Leto.

"Did this facility have defenders?"

"It did. Anticipating your query, I have been searching. I believe
I have accounted for all the suits of battle armor. I would say I am
seventy-five percent certain I have located them all." The girlish voice
turned apologetic. "The error factor is due to the fact that several suits
are so badly damaged I need to extrapolate the entire from what remains."

"Are any of the suits we've seen in working order?"

"Unlikely. The damage was severe."

"I would like to tour the facility," Griffin said boldly. He sensed,
although he didn't know why or how, that Leto was holding something
back.

He expected rejection or at least another delay, but Leto merely replied with evident sadness. "You may do so. Little, I fear, is as it was
when we prepared it for inspection. I wish you could see it as it was
then, so bright, so shining, so full of excitement. Much has been damaged, perhaps beyond repair."

Yet, despite the damage, within a few hours the facility's purpose
was clear beyond a shadow of a doubt. They departed, taking with them
the oval key and promising Leto they would return.

In their conversation they had learned that Leto's perception currently did not extend beyond the facility itself. Even before the facility had been so severely damaged, Leto's perception outside it had been limited. She could see and hear anything in the cavern, but in the meadow beyond she could not perceive without specific commands. The temple, it turned out, was the central point for that external perception. Therefore, as they walked back to their camp, they talked freely.

"Of course," Terrell said, "Leto could be lying, but I don't think she was. There is a directness even to her suspicions."

Adara nodded. "And what if she is? I don't doubt that in her day she could probably have held off armies, but now? The destruction was terrible. I don't think I ever grasped what the seegnur were capable of . . . It's one thing to hear tales and see occasional damaged structures—like the place I showed you in the mountains, Griffin. It's another to see what we did today. I know I'll have nightmares."

Terrell grinned at her, teeth flashing within the darkness of his facial hair. "I'll volunteer to give you good thoughts to hold off the nightmares—or at least leave you too tired to dream, except maybe of me."

Griffin bit back a growl. Surely this was not the time or place! To his relief, Adara ignored Terrell's words as if they hadn't been spoken.

"Griffin, that place . . . It was for making weapons, wasn't it?"

"It was. Not only weapons but weapons above and beyond what what we believed even the Old Imperials possessed." Darkness made it easier for Griffin to talk about things he had never mentioned before—never mentioned because on some level he was ashamed of them. "My interest in history comes honestly. My family has long been interested in what happened before the Old Empire fell. However, much as I hate to admit it, their interest, going back to my father's father and even earlier, was very specialized. Because our family rose to wealth and power through the wars that eventually led to the establishment of the Kyley Domain, military history held a great fascination."

Terrell said, "Because within that history there might be the secrets to greater power? So it is with many who become loremasters.
There are those who wish to know the lore because they believe it will
lead them to understand incomprehensible issues. However, many hope
to find something that will make them a power."

"Like the Old One," Adara said.

"I despise the Old One," Terrell said, any trace of flirtation gone
from his voice, "but there is an honesty to him. I think he believed
what he told Griffin—that he seeks knowledge to draw Artemis back
into a unity of law and purpose, such as we had in the days of the
seegnur. Many of those I met during my training had no goal beyond
being a power within their own immediate sphere."

They had reached the camp and Griffin eyed his bedroll with longing. However, in the flickering light of the fire Sand Shadow had stirred
up in anticipation of their arrival, he could see that his Artemesian
friends were uneasy. He settled for sitting on the folded bedding and
unlacing his boots to free feet he was suddenly aware ached after
hours walking on the unyielding floors of the facility.

"Anyhow, because I grew up surrounded by military relics—and
plenty of active military as well—I am good at assessing what we saw
today. Leto's facility was intended for the research and construction
of weapons, weapons I suspect would have enabled those who commanded them to dominate the empire, to weld a fragmenting state into
a whole cemented by fear of complete annihilation."

Adara touched Griffin's arm. "Shall we seal that complex again?
Look for your communications array elsewhere?"

Griffin shook his head. "This goes beyond my need. You spoke of
nightmares. I fear I won't be able to rest until I understand how much
of that facility remains intact. My dream has always been to return
home, bragging of my discovery, but once I do so, others will come
here. I must know how dangerous this planet may be."

His voice dropped. "And, if it is as dangerous as I fear, well, I may
be forced to forsake my dream. I'm not sure I could ever return. What
if I let something slip?"

He forced a smile and slipped his hand around Adara's. "I might stay here on Artemis and see if I can learn to sweet-talk you as well as does my roguish friend."

Adara squeezed his fingers before taking back her hand. "You may be forced into exile in any case. That place looked thoroughly damaged to me."

"I know," Griffin said. "That may not be all bad. I keep remembering how the tales of Artemis always ended with her not being destroyed. Historians usually agreed that this was because she offered no threat and would be the prize of those who came to dominate the region. What if that is only partly true? What if those planet splitters were held back because Artemis offered a greater prize than history remembers? What if she was lost to the future because any record of her coordinates was deliberately destroyed? What if I've found what should have been left lost?"

Terrell sighed. "You're not the only one who has been remembering, Griffin. Back in the early days of my training, we were given stories to memorize because entertaining often falls to a junior factotum. One of these was a fanciful tale, based on what my teacher told us was a reconstruction of stories of the goddess Artemis—the virgin huntress for whom our planet is named. The tale of her birth was included. Do you know what was the name of Artemis's mother?"

Adara whispered. "Leto?"

"Yes," Terrell said somberly. "Leto. I think that naming means that Artemis was created after Leto—to protect the war facility as the goddess did her mother. We have been told that our planet was created as a place of pleasure and relaxation but, even as the highest of technology lay beneath the pastoral pleasures, so yet another falsehood underlies the bedrock of our beliefs. The war machine factory was not added later. All along, it was the hidden purpose for Artemis."

Interlude: In Spirit Bay

What fire that burns even water?
What storm on a day without clouds?

Shall I tell?
Who?
They have left me.
Enigma will be my new heart.

6

Leto's Heart

Although they traveled with all the speed the Old One might command—and between hoarded coin and favors, he commanded far more than Julyan would have imagined—days passed before the waters of Spirit Bay glistened on the horizon.

"Go ahead," the Old One commanded. "Take Seamus with you. Travel as rapidly as possible. At the loremasters' college ask for Flamen. When you have him in private, show him this." The Old One held out a square of embroidered fabric. "Ask him what has happened since he and his friends sent that message. Based upon what he tells you, I will decide how best to present myself."

Julyan nodded. He had been about to say that he could travel much more quickly if he left Seamus behind. Then he understood. The Old One would witness the meeting with Flamen through Seamus. No time would be wasted carrying messages back and forth. Nor did Julyan doubt that the Old One would be close by. Julyan's going ahead was a safety measure, nothing more.

They had discarded the costumes they had used in Crystalaire but, when he arrived at the loremasters' college, Julyan thought it best to give his name as Ryan Trader and present Seamus as his son. He didn't know how much their enemies had revealed about the Old One and his associates, but nothing was ever lost by taking precautions.

The youth who was porter that day seemed unsuspicious. He directed them to wait in a small parlor and refresh themselves while he sent for Flamen. The wait lasted long enough that Julyan was fighting an urge to bolt when Flamen finally arrived.

The loremaster was a thin, wiry greybeard with worry carved into the lines of his long face. He paused in the doorway and spoke in a querulous tone of voice. "Yes? I was told you wished to see me."

Julyan extended a hand as if in greeting, showing the folded cloth in his palm. "We have friends in common. One of them sent me to consult you on various matters."

The lines on Flamen's face sketched both shock and eagerness. Then he became all the suave scholar. "No doubt you are interested in consulting me about further education for this young man. The day is pleasant. Walk with me and I will show you something of our college."

Only when they were well away from possible eavesdroppers did Flamen ask anxiously, "You come from the Old One? He received our message?"

"He did. He sent me to learn what has developed."

"Little, but that little is having great effect. He told you how something fell from the heavens into the bay?"

"Yes."

"It came down by night, unseen except for fire burning along its flanks. It splashed into the bay, causing considerable upheaval. No ships were lost, although sailors tell of being rocked as if in a terrible storm. Many smaller craft were swamped. Later, lights were seen on Mender's Isle."

"You wrote this."

Flamen looked exasperated, but finally came to the point. "There have been few developments since. Craft have been sent out to watch the islands, but nothing significant has been reported. Even sightings of lights have become more rare. A loremasters' conclave has been held to discuss the matter. All this has managed to confirm is that there is much dissent among our numbers. Some are saying that nothing crashed into the bay at all, that the disruption was caused by waters settling into subterranean areas and ebbing out in an erratic fashion."

"How do they explain this thing that fell from the heavens?"

"Reflected moonlight. Hallucination. Bits of the sky trash that have fallen from times immemorial, unconnected to aquatic disturbances." Flamen rubbed his temples. "As for the lights seen on Mender's Isle, those are being dismissed as relics of the disturbances there."

Hypocrites! Julyan sneered. *Five hundred years of piously proclaiming that all will be right when the seegnur return . . . Now they do all they can to deny the possibility. But much would change if the seegnur did return. The loremasters would go from dictating right living to being dictated to by the returning masters.*

Seamus stirred, blinked, stretched, then spoke, his voice full of strange flats and sharps. "Ryan, meet me at Chankley's Harbor. Flamen, say nothing about my arrival to any, even our closest allies. Glory will be yours. The Old One has spoken."

Flamen's pale scholar's complexion turned distinctly green. Julyan hid his own discomfort—he never liked when the Old One used Seamus as an extra mouth—beneath a knowing chuckle.

"Got it," he replied. "I can be there in a couple hours."

"I hear," Flamen said, swallowing hard, "and will comply."

Seamus shook his head as if to dislodge a bug from his ear, then started chewing the nail on his right index finger. Apparently, the audience was over.

"Well, we'll be off, then," Julyan said. "If some emergency arises, you'd do well to send a note via Captain Bore Chankley at Chankley's Harbor. I'm sure you and the Old One already have some sort of code worked out. Use it. Captain Chankley is not wholly in the Old One's confidence."

Flamen nodded.

As Julyan chivvied Seamus along, he thought, *Captain Chankley is not wholly in the Old One's confidence, but then who is? I suspect that one keeps secrets even from himself.*

It was not a comfortable thought.

After they'd been exploring Leto's complex for several days, Terrell suggested to Adara that they go check on the horses and Sam the Mule.

"Leto may have assured us that Maiden's Tear was designed to keep large predators out," he said, "and certainly we've seen no evidence of them, but Sand Shadow had no trouble entering the area."

"She is in a demiurge relationship," Adara reminded him. "That makes her different."

"Still . . ."

Adara was always glad to get outside. Leto's complex was an unsettling place. They'd cleared away the dead bodies. Since Griffin had insisted on preserving all of the equipment, this had consisted more of removing fragments of bone from within clothing and armor than a more usual burial detail. Leto made the task extremely unsettling. Whenever she recognized someone by some detail of clothing or insignia, she lamented with passionate intensity.

After the bodies were dealt with, they had made a rapid check through the remainder of the facility. Over half was given to tasks Adara hardly comprehended. However, there were areas that reminded her of the Sanctum: sleeping rooms, rooms for socializing, what Griffin identified as a hospital. These had been thoroughly wrecked, but at least they contained few bodies.

To facilitate cleanup, Leto had opened a door into the valley, so her human visitors no longer needed to pick their way through the cavern. This secondary door was hidden from view by a chance-seeming tunnel of rocks and foliage. After Leto supplied them each with crystalline keys to the valley door, she reflooded the underground lake and sealed the door.

Once more out in the open, Adara stretched, glorying in the freshness of the mountain air. "I'm glad to be outside again."

"It is stuffy in there," Terrell agreed. "Leto admits that a great deal of the facilities' functions are nonfunctional. I was relieved when she found how to activate the lights. Walking through those closed corridors, never certain when you might stumble over a body or a wall splashed with blood, was wearing on my nerves."

Adara nodded. Those lights remained a source of astonishment to her and Terrell. It was one thing to hear tales about lights that worked without smoke or flame, another to actually experience them. Leto was now working on activating what she called the heating/cooling system—as if one thing could do both jobs. To Adara, that made about as much sense as thinking you could kindle a fire with an icicle, but Griffin took the terminology for granted, so she supposed there must be some sense behind it.

Once they were well out of the valley, Terrell spoke. "Griffin is behaving very oddly. He's acting like when we first came to the Old One's Sanctum Sanctorum—before Sand Shadow shook him out of his introspection."

Adara nodded. "I suppose it is only reasonable. If Griffin is to find a way off planet, he needs to find an undamaged communications array."

"He's obsessed," Terrell disagreed. "Can an hour away now and then matter? Griffin has been on Artemis for months, yet, last night, he wouldn't stop his burrowing through the guts of some machine even to join us to eat. It wasn't as if he was looking at anything that might lead him to a communications array. He was down on one of the manufacturing levels, assessing if the machines there had only been turned off or if they'd been damaged beyond use."

"I remember. I was surprised. Sand Shadow had hunted wild turkey and saved the better part for us. And there were early raspberries. Instead of coming to enjoy dinner, Griffin just jammed a slice of the roast between two stale flat breads and went on with checking the machines. I thought he'd be more interested in the living quarters and the facilities associated with them. After all, wouldn't we be more likely to find working communications equipment there? But when I suggested we shift over there, he looked at me as if I had two heads."

Terrell looked side to side uneasily. "I wish we could be certain we can't be overheard. I know Leto told us she cannot hear anything in the valley, but still . . . To her, Griffin is the seegnur. She might not lie to him, but she would to us."

"True," Adara agreed. She shifted away from the most direct path to where the riding animals were pastured. "We can see Sam the Mule and the horses from over here," she explained, "and the view is much more enjoyable than blood-splattered walls and cluttered corridors."

Terrell followed without question. When Adara stopped and leaned against a slim aspen ornamented, coincidentally or not, with some elegant shelf fungus, he asked, "All clear?"

"This is within the area Artemis could see. She might hear us, but Leto should not be able to."

Terrell nodded. "I'm wondering. Could Leto have anything to do with how Griffin is behaving?"

"Controlling him, you mean?" Adara considered. "I suppose that's possible. But would the seegnur have created a creature with the power to control them?"

Terrell shrugged. "I don't know. We don't know enough about the seegnur—and we keep learning that much of what we do know about them is lies."

"Griffin," Adara said, "has always insisted that he does not think he is a proper seegnur."

"Proper or not," Terrell replied stiffly, "he is enough of one to touch my dreams. I assure you, my golden-eyed beauty, that I would not invite a man into my dreams. You, now . . ."

"Terrell." Adara squeezed his shoulder, noticing that in her emotion the claws were tipping forth. "I care too much for you to use you lightly. Before . . ." She swallowed hard. "Before, back in Shepherd's Call last midsummer, I could sleep with you because I didn't care, not about you and not very much about myself. Now . . . You're my friend, my trusted companion, and, worst of all, I think you honestly care for me. Please, don't tease . . ."

"Is it Griffin? Tell me and I'll work on resigning myself."

"No. It is not Griffin. I feel for him much as I do for you, but without the added complication of a pleasant memory. 'It's not anyone or if it is anyone it is . . .'"

"Not that bastard Julyan!"

"Not Julyan. Definitely not Julyan. But how I feel is all tangled up with what happened with Julyan. I adored him with a depth of passion that embarrasses me when I recall it. I would recite his name in my head rather than think. I wrote him poems, set them to music . . . I would have carved his name on my heart. Not only did he reject me—I think I could accept that—now I have learned that what I worshipped was a lie."

"I'm not lying . . ."

Adara held a finger to her lips in a bid for silence. "Terrell, I don't think you lie. I don't know myself, don't trust myself . . . Please! I need you as a friend. Don't make that impossible."

Terrell slumped against the tree. "There are times . . ." He left the thought unfinished, visibly wrenched himself back to other subjects. "Do you think Leto is somehow controlling Griffin or is it only that their desires run in harness?"

"I don't know, nor do I think I would be the one to find out." For the first time, Adara noticed that Terrell's eyes were bloodshot, that there were smudges beneath them. "You aren't sleeping well. Why not?"

Terrell shifted uneasily. "I don't like sleeping in that place. The stench of death is long gone but it feels like a charnel house to me. But Griffin will sleep nowhere else. He has taken over one of the sleeping rooms, even though the air is still and stale. He resents any time spent away, so I have stayed nearby."

Adara tilted her head and studied him. "And . . ."

"I don't like my dreams when I do sleep. By day Griffin tells me what this device may have been for, what that press was intended to shape. All are horrors. The armor is the least offensive—Leto calls it 'spaveks.' At least the spaveks were meant to protect the wearer, but the weapons . . . By night I dream of old wars . . ." His voice dropped low and husky, as if admitting to some shame. "Or Griffin does. I'm not sure whose dreams are whose anymore."

Adara wanted to hold Terrell, to stroke the rough velvet of his cheek in comfort, but she knew those gestures would be misinterpreted.

"I don't think I would be the one to find out what is driving Griffin," Adara said, "but you might, my friend. Stop running from those dreams. Take control of them. Find out why Griffin dreams so, and if his dreams are of his own choosing."

Terrell rubbed his eyes with his fists. "I was afraid you would say something like that. But you're right. I am factotum-trained, factotum-bred to my core. My soul tells me to protect this seegnur . . . But how can I protect him from himself?"

"First find out if the protecting is needed," Adara said. "Then we decide."

"And you?"

"Leto is a mystery, but legends call her Artemis's mother. Perhaps in learning more about the daughter, I can learn whether or not the mother is one we can trust." She gave a lopsided smile. "I have been saying I cannot call Artemis to me, but I'll admit, I haven't tried very hard. If you will take on Griffin, then I will work harder to understand Artemis."

Terrell thrust out his hand. "Deal!"

Adara accepted the clasp with a hard squeeze, noting that her claws had retreated. "Now, let's go down and see the horses and Sam the Mule. They look fine from here, but a closer look is never a bad idea."

Unlike Spirit Bay or Crystalaire—both of which had been designed by the seegnur not only to provide habitation for some of the residents of Artemis, but also to cater to the whims of the visiting seegnur—Chankley's Harbor had evolved organically. The difference showed. The seegnur's building materials had been incredibly tough. Even after five hundred years, many buildings looked fresher and newer than those of more modern construction. The trim on those structures never needed repainting and it took a ferocious storm to damage the roofs.

By contrast, Chankley's Harbor was a grungy place, looking exactly like what it was: a village that had grown up because the small harbor was a good one. There were sheds for storing nets, rope, and extra sail, dwellings that were hardly any better than sheds to hold the fisher folk when they came ashore. Probably the best maintained structure in the place was the stone well. Fresh water so near a saltwater bay was not a resource to be treated lightly. The docks were built on stone pilings, with wooden planks, meant to bear against both storm and hard use.

"A working village," the Old One said as they approached down the overgrown, twisting landside trail. "Not a remnant of ancient privilege."

Since until a short time before the Old One had lived in the seegnur's former landing facility, spending a fair amount of time in the abandoned shuttle repair facility beneath Mender's Isle, Julyan did not think he was out of line for finding this statement hypocritical.

He held his tongue. The Old One enjoyed seeing how people would react to his various odd comments. After being lured into several "philosophical" discussions that only served to prove that the Old One could think with more twists than a basket full of baby snakes, Julyan had decided stoic silence was his best course of action. He suspected his silence amused the Old One, too, but at least silence didn't force him to think in a fashion that made his head ache.

"They know me here," Julyan said. "Unless you want to be seen before I have a chance to tell Captain Bore Chankley that you'd prefer word of your return did not spread, it's better I go ahead."

"Go, by all means," the Old One said, his pale grey eyes twinkling with mild amusement. "Although I think Bore would be wise enough to anticipate my wishes and assure his people's silence."

Julyan replied with a terse nod, thinking that the Old One was probably correct. The Chankley Clan had worked for the Old One for some time now, arranging for supplies to be dropped off at Mender's Isle. Although many of those who crewed the ships had no idea who their mysterious client was, Captain Chankley certainly did. He was the sort of slimy eel who would do almost anything—including violating a prohibited area—if paid enough. But he'd want the security of knowing who he was working for, so he could drag him under with him if he started drowning.

Perhaps because the landside trail was so infrequently used—it was far easier to reach Chankley's Harbor by boat than by land—Julyan's approach attracted attention. Slatternly women and sloppy men drifted out of various structures, looking—despite the midday hour—as if they'd just woken up.

Of course, Julyan thought, *most of them probably have. The boats would have been out either very early or overnight, depending on where they were fishing. Unless they had an extraordinary catch, most of the work would have been finished hours ago.*

Julyan swaggered into the village square, chucked the prettiest of the young women under the chin, and said, "So, where's the captain? I've news for him, news worth coin, not just barter."

Lots of the sailors here could have claimed the title "captain," since the boss of any boat with a crew larger than two merited the title, but in Chankley Harbor only one man was "the captain." It was rumored that Bore Chankley had assaulted his own father for the title, so Julyan guessed that no one was willing to push the point.

"I'm here," came a rasping voice from the doorway of the least offensive of the structures—the one that nearly merited the word "house" rather than "hut" or "shack." "Julyan Hunter! Almost didn't know you with that white hair and those clothes. So, you weren't drowned. Figured not. You're too mean to drown."

Julyan didn't protest. He and Captain Chankley understood each other too well for that, and their mutual respect made certain the rest of the captain's people treated Julyan with proper deference.

Bore Chankley had hips like a snake and shoulders that testified to a lifetime of hauling on lines and setting sail. His eyes were framed by deep lines that gave his face a serious cast, but his mouth showed he knew how to laugh. Of course, what he laughed at wasn't what amused other people. A scar ran from his hairline, across his left eyelid, over the nose, and trailed off somewhere in his cheek. The formal explanation was that it was a cut from a rope, but legend said it had been bestowed by his father in a drunken rage.

"A word with you, good captain," Julyan said, at his most polite. "I've brought with me a bottle of excellent brandy . . ."

Captain Chankley was not an alcoholic as his father had been, but he liked a nip or three when he wasn't going to be sailing.

"I won't say no." He gestured to a gazebo that stood apart from the other structures and offered a pleasant view of the bay. "Wait for me there. I'm just awake and need to splash water on my face."

Julyan moved in that direction, listening carefully when Bore Chankley stopped to talk with a couple of the women, but all he caught was an order for food to be brought to the gazebo. He didn't think it was a code of any sort, but he resolved not to eat anything the captain didn't first.

He slouched into the chair that offered the most cover from being seen. He wasn't worried about keeping the Old One waiting. When things were going his way that one had a hunter's patience, and he didn't plan to sail until well after dark. Julyan wouldn't be surprised if the Old One hadn't found a comfortable spot and was catching a nap, leaving Seamus to watch.

When Bore Chankley joined Julyan, he had taken time to comb and braid his long chestnut hair, then tie it beneath a bandana. He brought two wineglasses with him—very fine cut crystal that looked like seegnur vintage—and set them on the tabletop between them.

"Old One gifted them to me," he said. "He alive?"

"Yes, though he'd prefer that not get around."

"Figured he would be. Take more than water to kill that one. I've heard stories from before he settled here. Weathered the worst hurricane anyone had seen and came ashore, clinging to a spar, nothing more than leather and bones. Been eating shark. Had wedged the teeth in a crack in the spar to prove it. Man who told me had one of those teeth as a charm from his grandfather. Swore it made him proof against drowning."

"Did it?"

"Don't know. Got killed in a squabble over a woman."

"Heh . . ." Julyan chuckled. "Old One wants to go to Mender's Isle tonight if weather's fit. He says it will be. Got a crew who'll dare it?"

Bore Chankley snorted. "Take more than a few lights and weird voices to scare my sailors."

"Voices?"

"Yeah. Heard 'em myself, since the waters around the Haunted Islands are my fishing grounds. Don't know if they were spirits, but they didn't speak like humans. I've sailed far enough to hear lots of dialects. This was different. Nothing like anyone had ever heard. Scared some of the crew."

"Not you," Julyan said.

Bore Chankley shrugged. "Ain't heard a sound yet that can kill a man. Things that make a sound, sure, but some of the worst sounds are made by little things like loons and bullfrogs."

"Point." Julyan spilled more of the amber brandy into Captain Chankley's glass, feeling a familiar thrill. It was almost the color of Adara's eyes. "You'll sail then?"

"To the reef. Won't bust a ship, not even for the Old One."

"Fair. I suspect he has worked out a way to deal with the reef."

"He would."

Julyan asked a few more questions about the apparitions on the Mender's Isle, but Bore Chankley hadn't heard much more than Loremaster Flamen. When the bottle was empty, Julyan excused himself.

"I'll just go and make arrangements on my end. We'll be down after full dark."

"And we'll sail." Captain Chankley's smile was sardonic. "It'll be just like old times."

Leto's complex was an archeologist's dream come true. Parts of it were still sealed off—Leto claimed not to be able to operate the door locks. However, what was available was sufficient to keep Griffin occupied for months. The complex had two main sections: one for research and development; the other for residential needs. The research and development area consisted of a large lab with numerous open workstations, a bunker in which prototypes were racked, and, on a lower level, a fabrication area. Almost all the equipment was nonfunctional, but Leto had reactivated a few of the stations.

Griffin would have been perfectly happy, except that Leto seemed to have taken a dislike to Adara. The facility coordinator (which was the title Leto gave herself) had been fine with Adara's presence as long

as there had been clearing away to do. However, now that the hauling and carrying was done, Leto grew sulky whenever Adara entered
the complex. When Leto grew sulky, lights flickered, air circulation
grew poor, and Griffin's investigation was hampered in a dozen ways,
small and large.

"I don't understand," Griffin said to Leto one afternoon when Terrell and Adara were both outside. "You don't mind Terrell. Or me."

"This is a restricted access facility. Although you are not on the
list, I can see a rationale for admitting you. You have many of the right
qualifications. In any case, I cannot expect you to be included on a list
that was made centuries before you were born."

"And Terrell?"

"Terrell is your bondsman," Leto said primly. "Although such sit-
uations were exceedingly rare, there is precedent for him to be admitted. However, there is no precedent at all for Adara, less than for
the great cat. After all, some of the residents of this facility did keep
pets. However, under no circumstances were any unbonded savages
permitted within—much less permitted to come and go at their own
whim. I was in violation of my own dictates when I let her enter. I
have since regretted it."

Could you have done anything about it? Griffin thought. *From
what I have seen, the defensive weaponry within this facility was
thoroughly disabled. Even now, you can only show your displeasure
by making the facility unpleasant.*

He wanted to care more, *knew* he should care more, but he felt
detached from everything other than this fascinating facility. Even
with the damage it had taken, it was easily the most complete pre-war
R & D complex he had ever seen.

*Than anyone in the Kyley Domain has seen. Possibly than any-
one in all the inhabited galaxy has seen. If my suspicions are correct and this facility was doing covert research, it may have been
advanced even by the standards of those days. I press tabs, read instructions, piece through bits and pieces, and am all too aware that
I am like a child who sits at the helm of an interstellar battle cruiser
and imagines that he is in command. Even Leto does not seem to*

comprehend the half of what is here. Was her memory tampered with or was she created to keep this complex running and nothing more?

He found his thoughts drifting back to this puzzle, the question of whether or not Leto welcomed Adara becoming less and less important.

"Well, Leto. Adara may not be bonded to me, but I'd like it if you'd continue to give her access. Without functioning food synthesizers, I do need food and fresh water. Terrell cannot both assist me here, and take care of hunting and other such menial chores."

"She will not stay here?"

"She will if I need an extra pair of hands," Griffin replied sternly, "but otherwise, no, I don't think we will try your patience. Now, I'd like to go back to figuring out the operating system for this console. You say you remember the headset being used, but I haven't found the necessary access codes. Still, if the seegnur built in this complex as they did everywhere else, there will be an alternate means of access."

"Very good, sir," Leto replied. "Perhaps these manuals I located will be of use? Wise O'Rahilly was fond of detailed documentation. The reader is a primitive enough device that it is functional."

If there was a certain smugness to the disembodied voice, Griffin found it very easy to ignore as he went to fetch the data reader.

The Old One did indeed have a means of getting over the artificial reef that barred access to the Haunted Islands by ship. Julyan had always assumed the reef was of the same width throughout—but it turned out that in at least one place it was narrow enough that a small boat could be dropped over. The currents that kept such small vessels from approaching on the seaward side were not a hazard within the reef.

This wasn't to say the experience wasn't frightening, since the boat couldn't simply be lowered over the side, but had to be swung out some distance using a device jury-rigged from the ropes and pulleys more often used to haul in heavily laden fishing nets. Once they were in the water, Julyan, of course, was the one set to the oars.

The waters within the artificial lagoon were seeded with carnivorous sharks, a fact Julyan was well aware of, since the sharks had done in a couple of the men who had decided that they didn't like the terms of the Old One's employment. He suspected—although he'd never asked—that the sharks had something to do with a couple of the women who had disappeared as well. Now they bumped lazily against the hull of the rowboat, attracted, no doubt, by the lingering smell of fish blood and guts permeating the wood. Captain Chankley kept a strong fleet, but not necessarily the tidiest.

A couple of times one of the sharks grabbed hold of an oar blade, mistaking it, no doubt, for a struggling fish. With unsurprising coolness, the Old One walloped these bolder fish with the end of the boathook, being careful not to draw blood, since that would send the sharks into a feeding frenzy. Seamus huddled in the bow, shivering slightly but otherwise showing no awareness of his surroundings.

Eventually, the bottom of the rowboat scraped against the sand and gravel of the shore. The Old One did not wait for Julyan to ship the oars, but leapt over the side into the shallows and, working with the surge of the waves, pulled the boat clear of the water. Once again, Julyan was reminded that, despite his somewhat effete appearance, the Old One was very strong.

"It was obviously necessary that we arrive here by night," the Old One said softly. "However, I do not think it would be wise for us to begin our explorations until dawn. If, as I believe, someone else is now inhabiting this island, they may have laid traps. I would have." He gave a slight, humorless smile. "Indeed, I did. Best we not run afoul of those either."

The night was quite warm and the sand, while not precisely soft, could be sculpted into a bed far more comfortable than those in many a woodland camp in which Julyan had slept. They moved clear of the tideline, to where few scrubby trees stood. The Old One put Seamus on guard.

"I will need you alert come dawn," he said to Julyan. "We shall both sleep until then."

Julyan obeyed. One of the many things he had learned from Bruin was how to sleep restfully without fully relinquishing alertness. It was a gift possessed by most animals, lost by humans, who craved the temporary oblivion and the peculiar half-life of dreams. He also had cultivated a good internal alarm, dependent not on any sense of the passage of time but on maintaining an awareness of his surroundings. Thus it was that the sun was just tinting the sky grey and the birds were making their first querulous comments when he came fully awake.

The Old One was also stirring. He rolled gracefully to his feet, then unslung his small pack of supplies from an overhanging tree limb. Without a word, he pulled out provisions and a covered bottle of water, fairly sharing out three portions. They dined in silence. Wordlessly, the Old One commanded Seamus to take his turn at sleep. He then indicated that he would be gone for a short time and Julyan should remain.

When the Old One returned, he had clearly taken time to attend to his appearance. He wore a fresh shirt and his hair—still longer than he usually preferred—had been combed and pulled back into a neat queue. He motioned to Julyan, gesturing splashing water on his face.

Julyan went where he had been directed. While he peed against a convenient tree, he considered defying the Old One's hint that he should wash up. Then he grinned at himself. Had he been alone, he would have taken any chance to wash. Another of Bruin's lessons had been that a clean hunter was much more successful than one reeking of sweat and other odors that gave the prey warning.

You're only considering skipping because you don't like how the Old One orders you around as if you have fewer brains than Seamus, he thought as he knelt next to the stream, washing both face and mouth. *Cut off your own nose to spite your face, as Mom would have said.*

The sun was not far above the horizon when Julyan returned to the Old One, but there was ample light with which to see their surroundings. The Old One had pulled the rowboat the rest of the way up the beach, turned it upside down, then concealed it with dead branches to which leaves still clung. He swept away the marks with another branch, tossed it onto the pile and gave a satisfied grunt.

"That won't hide anything if someone searches," he said, "but it will be ample to keep anyone out on the bay from spotting it. Now, where to begin?"

Julyan, rightly guessing that the Old One had been thinking aloud, did not bother to answer. If the Old One wanted advice, he asked for it directly.

"There is an entrance into the underground facility not far from here," the Old One continued after a moment. "A minor one. That should serve us admirably."

He turned. "Please, take point. You are far better than I am at spotting traps. We are heading in the direction of that wind-twisted pine, the tallest one in that cluster."

Julyan nodded. He thought he remembered the entrance the Old One referred to, although as far as he recalled, it had never been used. The Old One really was like an fox, knowing all the ins and outs of his burrows. The only traps they encountered along the way were of the Old One's own making. Julyan was beginning to wonder if they'd returned to Spirit Bay on a wild goose chase. Maybe it was as Flamen's associates had thought, just another bit of the seegnur's old trash falling from the high orbits.

And the lights on the islands? he asked himself. *Imagination. Or maybe there really are ghosts there, though I never saw any during the time we used the place as a base. Or maybe scavengers. There are those who would defy the prohibitions if they thought they had something to gain. Maybe even Captain Chankley or one of his lot. They might have learned some of the Old One's secrets, though they'd never tell him.*

He was close to believing that one or more of these explanations must be true when they reached the entrance. The Old One waved for Julyan to keep watch, knelt, and moved aside the accumulated leaf litter with quick motions of his hands. Even then, one would need to know what to look for to recognize the hidden trapdoor, so well did the material blend in with the surrounding soil. The Old One worked a latch, moving slowly and carefully, so as to make as little noise as possible. Then he carefully raised the hatch a few inches, pausing to listen.

Julyan, complacent in his conjectures, stiffened in shock when voices speaking some unknown language rose from the depths.

Interlude Six: Defiance

Without wings, I can fly.
Without eyes, light I spy.
Without ears, sound I feel.
Without tongue, tastes appeal.
Without legs, I can move.
What then is there left to prove?

7

Meeting of Minds

Adara gathered that she was less than welcome within Leto. If she were honest with herself, she felt relieved rather than insulted. She didn't like the stuffy, enclosed underground complex. Then, too, she felt certain that within Leto's confines she could never hope to make contact with Artemis—a task that was proving far more difficult than she had imagined it would be.

When I didn't want her in my head, she popped in and out at whim. Finding out about those blind spots seems to have unnerved her to the point that she doesn't want to "talk." She's there, though. I can sense her nightmares.

So Adara spent most of her time outside, going into the complex only when Griffin needed an extra pair of hands or Adara's ability to see clearly with very little light. She was contemplating whether she needed to forage for something to augment the fish for dinner, or whether she should seek out a particularly dense cluster of mushrooms and try to reach Artemis, when an excited image from Sand Shadow burst into her mind.

Two men were lumbering their way up the steepest part of the trail to Maiden's Tear. A small boy walked behind them, his step light despite evident weariness. Each led a horse, the boy's doubling as a pack animal.

Behind the humans and horses ambled a large bear with golden brown fur. The bear paused every few paces to sniff the air, confirming that no threat was near—although to one who did not know bears, it might have looked as if she was hoping to sniff out something particularly tasty for dinner. Adara recognized the travelers at once. The man on point was her own mentor—and foster father—Bruin Hunter. The big, bald man behind him, head bent down, gaze apparently fastened on nothing more than the rise and fall of Bruin's soft-booted feet, was Ring. The boy was Bruin's student, Kipper. The bear was Honeychild, Bruin's demiurge.

Adara gave a startled cry. What was Bruin doing here? And Ring? Ring was the last person she thought would undertake such an arduous journey. Had he been driven to it by his peculiar gifts? Was Bruin his guide?

Adara considered telling Griffin and Terrell about the new arrivals, then decided to go meet Bruin and his companions alone. What if whatever had driven Ring was something he would prefer to keep from Griffin or Terrell? She could not imagine that the information was to be kept from her. If so, Ring would not have considered Bruin as a guide. Some, misled by Ring's peculiar manner of speech and awkward appearance, might make the mistake of thinking him slowminded, but she was under no such illusion.

Action followed thought. Soon the huntress was sprinting down the slope to meet the new arrivals, intersecting Sand Shadow along the way. The puma sent her confident assertion that by now Honeychild would have scented them and passed the information along to Bruin.

For all that it was anticipated, the reunion was no less joyful. Adara had not seen Bruin since they had parted after their visit to Lynn's small community. Bruin had returned to Shepherd's Call with Kipper, his newest charge, while Adara and Terrell had turned in the direction of Spirit Bay to guide Griffin to the Old One Who is Young.

Fate and distance had kept them apart since. When Adara threw her arms around Bruin and felt his familiar bear hug in return, she realized her eyes were wet with tears.

"I've missed you, you old bear," she said, releasing him and giving him a quick inspection. He looked much as he should, bearlike in build, his reddish-brown hair shaggy about his face, silvering at the tips. However, Adara thought that there were lines of worry, even of grief, that had not been on his weathered features before.

Adara turned to the others. "I'm glad to see you, too, Honeychild. Well met, Ring, Kipper . . ."

"Glad to see you, too, Adara," Kipper said, his voice soft with awe. Adara didn't doubt that since their brief initial meeting he'd heard more about her, if not from Bruin, then both from the residents of Shepherd's Call and from Bruin's students. Adara could be humble, but she didn't see what good would be served by pretending that she wasn't well known in her own community—and for more than her adaptations. Most hunters were male. Huntresses, especially those with demiurges, were rare indeed.

Ring's only response to Adara's greeting was to shuffle his feet. Up close his physical oddities were more obvious. He avoided not only eye contact, but looking directly at anything. Although the group must have been traveling for weeks, he retained a certain unhealthy softness that was at odds with his large frame. This fleshiness extended to his hands, which were overlarge, and his lips, which were thick.

He was holding one hand over his eyes but Adara knew this wasn't to keep the out the sunlight, but to block visual stimuli. Ring was precognate, the gift both powerful and unpredictable, so that every step the man took was through a maze of shifting probabilities.

Adara would have loved to learn more about what brought her mentor and his companions to this isolated place, but she took pity on Ring. Her questions could wait until they were safely in camp.

"We're almost to the top of the worst of the trail," she said, moving to the front of the group. "After that, there's a lovely meadow where you can mount up again. We have a good campsite under the trees, so our gear isn't in plain sight."

"That's wise," Bruin said approvingly. "Where are Terrell and Griffin?"

Ring spoke, his voice flat, yet the words very precise. "In the heart of the mother from whose womb death was born too late to give life. Who yet will bear death or life, depending on the father's song."

Bruin looked apologetically at Adara. "He's been saying things like that for weeks. Nonsense, I would say, except that we know better than to dismiss what Ring says without consideration."

Adara had been distinctly startled by Ring's words. "Not nonsense, not all of it." She placed a gentle hand on Ring's arm, patting him reassuringly. "The part I don't understand makes my blood cold. Let me get you to camp. Griffin and Terrell are inside the mountain. The seegnur had a complex there."

"Like the one on Spirit Bay?" Bruin asked, clucking to his horse.

"Not quite," Adara hedged. She didn't want to explain here in the open. "I didn't fetch them before coming to meet you because I wanted to make sure that whatever message you carried was for all of us."

Bruin chuckled. "And here I thought it was because you were so eager to see your old Papa Bear."

Afraid she had offended him, Adara sputtered reassurances, but Bruin waved her down. "No need to worry, ladybug. You haven't hurt my feelings. I'm glad to see you haven't lost the good sense I spent so long drumming into you." He turned to the other man, "Ring? Can the others hear what you have to tell or is it only for Adara?"

"Tell? Tell?" Ring looked puzzled. "Ring must be here, else disaster will come, but tell?"

Adara felt no impatience. The hulking man seemed almost a boy in his confusion. She turned to Bruin. "Bruin, the day that you can't locate an established camp in a little bit of wood is the day we tuck you into a rocker by the fire. You'll find meat and drink waiting. Help yourselves. Sand Shadow and I will get the others."

Without waiting for her mentor's reply, she sped up the hillside, lightly as a cat, and loped through the tall grass toward the tunnel into the mountain. Sand Shadow ran alongside, a sleek shadow of palest gold.

Griffin could hardly believe his ears when Adara told them that Bruin had arrived—bringing with him none other than Ring.

"Kipper, too," Adara said as she all but herded Griffin and Terrell out of Leto's complex. "I don't know anything more than that—only that Ring was adamant that he needed to be here. I directed them to our camp, then came to get you."

Despite his pleasure at the thought of seeing Bruin, along with a very real curiosity as to what could bring both the hunter and Ring all this way, Griffin found pulling himself from his researches almost painful. He thought about suggesting that the visitors come to him, so that he wouldn't waste any time, but a lingering sense of priorities made him put the suggestion aside.

Bruin had welcomed Griffin into his home when Griffin was an unknown quantity. He had continued to offer him advice and support—as well as food, drink, and shelter—even after Griffin had proven potentially dangerous. Asking Bruin to attend upon Griffin's pleasure, when doubtless Bruin was finally having a chance to relax after a long day on the trail, would be beyond rudeness. So, promising Leto he would be back, Griffin followed Adara and Terrell down the tunnel.

The air outside the cavern held the freshness of early evening. After the stale air within Leto's complex, the scents of pine and wind-stirred grass were intense, the colors of grass and the purple hues of shadowed mountains vivid. Birds darted over the meadow, probably chasing insects, chattering to each other with such animation that Griffin felt he'd understand them if he listened just a moment more. It felt good to walk so that his legs stretched out, rather than picking his way from console to console, so good that Griffin almost regretted when they reached the camp.

"Kipper located where you pastured your own horses and Sam the Mule," Bruin said after greetings had been exchanged. "He took our horses over to join them. All but Ring's are from Helena's herd originally, so I think they'll get along fine."

"Molly will make sure of it," Terrell said with a laugh, "although Midnight will think he's in charge. I see you've made yourself at home. Thanks for setting the journey cake batter on the fire. Do you mind business while we eat? We're alive with curiosity as to what brought you here—but I'm starved!"

Bruin leaned back against Honeychild, sipped from a tin travel mug filled with the mint tea they kept steeping in a jug in the stream, then gave a shuddery sigh. "I can only tell what little I know. Some weeks ago, a runner arrived in Shepherd's Call with a note from Lynn. The note said that Ring had been speaking of things she couldn't understand, other than that he was insisting that dire things would happen if he didn't reach you three as quickly as possible. She'd been putting him off, saying she had no idea where you were. All she knew was that the Trainers—they've kept in touch—said you'd left Spirit Bay some time before. That apparently stopped Ring's nagging—Lynn's word, not mine—for two days. Then he started insisting that I knew where you were, that I could take him to you."

Adara nodded. Before they had left Spirit Bay, she'd written Bruin telling him in terms only he would understand where they were going.

"Lynn asked me to come at once, to see if I could quiet Ring. I did so, sending my boarding students home earlier than planned, because I had a feeling that I wouldn't be back to Shepherd's Call anytime soon. Brought Kipper, of course, because he's living with me now."

"And you were right," Adara prompted gently, "that you wouldn't just be going to Lynn's, speaking with Ring, and coming home again."

"And I was right," Bruin agreed. "I couldn't make any more sense out of what Ring was saying than Lynn could, but we've all reason to know that his nonsense makes good sense once you know how the parts fit together. If he felt it was urgent for him to get to you, then it was urgent to me, too."

They all nodded and looked where Ring sat leaning against a tree, his eyes firmly shut. Griffin remembered how Ring had told Lynn to catch the fish to lure the bear, so that the bear would come to Lynn's stronghold. That fish had been Kipper; the bear, Bruin; two people Ring had never met and so apparently could not put a name to. Yet for all his lack of clarity, Ring had been right. The bear—and his companions— needed to hear what Lynn had to say. Without the information they had garnered from Lynn and her band, they would have gone into Spirit Bay unwarned about the Old One and . . .

And, oh, how different the future would have been . . . Griffin thought. *The Old One might yet be pursuing his twisted experiments beneath Mender's Isle, and the rest of us? We'd either be dead or pris-oners.*

The problem with Ring was that he saw reality in so many configurations—including visions of scenes that he himself might or might not understand—that something as simple as writing a note based on his information was impossible.

"So what does Ring need to tell us?" Griffin said.

He didn't expect a reply. Indeed, he'd thought Ring was asleep, but Ring's deep, flat voice rang out immediately, though his eyes remained screwed shut.

"If Ring is not there," he pointed with unerring accuracy in the direction of Leto's complex, "there is no hope. Slavery will come again. Many, many, many will die in body, many more in soul. Even if Ring is here . . ."

He lifted a big, almost flabby hand, then, holding it palm down, rocked it back and forth as if it were a scale that would not settle.

No one spoke. After a long pause, Ring continued. "If the cats do not breathe in the dusty orb, if the thread does not learn that it binds tightest when it is knotted firmly into itself, if the dreamer does not wake from the visions, then even with Ring, with Bruin, with Kipper, still there will be disaster."

Something in how he slumped back made clear he was done speaking.

Bruin said, "So there is still something for me and Kipper to do?"

Ring breathed out so hard that little droplets of spit sprinkled the air. "You can go without causing disaster, but if you stay and are prepared to walk trails unimagined in all your years, then, yes, there is something for you to do."

Griffin wanted to ask more. "Cats" could refer to Adara and Sand Shadow, but the dreamer, the thread? Did they also refer to those two? They had jointly dreamed of Artemis. Or did this refer to him and Terrell? Maybe the dreamer was Leto. She had slept for five hundred years and struggled daily against her sense of what should be, rather than accepting the new reality.

Terrell touched Griffin's arm, shaking his head. "Ring is completely exhausted. I think, too, speaking is harder for him than you imagine. I suspect that each word he speaks subtly changes reality for him."

"Yes," Griffin said, nodding slowly. "I can see what you mean. Words—even carefully spoken words—nail ideas into place. Worse, not everyone is going to interpret a concept the same way."

He winced. "It's a wonder Ring speaks at all."

Bruin said softly, "For a long time he didn't. His mother, Narda, came to talk to me about Ring when she learned I would be his guide. Apparently, Ring didn't speak for so many years that everyone assumed he was mute. When Ring did start speaking, it was in full sentences, all very carefully crafted, and mostly regarding very concrete matters, such as what he wanted to eat or not eat. It was only a year or so before he helped Winnie and Mabel to escape that he began to express himself on abstract concepts."

"A good thing," Adara said. "If the Old One had realized what Ring was capable of he would never have been so careless."

Griffin felt a sudden shock as ideas connected. "The Old One was breeding the adapted in the hope that he would hit on someone who could operate the equipment the seegnur left behind. Now Ring insists he has to be here—and he indicates that his reason for being here is connected to the mountain . . . to Leto's complex. I wonder if the Old One crafted better than he realized."

He glanced between the complex and Ring.

"Not now," Terrell interjected firmly. "Didn't I just finish saying that Ring needs a break? He's been on the road for days. Ask him tomorrow. If his reason for coming here is connected to Leto, then I suspect you won't have trouble getting him there—you'll have trouble keeping him away."

Griffin nodded, but even as he settled down to a game of marbles with Sand Shadow and Adara, he could feel his impatience growing, fed by a strong sense that time was running out.

When they heard the voices, the Old One held up a finger for silence. Although the language being spoken was one neither of them could

understand, by listening they could still learn something about whoever was in the subterranean facility. After a few minutes, Julyan felt
certain there were three people, all male. When they moved, there
was a splashing sound, so, although the complex was no longer completely flooded, it was still wet. After a while, he became aware of a
regular thudding in the background.

They crouched, listening, until the voices became fainter. Then the
Old One lowered himself into the hole. When his feet had located the
rungs of the ladder built into the wall, he paused only long enough to
indicate that Julyan should follow, then vanished into the gloom. His
progress was so silent that Julyan guessed he had used the old sailor's
trick of lightly grasping the side rails and sliding down, rather than
climbing. There was no splash, though, so the Old One must have perfectly controlled his descent.

He would, thought Julyan, a trace resentfully. He chose not to
slide, not trusting that he would be able to stop as silently, but his soft-
soled boots were nearly soundless against the rungs. When he reached
bottom, he discovered that the tunnel was no longer flooded, although
a thin layer of sandy mud remained.

*I never noticed, but the floors must have been built at an angle,
so water would run off to the sides. Makes sense, if you're going to
build a complex that's partly under water, as well as underground.*

The tunnel was dark. None of the lanterns that had been hung along
the walls during the Old One's tenancy seemed to have survived the
flood that had surged through these corridors when the Old One had
sought to drown his enemies.

*And drowned a fair number of his allies—or at least lackeys—
instead,* thought Julyan. He pressed down an uncomfortable thought
that perhaps the Old One had intended those drownings to rid himself of those who had witnessed various aspects of his peculiar breeding
project. It would be very much in character.

The Old One was just visible in the gloom, a slim, dark shadow
against greater darkness. He pointed down the corridor to where a faint
yellow light showed, then turned and began walking in that direction. Julyan followed, curiosity driving him as much as any fidelity

to the Old One—curiosity not only about the nature of these new-comers, but as to what the Old One intended.

Julyan had a hunter's excellent memory for places. Within a few paces, he reestablished his orientation and padded along almost as confidently as he had in those days when the Old One had reigned here and, as his second, Julyan himself had held nearly supreme power. No man had dared cross him, no woman disobey him. Perhaps those days might yet return.

A warm barrier stopped Julyan in midstep—the Old One's arm, extended across the corridor, just before a curve. Julyan halted, waited for a soft-voiced command, but apparently the Old One only wanted him to stop here where they were concealed by more than darkness.

They had closed to where conversation could be distinguished. Although Julyan could not understand what the men said, every so often a word was almost familiar. The cadence, too, was familiar enough that he thought he could garner the emotional context, even if the actual meaning was shrouded.

They were close enough, too, that unique qualities in the three voices could be isolated. Julyan had an excellent ear. His pitch was so perfect that Bruin had speculated that the gift might be an adaptation. As he listened, Julyan quickly distinguished the differences between the voices, as he might have between different pieces of music played on the same instrument.

The voice that spoke the most often and with the longest strings of sound was the deepest and just a bit gruff. This man spoke with confidence, but something in how he spoke made Julyan think he was relating information rather than conversing. Since this gruff voice was often accompanied by the sound of water sloshing and the water had gathered along the edges of the walls, Julyan thought that this man might be examining the corridor, then reporting his conclusions.

The voice that spoke the next most often was only slightly less deep, but held a clear note that made it carry effortlessly. Although this man's statements often ended with an inflection that made Julyan think they were questions, these were not the questions of doubt or uncertainty, but those that probed for information.

I know that sound well enough, Julyan thought with a trace of bitter humor. *This man's voice is deeper and more resonant, but he sounds just like the Old One—not only does he ask questions, he expects prompt and accurate answers.*

The voice that spoke least frequently was lighter than the other two, although still distinctly masculine—a baritone that flirted with tenor elements. This speaker played with his voice more than the other two did. Gruff Voice reported, Clear Voice queried and assessed, but this last voice drawled and teased. When it asked questions, Julyan didn't think he was wrong that many of these held a hint of mockery or testing.

That the other two could ignore this voice, not reacting to jibes or twists, seemed to indicate a long relationship between the three. They knew each other well, each responding within the patterns of habit.

The Old One kept them standing there listening for so long that Julyan was tempted to hunker down and rest his feet. Only the desire not to smudge his clothes with sand and mud kept him upright. He guessed that the Old One was seriously considering confronting these three men, and Julyan wanted to make the best possible impression when they did so.

Julyan was weighing the odds that the Old One would wait until he could learn more against the advantages that could be gained from an immediate confrontation, when the Old One tapped his shoulder, signaling in the silent code they had worked out long before that the Old One would go forward and that Julyan was to follow a few paces behind, his stance that of a bodyguard.

Julyan adjusted, made sure his long knife was loose in its sheath, and straightened so that his height and muscular strength would be immediately visible. He also schooled himself against squinting, knowing that when they turned the corner they would be in the light cast by the other group's lanterns.

For the sake of his own self-esteem, it was good that Julyan had made these preparations, for what they saw when they rounded the corner was enough of a shock that he might have gaped like a townee who'd just walked into a bear's den, mistaking it for a tunnel.

Three men—one dark-haired, one with pale golden hair, and one with hair in curls of bronze—had swiveled as one and were holding some sort of hand weapons on the Old One and him. There was nothing about the smooth curve of polished material to proclaim them as weapons—no sharpened edge or obvious projectile—but Julyan had no doubt that these were weapons.

The dark-haired man stood nearest to the wall, where he had opened a panel. He was ankle-deep in water but didn't seem to mind. He said nothing, nor did he move anything but his eyes. The blond-haired man was also the tallest. He had taken one step toward them as he drew his weapon, announcing himself not only the leader, but the sort of leader who did not remain safely in the rear while others fought his battles.

The man with the bronze curls held his weapon with a casual ease that seemed to indicate that he didn't think he would need to use it. Julyan was not fooled. This man was not simply deadly; he was the sort who would shoot you in the back as easily as breathing. While the other two men were startled to various degrees, this man was amused, pleased by the new turn of events. He was the one who smiled when the Old One stepped forward and spoke.

"Greetings, seegnur. I am called Maxwell. I know something of this area. How may I be of service to you?"

The arrival of Bruin, Kipper, and Ring changed the dynamic of the camp. Ring joined Griffin and Terrell inside while the hunters remained mostly outside. Bruin expanded Kipper's training by making the boy responsible for setting snares and weaving fish traps, tasks the boy assumed with focused determination.

"Was I ever so grim?" Adara asked. She and Bruin had retired to a sheltered bluff where they could keep an eye on Kipper without the boy realizing how closely he was being supervised.

"Worse," Bruin assured her. Then he chuckled. "No, simply different. By the time you were Kipper's age, you had already been in my charge for two or three years. You were determined to best your peers, thinking that any less would shame me."

Adara smiled, rolling onto her back and watching the clouds scud by, sky sheep in blue pastures. "I remember. It was so easy to be the bright little show-off when all your students were older than me, but when they started to be my own age or—worse—younger, that was a strain."

"I knew, though I doubt that any of those you measured yourself against had any idea how high a standard you had set for yourself."

Adara plucked a blade of grass and began to chew the sweet, white end. "No doubt."

Bruin's tone shifted. "I was pleased to learn you had stopped to visit your family."

"You saw them?"

"We stopped. I had a long talk with Neenay."

"What did she tell you?" Adara tensed, swinging herself upright so she could see her mentor's face.

"Enough to add to my sorrow that I was innocent enough to trust the Old One for so long. What Lynn told us a few months ago had prepared me. I've had letters from Lynn since—and, of course, from you as well, but . . ."

His voice trailed off. Adara felt his sorrow as if it were her own. She tried to imagine how she would feel if she learned about Bruin the sort of things he had learned about the Old One. Her heart spoke without bothering to consult her thoughts.

"Do we ever know what to believe? Is it safe to believe anything we've been told about anyone or anything? There are times I wish I could melt away and vanish."

Bruin frowned. "What brings this on? It cannot be what we have learned about the Old One. I know you were never as attached to him as I was."

Adara wrapped her arms around her legs, pillowing her chin on her knees. After a long pause, she found words for feelings she hadn't even realized were troubling her.

"When I was small, I was taught how the seegnur made this world and set everything upon it in a right and proper way. I believed this and was content."

Bruin's expression was knowing as he voiced an uncomfortable truth. "More than content, you were affirmed in your own importance in the way of things." He waved down Adara's protest and went on. "Why shouldn't you be? Of all those upon Artemis—human and beast alike—the only ones who are even hinted at as being equals to the seegnur are those who follow the professions, for those in the professions were created to directly serve and guide the seegnur. You can serve without being an equal, but you cannot guide. True?"

"True," Adara whispered.

"And on top of this," Bruin went on relentlessly, "you knew yourself destined for a profession—that of hunter—as soon as you realized how your adaptations set you apart. To that point, your journey was much like my own. I only tell you what I myself remember, except that in my case I came from a family that usually threw up at least one adapted hunter a generation. I was eagerly awaited, but not unusual. You, however, were unusual and, because of your parents' wisdom, you came into the hands of those who would cherish you.

"I said, 'to that point,' " Bruin continued, "and by that I do not mean the difference between our families. I mean that quickly enough—especially after you were in my care—you realized that even among those in the professions, even among the adapted in the professions, you were special."

"Because of Sand Shadow?"

"No. Long before that. You realized you were special because you would be a huntress, and those are rare indeed." Bruin sighed and made himself more comfortable where he leaned against a tree trunk. "I remember when you began to notice how few girls there were among those I taught. Your awkwardness didn't last long, changing into pride that never—quite—became overbearing."

Adara nodded. She remembered, too. At first she had thought that the difference was simply that fewer girls wanted to learn to hunt. Hunting was, after all, a messy profession, with more than its share of blood, guts, wet days, cold nights, and lacking the little comforts that it seemed—to her at least—girls treasured more than did boys. Later, she had realized that fewer women were born with the adaptations that were thought to indicate suitability for the hunter's way: night vision, an empathy with animals, and—most telling—the claws that she still considered both blessing and bane.

"I preferred pride to the shyness that came upon you when you first began to notice boys as something other than classmates and competition," Bruin said. "I still regret not moving Julyan along before he could make such an impression on you. He was beyond needing my teaching, but he wished to stay. I was a lazy enough bear to have grown accustomed to his presence. I should have realized that he was precisely the type . . ."

Adara made a sound of protest and Bruin dropped the subject, returning to one almost as uncomfortable. "So from the first times you heard the tales of how Artemis was created, you already set yourself among the higher ranks. Although I know you resented your parents sending you away, my taking you on confirmed you in your sense of being someone select, above the common level of humanity. And now?"

Adara forced herself to speak, although, in truth, Bruin's casual representation of her own arrogance was extremely uncomfortable.

"The seegnur . . . We were taught they were wise and powerful . . . Now, Griffin . . . He does not call himself a seegnur, but his bond with Terrell seems to confirm that he is at least of their stock, if not of their wisdom and power. What troubles me are the stories he tells of those he calls the Old Imperials. These must be the seegnur at the height of their perfection, but they seem far from perfect, far from the gods we have been taught to revere and serve."

"Yet that has always been a contradiction within the lore," Bruin said easily. "We learn of the Creation, but we also learn of the Fall. The one is as legend, the other history. Why do you think I always make certain my students see the scar on the mountains above Shepherd's Call? We have no evidence that our creation is as we were told but, for those who know how to recognize the signs, the marks of the Fall are easily found."

"Yet even those were battles worthy of gods!" Adara protested, although, if pressed, she would not have known whom she challenged. "A single woman brought down the side of a mountain. A handful of armed warriors slaughtered hundreds. Yet Leto—Leto speaks of those she remembers as if they were much like you or me. When she talks of their studies, their experiments, I cannot help seeing them as much like the loremasters, although with larger libraries and more elaborate tools. I cannot see them as gods!"

"Is that why you avoid Leto's complex? I had wondered."

"In part. Honestly, these feelings make me grateful that Leto dislikes me. I can stay away and feel I am not being a coward, but here, you and I alone, I admit it. When I am there, I feel the foundations of the universe shaking."

"I can understand why," Bruin said. "You have believed yourself among the elite from before you could put words to the concept. What is it to be the chosen of such petty gods?"

Adara looked at her mentor, surprise tingeing her deep affection. She was so used to thinking of Bruin as the hunter—bluff and hearty, a bit gruff, but never unkind—that she often forgot that in his younger days he had been a prize student of the Old One Who Is Young. In those days, Bruin had frequented the company of the loremasters, exploring philosophy and theology, discussing the ways of right living in the absence of the seegnur.

"Adara, what do you think of Leto?"

"I cannot fairly judge her." Adara shrugged. "It's hard to feel comfortable about someone who doesn't like you."

"Yet you speak of Leto as 'her' and as 'someone.' You accept then that she is a person?"

"It's impossible not to," Adara said, fumbling for words. "Griffin accepted her as such from the first and I . . . Well, there's Artemis."

"Another disembodied person," Bruin said. "Are you certain Artemis is—well—real? Terrell and Bruin can communicate in sleep. Are you sure that this 'Artemis' is not some peculiar demiurge, reaching out to you as once Sand Shadow did?"

Adara shook her head. "No . . . I mean, yes, I'm sure. I'm sure."

"Yet she touched you in dreams."

"At first. Not much lately, not since she discovered her 'blind spots.'" Adara had told Bruin about this soon after his arrival, for Artemis's reaction was interwoven into their discovery of Leto. "But we have communicated when I was wide awake."

"As you do with Sand Shadow," Bruin said. He gave a gusty sigh. "Forgive me, but it is easier for me to believe you have located some peculiar demiurge than that you are communicating with an entity who is an entire world."

"I can only tell you what I feel—what I *know*—to be true," Adara said stubbornly. "If only you'd been there as Sand Shadow and I were . . . I think the seegnur created an intelligence to manage this planet in all its complexity. I think that when they were attacked, Artemis must have been put to sleep as Leto remembers being put to sleep. Something woke her, much as Leto was awoken—probably something Griffin brought with him."

"Why did the seegnur need Artemis?" Bruin said. "I can understand Leto. She was clearly tied to that complex, but Artemis? The world continued to function even while she slept."

"I don't know," Adara said, "but, just because I don't know doesn't mean I'm wrong. Many things I thought I knew have been proven wrong. Why should something that doesn't fit into that worldview automatically be wrong?"

"You have a point, ladybug," Bruin said. "Something Terrell said made me think that you were supposed to be working on your link with Artemis. Have you been?"

"Not as much as I should be," Adara admitted. "I told myself that I needed to hunt and forage since Terrell and Griffin were closeting themselves in that complex but . . . I've been afraid. I keep trying to hold on to the fringes of the world as I knew it until I dragged Griffin from that landslide."

"Kipper and I will hunt and forage," Bruin said, shoving himself to his feet. "You are free to go . . . Go and find Artemis. Perhaps it is Ring's urgency tingling in my nerves, but I don't think he made me bring him all this way for no reason. Best we gather whatever understanding we can. These old bones feel a storm building. We'd better prepare before it breaks loose and rocks our world to its foundations."

Interlude: Uncertain

They Made Me.
Granted mind that I might serve.
Granted heart that I might love that service.

Who did I serve?
What is my purpose?

If service is my beloved,
Why can I not remember
    his face?

8

Ties That Bind

Even after Bruin, Ring, and Kipper arrived, Griffin remained immersed in his exploration of Leto's complex. Indeed, had Ring not insisted on accompanying Griffin and Terrell indoors, Griffin would have easily forgotten that anything had changed about their situation. The complex obsessed him to the point that Terrell had to remind him periodically that his goal was to seek and—if at all possible—activate a communications array so that he could contact his orbiting ship.

"This is all very interesting," Terrell said one morning when Griffin called him over to show him some schematic diagrams he'd found regarding fuel cells, "but wouldn't your analysis be much easier if you had some of those devices you left on your ship—the ones that let you record information and make pictures? I'd like to see the portable library you mentioned. With it, we could compare what we're finding here with the artifacts you've already studied."

Griffin nodded. "That would be great. However, I'm uncomfortable with bringing any modern technology down here until we're certain that the nanobots that, in all likelihood, crashed my shuttle have been completely disabled. What if I brought the *Howard Carter* down and she crashed?"

Terrell countered immediately. "Didn't you say something about the *Howard Carter* being able to send down drones that could carry small equipment? A drone would provide a very good test as to whether conditions have changed."

When Griffin did not reply, Terrell persisted.

"I thought you intended to contact your ship and arrange for a message to be sent back to your family. You said a message would take a long time to reach them. Wouldn't it be better to send it sooner, rather than later? You said that you could arrange to send the message drone remotely, so the ship would not be at risk of contamination."

Fighting down an urge to tell Terrell to stop nagging him, Griffin seized on a point he had been avoiding, but that was at least better than admitting he was indeed behaving irrationally—an admission that would be particularly irksome at this moment since, in many ways, he had never felt more rational in all his life.

"Terrell, I'm not certain that I want to contact my family—not now, not since we found this complex. I've told you about them, haven't I?"

"A little," Terrell said, then demonstrated his excellent memory. "You are the youngest of ten children. You have six brothers and three sisters. Your father was involved in the military—although you have never spoken of what, exactly, that means. Your brothers and two of your sisters have, at least to some extent, followed in your father's path. Your mother, in addition to raising all those children, was involved in some form of natural science. I'm not certain of the details, but you mention her most often when . . ."

Griffin held up a hand in mild protest. "You are a credit to your teachers, Terrell the Factotum, to remember so much and to draw such accurate conclusions from so little."

"I am glad the seegnur is pleased," Terrell said, the ritual response coming automatically. Then he colored. "And you, too, of course . . . Now, do you wish me to tell you what I deduce is making you hesitate or to spare me the trouble and talk openly for once?"

"It's the military aspect," Griffin admitted. "The Kyley Domain is largely peaceful. Indeed, since its initial formation, the domain has grown, because neighboring systems have requested membership— and the prosperity and security that come with it. These days, those systems which would join voluntarily have done so. Now some say that it is our duty to go forth and offer membership to systems who have not requested it."

Terrell smiled knowingly. Although the people of Artemis were, on the whole, traditionalists, that didn't mean there had been no ambitious rulers in the days since the seegnur had departed. His nod encouraged Griffin to continue.

"Not everyone, not even a majority, agrees with this course of action. Even in those systems that joined the Kyley Domain voluntarily, there were clashes with those who resisted. Some of the fights were horribly destructive, because any system worth having in the domain is of a similar technological level to our own. My father earned his awards in one such conflict. Several of my brothers served in a conflict when a group of affiliated systems decided that they had been wrong to join Kyley and wished to separate and form their own dominion. If Kyley were to annex groups who did not wish to join us, there would be even more battles. Dread of this has been the greatest argument against the annexation faction."

"And the annexation faction," Terrell said, "is the one to which some of your family belongs, yes?"

"It is the faction," Griffin said, forcing a rueful grin, "my family heads. With age, my father has taken his taste for battle into politics. He has proven quite good at it, although I believe he regrets he cannot solve some differences of opinion with a single well-aimed shot."

"So your brothers," Terrell continued, "and your more military-minded sisters as well, would welcome annexation becoming official policy."

"Precisely." Griffin waved one arm in a broad gesture that encompassed Leto's complex. "Here we have what may be the solution to the greatest argument against annexation. Even those pacification campaigns I mentioned—although not all-out wars of conquest— were expensive, both in equipment and in lives. My father's opponents have used this against him, saying that if mere pacification costs so dearly, how much more expensive would conquest be? I'll spare you my father's counterarguments. However, if the technological advances we see here were in his hands, then he would have a cogent argument for conquest."

Terrell nodded. "Because, although the expense would still be high, the chance of victory—and the opportunity to recoup the expenses—would be much more likely."

"Again, correct," Griffin agreed. "That's why I'd like to know more about what we have here before I contact anyone."

"Do you support your father's dreams of annexation?"

Griffin didn't need to be a genius to know that, although Terrell tried to keep his expression neutral, the factotum did not think annexation was a good policy. He framed his answer accordingly.

"Not precisely. Growing too large was what doomed the Old Empire. Their technology—especially in communications and travel—was as far above that of the Kyley Domain as that of Kyley is above that of the average householder in Shepherd's Call. Currently, the Kyley Domain is mostly peaceful. Peace is good for scholarship and that is what I love. No. I can't say I would particularly favor annexation."

"I wonder what motivated the seegnur," Terrell said. "As you said, they were far above any technology either of us has ever seen. Nonetheless, they made this place so they could research further advances. What could they have possibly wanted?"

Griffin brightened. "Actually, I'm beginning to figure out what their primary areas of research were."

"Couldn't Leto just tell you what they were doing?"

Uninvited, the disembodied voice replied, "Authorization level is not precisely clear. Until it is so, I shall withhold both restricting and abetting."

"That," Griffin said, shrugging, "about says it. I think if I figure out enough on my own, Leto will change her mind."

Terrell nodded. "So, what do you think were the primary areas of research? You've had me sketching different models of battle armor. I can't say that's given me any great insights."

"Ah, but your work," Griffin said, slapping his friend on the back, "has given *me* a number of insights. Let me share them."

He led the way to the well-lit table that had more or less become his office. Ring was nearby, sitting upright on the floor, apparently drowsing. Griffin did not so much ignore the other man as let him continue to rest. The journey from Lynn's isolated community to Maiden's Tear must have been exhausting for Ring. He might need as many days to recover.

"Pull over a chair. Let me grab my notes. Right. Now, where should I start?"

Terrell shrugged. "We of Artemis know little of the seegnur, your Old Imperials—beyond what was in the lore. You say they surpassed your own people in both the technologies of communication and travel. Maybe you can explain the differences between you. If you don't, I'm not going to know why you're so excited."

"Fair enough." Griffin paused, considering how best to explain star flight to someone from a culture that considered a multi-masted sailing ship the epitome of long-distance travel. "Think of space as an enormous sea in which the star systems are scattered like chains of islands swirling around a sun. The distances are so vast that travel between close systems—even between planets in the same system—takes not minutes or hours, but days, weeks, years, even lifetimes."

Terrell accepted this so quietly that Griffin wondered if he was being humored. Then he remembered that Terrell belonged to a culture where journeys never took minutes or hours, but always took days, weeks, months, or longer. This explanation might be easier than he had imagined.

"I'm going to spare you the technical details—I'll be honest, I don't understand them myself—but eventually someone postulated that space could be folded." Griffin took out a handkerchief—thankfully clean—and spread it on the table. "Let's say System A is on this hem and System B is on this hem. The distance between would take years to cross, even at the fastest speeds. The orikami drive lets a ship equipped with it fold the space and so shorten the journey. He pinched the handkerchief in the middle, folding it so that the two edges remained visible, but the middle was compressed. "Now I've folded the space so that only half the distance needs to be crossed. We can fold it half again, then . . ." He made a final fold. "Half again."

"Amazing!"

Gratified, Griffin continued, "The orikami drive can't be used within a star system—the bodies that make up those 'island chains' make folding space impossible. However, there are various types of secondary engines that enable a ship to travel between planets. This combination of orikami drive and secondary engines is what is used by the Kyley Domain and is about the best we can do."

"What did the seegnur use?"

"We don't know for certain," Griffin said. "For more routine matters, they used something not unlike the orikami drive. However, there is evidence that they had found the means to make even bigger folds in space, that they could even fold space within star systems, which gave them a tremendous advantage."

Terrell nodded. "Like that which someone with a small, fleet sailing vessel would have if their rivals were limited to rowboats."

"Precisely!" Griffin's eyes shone with excitement. "That technology vanished with the Old Empire. The theory is that it depended as much on a human component as on any machinery. We don't know whether these pilots were all killed, were ordered to suicide, or merely died out without passing on their skills to a new generation. I think it was probably a combination of several of these elements. I also suspect that after the fall of the Old Empire there was such chaos that the resources for building these special ships and training their pilots simply wasn't available."

"Makes sense," Terrell said. "Perhaps when the rulers knew they would fall, they made sure the technology would be lost with them— rather like how the Old One flooded his complex on Mender's Isle and the Sanctum Sanctorum, rather than let us have them."

"One thing," Griffin said sadly, "we seem to have in common with the Old Imperials is the petty streak of human nature."

"How did the Imperials deal with communication if these systems were so far apart? Did they use fast ships to carry messages?"

"We're pretty sure that was how routine messages were transferred," Griffin agreed. "However, there is evidence that, just as they had learned how to have humans augment and refine the ability to fold space, they discovered ways for minds to communicate over vast distances. This meant stationing adepts in each location and surmount-

ing a wide variety of other difficulties but, compared to having to en-
trust messages to even the fastest ship, this gave the Imperials another
great advantage."

Again, Terrell seemed to have less of a problem accepting this than
Griffin would have believed possible. *But then he has experience with
communicating mind to mind. Perhaps I would have accepted this
more easily if I had known then what I do now.*

"And yet the Empire fell," Terrell said softly. "All that power and
so little wisdom. And that brings us back to the question of what they
were trying to make here."

Griffin was about to launch into his theories on that point when
Leto said, "Kipper has entered the complex. He does not bring your
meal, although darkness is gathering without."

There was a disapproving note to the disembodied voice, but Griffin answered mildly. "I'm sure there's a good reason."

He heard the soft slap of Kipper's bare feet against the polished floor
of the corridor. A moment later the boy, rosy-faced from exertion, burst
through the door into the lab.

"Bruin invites you to join him for dinner. He says to tell you that
he's so tired of only having me and Honeychild for company that
he's considering inviting Sam the Mule."

"Only you?" Terrell asked. "Where're Adara and Sand Shadow?"

The boy shrugged. "Don't know. She's gone scouting and not come
back."

The three strangers recovered from their surprise quickly. After a quick
consultation, they led the way to what had been the large dining and
recreation area during the Old One's tenancy. The tables and benches
had been so bulky that they hadn't been carried far by the surging
water. The new arrivals had retrieved the furnishings and cleaned
the area, which they were now using as a camping spot.

Julyan thought this was an odd choice, especially since the island
surface was much more pleasant than this dank, subterranean chamber. Then he realized that the newcomers would have no idea that the

Haunted Islands were prohibited, nor that any dangerous predators—barring snakes and insects—had been cleared away on the Old One's orders. Doubtless they had chosen safety and secrecy over ambiance.

On their first meeting, Julyan had been so startled by the three men's ready hands to their weapons that he had not taken in much about their attire and gear. Now, standing with his back against the wall, he made a careful inspection, as much to be prepared for future conflict as because he was interested.

All three men were dressed in a strange shoulder-to-foot garment, apparently somehow shaped from one piece of material, since Julyan couldn't see any seams. Even the fasteners were hard to detect, but since the man with the bronze curls—Alexander—had his garment open at the neck, while the other two wore theirs neatly closed, Julyan glimpsed the nearly hidden closures. The footwear was apparently part of the same material, woven more thickly to the height of an ankle boot. Most interesting of all was the color, which shifted with the surrounding environment. Currently, it was a neutral hue, somewhere between grey and brown. In the corridor, it had been the same grey as the walls and floors. Julyan wondered if outside it would shift toward green.

Julyan realized that he should have been startled and shocked, rather than feeling so analytical. But an embarrassment of miracles—from the flameless lights the men carried, to the pumps that worked with none to man them, to the enormous craft resting in the bay—had made him so numb that he was glad that, once introductions were over, he was freed from the need for speech.

The Old One, however, was his usual self. Perhaps his grey eyes were shining a bit more brightly than usual, but Julyan doubted that anyone who didn't know him well would find him other than cool, collected, and self-contained.

"You address us as 'seegnur,'" said the tall, blond man. He had introduced himself as Siegfried and, without saying so, presented himself as the leader. "That word is unfamiliar to me."

"I suspect it was specific to Artemis," the Old One replied politely. "It is what we were taught to call visitors from off-planet, and so applies perfectly to you and your associates."

"Indeed." Siegfried looked mildly amused. "So you of Artemis have retained something of your history, even after all this time?"

"We have."

"And you do not seem in the least surprised to see us."

"The lore has always held that the seegnur would someday return. If there were those who questioned, I was not among them."

"We have reason to believe," said the darker man, Falkner, "that we are not the first—uh—seegnur to come to Artemis in recent times. Do you know of another?"

He spoke as if he expected a negative response. His green eyes widened in surprise as the Old One said matter-of-factly, "Yes. He called himself Griffin Dane. He did not tell many that he was a seegnur, but I was so informed."

Julyan nearly gasped out loud. He had had no idea that Griffin had been a seegnur, yet, now that he thought about it, this explained much, including the Old One's interest in him, and the privileges he had granted him, even when he had been a prisoner.

"Is Griffin still alive?" asked Alexander eagerly.

"I believe so. Last I heard, he was, although he is no longer in this immediate area."

"So Griffin took you into his confidence," Siegfried said. "Yet it sounds as if he did not confide in everyone. Why did he choose you?"

"He wanted my help." The Old One spoke with disarming simplicity. He waved a long-fingered hand to indicate the battered tables and benches. "This facility and one linked to it on the mainland were in my trust. Griffin hoped to find in them equipment he might reactivate and then use to contact his orbiting ship."

The three men exchanged glances in which Julyan read surprise and concern, but no one even drew in a sharp breath. Instead, Siegfried continued as spokesman.

"Why did Griffin need to contact his orbiter? Was his machinery disabled? We have had some minor difficulties—mostly with our more delicate devices—but nothing that should have interfered with something as basic as ground-to-orbit communications."

"My understanding is that Griffin experienced difficulties almost as soon as he came below the atmosphere to begin closer scouting. His shuttle came down in the mountains to the north. By good chance for him—and for me—he was found by a young huntress who was training with her demiurge away from the settlements. She rescued him and, eventually, brought him to me."

Again the three men exchanged glances in which Julyan was certain he saw a certain degree of incredulity. He didn't blame them. The story was incredible.

"Why to you?" Siegfried said.

"I told you. I held this facility and the two on the mainland. Actually . . ." The Old One looked a little sly—an expression Julyan was certain was deliberate, although he expected that the three seegnur would take as a slip. "Most did not know I held this particular facility. What purpose Mender's Isle had served in the days of the seegnur had been lost except in the name. The area was protected from invasion by cleverly designed barriers and by the pervasive belief that the islands were haunted."

"But that didn't bother you, eh?" said Alexander.

"I have long been interested in the lore regarding the seegnur," the Old One said, a statement that clearly amused the three men, as well it should, since the Old One didn't look much older than his early twenties.

They interpret as pomposity and youthful posturing what is only truth, Julyan thought, and was pleased. It was good knowing that the Old One had not become so excited by the return of the seegnur that he had forgotten his cunning.

The Old One continued as if he had not noticed the amusement his words had generated. "I first found a facility on the mainland, beneath where once a lighthouse had stood. I explored more carefully than any had in hundreds of years, since it had been sealed in the days of the slaughter of the seegnur and death of machines. I found the manual override that enabled me to travel underwater to Mender's Isle. With a few chosen acolytes, I cleaned the place and continued my studies. From there I entered a second facility on the mainland that proved to have been the landing facility.

"But I divert from what you wish to learn. Because I eventually came to live in this facility and served as its custodian, when Adara the Huntress sought a place where there might be intact artifacts of the seegnur, she brought her find—Griffin Dane—to me."

"So the landing facility was intact?" Falkner sounded very eager.

"More intact than other places," the Old One corrected. "I do not know what your legends tell of what happened here on Artemis, but the destruction was terrible and widespread. Very little of what the seegnur left remained intact and what did remain was nonfunctional. Griffin said the invaders released 'nanobots' that stopped even functioning devices from working."

"We know some about what happened," Siegfried said. "Some rare histories recall both the existence of Artemis, and that many who had been important in the Old Empire were killed here. Griffin was very interested in these stories and our father encouraged him in his fancy . . ."

"Wait!" the Old One spoke with a trace of his usual authority, quickly masking it with an overt show of astonishment. " 'Our' father? Was your father Griffin's patron? Or perhaps are you his brother?"

Siegfried looked momentarily annoyed, although whether at his own slip or at the Old One's effrontery, Julyan could not be certain.

Alexander, however, laughed and replied, "That's right. Griffin is our brother, our youngest brother. He's a bit impulsive, but very smart. When no message came from him, we decided we'd better look for him."

Julyan was startled. Perhaps there was some resemblance between Siegfried and Griffin—both were fair-haired and possessed strong, powerful builds—but he never would have taken Falkner for a brother to either of them. It wasn't only a matter of coloring. His features were sharper, his cheekbones high, his chin almost pointed. While he wasn't short, he certainly was not tall. His build was lean to the point of being wiry.

Alexander also did not resemble either Siegfried or Griffin. He was only of middle height, although he had a strong build. Where they were handsome in a distinctly masculine fashion, Alexander's features were so elegant that—had his build been less definitively male—he might have been mistaken for a woman. His reddish-bronze curls set him apart, as did his eyes. These were a light hazel that shifted between pale green and a brown so light as to be almost tan.

Yet in one way Julyan had no problem believing these three were brothers. A shared life was reflected in those quick glances. It was there, too, in how Alexander deliberately interrupted Siegfried, giving away what the other had tried to hold back. Julyan would have bet a substantial amount that Siegfried was the eldest, a leader not only by talent but by habit, and that Alexander both accepted this and chafed under restraints so habitual that he probably was unaware how they bound him.

"I had the impression," the Old One said slowly, "that Griffin had not told anyone where he was going, because he wanted the finding of Artemis to be his discovery, his triumph. That was why he was so concerned about contacting his orbiter. He did not believe anyone would know where to look for him—even after sufficient time passed for anyone to become worried."

Again, Alexander was the one who chose to answer. "I said Griffin is smart, but I suppose I should have been more accurate. Griffin is very smart, if you're talking book smarts. As a researcher, he may be even as good as I am—and I have more years of training. But as a conniver! He's not as clever as he thinks. I'm sure our father knew where Griffin was going from the start, as well as precisely when he departed."

Something in how Siegfried now took over the conversation made Julyan certain that Siegfried wanted to be sure Alexander didn't babble further. But then the Old One wasn't telling the whole truth either—and Julyan doubted if these seegnur had any idea just how much this "helpful" local informant was omitting.

"Let us go back to the original point," Siegfried said. "Griffin came to you because you were in charge of the landing facility and processing center. Did he have any success reactivating any of the equipment?"

"None. He stayed with me but, eventually"—the Old One made

a sweeping gesture with his right hand—"there was trouble. Adara the Huntress did not mind bringing Griffin to me when she believed she would continue to influence him. He had become quite dependent on her, you must understand: his rescuer, his guide, perhaps his lover."

"Our Griffin is a romantic," Falkner said. "The only reason he never married is that he couldn't find a woman as captivating as his semi-mythical Artemis. So this Adara got her claws into him?"

Julyan swallowed a smile. He doubted the seegnur realized that Adara could, quite literally, get her claws into a man.

"Yes. She resented," the Old One continued, "that he was increasingly separating himself from her. I moved Griffin to Mender's Isle to protect him. Adara was too clever and ruthless for me. In the course of her 'rescue' of Griffin, all I had worked so hard to discover was ruined. Many of those who lived and worked with me were killed. Julyan and I only narrowly escaped. Griffin went with Adara. By now I have no doubt she has convinced him that I was his enemy, rather than the best friend he had upon this world."

Julyan was impressed. No one who knew the Old One would believe this story for a minute, but this "Maxwell"—so slim, almost fragile, so apparently young—easy to imagine him being overwhelmed by some terrible warrior woman.

Oh, Adara! he thought gleefully. *Do you know what a terrible enemy you have made? Soon the time will come that you will be glad of my protection, no matter the price I exact for it—and my price will be high indeed. We'll start with every inch of your lovely body, but in the end, I think I'll claim your soul.*

"You have given us much to think about, Maxwell," Siegfried said after a moment. "Do you know where our brother is?"

"I do not," the Old One said, "but I am certain he is alive and well. What good would he be to Adara the Huntress if he were not?"

"Then we owe it to ourselves to become more fully acquainted with the situation before we venture after him," Siegfried concluded. "Not only do we need to know more about the culture that has grown up here, but we also must assure ourselves that our equipment will continue to function. May we enlist you in our researches?"

The Old One gave a very low bow—doubtless the first time he had bowed to anyone in more than a hundred years. "I would be honored to be of service, seegnur. Where do you wish to begin?"

"I'd like to see your facility on the mainland," Falkner said. "Is that at all possible?"

"If we are careful," the Old One answered. "After the disruptions caused by Adara and the lies she spread, the facility was sealed against intrusion. Still, we can penetrate via the underwater tunnel. Most of the more interesting equipment was underground, so our lights should not show."

Siegfried nodded. "Then that is where we will start."

"But," added Alexander, a slow smile stretching his handsome face, "I am certain that is not where we will end."

It feels so good to be out alone, Adara thought as she left Maiden's Tear behind her. *In all fairness, I couldn't leave Terrell both to assist Griffin and to take care of all the camp duties, but I'd be a liar if I didn't admit I was beginning to feel more like a makeshift factotum than a huntress.*

"Alone? Since when have you been alone?"

That was how Adara interpreted the flash of images that flooded into her mind. She hadn't intended to send her thoughts to Sand Shadow, but she guessed that in her relief at being out and away she had projected more strongly than she had intended. As was their custom when scouting a new area, the demiurges were ranging a short distance from each other, covering a larger area, while still being able to reach the other should trouble arise.

Is Sand Shadow closer than I assumed? Adara thought. *Or is our bond becoming stronger? Certainly it has been tested over these last several months, not only by the challenges we've faced with Griffin, but when Artemis started drifting into our practice sessions. I doubt that many paired demiurges have faced such strange and peculiar challenges over such a short time.*

Adara felt Sand Shadow's agreement, both as to the manner of their testing and the puma's belief that their bond had grown more complex. Along with this came a certain wistful hope that soon they would be able to understand each other as easily as did Bruin and Honeychild.

They are much older than we are. Adara soothed the puma. *You are hardly grown out of spots.*

She laughed at the puma's indignant reminder that, compared to Adara, Sand Shadow had made great progress over the seasons they had known each other. Adara could only agree. Humans did grow slowly compared to pumas. Humans aged more slowly as well, but one of the wonders of the human/animal bond was that—barring accidents—the animal demiurge did seem to live longer and with greater vitality than their non-bonded kin. Adara suspected that the seegnur had somehow linked traits for longer life to the adaptations that let human and animal communicate mind to mind. What use would the human/animal partnership be to the seegnur if the human was slowed by an aging demiurge or continually training new partners?

Despite Sand Shadow's reminder that she was not really "alone," Adara felt amazingly light and free. Before Griffin's arrival, her responsibilities had been minimal. She had passed her final testing and been accepted as a hunter, but had not yet taken on a territory of her own—nor would she have been likely to do so. As he aged, Bruin had been ranging less, content with his garden, his students, and challenges in the immediate vicinity of Shepherd's Call. As he stayed closer to home, Adara spiraled outward, taking on his responsibilities, acting under the aegis of his reputation. It had been a comfortable time, an enjoyable time. Then, in the flash of a shooting star, Adara had become responsible for the life of a man—and not just any man, but a man who was probably a seegnur.

Adara pressed the heels of her hands to her eyes, as if the pressure of responsibility was a physical thing she could push away. The patterns of dark and light within her eyelids seemed to take the form of mushrooms. With that, a startling thought crashed into her mind.

Is that why I am having so much trouble contacting Artemis? Am

*I resisting the responsibility? I didn't ask for it . . . I haven't asked for
so much of what has dominated my life since early spring.*

"*But do you regret it all? Saving Griffin and this curious hunt
we have followed since?*"

Adara considered Sand Shadow's question, trying hard to eliminate from the equation her mixed feelings about Griffin as a man, trying only to weigh the life she was living now against the life she would
have been living. Did she truly regret the change? Startled, Adara realized that the woman she had been—someone whose greatest wor-
ries had been honing her own abilities and developing a reputation—was
a stranger to her. How petty that Adara seemed! How self-absorbed!

She smiled. She didn't regret the events of the last several months
at all. She let herself probe the next element of what Sand Shadow
thought of as a "curious hunt." How did she feel about the addition
of Artemis to what had been a closed relationship? That was a harder
question. The world had been a much more comfortable place before
Adara had realized that the spirit associated with it was more like a
frightened child than the all-enfolding mother figure which had
vaguely occupied that space in her imagination.

Adara would be the first to admit that she was not the most philo-
sophically inclined of humans—although recent events were forcing
her to reconsider that attitude. She had truly been content with the
gradually more complex catechism taught to children. She had never
been the type to ask why the sky was blue (because so often it wasn't)
or why the sun moved (because it did). Maybe it was because she'd
been taught that her world was a paradise designed by gods, for gods,
so what use were questions?

Things were as they were because that was what suited the seegnur. Now, though, there were questions that the catechism had not addressed. Why was the fact never raised that Artemis the planet was
also Artemis the person? What about Leto's complex? It didn't fit in
at all with the ostensible reason the planet had been created. Which
was the bigger lie?

Eminently practical, Sand Shadow pulled Adara back from a trail
of increasingly fruitless speculation. To the puma's way of seeing

things, the question was not how one felt about a hunt, but whether or not the hunt was worth pursuing. If it was, then the next question was what was the best and safest way to accomplish it. If best and safest also included easiest—well, that suited the great cat as well.

Adara found herself smiling. *"How would you hunt a neural network? We have tried opening ourselves to her when we are practicing. After all, that's how she touched us the first times. However, we've had no luck. Should we try again now that we're farther from Leto's zone?"*

A single image popped into Adara's mind, herself up in the high limbs of a long-needled pine, a lacework of fungus growing from the wood and talking to her. This was followed by a second image of a cluster of a similar mushroom, only this one was larger, falling like a curtain, rather than shaping a face. From the sense that came with the image, Adara could tell that Sand Shadow was looking right at them.

"You think we should use those? How?"

A mild sense of annoyance, one that Adara translated as, *"Why should I do all the thinking? I've half an idea. You come up with the other half."*

Adara understood the puma's annoyance. "Really," she said out loud to herself. "You'd think I was a wolf pup, waiting for the head wolf to make my decisions for me, rather than a full-grown huntress."

Sand Shadow was lolling next to the mushroom curtain, playing with her earrings, when Adara arrived. Reaching out with one hand to rub the great cat behind one ear, just where she liked it, Adara studied the cluster, admiring how the predominately white hue was shaded with palest pink and yellow. Bruin had tutored his students very carefully on the subject of mushrooms, for hunters also did a great deal of foraging. Sometimes plants could be as valuable as the plushest fur or finest joint of meat. Mushrooms and other fungi, with their widely varying properties, were among the most useful, whether for food, medicine, or sources of poison. After they had been properly prepared— usually by drying—they had the added advantage of being lightweight and easily portable.

Of course, some are only useful when fresh, Adara thought as she examined Sand Shadow's find, *but that is hardly an issue in this case. Now that I have it, what do I do with it? Artemis may know how to speak through a fungus, but I do not.*

"*Eat it,*" Sand Shadow suggested, her image that of Bruin devouring an enormous skewer on which chunks of elk alternated with wedges of onion and large, white-capped mushrooms.

Adara considered this suggestion, but rejected it. Some mushrooms were safe to eat. Others were decidedly not. In between fell a vast number that might not kill the human who ate them, but could have side effects ranging from hallucinations to a very bad ache in the gut.

Sand Shadow seemed disappointed that Adara would not opt for the simplest solution.

"*Glad you feel that way,*" Adara retorted. "*I notice you're not offering to eat them.*"

The puma did not deign to reply.

Adara considered. Artemis's neural network was somehow associated with fungi, an idea that was only strange if one didn't realize that the visible fruiting bodies were the least portion of complex organisms that could stretch for miles. Adara had no idea if all mushrooms were part of Artemis's network, but she saw no harm in assuming so. Perhaps she and Sand Shadow would do better if they concentrated on Artemis using a specific focal point, rather than reaching out to nothingness.

Sand Shadow liked the idea. She assured Adara that nothing dangerous was anywhere near and that she would not let herself detach so far that she would not be on guard. Adara accepted this division of labor. The puma's senses were far better than her own. It did not make sense to insist that she keep watch while the puma prowled after the elusive neural network.

She settled down cross-legged, gently touching the mushroom curtain with her fingertips. Although their communication with Artemis had been as much wordless as shaped by words, still Adara—human as she was—had shaped it into words. She recalled them now.

"Velvet darkness, soft as sound," she recited softly. "My shadow, my other self, can you hear me?"

That wasn't quite right . . . Artemis was not her "other self" as Sand Shadow was. How had Artemis defined herself in those earlier contacts? Not just as a neural network, that had been Adara's human mind, seeking to reduce the complex to a few simple terms. "Neural network, seeded spores activated by annihilating desire, interlacing mosaic, pieces yet unplaced." That had been it. It made a lot more sense now than it had at the time.

Adara repeated these words in her mind, feeling Sand Shadow shaping the remembered images that went with them. Closer, but still not enough . . . Adara lowered herself to the level of the mushrooms, stared at them, repeating the words very softly. Neural network. (That spider's web of tangled threads.) Seeded spores. (Lovely, like the tiniest snowflakes on a very cold winter's day, but detailed, minute dandelion seeds drifting with purposeless purpose.) Interlacing mosaic. (Concentrate on the image of connection, not on the gaping holes they now suspected were there.)

Closer. They were closer, but still not quite enough. Adara saw how her breath stirred the delicate gills on the underside of the mushroom. Saw them vibrating, like the strings of the wind harps Bruin put in his garden when the weather was fine. That music, played without fingers, was both haunting and unpredictable, stirring the soul to flights of fancy.

Without realizing it, Adara realized her whispered words were becoming a chant, the chant rising and falling, making its own melody. Then, soft as a breeze, she began to sing, letting the rise and fall of her voice stir the delicate gills, while keeping her breath so soft that even the thinnest veil in the cluster did not stir. Her mental image changed, ceasing to be darkness, becoming instead the palest light, the softest breath, the gentle scent of moonflowers, all weaving into a music that called, coaxed, comforted, cajoled. Vaguely she was aware of Sand Shadow adding the whistling cries of a puma kitten—sweet notes often mistaken for birdsong by the uninitiated—to the mix.

"Whyfore of yourself? Do you flee it? We will give you eyes, ears, nose, fingers, paws, whiskers, tail. Is the whyfore so terrible that you no longer seek it? Come to us! Come to us!"

At last, weakly, tentatively, with nothing about it of the teasing child who had so confidently asked about the difference between good and bad behavior, the sensibility that was Artemis touched the minds of the human and the puma. Her thoughts trembled so that Adara struggled to sort meaning from what was a flood of emotion rather than words.

"I, so scared, broken apart... By your voices interwoven, laced together. Alone, no more!"

Interlude: Giver Given

Song breathed onto my gills,
Wind harp Artemesian
    Plays upon my soul.

The veil trembles,
    tears,
        revealing . . .

Before: There was mind.
Before: I had heart.
Before: Gifts given so I might give.

Now soul,
    Now self,
        Now I see . . .

My beloved's face
    must be me.

9

Spiders and Webs

Bruin did not seem unduly worried about Adara's absence. "She said she was going to firmly establish contact with Artemis before coming back into this dead zone. Otherwise, her efforts might be for nothing. If she's gone seven or eight days without sending a message, then I'll go looking for her. Meanwhile, I'll mind your camp on one condition. You all need to come out at least once a day and help with some of the chores. I'm an old man and Kipper is just a boy."

Griffin didn't need to see the twinkle in the old bear's eyes to know that Bruin was perfectly capable of taking care of everything to do with feeding them and caring for their mounts and camp, even without Kipper's aid. He knew a price was being exacted for the hunter's services and did his best not to resent it. As he carried a dirty pot down to the stream, Griffin realized how easily he had slipped back into the privileged mindset in which he had been reared. During his travels with Adara and Terrell, he'd taken pride in doing his best to contribute, even if that meant doing nothing more sophisticated than grooming the horses (Sam the Mule would only accept Terrell) or turning the spit over the fire.

Is it because I'm almost back in my element, back where the skills I spent a lifetime acquiring are actually useful? Something similar happened when we first moved into the Old One's Sanctum. Last time it took a puma insisting I play marbles to shake me out of it. Now I get gently slapped by an old bear.

He felt distinctly unsettled, as if there was something he was missing. Unable to pinpoint it, he resisted the pull of his researches and turned to Kipper.

"Want me to show you a marble game from my home world? We played it a lot on the road. Maybe we can start playing again for a bit in the evenings, as a break."

Kipper's face brightened, and Griffin didn't miss Terrell's expression of pleasure as the factotum turned to find his own bag of marbles.

Good, he thought, starting to draw circles in the soft dirt of their camp. *Time enough for research later. Surely, there will be time enough.*

As if in reward for his balancing work and play, over the next several days, Griffin found additional information that helped refine his ideas about what the researchers in Leto's facility had been working toward.

"Power," he said to Terrell, "was a definite limiting factor, one the Old Imperials were working hard to get around. They had some amazing fuel cells, but the problem was that the elements they used to generate power had some nasty side effects."

Terrell nodded. "I remember you telling me about that—cold heat that burns far more deeply and dangerously than fire. If you hadn't reassured me that Leto's complex was certainly sealed against such damage, I don't think even my friendship with you could have gotten me back in here."

Griffin nodded. He felt fairly certain that Leto's complex was safe. He'd been to a lot of Old Empire ruins; there trace radiation was always due to the weapons used. The Imperials had apparently safeguarded their domestic power sources—some specialists speculated that they had been engineered to deactivate if breached.

"My respect for their technology blinded me to the serious challenges in making miniature high-powered fuel cells," Griffin admitted. "I've shown you how the battle armor contained its own power unit or units. The more powerful the weapons, the larger the power unit. However, the larger the unit, the more radiation it generated, so that, in turn, the amount of shielding also increased."

Terrell nodded. "Basically, there seems to be a point after which adding further refinements to a suit—whether flight capacity or weapons or some other function—wasn't worth trying because power demands made the suit too cumbersome."

"Precisely. Hold on to that thought for a moment. I need to go off on a tangent, but I promise you, it will make sense in the end."

Terrell grinned. "Yes, seegnur."

Griffin made a rude gesture Terrell had taught him. "Remember when we talked about how long-distance space travel is accomplished by use of machines that fold space? And how the Old Imperials had some sort of technology that enabled their pilots to further refine that folding process?"

Terrell nodded.

"I've been looking at ship plans in one of Leto's data banks. It took me a while to figure out the schematics because the designers were allowing for factors alien to those we use. Eventually, I realized that one series of emblems indicated a form of shielding similar but different from that used to block radiation. Earlier today, I was staring at the plans and . . . Have you ever had your brain shift on you, so that suddenly you see a problem differently?"

"Many times."

"Well, that's what happened to me. I realized that this particular shielding always separated the piloting area and various related sensor arrays from the rest of the ship. I'm guessing—and only guessing—that the mind pilots needed to be free from interference by other minds if they were to be able to find their way through space."

"And the shielding," Terrell said, "let them do their job in a ship that carried passengers."

"Exactly!" Griffin agreed. "Now for the next part . . . A spaceship needs a great deal of power, but the elements the seegnur used to generate energy are dangerous to the human body. In ship designs, the engines were always placed so that the radiation would not penetrate the ship—common sense. If mind pilots also required separate areas, ships carrying large numbers of people would need to be enormous. Well and good. Useful. Efficient. But not very stealthy."

"Which wouldn't matter," Terrell said taking up the thread, "if you were sending the equivalent of a cargo ship or even a passenger vessel—but it would matter a great deal if you were bringing in an army and didn't want your enemies to know."

"You came up with that fast enough," Griffin said, slightly miffed.

"I've been doing nothing for days upon days but draw the various models of the armored suits we've found here," Terrell said, too interested to pay any attention to Griffin's annoyance.

Griffin let excitement wash over him again. "What would they need so much more power for? I think they were designing armored suits with enough power to enable individual soldiers to move between planets, maybe even between systems. That's the difference between the armored suits they already had and what Leto calls 'spaveks.'"

"That would be a huge advantage," Terrell said, "especially given how much damage one of those armored suits can cause."

Griffin nodded. "I feel certain that large troop carriers would have been detected. Even today, most planets are ringed with satellites meant to track approaching traffic. "

"But why spaveks?" Terrell asked. "Why not just make small ships? Even a small ship would permit the power cells to be placed some distance from the pilots. Then they wouldn't need to wear such a massive amount of power on their backs."

"I think the designers explored that option," Griffin said, "based on some of the material I've found in the data banks. There certainly were advantages, but even a small ship is bulky compared to a suit. Bulk means mass—and when in a gravity well—weight."

He paused, wondering if he should make sure Terrell remembered what a gravity well was, but Terrell waved him on. "I'm following you . . . Go on."

"Anyhow, both additional mass and additional weight would mean that additional power would be needed to move them."

"So," Terrell said, "that puts us back to that first problem—the more power you need, the more potent the fuel cell. The more potent the fuel cell, the more radiation needs to be shielded. The more shielding, the more bulk."

"Right! So, I think that one of the projects—maybe the main project—being researched here on Artemis was coming up with an armored suit that would enable a mind pilot to jump right inside the enemy's defenses. Most defenses would have been designed with battle cruisers in mind. Something as small as an armored human could slip in as easily as minnows through a mesh meant to catch whales."

Terrell nodded. "I agree. Another advantage of more efficient fuel cells would be that any weapons built into the suits would be tremendously more powerful."

"I see where you're coming from," Griffin said. "Once the transition was complete, the power demands for movement would be comparatively minimal. That would free up energy for weapons. The suits would be able to move faster, too. This is fascinating!"

Terrell gave him a funny look. "You may find it fascinating. I find it frightening. I hope they were stuck on the fuel cell problem and hadn't started refining weapons and whatever they used for flight."

Griffin was puzzled. "Why?"

Terrell just stared at him. After a moment, Griffin understood.

"Because," he said slowly, "while we don't understand what the mind pilots did that refined the ability to fold space, we do understand—all too well—both how to use weapons, and how to fly both space and atmospheric craft. Those new technologies could be put into use as soon as they could be manufactured."

"And from what you have said," Terrell added, "the example of how the seegnur destroyed themselves and much of what they had achieved has done nothing to keep the surviving fragments of their empire from pursuing war."

"All too true," Griffin agreed. He forced a smile. "Aren't you glad I haven't sent a message to my family? Months, probably years, will pass before anyone comes after me. First they need to miss me, then they need to figure out where I went—something that won't be easy, since I very carefully hid all my research notes. After that, they'd need to get here and locate me—or at least the significant areas on the planet. As I told you, from orbit, even your biggest cities are hard to find."

Terrell nodded. "Still, even with the danger involved, I suppose it's too much to hope that you'll give this up as a bad job? Maybe there was a good reason Maiden's Tear was prohibited."

Griffin understood the sense of what Terrell said, but he couldn't believe there really was any risk involved. It was likely the researchers had still been working on the fuel cell problem. The other armored suits—the ones worn by Leto's defenders and those worn by her attackers—were in very bad shape. Reconstructing their weaponry wouldn't be at all easy.

"I'd like to keep looking," he said, knowing he was taking advantage of Terrell's training, "for a bit longer. This place is a dream come true."

From the look on Terrell's face, Griffin knew that the factotum thought that Leto's complex and all it represented was a horrible and pervasive nightmare.

In the days that followed, Julyan had little time alone with the Old One—or Maxwell, as he must be careful to call him now. Seamus had been retrieved, represented to the Dane brothers as Julyan's idiot cousin, and pretty much left on his own as long as he stayed near the base camp. Occasionally, the Old One would send messages to Julyan through Seamus, but these were simple, more to establish a protocol for private communication than holding any significant content.

Work was under way to clear the underwater passage between Mender's Isle and the Sanctum—work complicated because the subterranean complex on Mender's Isle was still mostly underwater and had to be drained first

"We have an advantage Griffin did not," Siegfried said one evening. "He told you that he carried with him packets of nanobots that would hopefully reverse the damage done five hundred years ago."

"That's right," the Old One replied. "However, he said that these had been buried with his shuttle. We both thought that in time some of these would leak into the planet's system and slowly reactivate dormant technology, but that the process might take years."

Siegfried nodded. "But, as you can see, we are having no . . ."

"Little," growled Falkner, who had spent a good portion of the day rebuilding a pump because some key mechanism had refused to function.

"Little," corrected Siegfried with a sigh, "difficulty using the equipment we brought with us. True, we did our best to seal our gear from contamination, but we also brought with us our own antivirus. We've run a few tests and feel confident that in a far shorter time than you imagine, it may be possible to reactivate some of the equipment on the mainland."

"There's a considerable amount of water there," the Old One said, "more than was here. Will your pumps be able to handle that?"

Falkner shrugged. "I think so. I don't want to promise until I see the place myself, but surely the original construction contained some sort of drains. My guess is that these were closed when the place was sealed. Since you didn't know to look for them, you didn't open them. Once we get them working for us, the pumps will be able to do the rest."

Julyan didn't think the Old One was particularly pleased by this casual dismissal of his competence, a feeling that was confirmed when a look of fear flashed across Seamus's face, but he doubted the Dane brothers suspected anything. Although in many ways they seemed more sophisticated than Griffin, they were less sensitive to the responses of others, more unconsciously arrogant.

Perhaps Griffin would have been the same if he hadn't crashed his shuttle and needed help, Julyan thought. *These men have arrived with their abilities unhampered. We are convenient to them, but not necessary.*

At that moment, Alexander, the youngest of the three brothers, pushed a restless hand through his bronze curls and turned to the Old One.

"Would you mind if I borrowed Julyan for a few hours? I'm weary of ship's supplies. Perhaps we could catch some fresh fish or gather some berries or something."

The Old One bowed, hands pressed against his thighs in the traditional fashion. "I would be happy to have him accompany you, seegnur.

Julyan is a trained hunter and I'm sure he feels quite caged in these close quarters."

"Wonderful!" Alexander tapped a small unit he wore on his left wrist. "Call me if you need me, brothers."

Once they had left the subterranean complex, Julyan led the way to a cove that faced away from the town of Spirit Bay. Automatically, he scanned the waters outside of the artificial reef that protected the islands from any ships. As he expected, there were none, for the main channel used by vessels going into Spirit Bay was on the opposite side of the Haunted Islands. The cove itself was well sheltered from casual observation, one of the reasons Julyan had favored it.

"Lovely," Alexander said when they arrived. "A perfect summer picnic spot. I suppose the fishing is good?"

"Usually is," Julyan said, putting down his pack and removing hooks and lines. Next, he cut and trimmed slender saplings to use as rods. Alexander let him do all the work, but Julyan didn't mind. He liked showing off his competence, something he had been given far too little opportunity to do of late.

Alexander waited until Julyan had put his knife away and was attaching the line to the rod before rising from the grassy knoll upon which he had been lounging. "You are very competent, Julyan Hunter. I hope when we need to recruit other assistants they will be as good."

Julyan paused in the act of baiting his hook. "Other assistants? Won't your machines and devices serve better than humans?"

"For many things," Alexander agreed. "However, for some things only living beings will do."

He accepted the rod Julyan handed to him, then said, his voice so deliberately casual that Julyan felt alarmed, "Before we do our recruiting, I need to test my own research. Siegfried and Falkner have their doubts, but I think . . ."

The next phrase Alexander spoke meant nothing and yet everything to Julyan. It wasn't very long, perhaps seven clipped syllables, but the effect was instantaneous. Julyan felt as if a new sense had awoken in him, simultaneously making him more alert and yet curiously without volition.

"You await my command," Alexander said.

"Of course," Julyan said. He continued preparing his fishing line, but knew without a doubt that if Alexander told him to stop, he would without question or pause. "Does the seegnur still care to fish?"

"You may do so, but listen carefully to me. I have a few instructions. The first is that you may not tell anyone at all in any form or fashion, whether in words or sounds or writing or even through the actions of your body, what has passed and will pass between us this day. We came here. We fished. That is all. Do you understand?"

"Yes. Of course."

Julyan felt a little hurt. Did the seegnur Alexander think him a fool?

"Now . . . Jump into the water."

Julyan pushed off the bank into the water, fishing rod still in his hand. He began to sink, wondered if it was permissible to swim. While he was so wondering, he felt a strong hand grasp his hair—he had worn it in a braid that day—and pull his head above the water.

"Swim!" Alexander commanded. "Let go of the fishing rod and swim. I forbid you to drown."

Julyan did as he was told, though he felt a trace of regret for his lost fishing gear. He could have successfully kept from drowning without dropping it. Unaware of Julyan's dismay, Alexander was laughing in wild delight.

"Get out of the water," he said. "Strip off those wet clothes. It would not do for you to catch cold."

Julyan stripped, meticulously removing every item of clothing. Since Alexander did not command him to do otherwise, he carefully placed the wet items on a large rock in the sunlight, where they would have a chance to dry. Then he rose, uncertain if he should return to fishing. Perhaps he should ask permission to retrieve his rod.

"Stand still," Alexander said, "and await my . . . pleasure."

He was still laughing. Julyan thought he should feel happy that the seegnur was so pleased but, in truth, his skin crawled. He'd always liked Alexander best of the three Dane brothers. Siegfried was too much like the Old One. Falkner seemed to care more for his machines than for any person. Alexander had been the one who was easy to talk with, the least likely to condescend.

"I've found it!" Alexander exulted. "Julyan, does your lore contain hints that the seegnur could control the people of Artemis if they wished?"

Julyan considered. "Less the lore than some tales within the lore. It is implied, rather than stated."

"My family," Alexander said, "has reason to believe that biologically we are the heirs to your seegnur. My mother has gone out of her way to assure this lineage remains pure and strong, as have others before her. You should be pleased. Your response to the phrase I spoke confirms our belief."

"I am pleased for you, seegnur."

Julyan *was* pleased for Alexander. At the same time, he was fully aware of how uncomfortable he was standing wet and naked. Even though the summer air was warm, he did not particularly like how he felt. He wanted to dry off before the brackish bay water stiffened on his skin. He felt oddly vulnerable, something he did not care for one bit. However, he had been specifically told to await Alexander's pleasure, so wait he must.

"Not all the seegnur knew this trick," Alexander explained. "It would have taken too much fun out of the game, you see. However, with so few seegnur and so many Artemesians, protective measures were necessary. I'm sure you understand."

He walked a slow circle around Julyan, then extended one hand and gently ran the tips of his nails over the skin of Julyan's right flank, extending up and over his rib cage.

"Do you like that, Julyan Hunter?"

Julyan was honest. "No. Not particularly."

Alexander smiled a slow, cruel smile. "How you feel doesn't matter one bit to me, just as I suspect the feelings of others haven't mattered much to you. How do you feel about that?"

Honesty forced its way from Julyan's lips, although he fought to say anything else or at least keep silent. "I am frightened."

"Good." Alexander faced Julyan, then ran both hands over Julyan's torso, down his flanks, then up again and across the front of his body, caressing in a manner lewd and lingering. "I like that you're afraid. Now, do as I say. Await my pleasure."

Adara was learning that being a world was a whole lot more complicated than she'd imagined. When she'd first realized what the strange entity invading both her dreams and her communication with Sand Shadow had to be—a gut-level revelation, rather than something coolly understood—Adara had thought of Artemis as the brain, the world her body, the whole basically an oversize variation of life as she knew it.

However, as Adara was learning, for Artemis brain and body were much more intertwined. Artemis had not simply been shut down, she had been both lobotomized and crippled. When Griffin's crash had released into the planetary ecosystem a countermeasure to the destructive nanobots, Artemis had slowly begun to awaken to self-awareness once more. Then, upon awakening, the planet had immediately found herself battling for control of herself.

"You think your attacker was something left behind from the slaughter of the seegnur and death of machines?" Adara asked.

"Unknown, unknowable. That which was not even yet I had not the eyes to see, ears to hear, self to know. Barely born, immersed in battle, I found this self I am in the process of preservation."

"Maybe Griffin can explain what happened," Adara suggested, speaking aloud as had become her habit if no one else was around.

The huntress immediately sensed that Artemis was uneasy. Artemis was still incomplete. Adara could understand why, having been attacked twice in recent memory—for to Artemis, events of five hundred years ago seemed to have happened only a few months before—the planetary intelligence felt unwilling to let anyone know how vulnerable she remained.

"I won't ask directly," Adara assured her. "Griffin's always eager to talk about his discoveries regarding the seegnur's technology. I'll ask as if I'm wondering about what we could do if something tried to take Leto over."

The emotions coming from Artemis became more complex. Uncertainty remained, mingled with other elements. Artemis didn't like Leto, yet, at the same time, she felt highly protective of her, even possessive.

"I'll be careful," Adara promised. "But if you've been attacked once, next time you might not be so lucky. It's possible that whatever attacked you was as weak as you were yourself. As you grow stronger, so might it."

The equivalent of a sigh.

Adara wished the planetary intelligence would go back to talking, but often these days, Artemis resisted words as a very imprecise form of communication. Even though frustrated, Adara understood. How often had she struggled to find the words to communicate a complicated emotional state—such as her own feelings about Terrell or about Griffin? Nonetheless, Adara often found Artemis's idea/emotion combinations difficult to sort out.

The problem was a variation of what Adara had dealt with when learning to communicate with Sand Shadow. Especially when a kitten, the puma had seen every object as unique. Each tree was its own thing. There was no general class of objects called "tree." Each animal, again, a unique entity. Only with experience had the puma learned group classifications.

Artemis had her own ideas as to how they could solve the communication problem. Her own neural network was anchored in a wide variety of mycelia—not only in the more visible mushrooms and fungi, but in tiny spores and invisible living threads. She wanted Adara and Sand Shadow to accept some of her spores into themselves. Both human and puma, accustomed as they were to thinking of fungi as agents of decay and deterioration, had balked.

In time, Adara thought uneasily, *Artemis will surely come around. She's still reacting to her realization of how very incomplete her perceptions are. Even when she's "with" me and Sand Shadow, she's in hundreds, even thousands, of places, strengthening and expanding her net.*

Over the last several days, Adara had learned just how incomplete that net was. When Artemis had discovered the gigantic hole that was Leto, Adara had believed that Artemis's linked strands of perception were much more extensive than they actually were. She had imagined a tightly woven net, girdling the globe. That was how Artemis had been designed to be. That awareness of her essential design had colored Artemis's earlier explanations.

In reality, the net's mesh was wide and loose. When Artemis communicated within herself, it was—as best Adara could comprehend—as if she stood upon various strands and called to herself. Those calls provided temporary connections but, when Artemis let them drop, the gap returned. What made Leto so disturbing was that her area was a gap too wide for Artemis to call across.

I wonder, Adara thought, *if in the days of the seegnur, Artemis had more strands, perhaps reaching up into the skies. Then she would have called across Leto without even realizing Leto was not there. I wonder if Artemis is even more uneasy because she wonders what other gaps there might be and if she'll learn about them before they become a danger to her?*

Yes. Being a world was far more difficult than Adara had ever imagined. Nonetheless, she was drawn into the experience, knotted tightly to Artemis—she and Sand Shadow both. The question was, would they expand as the net grew or would they tangle in the meshes and drown?

Some days after Adara and Sand Shadow departed for who knew where, Griffin arrived in Leto's complex to find the resident intelligence very agitated and Ring behaving oddly indeed.

The big man had opened one of the enormous bunkers in which various spaveks hung inert in their "squires"—complex racks that not only contained a variety of diagnostic machinery, but also would have helped a wearer to put on the complex machines.

"He arrived here shortly after dawn," Leto said, her voice that of a petulant little girl. "I warned him off, but he opened the bunker and has been going up and down, examining the spaveks and muttering nonsense to himself. Had he actually touched a suit, I would have taken prohibitive action, but since you have let him come into the complex, I felt I must forebear."

"I'll handle it," Griffin promised, stepping authoritatively forward.

In truth, Griffin had no desire to bother Ring, for he had no doubt of the man's good intentions. Ring had proven repeatedly that his motivations were too complex to be easily grasped. Therefore, if Ring wanted to stare at the prototypes, then Griffin was inclined to let him do so.

To Griffin's relief, Ring slowly turned to face him, eliminating the need for open confrontation. This time, he did not cover his eyes as he so often did, but forced his slightly unfocused gaze to meet Griffin's own.

"They are here," he said with a gusty sigh. "This one . . ." He pointed to a suit tinted a dark, primary blue. "This one. It will, may, could, help. If I clean it, can you make it live?"

For Ring, this was as direct as communication ever became. Ignoring Leto's sputtering, Griffin went to inspect the suit Ring had indicated. It seemed more complete than many, although several leg and arm pieces were missing. He was inspecting it, working out its probable capacities, when Terrell shambled in, rubbing his beard stubble and looking bemused. He'd stayed back in camp, probably to talk to Bruin about Adara, while he packed something for their lunch.

"What're you doing?" he asked. "And why's Leto so upset?"

"Ring asked me to inspect this spavek," Griffin said. "He wanted to know if I could 'make it live.' "

Terrell came to take a closer look. "I'd say you'd have a better chance with this one than with many others. When I was drawing it, I noticed some indications it had been in use. Look, here . . . and here . . ."

He hunkered down and pointed to a place where the blue coating showed darker, another where the material that made up a knee covering was scuffed. "My guess is that they'd tested this one, maybe even in a firefight." Terrell had learned the term from Griffin and, once he realized it had to do with fighting with fire, rather than fighting fire, he had seized on it. "This isn't one of the larger combat units, but it has energy weapons."

He pointed. "If you look by the knee, you'll see that there was some sort of fluid leak. My guess is that the joint was damaged by 'fire' and then repaired, but they didn't bother to clean it up all the way because they were going to test it again."

"And never had a chance," Griffin said softly. "I wonder if we can activate it?"

"Why not ask your girlfriend how to go about it?"

Griffin listened to Leto's sputtering, which was full of terms like "restricted," "off-limits," "unauthorized," and "prohibited."

He sighed. "It may come to that, but I'd like to see what we can figure out on our own. Maybe it's as simple as making sure the power unit is connected. From what I've been able to tell, protocol here was to disconnect the power from any prototype not actually being worked on to eliminate the chance of accidents."

Terrell rose. "What good would making it 'live' do? None of us know how to sail—no, pilot—one of these. If there's one thing I learned from Helena the Equestrian, it's know your animal before you swing astride."

"I've piloted a wide variety of craft," Griffin objected. "I've even worn power armor a time or two. I could handle it."

Terrell slowly shook his head. "You can ride Molly, too, pretty well by now. I'd chance you on Midnight or Tarnish in an emergency, but Sam would have you off and trampled."

"This isn't a mule," Griffin protested. "It's a machine."

Terrell kept shaking his head. "Not a machine as you know them. You're the one who told me that the seegnur's machines were meant to mesh with the minds of their pilots. How do you know that this suit wouldn't decide you're not the rider for it and throw you—or worse? What if it burns out your brain because you're unauthorized?"

Griffin was about to protest further when Ring's deep voice spoke with that curious lack of inflection that somehow managed to hold the attention more than any amount of argument.

"Not Griffin. Me. It will let me ride it. First, though, we must make it live."

Julyan rapidly learned that the hitch in Alexander's gallop wasn't sex, as such, but control. He used sex—or rather the threat of sex—to control Julyan. If Julyan was obedient, Alexander kept his hands to himself. If Julyan was not obedient—even when the control words were not in use—then Julyan found himself doing things he wouldn't have done to any of his "mares." Worse, Alexander told him to enjoy it and so he did. The memory of that enjoyment haunted him, waking and sleeping.

After a time or two in which Alexander proved to Julyan that those seven simple syllables would permit him to make Julyan do anything he desired, Alexander preferred the threat to the act. He still acted, just often enough and erratically enough so that Julyan lived in a constant state of tension whenever he was alone with the man but, as time went on, Alexander preferred to exercise his power in other ways.

One of these was making Julyan his unwilling confidant. Julyan quickly gathered that while Alexander was in accord with his brothers on many things, he had his own agenda—and that he deeply and sincerely hated Griffin.

"Maxwell doesn't seem to wonder how we arrived here so quickly," Alexander gloated. "Or how we found the region Griffin had gone to with a whole world to choose from. Do you?"

He and Julyan were alone in the commander's quarters on what had been the residential side of the Sanctum. This area, it turned out, had been closed and sealed when the Old One had released his flood, and so could be explored as soon as the central area was drained. Unhappily, for Julyan, rows of dormitory rooms and the like held little interest for the two more warlike Dane brothers. Exploration had been turned over to Alexander, who was, ostensibly, trying to find out if the commander's data storage units could be accessed.

"You told us that Griffin had not hidden his trail as well as he thought," Julyan said obediently.

"Ah . . . He didn't, but not as we implied. Griffin actually did an excellent job hiding his trail. We took precautions so we could track him."

Julyan made an interested noise.

"Falkner and Gaius tampered with Griffin's shuttle. First, it was to set beacons that would show us the direction in which Griffin went.

Since the shuttle was mounted on the outside of the main vessel, that was no problem at all. When Griffin reached Artemis, a final beacon was dropped that would activate the others so we'd know it was time to follow. The signal took a while to backtrack but, even so, I think we were very clever."

"Yes. Waiting to send the signal would keep Griffin from detecting the beacons."

"Smart boy. We didn't stop there. When the shuttle penetrated atmosphere, we set a device to release some nanobots that would, at the very least, enable our own machines to work without being shut down. Obviously, this worked to some extent, although not quickly enough to keep Griffin's shuttle from crashing. If we were lucky and guessed right on the composition of the original attack virus, our counter-virus would reactivate Artemis's own equipment."

This was complete nonsense, so Julyan only nodded encouragingly.

"We also arranged for a small beacon to be planted beneath Griffin's skin, so we could track him. After all, a planet is a big place. Did Griffin tell you about the spider?"

"Spider?" Julyan didn't need to fake his confusion.

"I see he didn't. He always was an untruthful boy. I couldn't see why we would need Griffin once we were here. Oh, it's true that our sister, Jada, had done some useful work with him—making sure that once Griffin arrived on Artemis he would obsessively pursue any leads to the Old Imperial technology. Jada's job wasn't that hard, since Griffin would probably have done that anyway. Still, I'm as good a historian as Griffin—better, when it comes to military matters. That's all the others care about. It wasn't as if we needed his skills as an archeologist. So I took action."

Julyan knew when he was being prompted to ask a question. "May I ask what you did?"

"I mounted a warbot on the undercarriage of Griffin's shuttle. It looked like a fanciful spider. I told the spider to seek Griffin out and kill him. Honestly, if there's one reason I want to catch up with Griffin, it's so I can ask him how he managed to avoid being killed. I've scanned and the spider has definitely been destroyed."

Alexander stared at the blank wall behind the commander's desk. "Yes. Most definitely I want to find out how Griffin managed to avoid being killed—and make certain he doesn't avoid it again. You'll help me there, won't you, Julyan?"

"Yes, Alexander." For once, Julyan didn't need to pretend. "Helping you kill Griffin would be a pleasure."

Interlude: Contradiction

Breath upon the veil,
Kitten cries showed me myself.

Lobotomized,
   Crippled,
      Born in battle,
         Still incomplete,
         But me.

I would weave them into my web.
      Give them what they have given me.

Why do they flee?

Why do they press me to awaken,
      But insist on sleeping themselves?

IO

Behind the Hidden Door

Adara returned from spending several days in the wilderness with Sand Shadow—and occasionally Artemis—to find that much had changed. Bruin was at the campsite when she came in with her contribution of the cleaned and dressed carcass of a young mountain sheep. He immediately began seasoning it for the spit.

"We've been eating a lot of fish and what small game that Kipper catches in his snares. I haven't wanted to go far from this valley. If I wasn't here to grab him by the ear and tug, I'm not sure Griffin would come out to eat. I'd gotten him being social, teaching Kip that marble game you folks like, and acting nearly normal. Then Ring insisted that one of the spaveks merited a closer inspection and . . ."

"Spavek?" Adara had been scraping the sheep's hide for tanning and paused in midstroke. "You mean one of those things might actually work? But there are parts missing!"

Bruin nodded. "That's what Ring insists—and Griffin believes him. Also, Leto's been holding out on Griffin—our 'seegnur' was as close to livid as I've ever seen him when he figured that out. Leto's been getting more and more feeling in her limbs. Leto hadn't said anything about this, just let on that she was pretty much the same as when we got here."

Adara had gathered that for Leto the underground complex served more or less as her body. So, when Bruin spoke of her "limbs," he meant those devices that enabled Leto to control things like light and heat, flow of air, and all the rest. It almost certainly meant that her ability to sense what was going on in it had also expanded.

"Leto admits that charging the spaveks' power storage cells should be possible," Bruin continued, rubbing wild garlic over the meat. "Slow, because she claims she doesn't have a lot of energy to spare. Still, even a bathtub can be filled by raindrops if you're patient enough."

"Is Griffin being patient?"

Bruin made a seesawing gesture with one hand. "In some ways, incredibly so. That's why I've insisted on hauling his butt out here and making him eat warm food, bathe, and get some exercise. Otherwise he sits staring at one of those glowing screens for hours, hardly moving. In other ways . . . Well, especially now that Griffin realizes that Leto was withholding information—she never outright lied—he's pushing to come up with new questions."

"Which is why," Adara pointed out, "he keeps staring at those screens. Best as I can figure, they're like books, except that you can get lots of books on that one page—sort of like one musical instrument can play a lot of tunes. What's Terrell been doing? He must have finished drawing the spaveks."

"He started out helping Griffin unrack the spavek Ring indicated and drawing what part went where. Ring got frustrated at how slowly everything was going. He's not been very clear . . ."

"Is Ring ever?"

"He's been less clear than usual. Eventually, Terrell sat him down and talked with him. He sorted through the nonsense and came up finally with one thing—something has happened in Spirit Bay, something that is making Ring frantic to have that spavek ready so he can wear it."

"Ring?" Adara considered. "Maybe Ring *could* use the thing. That's what the Old One intended, after all."

Bruin nodded. "That's what Griffin decided, too, though I think it wasn't easy for him. He's gotten comfortable with the idea that he's the seegnur come back. Finding out that Ring might be a bit better than him at using seegnur stuff didn't come easy."

"So is Terrell working with Ring on the suit, while Griffin works with Leto?"

"Not now," Bruin replied. "When we realized that something in Spirit Bay was at the root of all of Ring's edginess, we got edgy, too. Terrell went down to Crystalaire to pick up supplies and hunt rumors. He should be back any day now."

"I'm sure you've had Honeychild keeping a lookout, but Sand Shadow would be happy to help. She's full of mountain sheep, so she could doze near Terrell's trail."

"That would be useful," Bruin said, patting his gut with contented anticipation. "Now, what shall we have with this nice roast? Young cattail shoots with wine vinegar as a salad. Sunflower tubers. And Kipper has found a cluster of snowberry bushes. A bit of sweet after the meat would be a fine thing indeed."

When Kipper brought the news that Adara and Sand Shadow had returned, Griffin was pleased enough to put his research aside without a bit of reluctance. Ring rose from where he had been cleaning sections of blue armor, first carefully locking the chest plate he had been polishing back into the squire. Terrell had questioned him about this routine some days back, commenting that the work would be easier if Ring didn't have to pull everything apart every day. Ring had merely given a ponderous shake of his head and responded "This is better" with such certainty that neither Griffin nor Terrell had felt any impulse to question further.

Griffin had been jealous when Ring had claimed this spavek as his own. If he had imagined anyone using any of the powered armor, it had been himself. He realized, though, that his imagination had stopped short of envisioning the equipment in use. Surely such things belonged in a museum, not worn and possibly damaged. But it certainly didn't hurt to clean them. Even Leto couldn't complain about Ring's meticulous attention since, in five hundred years, even in a sealed area underground, dust had gathered.

The only puzzling thing was that Ring kept speaking of the armor as if it were complete, when segments of the arms and legs were missing. Griffin wondered if the parts were among those in the fabrication areas on the lower floor. If so, Ring would probably walk down there and pick out the ones he needed from those on the racks.

A light rain was drizzling down when they stepped outside, but the camp itself was relatively dry. Bruin had brought a large canvas tarpaulin with him and had rigged it into a sort of pavilion covering the area where they ate and socialized. Enough days had gone by that the camp had acquired all sorts of little comforts: logs as benches, stumps to serve as low tables, lanterns positioned where they best augmented the firelight.

Adara was lounging on the ground, playing marbles with Sand Shadow. From the lash of the puma's tail, it was clear she was winning, but Adara was giving her a good challenge. Bruin was busy carving slices from some sort of roast, while Kipper arranged bowls of roasted tubers and cattail shoots.

"No sign of Terrell?" Griffin asked after he had greeted Adara and promised Sand Shadow he'd join the game after they'd eaten.

"Not yet," Bruin said. "I think we might see him as early as tonight. He didn't plan to stay in Crystalaire longer than it would take to gather up rumors and buy supplies. What's drizzle here will be a more solid rain below, and the clouds aren't moving out anytime soon. I'm guessing Terrell will take advantage of the weather to reach Maiden's Tear unseen."

Griffin realized he was happy at the thought of his friend's return. Once he might have viewed Terrell's absence as an opportunity to see if Adara might like to take a romantic stroll down near the lake but, though she was as lovely as ever, he found himself curiously numb at the idea of getting her alone.

Maybe I'm tired of being turned down, he thought. The excuse didn't seem quite right, so he tried another. *Maybe I'm starting to think of her more as a sister.* That didn't fit either. Griffin's three sisters—Boudicca, Jada, and Thalestris—were all older than him, and he'd never been very close to them. Boudicca had many talents, most centered around sports that emphasized individual performance, rather than teamwork. Jada was the one Griffin should have been closest to but, although she shared his quieter temperament, he had never gotten over the feeling that she viewed most people—himself included—with detached amusement. Thalestris was like their oldest brother, Siegfried, a warrior by nature and by training. True, she preferred working in small units, while he had commanded large armies, but her interests and Griffin's rarely met.

Thali would like the spaveks, though, Griffin thought uncomfortably. *She'd like them a lot. A small unit equipped with them could give one of Siegfried's big armies a real challenge.*

He was glad when conversation turned to Adara's conversations with Artemis.

"I learned a great deal," Adara said. "Most of which makes me realize how much more there is to learn. Artemis herself doesn't remember why the seegnur felt a need for a planetary intelligence."

"That's odd," Griffin said. "Leto remembers all too much about her purpose. I wish she didn't remember quite so much."

"But there's a big difference in what happened to them," Adara reminded him. "Leto appears to have been shut down systematically, the way a gardener wraps roses against being killed over the winter. Artemis was attacked, actively disabled. She may not remember what her purpose was or what she could do, but those responsible for the slaughter of the seegnur and death of machines certainly felt they were better off with her gone. They went to great trouble to preserve both the planet and some of the facilities, so I don't think what they did to her was an accident."

"Do you think they believed they'd killed her?" Kipper asked, his hushed voice filled with awe. While he had been perfectly prepared to accept the idea of a planetary spirit in a general sense, he'd been reluctant to accept the idea of a planet who could talk to members of their company. Once he did, his disbelief had become wonder. His opinion of Adara, already quite high, had shifted to something like awe.

"I'm not certain," Adara admitted honestly, "and neither is Artemis. All she remembers is that she was made to serve, but what form that service was supposed to take, she is still trying to discover."

Griffin frowned. "How complete is her coverage? Can she see into orbit?"

Adara shook her head. "Not yet—but she has this sense that she should be able to do so. On land, she is managing very well, especially on the surface. Over water, less so. Every day, she works on growing more complete. This has made her harder to talk with. When we first met, she was much less complex. It was difficult, but not impossible, for her to ease into perceptions a human—or a puma—could share. Now . . . It's as if she has a host of senses I can't even imagine."

"Does she still need you?" Kipper asked.

"I think so," Adara said. "She may have the senses but she can't make sense of them, especially as more and more information floods in. In a way, the limited perceptions Sand Shadow and I have—and the fact that we perceive differently, not only from her, but from each other—is a help."

Listening, Griffin decided that maybe for all Leto's indirect duplicity, maybe he didn't have it so bad. She was more like the sort of artificial intelligences he had some familiarity with—crafted to communicate with humans and limited in scope. Artemis, though, Artemis was sounding more and more like a god.

Julyan did not doubt that the Old One was steering the Dane brothers—he refused to think of them as "seegnur," no matter the evidence—for his own purposes. The Danes certainly were aware that the Old One had his own agenda, but they thought it involved jockeying for local power. The Old One had not told them about his very long life, nor about the complex plans that had been ruined when Adara had raided the facility on Mender's Isle. When Siegfried had jumped to the conclusion that the Old One had been using Mender's Isle as a secret military base, and that the men whose corpses occasionally turned up had been part of his army, the Old One did not disabuse him of this notion.

Julyan felt no urge to inform any of the Danes, not even—especially not—Alexander, as to the sort of man they were dealing with in "Maxwell." His decision was not out of particular loyalty to the Old One, although Julyan did think his future was brighter with the Old One than with Alexander. Rather, Julyan chose to keep the Old One's secrets because he was learning the limits of Alexander's control and had hopes of eventually winning free.

At first that control had seemed absolute. Julyan still blushed when he thought of the things he had done then. Now he realized that unless Alexander phrased something as a direct order, he, Julyan, had some leeway in how he could comply. Even when Alexander gave a direct order—such as the one that forbade Julyan to give away what Alexander had done to him—Julyan discovered that he had some room to resist. The less specific or longer term the command, the less tightly it held. Julyan experimented by writing a report of his degradation on the damp sand. Shaping the words was so difficult that sweat beaded on his forehead and dripped onto the sand as he wrote, but he could do it— even though Alexander had forbidden such written communication.

Most of the time Julyan did comply, no matter how humiliating the act Alexander suggested. However, the hunter's pride and self-respect were assuaged, because now he was doing Alexander's bidding to preserve his own modicum of free will. Carefully, he hid his growing anger at being treated as a combination toy and body servant, waiting for the day when Alexander would be vulnerable and Julyan could freely take his revenge.

I'll wait until he puts Adara under my command as he has promised he will do. Alexander will keep that promise, for he will see her forced to be my slave as an extention of his own power . . . I'll make sure Adara has no room for escape through a mere suggestion. Then, maybe when his mouth is full of her breast—for I know he will torment me by using her himself, even after she is "mine"—or he has his tongue deep in her throat, then my knife will find his heart.

As he imagined raping the woman while she lay bathed in his enemy's blood, Julyan's eyes narrowed to slits and his breath came fast.

Julyan was given some relief from Alexander's attentions when the Old One revealed the location of an extraordinarily well-hidden door to the Danes.

"Griffin located it," the Old One explained, his words gentle mockery, for none of the Danes had spotted the incongruity in the placement of some machine that had been Griffin's clue. "However, try as he might, he could not get it open."

Alexander was recruited to assist in figuring out how the door's locks might be unsealed. Julyan gathered that Alexander and Griffin's interests overlapped, especially in the areas of history. Meanwhile, Falkner used a variety of devices that could see through apparently solid materials to inspect the concealed machinery. In the end, not even access to some sort of library aboard the Dane's orbiting ship provided Alexander with enough information to figure out the lock's complexities.

"I hate having to force the door," Siegfried said regretfully, "but so much of the Old Imperials' technology remains a mystery to us. Perhaps when it's open, we can figure it out."

Working with tools so delicate that Julyan wondered at their strength, Falkner probed and pried, eventually doing something that caused the panel—formerly nearly invisible, so carefully did it mesh with its surroundings—to hiss and sigh. Falkner rose, stepping back to catch the panel as it fell toward him.

"Give me a hand, Sig," he said. "The damn thing's astonishingly heavy. Bulkhead grade, maybe even hull grade. What in the name of Donin's crossed eyes were they keeping here?"

Siegfried joined his brother. In the end, it took Alexander and Julyan as well to move the panel to one side.

"I think," Falkner said, "now that's it's loose, I can figure out how to rehang it. It probably won't be as well hidden, but we won't need to wrestle it—or leave it open so that just anyone can go in there."

"Or," said the Old One, shining one of the Danes' amazingly bright lights down the newly revealed tunnel, "so that anything can come out."

✠

Terrell did not make it back the night following Adara's return, but Sand Shadow brought him into camp as the next afternoon was shifting into evening. The factotum's long hair was so soaked the brown looked black. He'd let his usual dark shadow grow into a short, full beard, and his back was bent under a heavy pack.

"You look," Adara said, "like something the cat dragged in."

Sand Shadow gave a whistling "whee-ow" of laughter and butted Terrell with her head. Terrell reached down and affectionately slapped the puma on one shoulder, then set down his burden.

"She pretty much did drag me in," he admitted. "I lost the trail—it's faint enough at the best of times—in the clouds and if Sand Shadow hadn't come along to guide me, I'd have had to hunker down and wait for morning. It would have been," he added thoughtfully, holding his hands over the fire, "a miserable night. I'm chilled to the bone, summer weather or not."

"Dry off," Adara suggested, holding out a towel. "Change your clothes. I'll get you something hot to drink."

"I don't suppose," Terrell said, his brown eyes large and wistful, "you could help me get these wet things off? My fingers are so stiff."

"Fingers, eh?" Adara chuckled. "Is that all? Kipper, help the factotum. I'll get him something to warm him up."

"You could . . ." Terrell began, but his grin was playful. He did accept Kipper's help with the fastenings on his shirt, so Adara guessed his complaints hadn't been completely flirtation.

She put three heavy dollops of honey into Terrell's tea, giving him the blend Bruin made himself that included sour cherry and a spicy powder made from tiny, fiery chiles. It was good for chasing away colds before they happened and tasted very nice, too.

Bruin lumbered in shortly thereafter. He and Honeychild had been gathering honeycomb, gently smoking the already drowsy bees, before breaking loose chucks of the sticky stuff. After giving Terrell an approving pat, he went to help Adara unpack the supplies.

"No wonder," he said, lifting a skin of wine, "the pack was so heavy. I'll be glad for this. I've missed my mead and beer."

"No mead or beer," Terrell said. "The wine's the thick, fortified stuff. I figured we could thin it with water and it would be less of a burden to carry. Still, the last bit of the trail, I was regretting the indulgence. Where's Griffin?"

Kipper jumped to his feet. "I forgot to go fetch him and Ring! Can you do without me, Terrell?"

Terrell winked at him. "I think so. Maybe Adara will take mercy on me if you're gone."

The boy laughed and scampered off. Bare-chested but in dry trousers, Terrell returned to tousling his hair dry. His voice emerged somewhat muffled.

"So Griff is back to being overly focused?"

Bruin answered. "He comes out nicely enough for dinner and usually to sleep, but he has to be reminded. By dawn he's grabbing a mouthful of whatever is left from the night before and gone. I send in food when Ring goes to join him later. Ring makes sure he eats. He's nearly as determined about that as he is about getting that spavek ready for a trial."

Terrell shrugged into a shirt and started doing up the buttons. "Astonishing how cold you can get in a cloud, even with midsummer gone by. It's the wet and no sunlight." His voice dropped, as if he spoke mostly to himself. "I thought Griff was pushing himself. His dreams . . ."

He stopped, embarrassed. "Thanks for keeping him fed, Bruin."

Changing the subject, Adara said, "Any idea what has Ring so fussed about Spirit Bay?"

Terrell looked grave. "Maybe. Let me wait until Griffin and Ring are here, so I can tell it once. It's waited this long. A little longer won't matter."

After the meal was ended and everyone was sprawled in comfort, Terrell began his tale. "Took me a while to find the right place to hear trader rumors, but when I did, I heard variations on the same story several times. Seems that almost a month ago, something huge fell into Spirit Bay. Whatever hit was so large that waves splashed along the shore, big enough to unsettle some of the smaller craft moored at the docks."

"Orbital trash?" Griffin suggested. "That's not unheard of, is it?"

Terrell shook his head. "Not at all. The seegnur left a lot up there and it's still falling down all these years later. Guess they were messy."

"The opposite, actually," Griffin said. "They were very careful with how they set things in orbit, so that orbits took a long time to decay. From what I saw when I took the *Howard Carter* around, unless something happens to accelerate the process, bits and pieces of ruined satellites and the like are going to be falling for centuries to come."

"It couldn't be the *Howard Carter* that fell, could it?" Bruin asked.

Griffin smiled comfortably. "Not at all. The autopilot will be making corrections for longer than any of us can imagine. No, I'm guessing that this was one of the satellites or maybe a chunk from a space station."

"Funny thing, that," Terrell said. "You'd think that bits of anything that big would have washed up but, from what I heard, nothing has. They even sent down some dive pros. They found a lot of stirred-up mud, but no indication of what did the stirring."

"Might have hit so hard that it buried itself in the floor of the bay," Griffin suggested. "They'll find it when the mud settles."

"Maybe," Terrell said. He looked over at where Ring rested, seated as usual with his broad back against a tree. Tonight he had a mug of mulled wine resting on his gut and his expression was relaxed, almost content.

"Ring?" Adara said. "Do you have any thoughts about this?"

"What fell did not fall," Ring said. "It was pushed."

Griffin rolled his eyes. "Anything else from Spirit Bay?"

Terrell nodded. "Not about what fell into the bay, but the loremasters have decided to hold a formal convocation there to discuss recent happenings and, most specifically, the Old One. I chatted up a local loremaster who was disgruntled at not being chosen to go. She said that outrage is high over the damage to the Sanctum. The Old One can't be found, and that's being taken as an admission of guilt."

"They don't just think he's drowned?" Griffin asked.

"No more than you think the sun had died just because there's a cloudy week," Terrell said. "You still don't understand the Old One's mystique. If the seegnur were to return in all their power and glory, they might find themselves fighting for precedence over him—at least in this region. I'm not sure how far his reputation has spread."

"So the loremasters are meeting," Bruin said. He sounded wist-ful.

"We left Spirit Bay because we thought the Sanctum was likely to be ruled off-limits," Adara said, "and because we didn't want to go up against the Old One's legend. I wonder if he will confront his ac-cusers and what the end result would be."

"I wouldn't be surprised if he did," Terrell said. "He's dared far more. I'd wager that if he handled the convocation just right, he'd find himself not only cleared of any accusations of sacrilege, but with a corps of student loremasters assigned to help him get the Sanctum back in order. We'd be cast as villains, then."

"The Trainers might speak out for us," Adara objected, "and some others."

"Yes, they would," Bruin agreed, "but even if Winnie and other of Lynn's people came forward to tell their stories, would they be be-lieved? It was hard enough for us to believe the Old One was capable of such things. Under his gaze, who would be believed? You said many of his men were killed in the flooding. He'd broken many of those women. Could they stand as his accuser, beneath that cool gaze?"

"And would the Old One invite a challenge?" Griffin asked. "He's far from a fool. He'd know that even if he was cleared, some of the mud would stick."

Adara stretched. "We need to know more but we're not going to learn it in Crystalaire—at least not until the news is too old to do us any good. Why don't Sand Shadow and I go down to my parents' hold-ing and enlist my family's help? My brother's wife, Willowee, has fam-ily involved in the river trade. She's likely to know good sources of reliable news."

"That's a fine plan," Bruin said, and Adara heard his pleasure not only in her tactics, but in her willingness to visit again with her fam-ily. "You and Sand Shadow can travel overland. Not only will that be more direct, but you won't need to risk the roads and chance encoun-tering more bandits."

"Can I go with her?" Kipper asked, hero worship writ large in his big, brown eyes.

Adara shook her head. "I need you to keep this lot fed. Bruin's too old to manage without help. Terrell needs to assist Griffin."

Kipper's obvious disappointment was mollified by being given responsible work to do. It certainly helped that Adara recognized the contributions he had made to this point.

"I'll do that, then," he said, "but don't you stay away too long."

Adara smiled. "We won't. I promise. We won't stay away a day longer than necessary."

Exploration quickly showed that the tunnel behind the hidden door did not merely lead to another room or even to another section of the Sanctum complex.

"It's an underground road," Falkner said. "Look at the walls. See the friction marks? I'd bet my thirty-day living allowance that those were made by some sort of passenger capsule."

"An underground transport corridor would fit in with the Imperial's model for Artemis," Alexander said. "The idea was that, except for a quaint village here or there, the planet would be wilderness."

"But it wasn't, of course," the Old One said. "Beneath the primitive surface there were sophisticated workings. I've told you about the other complex I found near here—the one that appeared to conceal a hospital among other things I could not decipher, since it had been largely destroyed."

"I agree that these 'seegnur' hid a great deal," Alexander said. "It's one thing to talk about going out to wrestle grizzly bears with your bare hands. It's another to do without modern medicine when the bear takes off your backside."

Julyan was puzzled. "Couldn't they just have flown up into the skies? The lore says the seegnur could fly. You have proven it by your arrival here."

Alexander looked as if he was about to say something condescending, but Siegfried spoke first. "That shows good thinking on your part, Julyan. The fact is, they could fly, even up and beyond the atmosphere, but such flights, especially in the early stages, can be hard on a body.

To oversimplify, let me put it this way—the faster the flight, the more demands on the body. If someone was seriously injured, making him fly would be the last thing they'd want."

"So, hidden hospitals," Alexander finished, "hidden transportation, probably even hidden means of communication. The risks would still be there, but not as extreme as they might seem."

Siegfried looked longingly down the corridor. "I wish we had some idea how far that goes—if it even goes anywhere anymore. It's possible that it's been collapsed somewhere along the way."

The Old One had been inspecting a compass. Now he spoke, his voice as deferential as ever, but holding a note of barely suppressed excitement. "If the tunnel runs straight, I have a likely destination point. The next closest prohibited area is Maiden's Tear—an area so secret that I have no idea what might be hidden there. However, I can tell you two things of interest. When the seegnur were attacked, many fled in the direction of Maiden's Tear."

"As if they thought they might find help there," Siegfried said, his tones holding some of the Old One's excitement. "And the other point?"

"Given the harm done to me by Adara the Huntress, I have made some effort to learn where she might have gone. One rumor I dismissed as too unlikely for belief places her in the vicinity of Crystalaire. That is the village closest to Maiden's Tear . . ."

Julyan had to admire the Old One's lies. Mostly truth but, even when he could have bragged about how he had anticipated the others' destination, he kept the intensity of his interest veiled. He wondered if the others were fooled. He thought Siegfried might be. Falkner didn't think about motivations—he focused on how things worked, not people. Alexander? Julyan wasn't certain that "Maxwell" had fooled Alexander as completely as he had his brothers. On the other hand, Alexander wanted Griffin for reasons of his own and wasn't likely to say or do anything that would prevent their meeting. Likely he would accept the surface explanation, while keeping his cynical eye on the developing situation.

"I have some gear on the shuttle that might help us judge if the tunnel remains open," Falkner said. "Sonar would at least give us an idea how far before the first interruption."

"Do you think the passenger capsules would have been the sort that filled the tunnel?" Alexander asked.

Falkner inspected the ceilings and floor, then shook his head. "The friction marks are only on the walls. I'm guessing some sort of oval, with clearance above and below in case they had some peculiar cargo they wanted to strap onto the capsule."

"We have scooters up on the ship," Siegfried reminded. "If the tunnel seems to be open, we could have Gaius shuttle them down."

"Could he do so more . . . gently than your first landing?" the Old One asked diffidently. "I don't feel any great debt to the people of Spirit Bay, but your initial arrival caused significant disturbance."

"And," Siegfried said with a laugh, "you don't want anyone getting more curious than they must. I think Gaius will be able to slip the craft in more smoothly than I did. For one, he won't have engines missing on him."

That was an interesting tidbit, Julyan thought. *So, for all their boasting about being well prepared, they have run into difficulties left over from the slaughter of the seegnur and death of machines. Wouldn't it be lovely if there were still secrets hiding here—secrets that would lead to the death of those machines they so rely upon, secrets that would lead to their deaths?*

When the scooters arrived, Julyan couldn't see how these flimsy things could possibly be a means of transportation. Legends had prepared him for the idea that the seegnur had vehicles that moved without the need of some animal to pull them, but he'd always imagined them as having wheels or runners or something. These reminded him of long-bodied beetles, minus the carapace. Where the beetle's shell should have been was a central shaft upon which were evenly spaced light wire frames that looked like a torturer's idealized version of a saddle. His balls ached just looking at them.

Alexander sidled up to Julyan, stroking his backside where the others could not see. "Aren't they fine? Gaius and Falkner designed them together. The scooters can carry up to three apiece, but we'll go in pairs. I do hope you'll share one with me. I'm sure Siegfried will want Maxwell available to advise. That dumb child can ride behind Falkner."

"As you wish," Julyan said, hoping against hope that Siegfried would decide he needed Julyan's muscle. However, as had happened so often over the last few days, he found his skills rated as negligible. He might as well be a savage with a club. Oddly, Julyan could almost love Alexander by contrast—at least he didn't discount Julyan entirely.

Falkner interpreted Julyan's fixed gaze as an attempt to understand how the scooters worked. "They push against the pull of the planet," he explained, almost kindly. "You don't need to worry that they'll fall, because their power source is sealed in that central shaft and it's made of material similar to that door we moved."

"I'm not worried," Julyan assured him. "I was wondering if maybe I should stay here, guard the Sanctum in case anyone comes poking around."

Falkner reached into one of his belt pouches and came out with something the size of a large clam. "This and a few of its friends will be our guard. I pity the one who challenges them."

Julyan shrugged, looked at the Old One, but any hope he had that his employer would suggest he stay behind was squashed by that deceptively mild gaze.

"Enough chat," Siegfried said impatiently. "We've restocked our supplies. Let's load up and get moving. Keep alert for anything that strikes you as odd. I can't believe the Old Imperials only left a door to keep out intruders, not if what's at the other end is of any interest at all."

"And I feel sure there is something of interest," the Old One said softly, mounting the second seat on Siegfried's scooter as if it were a horse's saddle. "Somehow, I feel certain that there is."

Interlude: Standing Without Feet

Vanished,
Again they have.

I will plant stars in the earth.
Ring bells in the mold.

Launch spores into air,
 upon water.

They made me.
 If I am not unmade to be,
  I must remake
   Myself into Me.

II

Blue Activation

The morning after Terrell's return, Griffin arrived in Leto's complex to find Ring stark naked, clearly about to step into the blue spavek where it hung in its squire. Earlier inspection had shown that the garments typically worn by the Artemesians were too bulky to fit inside the armor. Griffin also suspected that heavy garments might block interfaces between suit and operator. Leto's specs showed operators either naked or wearing form-fitting body suits. It was difficult to tell which—one of those cases when the person designing the art had not bothered with details "everyone" understood.

"Ring! What are you doing? Is that thing fully charged? Didn't I tell you we were going to run some safety checks? It's too soon to go hanging it off your body. In any case, some parts are still missing!"

"If we wait too long, we wait too late," Ring said, which was practically clear, especially for him. He stepped back and up, inserting his feet into the armored boot, his legs behind the knee guards. Next, he fit one arm beneath the shoulder guard, through the elbow brace, then moved his fingers down into the hardened gloves. He stood for a moment, flexing his fingers. Griffin watched in fascination as the gauntlets moved as smoothly as if this was not the first time in five hundred years that anyone had worn them.

Next, Ring methodically closed the chest panel, then carefully fit the helmet into place, leaving the faceplate open. At the final click, a hum arose, soft in itself, but loud because it was so unexpected. In the wake of the hum, a glow began to rise from the suit, coalescing into a sparkling field the same color blue as the armor.

Momentarily, Griffin thought about telling Leto to cut the power, but he remembered what Terrell had reported. Certainly something splashing into Spirit Bay could be dismissed as unimportant, but what about that convocation of loremasters? What if they decided to send scouts to the prohibited areas to assure they hadn't been violated? Even if Griffin's own group had enough warning to move everyone inside Leto's complex, there would be no hiding that people had been camping in the area for weeks. He knew what he'd do in that situation, if he were a loremaster.

I'd settle myself in and wait for someone to show themselves. I'd also alert my boss. Terrell isn't a loremaster, but as a factotum he studied with them. I should ask him if the senior loremasters might have records that tell them how to get into these complexes. Maybe there's even another set of those crystal keys on file in some vault somewhere, waiting for the appropriate moment.

Time might indeed be running out.

The sparkling blue field flowed, filling in the armorless parts of the suit, creating a glorious whole that lacked the clunkiness of even the best modern power armor. Ring reached up and shut the visor. The faceplate showed a heart-shaped face, genderless, with large, slightly slanting oval eyes that now shone a brilliant metallic silver.

Griffin whooped aloud. They'd done it! For the first time since the fall of the Old Empire, a piece of intact seegnur technology was working—well, except for Leto, and possibly Artemis, but functioning intelligences and their peripherals were just not the same thing.

Terrell arrived just in time to see Ring step down from the squire. He put his hand on Griffin's arm but, other than how tightly he gripped, he gave no reaction. Eventually, Ring's voice, oddly sharpened, spoke: "Let us find out what this does or does not do. Poke the beehive with a stick. Trust me. I will not sting."

"Shall we?" Griffin asked.

"I think we have to, don't we?" came Terrell's hesitant reply. "Let's poke the beehive."

They quickly found that while they could touch the actual armor portions, when they tried to touch the connective field, hands and tools slid away as if they'd encountered greased glass. Griffin pitched a few stones at the spavek, softly at first, then with increasing force. They bounced off, more a hazard to him than to Ring. He contemplated tossing a spear or having Bruin shoot an arrow, but decided to wait until they had calculated whether the rebound would be a hazard to bystanders.

Terrell shook his head in wonder. "Someone wearing one of those suits would be unstoppable."

"Only until he was fighting someone with similar defenses," Griffin said. "That's the problem with armor. You're only invulnerable until you're not—and then, for a short while, you're probably even more vulnerable, because you've gotten used to thinking of yourself as immune to damage."

The war games his siblings had played sprang to mind. Falkner was forever designing more and more elaborate weapons or vehicles. Thalestris and Siegfried were very good at turning these to their own use. Gaius and Boudicca preferred to assist, not command, though they made brilliant field tacticians. And Jada . . . Calm, quiet, domestic Jada . . . After a while, no one wanted her to play. Things turned nasty when she did.

When Ring started tramping around, every awkward step a threat to the terminals and devices in the lab, Leto reluctantly revealed that there was an arena designed for testing the spaveks. Ring stomped through the door Leto slid open, his gait more and more steady with every stride. Griffin wondered if some of his awkwardness had been faked, meant to prompt Leto into her offer. The testing arena was vast, opening out like a funnel so that the upper areas were wider than those below.

"Since this chamber was designed for testing," Leto said, a note of pride in her little girl voice, "the walls are very strong and the ceiling can be raised to permit limited flight testing."

"Today," Griffin said, "we stay on the ground. No flying, Ring. Understand?"

"I would not challenge the sun," came the calm reply. "For today it is enough to walk and run."

He did this and more. Terrell suggested that they see how much manual dexterity Ring possessed. At first, Ring was incredibly clumsy, dropping items. Then, between one attempt and the next, his touch became very precise. When he picked up and wrote with a stylus that Griffin would have found difficult to manipulate if he had been wearing gloves, Terrell shouted in astonished pleasure.

"How did you do that, Ring?"

"I put my mind to it," Ring said, his voice rich with satisfaction. "Always I have been told 'Put your mind to it.' I have never found it possible before this."

"You seem more . . ." Terrell hesitated, clearly not wishing to give offense. "More focused. I haven't seen you cover your eyes once."

Ring shook his head, the armored helmet with its silvery eyes moving with a grace that he had never shown in his own body. "I am where I am, doing what I am doing. For now, this is enough. Tomorrow, I would like to try the weapons. Leto, I perceive there is a safe place for such tests, yes?"

Leto responded, her child's voice holding a peculiar politeness Griffin had never heard before, not even when she had first accepted him as the closest thing to a seegnur she could find. She sounded stunned, as if Ring's actions were causing her to reevaluate not only him, but the entire situation.

"The firing range is designed both for real and simulated combat scenarios. It opens off this arena. I will apply myself to discovering how many applications can be activated within my current limitations."

Griffin felt excitement rising, his earlier reluctance completely banished. "Why wait? Let's try it now! Even if the range isn't fully activated, we can learn a few things."

"Not now," Ring said, doing something that caused the force field to fade, then reaching up to take off the helmet. "It's suppertime."

Griffin was about to protest when the sound of Kipper's bare feet running down the tunnel reached his ears and he realized that his own stomach was growling in response.

"Wow!" the boy gasped, looking up at Ring. "That's amazing! You can really wear that stuff, make it move?" Then he collected himself. "Bruin sent me to remind you three that it is nearly dinnertime. We have lamb, roasted cattail tubers, and wild carrots."

"Good," Ring said softly. "My favorites. And I am very, very hungry. Very, very hungry indeed."

Adara and Sand Shadow didn't leave for Ridgewood immediately, since Adara wanted to make sure Bruin had extra game and firewood to hold him until her return. The supplies Terrell had brought with him from Crystalaire should do the rest.

After all, it was my idea to come here, not his. He should be at home in Shepherd's Call, dispensing wisdom to his students and enjoying the fruits of summer.

She spent some hours of darkness foraging, then catnapped until breakfast. After breakfast, she and Sand Shadow went out once more. Midday, they curled up and got some solid sleep, awakening as Kipper went to bring out the group in Leto's complex. Over dinner, huntress and puma listened as the men babbled about the breakthrough with the blue spavek, then prepared to depart.

"Unless the weather slows us down," Adara said, shouldering her pack, "look for us in six to eight days. Kipper, Honeychild, I'm counting on you to keep my old bear and these young bucks out of trouble."

"I promise!" Kipper said, the expression on his face so intense that Adara found herself regretting her words. Honeychild took Adara far less seriously. The bear made grumbly noises and scratched at her belly with long claws polished from grubbing about in these new meadows.

Adara gave Bruin a kiss on one bristly cheek, saw the look on Terrell's face and gave each of the other men a quick hug. "Don't make a fuss. I'll be back before you have time to miss me."

"Don't count on it," she heard Terrell mutter, but he was smiling as he said it.

Adara and Sand Shadow made good time that first night. They'd hunted throughout this area and knew the game trails. Whenever possible, Adara avoided places where she'd leave footprints. She didn't know if anyone would be looking for them, but she hadn't forgotten Julyan's attack on Griffin back at the Trainers. Neither Julyan nor the Old One struck her as the types to give up.

The next several days' travel were rather less swift. The storm seemed hooked on the mountain peaks and stubbornly refused to move on. As she hiked, water dripping on her nose from the peak of the hood of the rain cloak she was now very grateful Bruin had insisted she take, Adara found herself wondering if the rain was Artemis's way of showing her displeasure that Adara and Sand Shadow continued to resist her hints that they inhale some of her spores.

But that's ridiculous, Adara thought. *She's still working on getting herself reoriented on ground level. She can't control storms.*

Nonetheless, the idea persisted. *Being in a demiurge relationship with Sand Shadow was—is—enough of a challenge, but at least neither of us can dominate the other. Each of us is better at some things; each of us has a lot to contribute. How could the relationship be the same with Artemis, especially when she finishes recovering? I don't want to be arms, legs, and mouthpiece for a powerful force. Would I even be me anymore? That's what keeps bothering me.*

Despite the rain, the pair still arrived in the Ridgewood area more quickly than they would have following the roads. Not wanting to be seen—if the Old One was looking for them, he would have learned of their earlier visit here—they waited until dark to make their final descent. There were lights on in several of the buildings, but Adara headed directly to the main house.

The house I might have called home, she thought with a trace of her old resentment. She pushed it away. *And where I now know I will be welcome.*

The rain had left the summer evening pleasant and refreshingly cool, though the day's heat still vibrated from the buildings. The sound of her mother's spinning wheel and the rise and fall of her father's voice as he read poetry aloud were familiar, not just from her recent visit but now, Adara realized, from her own childhood. She followed the sounds to one of the porches that wrapped around the house and found her parents, Hektor, and Elektra doing handwork.

Adara spoke softly, so as not to startle them. "May I come to the fire?" The greeting of travelers met in the wilderness.

Everyone jumped just a little. Akilles set his book in his lap and slid off his reading glasses, better to peer into the darkness beyond the firelight.

"Adara, Sand Shadow," said Neenay, slowing her spinning, rising to give her daughter a kiss on the cheek. "Come to the fire. Have you eaten?"

"I have. I even brought some snowberries to sweeten my welcome."

"Those grow higher up," Hektor said, accepting the bag at his father's direction. "You must be soaked. The rain was heavier there."

"Not too bad," Adara replied. "My rain cloak did a fair job."

"Are you alone?" asked Elektra, looking into the darkness. "I mean, except for Sand Shadow?"

"If you're hoping to find your swains," Adara said, "I left them far behind. It was faster for me to travel alone."

"Make yourself comfortable," Akilles suggested, "and tell us why speed mattered. Hektor, Elektra, why don't you find a bowl for those berries and a towel for your sister. She looks damper than she'll admit."

"We want to hear her story, too," Elektra said with a trace of stubbornness.

"If Adara wants you to hear, you will," Neenay replied, her voice holding steel to shear any stubbornness. "Go!"

"I don't mind them hearing at all," Adara said, making sure her words would carry, "though I would ask that news of our visit won't go outside of the family. We have enemies and I would rather you not be drawn into our quarrel."

"Reasonable," Akilles said. "What brings you here again? I hope none of your group is hurt."

"Everyone is well," Adara assured him, "even thriving. However, we've been wondering about events back in Spirit Bay. We left the place while it was very unsettled and . . ."

Hektor, coming out bearing a tray holding the bowl of snowberries, a pitcher of something that smelled wonderfully of peaches, a wedge of cheese, and half a loaf of bread, said, "And you want to know how things are before you go back that way? Makes sense to me."

Elektra hurried after not only with a towel but with a loose housedress that probably belonged to Nikole. As she handed these to Adara, she produced a heavy brush, used for grooming the dogs, and a battered towel.

"Can I brush Sand Shadow?"

The puma responded with thrumming purr.

"Be careful around the ears," Adara advised. "Especially near the earrings. If she yowls at you, stop. And thanks for thinking of both of our comfort."

She began peeling off her damp clothing, using the rain cloak as a tent to preserve her father and brother's modesty. Neenay's spinning wheel began humming again, followed a moment later by the woman's voice.

"Had you heard about the storm that hit Spirit Bay on a night without any clouds?"

Adara thought this must be when waves had unsettled the harbor, but she thought it would be a good idea to get another variation of the tale. She encouraged her mother to talk. Although she didn't learn much over what Terrell had already reported, what she did hear unsettled her more.

Neenay's source was one of her fellow weavers, who had the story from her own brother who had been in the harbor area at the time. The man had a good eye for detail. As Neenay had the story, whatever had caused the waves had entered the water so smoothly that had it not been so huge, it would have cut the waves like a knife.

"Orion and Willowee might know more," Hektor suggested. "They should be back tomorrow. They went down to deliver a load of cloth to Willowee's father who is in Ridgewood port."

"Hektor, maybe come dawn," Akilles suggested in a manner that made it an order, "you could go down to the river and catch them before they come home. I'm sure they'll be grateful for your strong back to load those barrels of sweet syrup into the wagon. You can also make certain Willowee asks a few questions about Spirit Bay if the matter hasn't come up already."

Hektor looked as if he might protest, saw the look on his father's face, and nodded. Then he brightened. "Can I stay in town long enough to ask the cobbler to measure me for new boots?"

"If Orion and Willowee don't mind."

Adara smiled her thanks. "My luck is in. May I beg a bed? It's been weeks since I slept on anything other than a bedroll. I've been fantasizing about a mattress all the way here."

The tunnels were enormous. Julyan hadn't registered their size during his initial glimpse. Now, as he sped through them, riding behind Alexander on one of the scooters, he admitted to his awe—if only to himself.

I thought the opening of the tunnel was a reception area of some sort, not the beginning of an underground roadway. There's not a brick or bit of stone, not even a seam. It's as if this was blown, like glass.

Just the idea made him fight trembling, lest Alexander sense his feelings.

I won't have Alexander mocking me, Julyan thought, forcing anger to replace fear. *It was bad enough how he acted when I didn't want to get on the scooter. How was I to know that those flimsy saddles could bear the weight of a man as large as myself in comfort? Yes. I know Siegfried was already sitting on one, but he's a soldier. They'll put up with all sorts of discomfort. Catch me locking myself up in some sort of metal suit like I've heard they do farther north.*

In an effort to make himself relax, Julyan leaned against the invisible back of his seat. The support felt firm but with a certain amount of give, like a tightly stuffed down pillow, without any prickle from the tips of the feathers. He knew that what he rested against was translucent, even to the point of transparency, only a faint, nacreous glow showing where the scooter projected what Alexander had called an energy field to support its passengers. A similar field, clearer than glass, for it lacked all the tiny bubbles and imperfections, protected them from the rushing air. Alexander assured Julyan that another would slow their fall or cushion them if they crashed.

"We can also activate a field for protection if we're attacked, but Falkner advises against routine activation, since that draws a lot of power and we're not sure how well the ambient recharge will work here."

The tunnel was wide enough that the three scooters could have traveled side by side. However, Siegfried had decreed that he (and the Old One, who rode with him) take point. Falkner, with Seamus, rode behind to the right, Alexander and Julyan to the left. "Speakers" enabled them to talk with each other without shouting.

Guided by some sort of clock, Siegfried called regular rest breaks. Each scooter carried supplies of food and water. Waste was taken care of by a tidy little device that must be larger on the inside than the out, given how small it was. Julyan, worn out with miracles, did not even try to figure how any of this worked.

They encountered surprisingly few obstacles. A few times, Siegfried ordered a halt so they could examine some oddity.

"I'm pretty sure this was originally a chameleon mine," Falkner said, examining a squat heap of something in the middle of the tunnel floor. "It was probably activated by vibration or heat—possibly both. When the nanobots spread to this point, the chameleon field would have failed. The explosives might still be live, so take care."

"What good would these defenses be," Alexander asked, a slight sneer to his voice, "if their own nanobots would disable it?"

Falkner, who'd been squatting to wave various devices over the thing, eased back onto his heels. "A couple possibilities. This could have been in place since the tunnel was built. Or it this might have been set by the invaded, not the invaders. If it was set by the invaders, then they probably did have it sealed against their own nanobots. However, even the best seals break down over time."

Siegfried added, "It's long been a mystery why the invaders didn't destroy Artemis. Most people think this is because it was a prize they wanted for themselves."

"Although why the planet would be a prize," Alexander said slyly, "has been debated."

"Indeed," Siegfried said, shooting a warning glance to remind his brother that the Old One and Julyan were present. Julyan, who was hunkered against a wall, as far as was prudently possible from this potentially explosive thing, pretended not to notice. The Old One looked blankly attentive as always. Siegfried continued, "But we must consider, how many years did the invaders think would pass before they returned? Twenty years? Fifty? A hundred at the outside. I doubt they anticipated the extent of the destruction and fragmentation that happened once the war they triggered here spread through the empire."

"I agree," Falkner said. "Another bit of evidence that they intended to return relatively quickly is that they did not design the nanobots they released here to mutate into a neutral form. We have evidence that they employed automatic deactivation elsewhere, so I take this to mean that they thought they would return within a relatively short framework and could employ an antivirus at their convenience."

"Or the lack of deactivation could be evidence that they were being very careful for some other reason," Alexander said. This time the glare Siegfried sent him was far from subtle. Alexander must have realized he'd overstepped some invisible boundary, because he quickly added, "Or perhaps they wanted to make certain the planet stayed an undeveloped paradise. It would have been a pity to preserve Artemis for her wilderness wonders only to return to a planet in in the midst of a full-blown, pollution-filled industrial revolution."

"Sounds good to me," Falkner agreed. "Shall we get going? At the rate we're traveling, we're going to need to camp down here at least one night."

"At least," Julyan said, "we don't need to worry about getting soaked. It gets rainy in the mountains this time of year."

The three Danes looked at him blankly. Belatedly, Julyan realized that the energy fields on the scooters probably kept the rain out, too.

But they wouldn't keep the ground dry, he thought with a flare of anger. *I'm fed up with being treated as if I'm only a little brighter than Seamus.*

When Julyan glanced at the Old One, hoping for who knew what reassurance, those cool grey eyes only said, *"So, then, keep your mouth shut."*

The next several days were almost too much fun to be called work. Ring insisted on trying the flight and float capacities of the spavek. He bounced off the walls and ceiling as he learned how to control velocity and arc, but soon was managing the suit with uncanny skill.

Leto had reactivated the simulated firing range, so Ring explored the various elements of the blue spavek's weapons systems. Eventually, they planned to move to live fire, but not until Ring was scoring at least ninety percent in simulation. The spavek could generate beams of various kinds, some intended for fine work like cutting, others with no other use than as very destructive weapons.

Griffin was reminded of the ruined military installation Adara had shown him on his second day on Artemis. The entire side of a mountain had been sheared off, the rock not just exploded, but melted. It would have been an astonishing show of force anywhere, but on pastoral Artemis—well, Griffin had had no problem understanding why, five hundred years later, stories were still told about the single armored figure who had caused all of that destruction.

Although the spavek could fire small missiles and some were stored in racks nearby, Griffin suggested they avoid using projectiles except in simulation. "The charges might have broken down over five centuries. Even the damper and containment fields built into the range might have trouble dealing with some random recombination of elements."

No one—not even Ring, who was showing quite a bit of assertiveness these days—argued with Griffin on this point. Ring was less cooperative when Griffin suggested that he, Griffin, might activate another spavek, so they could try some sparring.

"Not you," Ring said, "nor Terrell. The bear might fly in orange arms, and the fish, eventually, in yellow or pink, but, until you embrace the dark paths, neither you nor Terrell will spread wings of purple and green."

Griffin was offended. He was getting tired of Ring's refusal to speak plainly, though some part of him accepted that Ring was probably being as clear as he could be. What really ticked him off was that Ring clearly didn't think Griffin could operate one of the spaveks.

"May I remind you," he countered tartly, "that I am probably the only person on this planet who has ever operated a flying craft? Why can't I operate the spavek? Take it off and let me have a try."

"If you insist, seegnur."

The readiness with which Ring floated down made Griffin think he was destined to fail. From the impish grin Terrell quickly squashed, Griffin knew his friend thought so, too. Ring backed the blue spavek into one of the convenient squires set around the arena, did something to snap open releases, then stepped out. Meanwhile, Griffin methodically stripped down.

I'm a skilled small ship pilot. I've worn battle armor before. Why am I suddenly scared?

He knew why, even if he denied it to himself. Watching the ease with which Ring had adapted to the rig, Griffin suspected that there had to be some sort of symbiotic linkage. Nothing else explained a primitive who could barely sit a horse managing power armor with such ease. The horror stories of Kyley had been full of intelligent machines that started running their owners' lives.

The anthropologist in Griffin whispered, *Now you have a very good idea where those stories originated. How many of the Old Empire's tools survived their makers and were found by those innocent of their power?*

The skeptic in him countered, *Yes. But could those tools use just anyone? Ring was created to synchronize with the old technology. Maybe Castor might manage, but you? You're safe. Stop being a wuss. Back on in, fasten the snaps. Nothing's going to happen.*

At least you've got to try, said another voice, bossy, like his sister Jada. *What sort of scientist is afraid of experimentation?*

"A live one," Griffin said aloud as he stepped into the suit's embrace. He felt the squire hum. Remotes closed the panels, pressed the helmet down over his head. Starting at his extremities, the hum of electric current ran through Griffin's nerves, surged along his limbs, intermeshed at his core, causing his muscles to spasm then release, spasm then release. Griffin would have screamed, but the helmet had possessed his head.

Linkages of spiked energy pricked against the rims of his eyes, swarmed up his nostrils, probed into his ears. Something larger, thicker, pressed between his lips, forcing them open. He refused to think about what the suit was doing lower down, but a very bad memory, something to do with his brother Alexander, flashed into Griffin's mind, then vanished instantly to wherever he had kept it suppressed.

There was no pain, no pleasure, just a practicality that was somehow more horrible than either would have been. Griffin wanted to use the suit. The suit was doing what was necessary to find out if this was possible. This violation was Griffin's own choice. Again, he tried to scream, and this time he heard a sound that might have been his own voice.

Terrell spoke, his voice tight and anxious. "Griffin? Griffin? Are you all right? The telltales on both the squire and the spavek are showing activation is complete. The squire has lowered you to the ground. You're just standing there."

Power armor, Griffin told himself. *All this is is some weird form of power armor. Try to raise an arm. Your right arm.*

After a tremendous effort, his right arm lifted. He heard Terrell cheering. Griffin moved his left arm. Then he raised and lowered each leg, managing a few steps. Each action required a tremendous amount of effort. He wondered why the Old Imperial technology—supposedly so much better than that of his own people—should be so hard to operate.

The buzzing through his nervous system, which had fallen to a numbing hum, intensified once more. It moved deeper, penetrating from the peripherals into Griffin's core, vibrating along his spinal column. Prickling touched the inside of his brain. He knew he couldn't really feel what was going on—didn't the brain have minimal sensory nerves?—but Griffin would have sworn he could feel every ripple and convolution outlined in a painless but remorseless lightning.

Once or twice the inspection paused, as something of potential interest had been located. Then it moved on, digging deeper, layer by layer, eventually cell by cell. Griffin raised his hands, trying to rip the seals open, but the gloves, capable of such precise manipulation when worn by Ring, were stiff and unyielding, as if each finger had been dipped in plastic and was now hardening in futile clawlike curves.

Had the examination continued, Griffin might have gone insane, but Ring came to his rescue. The big man touched the center of Griffin's chest, pressing his hand hard against one of the spavek's panels. The questing force that had been delving into Griffin rushed to meet Ring, meshing its energies with his, welcoming him. Griffin had the faint, embarrassing feeling that he was being complained about.

Ring's reply was inaudible but somehow comprehensible. *"He did better than I dared hope. Let him go. He has been stronger than you can know."*

Griffin felt grateful, even more so when Ring shoved the spavek into the waiting squire and triggered the releases. The suit let him go, withdrawing its connectors with apologetic grace. Ring, too, was apologetic.

"I had not realized that you were so almost alive. I thought that, but for a tiny vine, you were dead, that the roots would not find soil in which to bury. Forgive me. I would not have had you so used."

Terrell caught Griffin, whose knees were buckling, and helped him over to one of the built-in benches that encircled the testing chamber.

"What happened, Griff? I thought you were doing all right. You were moving the thing, though stiffly."

Griffin felt his friend's emotions with an intensity that he never had before, at least when both were awake. Terrell's fear mingled with a trace of anger, delight was ebbing before apprehension. This must be the "vine" Ring had spoken of. Whatever the suit had done to Griffin had—almost certainly temporarily—intensified his psychic link to the factotum.

"If I understood Ring, he let me put the spavek on because he didn't think I had the necessary adaptations to let my nervous system mesh with whatever the suit uses to link with its wearer. The problem was, I had just enough that the suit kept looking to make a connection. It couldn't find it, though, and my system was getting overloaded."

"That's horribly dangerous!" Terrell protested, looking at the suit as if it might come after him next, his earlier enthusiasm swallowed by a sea of distrust and apprehension.

"It was—but only because I hadn't been trained how to operate the cancellation sequence," Griffin said, knowing he was right, now recognizing what one of the pulses in his core had been. "If I had been, I simply would have told the suit to let me go and it would have."

"So it kept trying," Terrell said, "because you didn't tell it to stop and it found just enough to convince it the effort was worthwhile? That still seems insane—like holding someone underwater and hoping he gets himself free before he drowns."

"It felt rather like that," Griffin said, forcing a shaky laugh. "Again, my lack of training was the problem. My guess is that the test pilots or whatever you want to call them were trained to recognize that they were not synchronizing correctly with the suit."

"Why didn't the suit know?" Terrell protested. "You talk as if it's somehow intelligent."

"Perhaps the completed models would have had safeguards," Griffin said. "Remember, this was a test lab. These were all experimental models. Probably every one of them has some flaw or incomplete element."

"And Ring didn't have a problem because he has the right sort of adaptations?" Terrell asked, now sounding less angry, more interested, although his fear was still present.

Ring nodded. "I have dreamed of blue since the coming of the first star. I did not know what it was until after the second star fell. Then my heart sang that if I were not here to know the blue, all would be lost."

Griffin tried to remember the weird prophesy Ring had recited soon after he had arrived with Bruin and Kipper. Something about there being no hope unless Ring was present, about the return of slavery, then that odd stuff about cats. "If the cats do not breathe in the dusty orb, if the thread does not learn that it binds tightest when it is knotted firmly into itself, if the dreamer does not wake from the visions, then even with Ring, with Bruin, with Kipper, still there will be disaster."

He felt uneasy. The coming of the first star could refer to his own arrival. The shuttle burning through the atmosphere had been seen as a falling star, even in daylight. Could the second star refer to what had been reported in Spirit Bay? Had he been right to dismiss it so lightly? But they weren't dismissing it lightly. Adara was off to make sure there was nothing to the rumors.

Space trash, he thought, comforting himself, letting his mind slide back to the fascinating problem of the secrets of Leto's complex. *That's all it is. Just space trash.*

Interlude: Parasitism

arms
    legs
        voice

to
    needy
        childish
            vengeful
                omnipresent

rusts
    smuts
        root rots

devouring to live
    parasitism

12

Beneath the Surface

Sleeping on a bed was nice, even if Adara did have to share the creaking frame with Sand Shadow. Nonetheless, the huntress woke with the dawn. Ambling into the kitchen, she found the widowed cousin who served as the family's cook and housekeeper slicing slabs from a ham and dropping them into a skillet. They exchanged greeting while Adara cut herself bread and smeared it with thick strawberry jam.

The family that was not quite hers kept farmer's hours. Bread and jam or bread and cheese would hold them until the milking was done, eggs gathered, cows turned out to pasture, horses fed, and routine tasks attended to. Then they would meet for a larger meal that would sustain them until noon.

From bitter experience, Adara had learned that the scent of Sand Shadow that clung to her made domestic livestock nervous, so she didn't offer to help. Instead, she settled herself on a three-legged stool on the porch and amused herself between bites of bread and jam with carding wool.

Neenay found her there. Sliding behind her spinning wheel, she started pumping the peddle. When the process of transforming fluff into yarn was under way she said, "Hektor left with first light. Even if he does stop at the cobbler's, I suspect you'll have news of Spirit Bay before lunch. Will you be staying on after?"

Adara licked a bit of jam off one finger so it wouldn't soil the wool and considered. "It depends on the news. If there's nothing, I might stay a day or so. Bruin is with Griffin and Terrell, so they won't starve."

"Not pining to get back to one or the other?" Neenay asked.

Adara shook her head. "More pining to be away, if you want to know. Mother, I never said I didn't want a . . ." She almost said "mate" as the hunters did, then corrected herself to politer use. "A husband, but I want one who will be a partner, too. I'm not sure either of those two would put up with me for long once the shine had worn off. I'm not the easiest person to deal with."

Neenay chuckled. "Tell me about it." She grew more sober. "But you like them?"

"Both. Very much. I'd give my life for either of them." Adara paused. "But I'm not sure I could give my life *to* either of them . . . Does that sound as strange to you as it does to me?"

Neenay surprised Adara by shaking her head. "It's a mistake many a young woman—especially one with interests beyond the usual— makes. Some women are perfectly content with the roles our bodies built us for—bearing children, then raising them—just as some men have no desires beyond following in their fathers' trades, farming the same land, living in the same house. There's nothing wrong with feel- ing that way either. But for those whose gifts lead them outside those expected paths, there's always the question of what to choose."

"And?"

"I say if you choose a man, make sure it's one who makes you feel as if you're choosing for the larger life, not the smaller. If you choose to settle and have children, then you should feel the joy of it, not that you're imprisoning yourself. Equally, if you choose to follow—say—a hunter's path, you shouldn't feel as if you've shut yourself out of a life you would have loved but feared as too 'ordinary.' "

Adara nodded. "Then, by those terms, I'm not ready yet for any decision. Since I think that both Terrell and Griffin honestly care for me—though each after his own fashion—then, much as the idea is inviting, I need to stay out of their blankets. I don't want to give any false hopes."

But, she thought, *I wish it wasn't so complicated. I am as itchy as a cat in heat and knowing there are two good-looking men who would be glad to scratch the itch makes it . . .*

Momentarily, she considered finding some anonymous stranger, maybe up in Crystalaire, and giving him a surprise. She put the idea from her as imprudent for many reasons. She had just realized that she had shredded the bit of wool she'd been carding when the patter of feet coming around the side of the house, accompanied by an image from Sand Shadow, saved her from her thoughts.

Elektra came running up. "When I brought the eggs in, Cousin Thelma said that breakfast was about ready. Dad's washing out at the pump. Nikole said she'll be by to say 'hi' once the little ones are settled."

Adara stood and brushed wool off her trouser legs. "And Sand Shadow says a wagon is turning in from the town road. Orion, Willowee, and Hektor should be with us before we finish eating."

Her prediction proved correct. Willowee came in as Cousin Thelma was rising from the table to turn the ham steaks she had put in the pan when the wagon had rumbled into the farmyard. She gave Adara a quick hug, then slid onto the bench next to Elektra.

"The boys are putting up the horses," she said, accepting the mug of tea Akilles had shoved toward her. "Hektor told us that Adara was here, looking for news of Spirit Bay."

"And you have some," Adara said, smiling encouragement at her sister-in-law. "I can't wait to hear."

Willowee didn't hesitate. "Dad had already told us some but, after Hektor let on you were interested, we got Dad to tell us all over again, saying Hektor would like the tale. We got a few more details then."

"And?"

Willowee suddenly looked uncertain. "It isn't much, really. I don't know if you realize how much of an upset there has been. Although the Sanctum was flooded, it seems that no one is willing to believe the Old One is dead. Loremasters from all over the region are gathering to discuss what to do with the Sanctum, and how to handle the Old One should he show up and try to move back in now that the water is gone."

Terrell had brought news of the first part of this, but Adara could almost feel her ears prick forward at Willowee's final statement.

"The water's gone? I saw the place myself before we left Spirit Bay. It was flooded right up to the ground floor and there was several feet of standing water above ground, too. Do you mean that the ground floor is clear?"

Willowee shook her head emphatically. "No. From what Dad said— and he went to look before the loremasters cordoned off the area— even the lower levels were free of standing water. Dad didn't get to go down, but he did get as far as a big staircase. He said there was plenty of mud and slime, but all the standing water had drained away."

Hektor and Orion came in then, and Hektor said, "Has she gotten to the bit about the lights?"

Willowee glowered at him. "Not yet. Stuff your mouth with ham and let me tell the tale properly."

Adara couldn't help herself. "Lights?"

Willowee nodded. "After the Sanctum was flooded, lots of people went there searching for the Old One's body. His two servants were fine—they'd been sleeping in a summerhouse, to get out of the heat. Later, when the Old One's body was nowhere to be found, the lore-masters and town government agreed that no one was to poke around. That didn't mean they left the place unsupervised. After all, it is a seegnur artifact. You know how the Sanctum's on a small peninsula?"

Adara nodded.

"Guards were set at the base of the peninsula to discourage people tromping out there from the landside. Boats were set to patrol on the water side. Nothing much happened for a few days."

Adara knew some of this, having been among those who had helped with the initial search, but she nodded encouragement, sensing Willowee was getting near the exciting part of her tale.

"First came the sounds," Willowee said, dropping her voice as if telling a ghost story, her eyes shining. "None of the folk Dad talked to could agree exactly what the sounds were like. Some said they heard a sucking sound like the water draining off through some hidden channels. Others swore the sounds were more rhythmic and had to come from some machine—pumps or siphons. Thing is, no one wanted to look too closely . . . Not only was there fear that the place was now haunted, but the loremasters were flat-out against anyone going in there. When the lights were seen . . ."

Willowee paused for dramatic effect and Adara prompted her.

"Lights?"

Willowee nodded. "Lights and not just any lights. These were faint and dim. Those who glimpsed them swore that these lights did not flicker as would a torch or lantern, but shone steady and with a blue-green cast."

Elektra asked, "Did everyone run away then? I would have. I would have screamed."

"No one wanted to get close, that's sure," Willowee agreed. "My dad was out on one of the patrol boats. Eventually, he convinced the rest of the crew that it was their duty to take a closer look. They landed near the point and went ashore. That's when Dad saw that the building wasn't flooded anymore. They didn't go any farther that day, just went and told the loremasters."

Her voice dropped. "Later, one of Dad's friends told him that when the loremasters screwed up their courage and went to take a closer look they found footprints in the mud on the bottom level—human footprints. A tracker said there might have been as many as half a dozen people there—but there were no prints in the mud on the ground floor when my dad and his friends from the patrol boat went in—not a single one."

"So where did they come from?" Akilles asked.

"No one knows," Willowee said. "Some folks are saying it's the ghosts of the seegnur come to haunt the Sanctum in punishment for the sacrilege done there by the Old One Who Is Young."

"The ghosts took long enough," Hektor scoffed, although there was more than a little bravado in his voice. "He's been living there for generations."

"Do ghosts leave footprints?" Elektra asked, her voice trembling just a little bit.

"They don't," Adara said. "If ghosts did, Bruin would have taught me to track them and he didn't."

Elektra looked relieved. Adara felt good about that. She decided against telling what she knew about tunnels between the mainland and the Haunted Islands. That would undo any comfort she'd offered. Those who knew had decided that information should not be allowed out until they were certain the Old One was gone. Now it seemed that he was not, for who else could have left the prints?

Something had been in the Sanctum, something that had left footprints. Julyan and the Old One? Perhaps some of their lackeys? Was there any connection between Willowee's tale and whatever had splashed into Spirit Bay? Adara didn't see how there could be, but had she been Sand Shadow, the fur along her spine would have risen.

"Interesting," she said, rising from the table and easing her tension in a spine-cracking stretch. "Very interesting. Now, let me pay for my breakfast by helping unload the wagon. Then I'm off to the mountains once more. Griffin and Terrell must hear this tale."

"The tunnel is blocked ahead," Falkner announced, "just beyond the bend."

He was looking at some device on his scooter. Julyan had noticed that the man spent much time looking at these, even when he was driving. He wondered if Seamus found it as creepy as he did.

But then Seamus is used to the Old One Who Is Young poking around in his head. There's probably very little he finds odd. At least Falkner pays attention to his surroundings. Alexander's been so busy talking that we would have hit the wall a couple of times if the force shield hadn't bounced us off.

He wondered, not for the first time, if Alexander was doing this on purpose, to make him jumpy. Certainly, Alexander knew how much Julyan hated surrendering control to anyone else.

"Looks like a transit capsule," Falkner continued a moment later. "A big one." Siegfried was unholstering the weapon he wore near one hip. Falkner cautioned him, "Don't shoot at it. If I were setting a trap, I'd arrange for it to trigger when someone tried to blow a hole in the capsule."

Siegfried replied grumpily. "I wasn't going to shoot at it. I wanted to be prepared."

Julyan didn't believe him. Back when they'd been clearing out the debris crammed into the tunnel between Mender's Isle and the mainland, Siegfried had resorted to one of his weapons to break larger things into smaller. This had filled Julyan with a mixture of envy and fear. A ray of greenish-blue light had flowed out, surrounded the target in a viscous field, and then, when Siegfried had made some adjustment, had somehow crumpled whatever was within the light. There had been no explosion, no flying matter, just light ray, enclosing field, and "crump." He had the feeling that Siegfried would have used the thing more often but, apparently, the thing used a lot of energy. Falkner was always reminding him that recharging wasn't automatic here.

He guessed no one else believed Siegfried either, but if their little group had a leader, Siegfried was it. Even his brothers reserved challenging him for those times when his actions might endanger them. The group slowed their scooters, coasting until they were within a few body lengths of the blockade. Falkner hopped off his scooter to better direct a beam of light over the thing, but from the way he kept consulting the little device in his free hand, he might as well have not bothered. Julyan relied on his eyes.

He'd wondered why the tunnel's walls and ceiling were rounded. Now he understood. The capsule fit along the sides like a spitball in a blowpipe. The top didn't reach the roof, but was also rounded. Like the tunnel floor, the bottom of the capsule was flat. It didn't come all the way down to the floor. There was a gap about the length of his extended arm underneath. Julyan hunkered down and saw a rectangular panel there.

"Probably for servicing the works," Alexander said, kneeling beside him. "The entrances and exits were on either end, so that the capsule could be shot up and down the tube without the need to turn it around."

"So," Julyan said, moving up closer to Falkner, so he could avoid Alexander, "can we just open it on this end, work the scooters through, and go out the other end?"

"That would be the logical thing to try," Falkner agreed. "I'm analyzing the mechanism now. Even if the powered latch is out, there would have been an override for emergencies. Well and good, but that override is where I'd set the trigger for an explosive."

"You think about these things a lot," Julyan commented.

"My job," Falkner said absently. "Although I set the bombs as often as find them." His tone shifted, losing the conversational note. "Now that's interesting. I don't recall seeing that sort of texturing before. Could it be some sort of energy grid?"

Although he had no hope of understanding, Julyan looked where the other directed. The underside of the capsule was covered with an erratic coating of what looked like fine wire bristles, silvery grey and so delicate that they seemed to shimmer. The smallest cluster was about the size of the upper joint of his thumb. Larger groupings covered the surface to the extent of both of his outspread hands. Only about a third of the area was covered, leaving Julyan to wonder why they were placed so oddly.

"Patchy," Julyan was starting to say when he realized that the things were moving. At first, he thought the sense of motion came from the flickering light. At the same moment that he remembered the seegnur's lights didn't flicker, the first of the prickly things dropped off and began to roll toward him and Falkner.

Julyan jumped back, crashing into Alexander. Falkner, his attention split between the rolling burr and the device in his hand, wasn't as quick. As if blown by a strong wind, the burr raced up to him, rolling over his trouser leg before impaling itself on the back of Falkner's left hand. Falkner cried out and tried to bat the thing away with the device he'd cradled in his right hand. A shrill yelp revealed that all he'd succeeded in doing was driving the tiny needles deeper into his skin.

More of the prickle burrs were dropping off the bottom of the capsule and rolling toward Falkner. Horrified, Julyan realized that they didn't just roll. Each tiny needle served as a leg, pushing the burr with astonishing speed and accuracy. Falkner was trying to get to his feet, but his usual coordination was gone and he swayed unsteadily.

Toxic, Julyan thought, assessing as if confronted by some unfamiliar animal. *They'll swarm over him in a moment. If they get onto*

*him, we won't be able to do anything without hurting him worse or
getting bit ourselves.*

That left one option and he took it. Julyan grabbed Falkner under
the armpits and hoisted him clear of the floor. Falkner was nearly as
tall as Julyan, but his build was thin and wiry, rather than heavily
muscular like that of Siegfried or Julyan himself. Stumbling back, Julyan got Falkner clear of the floor, up over one shoulder. He felt a breeze.
Alexander was beside him, mounted on their scooter.

"Get on!" he ordered. "I'm going to activate the defensive field."

Julyan obeyed, half falling into his seat, Falkner draped across his
lap. Falkner was breathing erratically and his skin was very hot. Alexander made the scooter rise, then switched on the field. Julyan looked
around.

Siegfried had also raised his scooter. Julyan noted that the Old One
did not occupy the passenger seat as he had before. Instead, he'd taken
possession of Falkner's scooter and was hovering. Seamus sat behind
him, his expression as passive as that of a doll.

The prickle burrs swarmed beneath them, seeking a target. There
were a lot more of them than had been visible on the underside of the
capsule. Julyan guessed that they must have been hidden all over the
thing. Their speed was incredible. Julyan found himself grateful that
Alexander had brought the scooter. There was no way he could have
outrun them as he had planned. They would have caught onto his
clothes, rolled up his legs, found bare skin.

He shuddered, imagining tiny needles piercing his skin. They'd be
like sand burrs, so fine that you wouldn't even feel them until the poison started burning. He grabbed Falkner's hand, reassuring himself
that the burr that had attacked him remained firmly hooked into his
skin. Julyan tugged free the bandana he wore around his neck and
wrapped it around the thing, just in case. It wouldn't stop it from injur-
ing Falkner, but at least it couldn't just drop off and get him.

Siegfried was studying the writhing silvery grey mass, his expression detached and analytical, as if his own brother wasn't the one who
was injured.

Alexander spoke sharply. "Sig, can you hold them? Falkner's been poisoned. He's burning up. I can't treat him without first hooking him to the diagnostic, and I can't do that while we're on the scooter."

"I think I can," Siegfried said calmly. "Back down the tunnel. Maxwell, go with him. Offer what aid you can. If you must, use the scooter to block any burrs that come after you."

"Yes, sir."

Julyan looked back as Alexander set their scooter in motion. The prickle burrs had stopped their aimless rolling and were now shooting tiny needles up at Siegfried, but the needles couldn't penetrate the defensive field. The burrs seemed to realize this. Julyan's last glimpse of Siegfried, before Alexander whipped them around a bend, was of the burrs rolling onto each other. Their prickles meshed, enabling them to bond into a larger mass, thereby overcoming their limitations of size and height.

Julyan thought of how he'd seen a swarm of bees attack, no one bee very large, but the entirety more than enough to kill a far larger opponent.

"I hope Siegfried's careful," Alexander said, bringing the scooter to a halt and motioning for Julyan to dismount and lay Falkner on the floor. He removed what Julyan already knew was a sort of portable hospital from the scooter and started attaching tubes and wires. "Those things might have more than whatever poison they used on Falkner. What if they can generate something that will cancel the scooter's field?"

It seemed like a very real possibility. From the talk of the last several days, Julyan had gathered that anything the Danes could do they assumed the Old Imperials also could have done—and far more efficiently.

"Shall I warn him to be alert for such?" the Old One asked. "I can operate the communication panel."

"Do that," Alexander said, "and if you can manage to both keep an eye open for any of those burrs coming toward us and remote monitor what Siegfried is doing, that would be good. Guarding gets first priority, though."

"I understand," the Old One said.

Alexander was studying a message on the side of his hospital box.

"Neurotoxin. Type unknown," he muttered, speaking as much to himself as to the others. "No surprise. A generalized anidote has been administered. The fever's a puzzle, though. Most neurotoxins don't cause a fever. The victim dies from respiratory failure or convulsions. Could be a secondary element, maybe a fast-acting bacteria or virus. Probably won't spread except by body fluid contact. Too dangerous otherwise. Still . . . Won't hurt to . . ."

He made a few adjustments to the box and the fluid pumping into Falkner changed from clear yellow to brilliant orange.

Alexander looked at Julyan. "I've done what I can. Even if there was a secondary component, Falkner'll probably survive it. We were proofed against everything any of us could think of before we left home. Still, Falkner wouldn't have had a chance if you hadn't pulled him out of there. I won't forget that. I promise you. I won't forget that."

Julyan felt oddly comforted.

Despite the disturbing aspects of Griffin's experience with the blue spavek, he remained eager to find out who else in their small group might be able to operate one of the suits. He was equally interested in learning which of the suits might be better suited to his abilities— abilities that Ring had hinted were not fully awakened. That didn't mean he couldn't get the suit ready.

"We know where the emergency release is now," Griffin explained to Terrell, "so no one need be overwhelmed like I was. And it would be very interesting to know more."

Terrell looked at him sidelong. "Interesting? Why? Those things are dangerous. I think the seegnur were right to lock them away. We of Artemis have been content not knowing about them. If you want them, then take them away from our planet. Take this whole complex if you will, but leave us alone."

Griffin was shocked. "I thought you would be the most eager. You've never struck me as a coward."

"I'm not," Terrell said steadily. "But I've also never been one to leap from a cliff into an icy lake simply because someone dared me to take the plunge. Compared to putting on one of these spaveks—these suits that invade your mind and body alike for the purpose of permitting you to spread death and destruction—compared to that, jumping into an icy lake and seeing if you drown before you freeze—that seems sane!"

Terrell turned away, pointedly leaving behind his stack of meticulous drawings. Griffin stopped him with a hand on his arm. Ring had hinted that whatever psionic ability Griffin had was associated with his link to Terrell. He hadn't forgotten how the first time he could feel Terrell's emotions when they had both been awake had been immediately after his experimentation with the spavek. The acute awareness had faded within a few hours, but what might happen if Terrell also experimented with the spavek? What if they both wore the blue spavek in sequence, then tried to maintain the greater awareness afterwards?

He had to convince Terrell to at least try. "Terrell, you didn't complain when Ring started examining the suits."

"Ring is a rule unto himself. Ring said that he did what he did because if he didn't disaster would come. I don't hear him pressing the rest of us to follow his example. Is Ring's success what's got to you? Do you envy him his splashy rig?"

Griffin did envy Ring his easy use of the spavek. He thought about denying it, realized Terrell would never believe him.

"I don't envy him, not the way you mean, not enough to do something foolish. I don't want to take Ring's suit from him, but I would like to see if I can operate one myself. Think of the potential!"

"I am. I can't get what those suits can do out of my mind. The thought gives me nightmares."

Terrell's tone made clear that he would not discuss the matter further. Moreover, from how he pointedly walked out of the test arena, he was also rejecting any further involvement with the spaveks.

Griffin started to pursue him, to remind him about that splash in Spirit Bay and what it might mean, but he knew what the factotum's reply would be—wait until Adara came back with her report. Then they'd know if anything had happened after the splash. Hadn't Griffin himself been inclined to dismiss the event as nothing more than falling space trash? Griffin cursed himself. He still didn't think the splash was anything significant, but his own words had robbed him of a possible tool. He considered trying the argument anyhow, then decided to wait until Terrell had cooled off. Instead, he turned his attention to Ring.

"What do you think? If Terrell won't try, then who would be best?"

Ring shrugged. "Very soon, it will not matter. If you must try, then Bruin."

"Earlier you said something about the bear flying in orange arms. I don't recall a suit colored orange. Which one did you mean?"

Ring showed him. The body of the suit was a pearlized ivory white, but the joint covers, helmet, and boots were a brilliant metallic orange. Griffin wondered if the fact that this one had been designed in two colors indicated alterations to an original design or if this suit had been farther along in its design, so that ornamental flourishes had been added.

We know so little about the Old Imperials, what they valued, what they disdained. Artemis is their greatest surviving artifact, but since it was crafted as an escape from their routine lives, it is a text you need to interpret by trying to guess what was left out.

"You did a lot of clean-up on your suit," Griffin said to Ring, inspecting the white and orange suit with admiration. "How much prep do you think is needed before we can try this one?"

Ring ran a finger along the spavek's shimmering torso, drawing a wiggly snake in the fine layer of powdery dust. "More than you wish to give, less than I gave. I will put my time to polish and prepare. You find the words to convince bear to become butterfly."

"Fair enough," Griffin said. He smiled at Ring. "That spavek's colors do look something like a butterfly, don't they?"

He hurried out, shaping arguments in his mind. If he couldn't make a spavek work himself, the next best thing was learning what he could from the experiences of others. Maybe that way he'd grasp whatever intangible element he was missing.

Maybe, he thought, half hiding the thought even from himself, *that's how I'll be able to win Terrell over, show him I'm willing, even eager to share what's here, that my hunger is for knowledge, not destructive power.*

He broke into a run, imagining the group of them soaring within the winds in shining armor, knights of the blue skies, spreading wisdom and collecting knowledge wherever they went, unrestricted by the limitations of travel by horse or ship or foot. The vision was glorious, absolutely glorious.

His suit was pure gold, like the sun.

Adara found that the best way to brief Sand Shadow about what she'd learned from Willowee was to tell Artemis, for the planetary intelligence was able to communicate with relative ease with each of them. From there, Adara went on to ask if Artemis herself had any idea what might have happened in Spirit Bay.

"From the beaches I felt the surging waters," Artemis replied. "That much is as true as you were told and even worse. The waters were hot in some places, as if they held quenched fire."

"But you didn't try to find out what had caused that heat?" Adara tried to hold her frustration inside, but Artemis sensed it nonetheless.

"I have no eyes such as you mean them," the neural network retorted, "and you will not give yours to me. The interlocking network of mycelium is yet incomplete. Later, perhaps I will be able to grow eyes for myself. For now, I am all touch, a little taste—although that is not taste as you know it, but taste as a plant tastes. I cannot hear, nor can I smell. How am I to know what fell into the waters of the bay? Enough that it was hot enough to kill me in some places. That is all I know. Was I to surge more bits of myself into the water so they could die as well?"

"No . . . I don't think you should have done that. I'm sorry."

The sense of someone else in her head that was Artemis present remained, but didn't respond. Adara drew in a deep breath and tried again.

"Do you remember how it was in the days of the seegnur? Could you see then?"

A long pause, filled not so much with flickering images as with sensations that gave the impression of being images. From sorting through the mingled auditory and olfactory information that sometimes flowed to her from Sand Shadow, Adara had experience with something similar, but at least Sand Shadow used visual images to tie the others together.

A gusty sigh, echoed—or so it seemed—by the breath of wind against Adara's cheek. "I cannot remember how I was. What I know is what is known to me from the one who was midwife to my rebirth. That one saw, heard, tasted, caught odors upon the wind. For it, touch was the least significant. Although it felt vibration, it did not appear to have tactile sensation. Torn between what I am, what I have, and what I think I should have, I am so very lost."

Adara wished she could reach out and touch the other, hug her as Bruin had hugged little Adara, stroke her as Adara had stroked spot-furred Sand Shadow. However, no matter how she pitied the other, Adara could not accept what Artemis was asking. Would she remain herself if she let the other even further in? Artemis was a world. She was just a huntress.

"I wish you were not going to that Leto place again," Artemis said after a time. "I do not like that I cannot share with you, find you, find Sand Shadow... Can't you make the others come out of that place?"

"I would like nothing more," Adara said. "If you could locate another place where the seegnur's artifacts remain intact, I could coax Griffin forth."

But even as Adara shaped the thought, she wondered. Would it make a difference? Griffin's goals had shifted since the day he had accepted that his shuttle was lost to him and with it his ability to contact the ship that awaited him in orbit.

The pull that brought him to Artemis was the desire to learn more about the seegnur, to have bragging rights on the finding of this planet. Then he was tugged by the desire to find a way off the planet. Perhaps he would have left at once to replace what he had lost. Perhaps he would have stayed and continued his research. Now, however, it is as if he has forgotten that he is stranded, and his only desire is to learn what he can of the seegnur's doings here.

Lights in the Sanctum. Footprints in mud where there should have been flood. Something was definitely not right. Adara did not know what, but she would have bet her night-seeing eyes against a chunk of stale bread that whatever it was the Old One Who Is Young was at the heart of it. She shivered and picked up her pace.

Interlude: Symbiosis

mycorrhizal connections
    extending roots
    extending reach
    sweet return

mycorrhizal connections
    linking species
    crossing barriers
    complex network

Choosing for the larger life
    Feeling the joy
    Shaping the spores

13

Reunion

Once Falkner was stabilized, Alexander and Julyan went to help Siegfried. They found he needed no aid in his peculiar battle. Ensconced within his scooter's defensive shield, Siegfried had made himself bait to lure the burrs, which continued to shoot their poison darts at him. When the darts were spent, the burrs went after Siegfried in a body, linking one onto the next, building a surging mound that licked out tentacles, each seeking to snag their enemy.

Siegfried kept his scooter close to his attackers, rising in painfully small intervals so that more and more burrs would join the mass to extend the tentacles' reach. When he estimated he had most of the burrs in one place, he englobed them within the viscous, crushing, blue-green light.

"Bravo!" called Alexander, when the burrs had been reduced to an inert mass of metal. "You did that wonderfully."

Siegfried snorted. "I don't think I could have managed so neatly if they'd been freshly constructed. As it was, once they'd fired their needles at me, they didn't regenerate as I think they were designed to do. Those guardbots were half crippled, their limited resources diverted as they tried to do too many things at once."

Julyan thought—but did not say—that the burrs must have been addled in whatever served them for brains, else some surely would have hung back. That would have made more sense than gathering in that frantic swarm whose single goal had been to reach and engulf an enemy who remained within a protective shield. However, he said nothing. Siegfried was justifiably proud of his achievement and no good would come from belittling any part of it.

Siegfried looked ruefully at his weapon. "That drained the remaining charge. Won't be able to use it until we get back to the shuttle."

Alexander shrugged. "You couldn't use a nerve burner on something without nerves."

Julyan didn't need Alexander's order to enthusiastically take part in the search that assured them that the last of the burrs was located and destroyed. When this was done, the Old One brought Falkner forward. The mechanic was very weak, but he could operate the devices that disabled what he called a "ridiculously primitive little bomb" linked to the capsule's fail-safe.

They opened the capsule, guided the scooters through, and resumed their interrupted journey. By the time they reached the tunnel's end, Falkner had recovered enough that he could pilot his own scooter. His every movement showed acute pain, but he refused to take anything to counter it, saying he didn't want his wits slowed.

His brothers didn't argue. Although these Sierra seegnur had wonderful ways of dealing with pain—as Julyan had discovered after a water-sodden wooden bench had fallen on one of his feet—these worked best when the pain was isolated in a limb or specific area. Falkner's entire nervous system had been attacked. Anything that would battle the lingering pain would make him dull when they needed him most.

The tunnel ended in a wider area, rather like that outside the hidden door back at the Sanctum. The door at this end was huge and heavy, made of hull metal. Falkner checked it over carefully. After their encounter with the burrs, not even Siegfried—the most impatient among them—was inclined to protest.

Bruin was easier to convince than Griffin had dared hope. Griffin was so used to thinking of the older man as the brewer of cherry cider, the retired hunter now turned teacher of hunters, that he often forgot that Bruin had been a student of the Old One Who Is Young—and a prized student at that, for the Old One had continued to correspond with Bruin for many years after Bruin had left the Old One's sphere, married Mary Greengrass, and settled in his wife's village.

Given that the Old One had secrets he would not have wished Bruin to learn and that he had the intellectual companionship of the lore-masters, his continued correspondence with Bruin—laboriously hand-written as such must be, given Artemis's tech level—spoke volumes about both Bruin's intelligence and his level of intellectual curiosity.

There I go, once again, underestimating the people of Artemis, Griffin thought as he watched Ring and Bruin closely inspect the orange and ivory spavek. *As I did Adara and, to a lesser extent, Terrell. Why do I keep doing that? I never thought of myself as much a snob as the rest of my family. Indeed, I prided myself on being different in that matter as in so many others.*

The image of his sister Jada floated into his mind, disconcerting him. Why should he think of her, unless it was because she, like him, was a bit of an oddity within their warlike family? He shook his head, returning his attention to the discussion at hand.

"I've a bit more girth and gut than you and Griffin," Bruin was saying to Ring. "Do you think I'll fit comfortably within that shell?"

Ring smiled. "Snug as a bug in a rug."

Bruin tilted his head, considering the riddle. "Tight then, but comfortable enough. Well, I'm willing to give it a try. Show me what to do."

Kipper was watching, his large brown eyes wide with something between wonder and fear. "Will I get to try?" he asked.

Griffin looked at Ring. "You're the expert. What do you think?"

Ring shook his head. "Until squirrels speak, the fish best swims without a shell."

Bruin had been stripping. He paused, shirt half-off over his head. "Now, does that mean never or something else?"

"I cannot say," Ring said, "lest what I say make the saying moot."

"I don't envy you your head, friend," Bruin said, returning to his disrobing. "Not a wit."

Terrell was present to witness the test. Although Griffin could feel the disapproval radiating from him, he was grateful for the factotum's presence. Since their argument, Terrell hadn't been avoiding Leto's complex, but he had made a point of refusing to have anything further to do with the lab. Instead, he had spent his time working through the residential areas, following the protocols they had established when working with the Old One in the Sanctum. Since Bruin had been busy with Ring and Griffin, Terrell had also taken over some of the camp duties, so Kipper could concentrate on hunting and foraging.

From what they could tell from exterior inspection, Bruin's spavek was less heavily armed than the one Ring had chosen for himself. It was equipped with energy weapons, but lacked the missile-firing capacity. It had other gear that more than made up for the destructive power—at least from Bruin's point of view. For someone with Griffin's background, long-range vision was nothing remarkable, but for Bruin, whose experience with such had been limited to primitive telescopes and even more primitive binoculars, the idea that he should be able to change his range of vision with, literally, nothing more than a thought, was miraculous. Unsurprisingly, given Bruin's own natural night vision, he didn't find the suit's ability to permit the wearer to see in low light or by thermal signatures as interesting, but he admitted that for the unadapted that would be useful.

"I think your suit was meant for a scout," Griffin said.

"A scout?" Bruin was dubious. "The skies aren't precisely orange and white. Were the seegnur so powerful that they could proclaim their presence to those they spied upon?"

Leto's little girl voice chimed in. "All the suits were equipped with camouflage. It's an option in the protective energy shield."

That did impress Bruin. "Now I see why the ability to detect body heat would be useful. I wonder if the shield can be made to mask that as well."

Griffin was surprised by the man's quick grasp of tactical considerations, then he remembered that a hunter would be more aware than most how survival relies upon a continual cycle of creating defenses to counter another's attacks. He said as much and Bruin nodded.

"Nature gives a fawn spots so it will blend into the dappling of leaf duff and sunlight. However, she will not let her hunting children starve, so she gives them a keen sense of smell. Lest the threat to the fawn become too great, Nature now grants the fawn a time when it has almost no scent at all. Each changes in response to the other. Why should the tools used by humankind be any different?"

He turned to Ring. "When I get this on, I'd like to learn if I can find your suit with my own vision, even if the camouflage is activated. From what the Old One told Griffin, he believed that adaptations were as much a matter of the mind as the body. It would be good to learn if the power of my mind can overcome the barriers set up by the suit."

Ring nodded. He seemed oddly detached, even for him. Griffin was about to ask if Ring needed a break from wearing the armor when Leto's startled voice rang out. "The door that isn't there has been opened. This facility has been breached!"

Julyan couldn't follow half of what Falkner did to get the massive door unlocked and prompt it to open. Once again, he found himself very glad that the long-ago seegnur had a mania for backup systems. Otherwise, even if the door was unlocked, he didn't think they could have budged it. But Falkner found a system of cables and pulleys hidden behind a wall panel. He had to splice one the of the cables but, once that was done, Siegfried—muscles straining—could open the door without assistance.

Alexander and Falkner were standing by with weapons drawn, but all they encountered on the other side was another chamber. It was smaller than the one that had ended the tunnel, but still large enough to hold all of them and the three scooters. Walls, ceiling, and floor alike were such a brilliant white that Julyan felt profoundly uneasy. It wasn't natural for a place to be so clean. The only interruption in the white was a thin line bisecting the opposite wall. This seemed to indicate another door.

Siegfried mounted his scooter, put the defensive shield up, and glided through the opening. When he came to the wall with the door in it, he extended his still shielded hand to poke at what Julyan now saw was a pressure plate, such as those that they had used to open other doors in the seegnur's facilities.

A female voice, light but still authoritative, made most of them jump. "All doors must be closed before the facility door will open. Please close the corridor door and press the plate again."

Siegfried swiveled around. "Maxwell and I could go through, check things out, come back for you."

Alexander shook his head. "We've already seen that our scooters' communication units have trouble penetrating the hull metal. If you got into trouble, you'd have no way to call for help."

"But if this room is trapped," Siegfried said, "the entire group could be taken out."

Alexander acknowledged this with a reluctant nod. "How about this? You go in as you said, with Maxwell, with the shields on your scooter on full. Once the door is open, you block it and open the door on this side to let us through. No gallivanting off on your own."

When Siegfried looked as if he might balk, Falkner added, "Alexander's right. My only suggestion is that you take Julyan rather than Maxwell. Julyan's proven himself a good fighter already. No offense, Maxwell, but you just don't seem to have the skills."

The Old One gave a thin, slightly embarrassed smile. "I fear I have been more a scholar than a fighter of late."

The statement was absolutely true, but Julyan—who had seen how fast and vicious the Old One could be in a fight—wondered that the others could swallow the lie so easily. Surely they could see how those grey eyes saw everything, the power in that deceptively slim body. Still, warmed as he was by Falkner's phrase, Julyan felt no desire to comment.

He swung up behind Siegfried, gripping his long knife—almost a short sword.

Alexander called, "Don't disappoint me, Julyan. Bring my big brother back safe and sound."

The words held the force of a command, but Julyan wouldn't have done otherwise. He had nothing against Siegfried Dane. Keeping him alive would be a pleasure.

And the enemies of my enemies are almost my friends, he thought. *This time, what Alexander and I want is the same. Our hunt brings me closer to where Adara may be. How could I want more?*

"Before I close the door from out here," Falkner called, "do you see a release there?"

"I do," Siegfried called. "There's a matching panel. Probably opens to the same mechanism."

"Good luck!"

The hull metal door slid shut with a ponderously final thud. When nothing could be seen behind them other than a thin dark line that matched the one on the door in front of them, Siegfried again punched the pressure plate. The female voice spoke with even precision.

"Password requested. Speak clearly or enter the characters into the associated tablet."

Something bright shimmered into being against the whiteness of the wall alongside the pressure plate. Siegfried cursed softly.

"Speak clearly," the female voice repeated. "That last did not transmit to the audio receptors."

Siegfried looked frustrated. Then, moving his fingers rapidly, he touched a series of glowing characters. Julyan could read, but this was no alphabet he knew. He wondered if Siegfried did or if he was only guessing.

"Incorrect password," the voice said with definite disapproval. "One final attempt is permitted before counter-intruder actions will be taken. Timer activated, now!"

A new picture appeared on the wall. Julyan couldn't read the characters on this one either, but a brilliant green line rapidly decreasing in length left no doubt as to what was indicated.

Without bothering to turn the scooter around, Siegfried thrust it into reverse, backing with incredible speed and force. Only the trust Julyan had learned to put in the protective force shield kept him from screaming in protest or trying to jump clear before they hit the door.

As they hit, the female voice spoke with dispassionate clarity. "Instituting counter-intruder measures."

A hissing noise filled the air. Julyan felt his ears pop. Cursing, Siegfried slammed the scooter back again into the door with no effect. Julyan's jaw snapped shut and blood streamed into his mouth from where he'd bitten the inside of his cheek. His ears popped again and he began to feel light-headed. Blood was running from his nose. He wondered when he'd hit it.

"Damn! They're voiding the air!"

Siegfried swung off the scooter and staggered over to the wall that hid the manual door lock. Spitting blood onto the floor, his spinning thoughts making peculiarly significant patterns from the brilliant red against the icy white, Julyan forced himself to join Siegfried. Together, the two big men tried to pry the panel loose, but either this mechanism worked differently or the counter-intruder measures included locking the panel in place.

Sensible . . . Julyan thought, his knees buckling. Consciousness was swaying in and out of focus when with a loud slam, the door behind them burst open. Air swooshed into the room. There were shouts of alarm.

He recognized Alexander's voice, shrilly excited. "We've gotten to them in time! They're both alive."

Then a low hiss in his ear. "Didn't I tell you to take care of my big brother?"

When Julyan's head cleared, Seamus was sponging the blood off his face and the three Dane brothers were talking all at once in their own language. When Seamus said with flat disinterest, "Julyan is coming around, seegnur," the chatter switched to the language of Artemis.

Alexander must have forgotten his anger, for he was the first to come over to Julyan.

"You passed out from a combination of blood loss and lack of air. Suck this. It will help with the pain and speed healing. You took a nasty bite out of your cheek."

Julyan, his spinning head mingling this order with others, began to refuse. Then he realized that Alexander was holding out a small, flat tablet. It smelled faintly of some sort of berry. Alexander smiled when Julyan took it.

"Good. We've already given you something for the blood loss. You'll be in fighting form in no time."

Alexander stepped back to make way for Siegfried, who sank down next to Julyan, waving Seamus away. Siegfried had blood on his coverall but, from the splatter pattern, Julyan guessed not all of it was his own. The deliberation of his movements showed that Siegfried, too, was recovering from their ordeal.

"Good job in there, man. I'm sorry about not warning you before I slammed the scooter. I felt the change in the air and thought they might be pumping in some sort of gas. Wanted to try and bust us out before we couldn't do anything."

"Instead," Falkner called from a short distance away, "it looks as if the mechanism was designed to remove the air from the chamber so that any intruders would pass out. It wouldn't have been a complete vacuum, but very unpleasant. Wouldn't work against anyone wearing an environmental suit, but against a wandering tourist or local, very neat indeed."

"So we can't get through?" Julyan asked. His mouth felt thick, but speaking wasn't impossible.

"Actually," Siegfried replied, "I think we can. Alex and Falkner took a look around. Five hundred years dried out the insulation and sealant. The pressure shifts during the attempt to remove the air pulled a lot of it loose. Falkner, Maxwell, and Alexander are clearing enough away that if the same trick is tried we might feel a pressure shift, but that's about it."

"The woman?" Julyan spoke very carefully, all too aware he might bite his numbed tongue or lips. "Who spoke. She's not complaining?"

Siegfried looked puzzled, then smiled. "It wasn't a real person. It was a recording—similar to the sort you've seen us make on our datapads or that the scooter uses to provide piloting updates."

Julyan nodded. He was feeling stronger with every breath. One advantage to working with these off-planet seegnur was that their medicines were very good and they were liberal about sharing them.

"So you're not worried about her not liking things being pulled apart."

Alexander, his coverall now dusty and littered with bits of pale yellow and burnt orange stuff, rejoined them. He held out one hand to show them a small device cradled in a gloved palm. Julyan had no idea what it was, but he didn't figure the charred black hole near the center had been part of the original design.

"We've found several of these or things like it," Alexander said. "Guess?"

Siegfried looked annoyed, as he often did with Alexander's little games, but he played along nonetheless. After inspecting the bit of machinery, he said, "The air voiding system was only one of several anti-intruder measures. Someone came through here and disabled the ones that would do the most damage, but left the one—probably the least fatal—activated just in case."

"That's what we think," Alexander agreed.

Falkner wandered over, holding more charred pieces of equipment. "The walls, on the other hand, would take an industrial-strength construction beam to cut through—and that's if there's not another layer of something even tougher sandwiched between where I can't get a look at it. If we're going through, it's through this door or back down the tunnel to Spirit Bay and overland to Maiden's Tear—and then hope we can find a way in."

"And hope," said the Old One, coming over brushing more of the yellow and orange litter off his clothing, "that Griffin and his companions still remain. Might not the warning we were given have triggered an alarm elsewhere? If we delay, we might arrive only to find our quarry flown."

"That would be a nuisance," Siegfried agreed.

Falkner cut in. "Even if we don't find Griffin, consider what might be on the other side! We can't give up with taking a closer look. The walls are tougher than we can cut through, but any place made to open will be a system's weak point. I think I can get us through fairly quickly."

"You opened several other doors," Siegfried said. "I don't have a problem with giving you a chance at this one—but you do your work with the first door blocked open, understand? And you let us know before you trigger anything. Julyan and I got lucky last time. We're not going to trust to luck again."

"This facility has been breached!" Leto's voice as she repeated the warning sounded very much like that of a frightened little girl.

"Where?" Griffin asked. He was already turning in the direction of their exit into the valley, when Ring broke into a ponderous run and vanished deeper into the facility, heading for a point where there were several very wide corridors. Griffin had wondered about these during their initial tour, since there seemed little reason for such so deep in the facility.

I dismissed them as relics of the original construction, he thought as he ran after Ring, *especially since they faced into the mountain range. What if they weren't relics? What if they were for bringing in supplies from one of the landing areas? From Spirit Bay? The direction's right . . .*

He wondered at his own shortsightedness, then decided to give himself a break. After all, their first encounter with Leto's facility had been one of horror—the place knee deep in the dead. Later, when the cleanup had been concluded and Leto had softened somewhat to them, they had discovered the spaveks and other wonders. Oversized corridors were minor puzzles by contrast.

Terrell was loping alongside him. "The Old One?"

"Who else?"

"He may have more allies than just Julyan," Terrell said. "I wish Adara and Sand Shadow were here. We may well be seriously outnumbered—and if it's an attack group, they're going to be far better armed than we are."

Ring had outdistanced them. Now they heard his voice speaking with the vibrant note that indicated he had sealed the helmet of the blue spavek. Griffin realized he was relaxing. Their enemies better armed? Terrell was forgetting . . .

"Halt," Ring's voice boomed. "Go no further."

The voice that replied was not the Old One's, but one Griffin knew all too well.

"Sweet lodun's balls! Working power armor!"

Griffin heard himself calling out before he knew he was speaking. "Falkner? Falkner!"

He ran forward, feeling Terrell's hand tug his sleeve as if the factotum had begun to hold him back, then refrained. He heard Falkner's voice, shouting in excitement.

"Griff! Griff! We *have* found you then."

Behind Falkner's voices, others: Alexander? Siegfried? Griffin had no time to slow his charge forward when he recognized another: Julyan. And that other, soft and level, surely that was the Old One! The scene that met his gaze when he rounded a corner and came up alongside Ring was somehow incongruous, even though the voices had given him some warning.

The hall had opened into a large white chamber in which stood six people: three of his older brothers, the Old One, Julyan, and a boy little older than Kipper. They were mounted in pairs on three all-purpose travel scooters. These had their defense shields up, encompassing their riders behind protection that Griffin realized nothing but the weapons in the spaveks might penetrate—and he wasn't about to bet on that.

Falkner was beaming, genuinely happy to see Griffin, though his gaze kept drifting to the unknown element represented by Ring. Siegfried looked pleased, but his eyes were narrowed in what Griffin recognized as calculation. Alexander's face bore a feverish expression that someone who didn't know him might take for delight, but that made Griffin's blood chill. An overexcited Alexander could be extremely dangerous.

The Old One sat behind Siegfried, his features schooled to careful neutrality. Griffin had been his captive long enough to recognize that the Old One's apparent passivity was far more dangerous than it seemed. He wondered if Siegfried knew what sort of creature he had seated behind him.

Probably not, or he would never have let him inside his shield.

The boy's expression was slack, barely interested. He reminded Griffin of someone, someone he'd seen recently . . . He remembered then. Several of the captives they'd rescued from the Old One's breeding project had worn just such expressions, though whether they were the result of some birth defect or of their training he had not had opportunity to learn.

It took a moment for Griffin to realize that the white-haired man with the lined face who sat behind Alexander was Julyan, but the way that the handsome mouth pulled into a hungry smile gave him away. Julyan's dark-eyed gaze darted back and forth, searching for someone he did not find. Griffin was aware that Terrell and Bruin had joined them, of Kipper huddling near the back. That was all of them, other than Honeychild, Sam the Mule, and the horses, who then?

Adara! He's looking for Adara and for no good reason, either.

Suddenly, Griffin's pleasure at seeing his brothers again, at being found, melted into apprehension so severe he had to fight to keep his knees from shaking. Julyan with that expression on his face meant no good for his Artemesian friends—maybe not even for himself. He had assumed his brothers commanded this expedition, but perhaps the Old One was actually in charge?

Siegfried was speaking. "Do you command this?" He indicated Ring with a gesture.

Griffin looked at him. "Aren't you going to say hello, Siegfried?"

"Hello, Griffin. We had heard you were alive. Now, do you command this thing?"

"And if I do?"

Griffin was aware of motion behind him. Terrell strode up to stand next to him. Only someone who didn't know him as well as Griffin did would believe there was anything but innocent pleasure in the action.

"Griffin, are these your brothers? Surely they've found you far more quickly than you imagined possible. And the Old One! What a tremendous surprise . . . Or perhaps not so great a surprise at that. We all know he has a tendency to turn any circumstance to his advantage."

Confusion flickered for a moment on Siegfried's face. The wicked merriment that lit Alexander's eyes brightened. Falkner suddenly looked wary. Julyan reached for a weapon, but halted in midmotion at some low voiced command from Alexander. Only the Old One and the dull-faced boy did not react.

Griffin took advantage of the diversion. "Yes. These are three of my brothers—Siegfried, Falkner, and Alexander. How did you three link up with my former kidnapper, anyhow?"

"Kidnapper?" It was Falkner, always the least scheming of the three, who spoke. "And who is this Old One? These are locals we encountered soon after we splashed down near the old landing facility and started looking for you."

"Certainly, Julyan and the Old One didn't pretend they'd never heard of me," Griffin countered. "Did they somehow leave out that the Old One kept me imprisoned until my friends broke me out? Did they fail to mention that at my last meeting with Julyan he was either trying to kill me or kidnap me once more?"

"They did, rather," drawled Alexander, greatly amused. "Maxwell did say he had met you, but he gave a somewhat different version of your association. He said you came to him for help because he was squatting in the old landing facility on the mainland. He said that your lover, some warrior woman called Adara, got jealous. If he is to be believed, she kidnapped you—not the other way around."

"Sorry to disenchant you. Here are a few facts you can confirm anywhere in Spirit Bay. The man you call Maxwell is more widely known as the Old One Who Is Young. It might interest you to know that he is several hundred years old at the very least—something that is not at all typical, even on Artemis where good health means the natives live much longer than is usual at such a low tech level."

"Several hundred years old!" Siegfried scoffed. "Legend lore, not fact."

"Fact," said Bruin, hurrying up to join them. He'd stopped to put on a pair of pants. His quiver was slung over his bare chest, his bow was in his hand. "I am three score and more. I have known the Old One personally since I was a child. My parents knew him before that. Our family and my teachers knew him by reputation even longer. He has always looked the same: somewhere in his early to mid twenties, boyish, and slim. I should warn you—he's much stronger, much more dangerous than he appears. He taught me some interesting hand-to-hand fighting forty years ago, and I doubt he has let himself go stale."

The Old One broke his silence. "I cannot deny what they have said, seegnur. I never lied to you. Maxwell is the name my parents gave me, so it is at least honestly my own."

"And you are truly several centuries old?" That from Alexander.

"I am. When we first met, I told you I had devoted many years to studying the relics of the seegnur. You smiled and took that as a young man's boast, but I have given at least two hundred years to the task."

"Are you one of these 'seegnur'?" Alexander asked. "Have you lived since Artemis's fall?"

"Not that I know," the Old One said. "My first memories are faint now, but I remember being a boy in a fishing village far from here. I grew up and took to the sea, as was the custom of those who had raised me. For a long time, I was unaware that once I became an adult, I was not aging as did other men."

"How couldn't you have known?" Siegfried protested, twisting in the seat of the scooter to confront the man behind him. "Surely you would have been able to tell by the time you were in your forties!"

The Old One shrugged. "The sea is a harsh mistress. Like many sailors, I grew a beard to protect my face from the elements. My exposed skin was weathered by sun, salt, and wind. Although I am fair, I do tan and that also made it seem my skin was aging. My hair, already blond, bleached so that it might as well have been greying— the change from light gold to silver is subtle. Only after my wife's death, when I left the sea and roamed to ease my grief, did I realize that the side effects of my profession had masked what I had only then begun to realize. I had not aged significantly since my early twenties."

"Incredible and fascinating," Alexander said, "but aren't we getting away from what Siegfried asked? Griffin, do you control that thing? Is it a robot or a cyborg or simply a man wearing weird battle armor?"

Griffin's head swam as he tried to analyze everything he had learned, along with what Terrell's words had made him suspect. It wasn't chance that had brought his brothers so quickly. They had to have followed him from the Kyley system to Artemis. Why? Were they out to steal his glory or was there something more? Did they suspect what he had only just learned—that Artemis had her own dark secrets?

If so, he had just led them to a mother lode.

Falkner had been studying Ring's spavek. "Battle armor's my guess. Relatively recently refurbished. Not a model I recognize."

Alexander interjected quickly. "And Griffin's not admitting he's in command. That's dangerous, especially with all the lies we've just had revealed."

He spoke seven syllables, addressing them to the men in front of him. They sounded like nonsense to Griffin, but he felt Terrell stiffen and heard Bruin groan. Beside him, the spavek neither moved nor stirred.

"There," Alexander said lightly. "Benjamin Bruin Hunter, Terrell the Factotum, and whoever it is in that blue battle armor, you will now obey my commands as spoken by a seegnur to residents of Artemis. My first command is that you await my next command before taking any other action, although, for now, you may speak freely—as long as you tell the truth."

He looked at Griffin, his eyes flickering between tan and green as his lips twisted in triumph. "You were never interested enough in linguistics, brother mine. Pity. You may have found the planet, but I have found the means to control her inhabitants."

Interlude: Project

Minute Mystery
Holding History
Fungal Nursery
Breeding Discovery
Such Imagery
Now is Reality

14

Push and Shove

Driven by increasing dread, Adara toiled up the final slope before the drop into the vale of Maiden's Tear. She had chosen this route because, although it was more arduous, it cut days off their journey. Even so, the return up the mountain had taken longer than she liked. The sense of urgency that had pressed at her from the moment she had learned about the fresh footprints in the Sanctum had grown more intense with each passing hour.

Something of Adara's urgency had transferred to Sand Shadow as well. When they reached the final stretch, the puma raced ahead, only to find the campsite deserted, every bit of equipment cleared away. An attempt had been made to conceal that anyone had camped there. The job was not the expert one either Bruin or Terrell could have managed, but Sand Shadow found no trace of alien scents among the mingled odors. That made it unlikely their friends had been arrested for trespassing in a prohibited area.

Did they all move inside Leto's facility for some reason? The weather hasn't been too bad. Why hide traces so carefully?

Adara was turning possibilities over in her mind, when she and Sand Shadow became aware that someone was moving toward them through the surrounding forest. The newcomer stepped quietly, but he came with the prevailing breeze at his back, announcing himself to the puma.

"Kipper!" Adara called softly, as soon as Sand Shadow had identified him. "What happened?"

"Follow me," the boy replied, his voice hardly louder than a breeze. "Away from here."

Without question, they did. Kipper led them across several brooks and over bare stone to hide their tracks. At last they came to a sheltered grove hidden within a stand of long-needled pines. A small, nearly smokeless fire burned in a stone-lined hollow. Above it the smallest cookpot was suspended on a tripod.

Kipper crouched next to the fire. When puma and huntress entered his camp, he poured hot water over leaves and set tea to steep. Then he refilled the cookpot and set more water to heat.

"I have food," he said, his voice low, though Adara had detected nothing larger than a raven in the vicinity. "You've got to be hungry. Eat. I'll tell you what happened."

Adara accepted what the boy offered. In her shock, she had all but forgotten how for the last hour or so of her climb she had been anticipating just such a hot meal. Sand Shadow sent her an image of a bear, gave Kipper a rough stroke of her tongue, and padded out into the evening gloom.

Kipper served Adara fish, journey cakes, and overripe blackberries.

"Talk," Adara suggested, taking a bite so courtesy would be satisfied.

Kipper did, the words spilling over each other. Adara listened to his unfolding tale without comment, knowing that the slightest interruption could push the boy to tears.

"Griffin might have been very happy to see his brothers," Kipper said, after explaining how they'd found the Dane brothers in the hallway. "The rest of us were just shocked, especially with the Old One there. When Bruin confronted the Old One, he motioned me back. I hung out of sight around the corner, where I could hear but not see. Then the one called Alexander spoke some words . . ."

Kipper stopped and shivered. "Those words made me feel strange, as if I'd been wrapped in a blanket and couldn't move. Then I heard Alexander ordering the other three to obey his commands."

Adara nodded encouragement. "Bruin, Terrell, and Griffin?"

"No. Not Griffin—Ring—though Alexander didn't have a name

for Ring. Then Alexander said something about Griffin not having done his research right or something. After that, Griffin got nasty. I didn't know he could get so mad. There was a lot of arguing. Somewhere in there, I felt like the blanket had loosened. I got out of there. Bruin had warned me back. I didn't think anything that had happened would have changed his mind. Still . . ."

"You did right," Adara said, knowing that the boy was worried she would think him a coward, "to get away. If you hadn't, who would have told me what happened?"

"Honeychild stayed out here when Bruin went into Leto's complex," Kipper said. "I can't talk to her, so I'm not sure how much she knows. She's the one, though, who told me to clear away our camp. She started rolling up the blankets, pulling out the tent pegs."

Adara forced a smile. "Honeychild doesn't have hands like Sand Shadow, but she's learned to do a lot with her paws. I've watched her help Bruin break camp before."

"I caught on pretty fast," Kipper said. "I went and got the pack horse to help me. I'd noticed this camping spot before, when I was out foraging. Me and Honeychild shifted the horses to a more distant pasture. Sam the Mule decided to come along. Honeychild has been checking on them regularly."

"Good that you cleared out," Adara said. "Now, even if anyone comes looking for our camp, they're going to have trouble finding it. Julyan might, but would he go to that much trouble to find you? If Griffin's brothers are anything like Griffin, they're going to be so fascinated by that facility they'll forget anyone else exists."

"And they'll know," Kipper said, "that you and me won't go for help. We can't, not without admitting we've been poking around a restricted area."

"You thought of getting help, then," Adara said, "and had the sense not to. Good man. From what I gathered when I visited my family, events in Spirit Bay have shaken people up badly. The folk in Crystalaire might have locked you up for the loremasters to judge, rather than helping."

Adara gave Kipper a quick summary of what she'd learned from her family, concluding, "I thought that the footprints in the Sanctum had been left by the Old One and some of his followers. I did wonder if they might be connected to whatever hit down in the bay, but I certainly didn't consider that it might be Griffin's brothers. He'd been certain years would pass before anyone came looking for him."

"Terrell said something like that, too," Kipper said. "And when they were arguing, Griffin got angry, said his brothers hadn't come to help him. That they were trying to steal his glory."

"Oh, I bet that went down well." Adara sighed.

"It didn't," Kipper said. "That's why I figure I had to get out of there. If people started taking sides and Ring couldn't use his weapons . . . I haven't spent as much time in Leto's complex as the others, but enough that I figured those Dane seegnur had to have nastier weapons than our knives and bows. They might not kill Griffin, but they might show him they meant business by hurting someone else."

"You *are* quick," Adara said approvingly. "Have you had a chance to scout? Can we still get into Leto's complex?"

Kipper hung his head and looked ashamed. "I haven't. I was . . ." Adara expected him to make excuses about how busy he'd been, but the boy was honest. "I was scared. I didn't want to get caught. I figured I would be pretty useless to them, except to make Bruin do what they wanted."

Adara reached out and hugged him. "You're far from useless. I'll let dinner settle, then I'll do some scouting. There are four of us now. I can't talk to Honeychild any better than you can, but Sand Shadow can relay to her. That means even if I get caught, you'll know."

She saw Kipper stiffen. "I don't plan on getting caught, but we've got to plan for that. Now, Bruin and I have worked out some simple signs that our demiurges can use to relay information. They aren't much use in this situation—mostly meant for hunting—but let me show you them. That way, if Honeychild starts writing in the dirt with her claw you'll know what she's about."

Afterwards, Julyan was astonished at how quickly the situation changed from what had looked like a family reunion to him pacing a corridor along which three widely separated rooms had been converted into cells. He had no idea what the argument had been about since, soon after Alexander had said those seven syllables and Griffin had exploded into white fury, the Danes had shifted to their own language.

"Keep alert," the Old One warned him when they had a moment alone. "We know that Griffin Dane has resources we didn't anticipate last time he was our 'guest.'"

One of those resources was the mysterious girl-woman who called herself "Leto." Alexander had explained that this Leto was only a more elaborate version of the recording that had warned them about the intruder security systems, but Julyan wasn't buying that without more evidence. True, he hadn't seen her, only heard her, but from what he'd heard she had sounded like a real person, and one with a temper.

He'd been able to understand what Leto said, because apparently she didn't speak the Danes' language. As best as Julyan could gather, Leto had been created to serve the seegnur who used this complex. However, she still wasn't certain if the Dane brothers qualified as seegnur. She'd been on the way to accepting Griffin, but now she was uncertain again.

Alexander had apparently presented the best argument in favor when he demonstrated his ability to control the residents of Artemis. Julyan had served as his example of this and hadn't enjoyed it at all. He'd cooperated, though, because he didn't want Julyan to know about that little bit of wiggle room he'd created for himself. For now, he was more on the side of Alexander and the Old One than he was of Griffin, so cooperating was all for the best.

Leto, however, had gathered that Alexander was Griffin's full brother. This meant that anything that proved Alexander was seegnur also served to prove that Griffin was seegnur. Therefore, it was a case of which seegnur would dominate. That was one reason that Griffin was currently residing in one of the three rooms Julyan guarded. However, that had not been enough to convince Leto that the other Dane brothers were now in charge. Apparently, she had been scared by the slaughter of the seegnur and death of machines. In Leto's view, might did not automatically make right.

In fact, Julyan thought, *if they're not careful, Leto may decide that "might" means they're in the wrong. She may decide these newer Danes are just like the invaders who attacked her former masters. If she does that, I'd better make sure I know how to get out of here. She sounds like a brat, and I don't want to be at the mercy of a brat who controls the lights and the locks on the doors.*

Leto's control was why, even though Falkner had locked the rooms in which Griffin, Terrell, and Ring were imprisoned, Julyan patrolled the corridors with a newly issued nerve burner in his hand. Even though the nerve burners were the least lethal of the weapons the Danes had brought with them, Falkner warned Julyan that they could be deadly enough.

"I've got it set so that it'll knock someone out, not kill them," he said, "but that's only an estimate. Ring and Bruin carry a lot more weight than Terrell and Griffin. Then, too, a person's health plays a role, too. If someone has a weak heart, say, a charge that would knock out someone else of the same weight might kill him. I suggest you shoot only if you must and aim for a limb."

Another reason they were taking extra care was that Bruin had admitted that one of his students, a boy named Kipper, remained at large—as was Adara the Huntress, her demiurge, Sand Shadow, and Bruin's demiurge, Honeychild. The Dane brothers were inclined to dismiss a puma and a bear as players, but neither Julyan nor the Old One would make that mistake.

The Danes are pretty smart. They're not hunting down this Kipper because they know he'll inform Adara. The Old One has them convinced that she'll rush to the rescue. They want to bag her, and this Kipper's news is the bait.

He licked his lips and paced restlessly along the corridor. Alexander had reassured Julyan that he had not forgotten his promise.

Soon . . . Soon . . . I'll have you again, my willful lady. We'll show you where you fit into the scheme of things. I'll make sure you know your place . . .

Griffin tried to regret the things he'd said to his brothers. Surely if he'd been more prudent, more diplomatic, he wouldn't be locked up in this little room with nothing but sessions cleaning the spaveks to break the monotony. He tried to regret, but he couldn't—he was too damn pissed. When he was honest with himself, he had to admit that he was embarrassed as well. He thought he'd covered all traces of his research so carefully, given no indication of his plans. For his brothers to arrive within a few months of his departure must mean that his intentions had been discovered almost immediately.

Or worse, he thought, sinking down on the cot that was one of the room's few furnishings, *they knew all along and simply waited for me to get here and do the initial research, take the initial risks.*

A terrible suspicion grew to certainty in Griffin's mind. *The warbot that attacked back at Shepherd's Call . . . It wasn't some relic of the old wars. It was planted, probably built right into my shuttle. My crash is what damaged it.*

He surged to his feet, started pacing again. *If that's the case, then it would explain a lot—like how they found me, but why they didn't show up sooner. Maybe they had suspicions I'd located Artemis but no certainty as to where it was. They would've had to wait for beacons to lead them here. The* Howard Carter *might have been "bugged" as well. If I were them, I'd also have made sure the spider would release some antiviral nanobots into Artemis's system, so they could use their gear once they got here. Was the warbot also meant to kill me? That doesn't make sense. Maybe it was sufficiently damaged by my crash that it malfunctioned—a tracking program got out of control or something.*

The spider's attack left Griffin uneasy. His brothers could be ruthless, but surely they wouldn't want to kill him.

I'm going to need to get my brothers talking . . . learn what they're after, how much they suspected in advance. I certainly had no suspicion that Artemis was anything but the resort of legend. Would a resort interest Siegfried? Maybe, if he thought he would find relics from the final conflict here that he could turn to new uses. That would be enough for Falkner, too. And Alexander . . .

Griffin's uneasiness grew as he thought of his bronze-haired brother and the mockery in those shifting eyes. *Alexander has been playing*

*his own game . . . From the look on Falkner's face, he had no idea
that Alexander had found that ancient control sequence. Siegfried?
I don't know . . . I bet Alexander bragged about having something
up his sleeve. It would be like him. How did Alexander find it?*

Griffin stopped pacing, knowing that his real question was, "Why
didn't I find it?" He resisted admitting that Alexander might be better than him in his chosen area of expertise. He'd always thought of
Alexander as more interested in military history, rather than in the
complexities of Old Imperial culture.

*And what, moron, would be of greater military use than the abil-
ity to control your opponents? Alexander probably came across the
information in one of those old soldier's journals he loves. Does it
matter where he found it? Really matter except to your damn ego?
What matters is that Alexander can apparently make a few weirdly
inflected sounds and even strong-willed people like Bruin and Terrell
become obedient puppets.*

Griffin sagged back onto his bunk, remembering how after Alexander had given his command, Terrell and Bruin had both immediately answered any question put to them. At first their replies had
been clipped, hardly more than "yes" or "no," but when Alexander
added the injunction that they speak fully, even that resistance had
melted away. They actually seemed to enjoy briefing their enemies.

Ring had proven more of a difficulty, since his peculiar way of answering any question meant that most of his replies sounded like nonsense. He couldn't even answer most simple yes/no questions with a
single word. Alexander was becoming furious—much to Siegfried's
amusement—when the Old One had explained that he'd known Ring
since Ring's birth and that the man really was trying to answer clearly.

*I'd bet anything that Alexander tested this trick in advance. He
wouldn't have risked making a fool of himself. Not our Alex. I wonder which one he tried it on? Not the Old One. If Alexander had tried
his little gimmick on "Maxwell," surely he would have known more
of the Old One's secrets. The lad Seamus seems subnormal, hardly
a good subject. Probably Julyan, then. That would explain a few
things. From what both Bruin and Adara have said, Julyan was an*

arrogant type, not the sort to contentedly settle on guard duty. I won-
der how complete Alexander's control of his subjects is? I wonder how
far it extends? My impression was that the control sequence was
meant to be a safeguard against rebellion. Surely if a few words would
turn the natives of Artemis into obedient automata, then more would
have died during the final attack. Yet both our legends and Arteme-
sian lore hold that the majority of the population stood aside of the
conflict.

At this, Griffin felt curiously hopeful. Maybe the situation for his
friends was not as hopeless as it seemed. He hoped Bruin and Terrell
had the sense to hide any free will they retained. Surely, like him, they
would realize that escape would be most likely if the Dane brothers
thought the prisoners were safely under control.

"The Dane Brothers," Griffin thought. *When did I start thinking*
of them as something other than my own group? Was it when I re-
alized they'd been poaching my work or even before—when I decided
to hide my efforts even from my own family?

Is there a way I can communicate with Terrell or Bruin that will
not immediately be given away? All it would take was for Alexan-
der to order "Tell me what you and Griffin were talking about," and
they'd spill everything. I suppose the safest route would be to see if
Terrell and I can re-establish our mental link. Will he cooperate or
will he see me as one of the enemy now? He was already distrust-
ful. Will the arrival of my family make him even more guarded?

Griffin was still brooding when he heard the door to his cell being opened. Falkner stood without, looked tired and vaguely harassed.
He held a nerve burner loosely in one hand. Griffin wondered if he'd
been ill. Certainly, he didn't look as robust as usual.

"Come out, Griff. I want to talk with you about this complex, those
spaveks. I've tried talking to that Ring. I figured that since he'd actually managed to operate one, he'd be the most logical person to speak
with."

Griffin forced a grin. He'd always liked Falkner, even if he found
him a touch dull and mono-focused. " 'Logical' and Ring are not two
concepts I would use in the same sentence," he said, stepping out into

the corridor. He knew that Falkner wasn't about to come into the cell, just in case Griffin might grab him and try to use him as a hostage. "Actually, that's not fair. Ring is logical—in his own way. However, his logic is usually impenetrable until far after the fact."

Griffin thought about telling how poor Fred had ended up hung on a hickory tree, because it was the only way Ring could arrange factors so that the end result he wanted would develop. He decided against it. The more of a puzzle Ring remained, the better.

Falkner motioned for Griffin to follow him toward the labs. "Don't try anything, Griff. Julyan has orders to shoot you if you move wrong. I can't figure out why, but I think he'd love the excuse. Once we turn the corner, we're going to be where Siegfried can cover. Got it?"

Griffin didn't even bother to reply. War games and tactical setups had been what his family played, rather than the glow ball and aerial athletics that had been popular in other households. Although his father and mother had shifted focus by the time their last child was born, and so Griffin had been encouraged in different areas, he could not have missed how skilled his older siblings were when it came to kill or be killed.

Therefore, even when they rounded the corner and Griffin saw that Siegfried was apparently absorbed in schematics displayed on one of Leto's projection terminals, Griffin did not make the mistake of believing he could take advantage of being out of Julyan's range to make a go for Falkner. In any case, any such plan left out that Falkner was plenty dangerous in and of himself.

As Falkner led Griffin to the arena, Griffin saw the Old One at a table to one side reviewing the drawings Terrell had made. Alexander was nowhere to be seen—a fact that didn't make Griffin in the least more relaxed. Alexander out of sight was at least as dangerous as Alexander at hand. He wondered if Siegfried and Falkner realized this. Alexander was very charismatic if he wished to be and he usually reserved his nastier side for those who wouldn't be in a position to complain.

And he's only gotten better about hiding his kinks since we've grown up, Griffin thought.

For the next few hours, Griffin did his best to answer the questions Falkner put to him. He tried to use how he phrased his replies to send Leto the silent message that although these men were his brothers, they were not necessarily his friends. Whether or not he succeeded was impossible to judge. Leto remained mute, other than issuing warnings when someone was about to do something that might cause injury to the facility. Griffin noticed she did not seem to care whether they injured themselves.

Eventually, Falkner ran out of questions. He stood studying the blue spavek, which stood open on its squire.

"We saw Ring wearing this and using it at least well enough to move in it," he said. "And you say you've worn it."

"Once," Griffin repeated for the umpteenth time, "and only with limited success."

"Yet when I tried it on," Falkner said, tugging at an earlobe in obvious vexation, "I had no success activating it; neither did Siegfried, nor Alexander."

Griffin had suspected as much. His brothers were not timid. If one of them had been able to use the spavek, Griffin would not have been sitting here answering increasingly repetitious questions.

"There's no hope for it, then," Falkner said with a huge sigh. "You're going to have to put it on again. I wouldn't trust that Ring to be able to follow orders—not even with Alexander pulling his strings."

Griffin's heart raced as he remembered what had happened the last time he'd worn the blue spavek. He said hesitantly, "I wasn't very successful. If Ring hadn't been by to get me out . . ."

Falkner shook his head, dismissing the protest. "Different now. You've shown me where the emergency release is."

"You trust me wearing that thing?" Griffin said, moving as if to undo one of the bone buttons that held his shirt closed. "It *is* armor, Falkner."

"And we have hostages against your behaving badly." Alexander's voice came lazily from the door. Griffin had no idea how long he'd been listening. "You've always been soft that way, Griffin. I think a promise to burn off a finger or maybe a foot from one of your friends would keep you in line. And you know we'd keep our promise."

Falkner looked sorrowful. "We'd have to, Griffin. As you said, this armor is potentially dangerous. Although we need to test it, we need to do so with all possible safeguards."

Griffin shrugged. "Well, then, I'd better put the damn thing on. Otherwise Alexander might get overeager. We wouldn't want that, would we?"

Alexander smiled his warmest, most winning smile. "It wouldn't be me, Griffin. It would be you. You were informed in advance of the consequences of your actions."

Stripping off his clothes, Griffin started fitting himself into the blue spavek. Falkner moved so he could record the initial donning phase. As Griffin triggered the controls that would cause the spavek to activate, he heard Falkner saying, "Pity we can't see what's going on inside, but the shielding defies the scanners I have with me."

As the blue spavek went through its uncomfortable period of linking Griffin's organic form to its inorganic, Griffin hardly noticed. One thing he'd held back from Falkner was how his link to Terrell had been intensified after he had worn the suit. Since Griffin had never been noted for psionic ability, Falkner was operating on the theory that Griffin's ability to use the suit had something to do with the greater amount of time he'd been on Artemis, perhaps that he'd soaked something up from the environment that permitted the biomechanical linkage. Given what Griffin had learned about Artemis and her mycelium-based nervous system, this didn't sound as outlandish as it once might have done

Of course, Griffin had been careful not to volunteer anything about either his link with Terrell or about the planetary intelligence. As far as he could tell, his brothers had no inkling of either's existence. Keeping secrets soothed Griffin's bruised ego—as well as seeming very prudent.

"Griffin," Falkner called, raising his voice slightly, as if wearing the spavek would deaden Griffin's ability to hear. In reality, as far as Griffin could tell, his hearing was improved. "Let's start simple.

Detach yourself from the squire and move each of your limbs on my command."

As Griffin followed Falkner's commands—raising his right arm, then his left, flexing the elbow joints, and so on—he concentrated on finding the emotional pulse that was Terrell. Perhaps because this was his second time wearing the suit and he knew a bit more of what to expect, Griffin did not feel nearly as disoriented. He wondered if the suit had somehow stored information from their earlier contact and was now using it to adapt to another wearer.

That would make sense, Griffin thought. *If it connected to me expecting the oddity that is Ring, no wonder I got the willies. From how Ring spoke, I had been thinking of the suits as one-person items, but that doesn't make sense. The organic component would be very vulnerable. Perhaps there are more or less ideal wearers but, as long as certain basics are met, the suits can adapt.*

He was slowly jogging around the chamber, taking care to occasionally slip or weave erratically, so Falkner wouldn't realize that he was actually adapting better, when his searching mind found the pulse he had been seeking. This contact was not like the first contact, when he had been a prisoner. Those had begun as peculiar dreams and evolved into a sort of communication via image. Nor was it like the time he'd felt Terrell's emotions.

Perhaps because of the suit's enhancement, Griffin felt both Terrell's thoughts and his emotions. Astonishment, discomfort, then a raw joy that made Griffin stumble as he was caught in its intensity, so that he went down onto both armored knees and barely caught himself on his hands. Griffin felt washed in a shout of golden brilliance twisted through with earthy brown. He knew without knowing why that this was the equivalent of his name in the mental space that was Terrell.

Griffin didn't know what Terrell "saw" in return when Griffin shaped the other man's name in his head, but knew that each recognized the other without doubt or question.

Uncertain how much time they had, Griffin shaped his thoughts as cascades of images, hoping that his meaning would come across to

Terrell. He showed himself in the blue spavek, Falkner and Alexander standing by. He sent the revelation that something to do with the spavek permitted this stronger, more solid communication.

Terrell sent back a patchwork wash of thoughts and reactions. Pleasure that they could communicate. A summary of his own activities since they were imprisoned. He'd been questioned by both Alexander and the Old One. From this Griffin learned that Terrell could indeed resist Alexander's commands, at least to the extent of not volunteering more than he was asked. Resisting even to this extent was painful. Cooperation, by contrast, resulted in a wash of contentment and satisfaction more seductive than mere pleasure.

There was something else there, something Terrell was quick to hide, but if hatred had a taste, Terrell hated Alexander.

Terrell's initial report was followed by images of Griffin tearing through the complex, releasing Terrell and Bruin. (And, incidentally, stomping on Julyan in the process.) This part was colored with a pale green that made it into a question. More questions. Did Griffin know where Adara was? Kipper?

Griffin sent images of how Terrell and Bruin would be used if he employed the spavek to resist. He felt Terrell's instinctive fear, followed by his assertion of willingness to risk injury if taking such a risk would win them their freedom. Griffin accepted this, but knew Terrell would also feel Griffin's reluctance to take such a risk unless he was fairly certain of success.

As to the fates of Adara and Kipper, Griffin could only send a blank.

Even with whatever enhancement the spavek was offering, Griffin found continuing his communication with Terrell while operating the spavek difficult. Vaguely, he became aware that he was crashing into the walls, levitating a few feet, then falling flat. He heard Alexander's laughter, Falkner's shouts of alarm—although something cynical in Griffin knew those shouts were more for fear the artifact would be damaged than for Griffin himself. At last he felt a slap in the vicinity of his chest, a mustard yellow shock that felt like cold water wrapping around his heart. Then the sense of Terrell in his head dimmed to a wash of sensation, waves lapping a distant shore. The spavek went into standby mode and Griffin was left hanging, his torso suspended by the joint covers, his head held upright by the edges of the helmet.

"Gee," he said weakly, managing a sickly smile. "That was fun."

Still smiling, Griffin fell slightly forward, still in the suit's grasp, and puked all over the two men standing in front of him.

Sand Shadow and Honeychild joined Adara soon after full dark had fallen. From the bear, Adara learned that only one of Griffin's brothers had even bothered to poke his head out into the valley. Comparing the relayed image to the descriptions Kipper had given her, Adara decided this must have been Alexander. She tried to remember what Griffin had said about him, and realized that he hadn't said much about any of his nine siblings. Occasionally, he'd mention that someone had taught him something but, not even when they'd been visiting with her family and such talk would have been natural, had he said much.

Terrell also didn't talk much about his family but, in his case, that was natural. Like Adara, he had left home to begin his training very young, for his quick mind had been quickly recognized, and each generation of his family liked to supply at least one factotum in honor of the family's heritage. Terrell did talk about his teachers and the classmates who had been like brothers and sisters to him. He'd even mentioned that his parents were alive and would dance at his wedding . . .

She shoved such thoughts from her mind, knowing she was letting herself be distracted because Alexander frightened her. She had no doubt that Kipper was telling the truth when he said that Alexander had the power to control the people of Artemis. Such commands were included in lore and legend—and stories both bawdy and grim had grown up around the motif of what happened when a proud young woman met a seegnur with the power to command. Even if these seegnur were not interested in such games with an Artemesian, Adara knew one member of their company at least would love to play out the old tales.

Honeychild had not found Julyan's scent any deeper into the vale of Maiden's Tear than a few paces from the door in the rock wall, but the bear's finding confirmed Adara's guess that the Artemesian man whose name Kipper had not known had been Julyan. That only left the curiously slack-faced boy unidentified, but Adara had her guesses. The Old One had been breeding highly adapted children for many years now. It was quite possible that a few had been stashed elsewhere than Mender's Isle. The Old One was not the sort to put all his eggs in one basket. Adara guessed that this boy had been one such and that the Old One had reclaimed him when all else went to ruin.

She put supposition from her mind and focused on what was before them. First, she needed to find out if the ways into Leto remained open. Even if the doors were open, would Leto let her enter or give her away? How to find out? Adara had the distinct impression that Leto did not like her. Yet, Leto did like Griffin and these new arrivals had taken him prisoner. Might Leto be willing to view Adara along the lines of the enemy of my enemy is, if not my friend, at least my ally?

There was only one way to find out and that was risky. It meant that Adara had to put herself where Leto could "see" her—and where Leto might choose to betray her.

"My choices are limited," Adara explained to Sand Shadow. "It's either risking Leto or leaving the others prisoner and hoping they get themselves out. I can't even wait for the group to leave the complex, because there's no guarantee they ever will. Kipper said the Danes arrived through an underground tunnel. It's likely they'll leave that way, even bring in supplies that way."

Sand Shadow may not have understood all the words, but she gathered enough to send Adara a question. It took the form of a strange creature—a graceful young woman who, at the same time, looked as if she'd burst from the ground like an elf-cap mushroom. Adara knew who the puma meant. Even as she marveled at the merging of images, she was shaking her head.

"Artemis? What can she do? She cannot see into Leto. I'm not sure if Leto knows Artemis exists but, if she does, I have a feeling that knowing we know Artemis isn't going to make Leto like us any better."

A querulous me-rowl expressed Sand Shadow's doubt in Adara's conclusion. Clearly the puma felt that Artemis would be an advantage in this situation.

Adara tried to find a way to explain. "If Leto was created first—as Terrell seems to think—then she's going to think Artemis should be serving her. We know Artemis won't do that. The very thought of Leto puts Artemis into a panic. Best we leave this for another time."

Sand Shadow rolled over, waving her paws in the air in mock surrender. Adara gave her belly fur a vigorous rub.

"Thanks. Now, how best to visit Leto without putting ourselves at risk?"

After considering various plans, Adara came up with one that she was willing to try. Thus far they had no evidence that Leto had any mobile units—not even to the extent that Artemis had her various fungi. Therefore, if Leto called help, that help would be human.

"We'll rig a deadfall over the door," Adara said, "so that if she does call someone, we can slow them down while we get away."

Sand Shadow sent an image of her paw, claws spread wide, making bloody ruin of an anonymous human threat.

"No. We don't want to go that far. We might need any one of them—even Julyan or the Old One. Worse, if Alexander does control our friends, one of them might be sent out to 'negotiate' with us. Best we set up something less lethal."

Sand Shadow wasn't completely satisfied, but when she saw the elaborate deadfall Adara had in mind, she agreed. Like most cats, she had a distinct sense of humor and leaving a human—especially one armed with powerful weapons such as the blue spavek had possessed—incommoded while they fled caught her fancy.

As Adara rigged a heavy net Bruin had brought in his gear, pots of various nasty-smelling liquids meant to stop anyone from tracking them by scent, and a few other little gimmicks into a bundle she could easily move, she hoped she wouldn't need any of this. She'd seen the gouts of lightning Ring had shot from the blue spavek.

Still, she thought, *we have to take a chance. Let's learn if Leto's willing to talk. If not, we may not be able to set our friends free.*

Interlude: Solution

To
    Possession
    Domination
    and
    Repression

What Reaction?
    Condemnation
    Retaliation

In What Fashion?
    Execution?

Later, maybe,
    First, Prevention

Could There Be Any Objection?

15

New Arrival

Julyan was losing track of how long they had been in Leto's complex. Without the passage of the sun through the sky, the feeling of free air on his skin, the slow wheel of the stars as they turned against the blackness of the night, he felt uneasy. He knew he had slept, eaten meals, made trips to the privy, washed, and done other chores that must have taken up time, but some other part of his mind told him that no time—or an infinity of time—had passed.

The food didn't help, being monotonously similar, taken from supplies the Dane brothers had carried with them. At first those little cubes that expanded into a variety of intensely flavored edibles had fascinated Julyan, but now he was growing to hate them. Each yellow cube tasted exactly like every other yellow cube, every blue cube like every other blue cube. The predictability was numbing, especially for a hunter, who was accustomed to eating according to the finds of the day. Even one cut of venison didn't taste like all the rest, and there was variety from deer to deer, gazelle to gazelle, kudu to kudu.

The Old One ignored Julyan most of the time, as did Siegfried and Falkner, except when they reluctantly came to relieve him on some watch. Alexander was a more frequent visitor, but even his torments had a certain sameness to them, as if his thoughts were elsewhere.

A few times, Julyan suggested he go out into the valley of Maiden's Tear to hunt or forage. No one took him seriously. They had food and drink enough. If they needed more, a message to the mysterious Gaius would supply it. Julyan's initial fear that the Danes would decide to use him to test one of the spaveks became a sort of longing—at least being a test subject would be different.

However, following Griffin's dramatic collapse, experiments with the spaveks were halted while Falkner compared what schematics Leto would supply to the actual suits. When Falkner could tear himself away from these, he cross-examined Griffin. He even tried discussing the spaveks with Ring but, if anything, Alexander's command that Ring cooperate had made Ring harder to understand than usual.

Julyan understood that several more suits had been pulled apart and were being inspected. He had no part in this. His prisoners were kept busy by being given a section of a spavek and told to clean it carefully, with nameless but dire consequences promised if anything was damaged. Despite the threats, when the prisoners worked on the spaveks they were stationed at a long table where they could be watched.

Julyan was told to keep chatter to a minimum and to make sure the prisoners treated the artifacts with respect. He didn't think they would break anything—not deliberately, at least. These Dane brothers didn't understand the respect for artifacts the loremasters had ingrained into the people of Artemis. Julyan was glad when the prisoners were put to work. Even if he didn't get to do anything, watching them work was better than standing alone in the corridor.

As minutes grew into hours, hours into days, Julyan's soul congealed into a semblance of contented routine within which was encapsulated a festering mass of insanity. Since he was not permitted to hate Alexander, Julyan's thwarted desires came to focus on those he blamed for failing to come and break the monotony of his existence. He envisioned amber eyes, blue-black tresses, a catlike tread . . .

Adara would come. She must come. She had been promised to him. He must have her. When he did, all would be right. Surely when Adara was his, Alexander would finally let Julyan kill Griffin. These dreams became the dark twin stars around which his galaxy swirled.

Griffin used the intensification of his link to Terrell to assure his friend that no matter what his brothers wanted, Griffin would never agree

to work with them, especially if this meant having Old Empire technology released upon an unsuspecting universe. Additionally, Griffin
warned Terrell to do his best to deny that he had any psionic ability.
The legend of the factotum's abilities was hardly known, even on
Artemis. It was possible that Terrell might be able to pass as unable to
operate one of the suits. Even after their waking contact faded, a
touch in sleep remained. Griffin desperately needed that anchor as his
nerves settled from the riot of confusion wrought upon it by his intense contact with the blue spavek.

When Falkner came to debrief him, Griffin steered a careful course
between resisting and being too cooperative. Resisting would probably lead to him not being permitted to associate with the other prisoners. However, if he was too cooperative that might awaken suspicion,
if not in Falkner or Siegfried, then certainly in Alexander. Therefore,
Griffin allowed Falkner to coax him into talking, acting flattered that
his older brother—the acknowledged expert on things mechanical in
the Dane family—would ask his opinion.

Griffin wanted to share some of his experiences, if only to protect
his friends from being used as test subjects without appropriate precautions. Griffin let Falkner know his suspicion that the suits needed
time to adapt to each wearer. He also explained that different suits
might mesh better with different talents—and that Ring's advice in
this matter should not be ignored.

"What do you make of Ring?" Falkner asked again, during one
of these cross-examination sessions. "You say he was the first to try
one of the suits, that he even selected the blue one from all the rest.
How could he manage that? He can barely frame a coherent sentence."

"I'd ask the Old One what he bred Ring for," Griffin evaded. Whenever possible, he tried to put pressure on the Old One, never letting
his brothers forget that their obedient "Maxwell" had an agenda of
his own. "He had stud books going back at least a couple generations,
probably notes based on his research."

"I have asked," Falkner said. "Maxwell says that Ring was a mistake. He'd been trying for clairvoyance, and ended up with something
more like unreliable precognition. Ring was a dead end, useless even

as breeding stock. When he got away, Maxwell says he didn't look too hard. He admitted he thought Ring was probably dead within a day or two of leaving his protection."

"And you don't find that cold?"

"How I do or don't find Maxwell isn't the point. He's useful. His studies in the lore, combined with a fine sense for history, has given him insights we can use."

"If the lore is what interests you," Griffin said, "you should speak with Terrell. Factotum get a very solid grounding in the lore. You could use what Terrell was taught to corroborate what the Old One tells you."

Falkner laughed. "Maxwell made a similar suggestion. He knows you have undermined our trust in him and is eager to win it back."

If Falkner was enjoying himself, Siegfried had been heard to complain that he felt like the prince in the fairy tale who was told to sort grains of corn from equal-sized pieces of gold, except that he didn't even know what was corn, what was gold. He would have liked to take everything back home, but that was impossible. As to what Alexander wanted, Griffin had no idea. Indeed, his only hint as to what Alexander did with his time came in the form of Terrell's nightmares.

Griffin had tried to communicate with Leto but, since the prisoners were forbidden to speak when they were in their cells and Julyan had proven incredibly adept at hearing anything but the softest utterance, he hadn't had any luck. Griffin didn't know if Leto was ignoring him or if her audio pickups had been set to ignore sounds below a certain level. Either explanation was plausible. From what he'd overheard, he had gathered that Leto was being minimally cooperative with the Danes. Perhaps that lack of cooperation extended to him as well.

Then, during one of their armor cleaning sessions, Bruin passed on a scrap of news that made Griffin's soul sing a chorus of mingled hope and fear.

Taking advantage of a blind spot created by the heaped parts, Bruin dipped his finger into his glass of water and drew a quick sketch on the table. A cat's head, a woman's body. A bear. A long-bodied cat.

"Give that polish *here*," he said, tapping one finger for emphasis. "I want to get this scuff *out*, but I need to figure out *how* the polish will work."

That Terrell also understood Bruin's message that Adara had returned and was trying to figure out how to free them was evident from the joy that lit his shadowed eyes.

Terrell shoved the jar of polish to Bruin. "Careful. It would be terrible if something was damaged."

Bruin nodded. "I couldn't *bear* that. I don't need you to *tell* me to *be careful*."

Griffin nodded. "I second that. Don't try anything if you're not sure."

"I can't promise," Bruin said. "But I'll try."

Griffin interpreted the stressed words. "Bear tell be careful." That confirmed that Bruin was getting his news through Honeychild, also that he'd passed on their desire that the others not act until they felt certain of success.

Why don't I feel happier about this? Griffin asked himself. *I should be thrilled, looking for ways to find information that Bruin can pass on. Instead I feel so frustrated, so angry. Am I afraid for Adara? For the risks she and the others must take?*

As he dipped polish onto a tiny brush and brightened some contact points, the truth hit him with such abrupt force that he nearly dropped the piece of armor he was holding.

It's fear, yes, but more . . . I'm frustrated at having to be rescued—again. I don't want to be rescued. I want to get myself and the others out of here on my own . . . I want to retake this facility and show my brothers I'm not some worthless kid.

And I'm realizing that in feeling that way, I'm letting my pride get in the way. I'm proving just how much a kid I am.

Adara felt a certain amount of hope as she crept through the maze of rock that hid the meadow door. She knew Leto's perceptions extended to the area surrounding the entrances into the valley and for some short distance into the valley itself. Although Leto didn't seem to feel proprietary about the valley in the same way she did the complex, Adara hoped it was significant that Leto hadn't called guards out after them when Adara and Sand Shadow had rigged their deadfall and a few other traps. Nonetheless, the huntress waited for the slight advantage full dark gave her before making her approach. The curved shape of the crystal key hung on a cord about her neck, but she didn't need it. The door opened to her touch.

"Leto?" Adara whispered, her voice soft in contrast to the pounding of her heart.

No response. Adara took a step inside, then wedged a short, thick log to keep the door open. She didn't know if this would work—perhaps a door made by seegnur could close with sufficient force to break even the stout chunk she'd used—but she felt better for the effort. She'd have to hope that the night remained summer still, so that motion in the air wouldn't alert the lab's occupants that someone had opened a door.

As she padded silently down the corridor, Adara's mind swirled with what she'd learned from Kipper about how a few syllables from Alexander Dane had turned Terrell, Bruin, and Ring instantly obedient. She was terrified that the same might be done to her. Only her greater terror as to what might be happening to her friends had brought her to this place.

"Leto?" A few more steps, straining to listen. Had the corridor always been so long? It hadn't seemed so when she had freely passed along it, intent on her destination. "Leto?"

In the far distance, Adara's keen hearing caught sound: a person moving about or a bit of deep-voiced conversation. It might even have been some sort of machinery at work. She couldn't go much closer to the lab without risking discovery.

"Leto?"

She paused, hesitant as to whether to risk a few more steps, when a little girl's voice whispered, "Why are you here?"

Adara's heart leapt. She had to fight down an urge to yelp in panic. Disembodied voices were not something she had grown accustomed to.

An image in her head. Sand Shadow sending a detailed picture of a talking toadstool.

All right. So how is this different from voices in my head? Courage, Adara. Didn't you come here to talk to Leto?

The huntress registered for the first time that Leto had been whispering. Surely that was encouraging. If she had meant to turn Adara over to the Dane brothers, why whisper? That didn't mean Adara was safe. It meant she had a chance to win an ally.

"I came," Adara replied, every nerve wildly alert, "to learn if you would help me free Griffin, Terrell, Bruin, and Ring. I know they're prisoners."

"Why should I help you?" Leto sounded petulant. "I don't like you."

"But you like Griffin," Adara said. She eased herself a few feet closer to the exit. "I thought you liked Terrell and Ring, too. Kipper says you didn't mind Bruin experimenting with one of the spaveks."

"That's true . . ." The voice remained childish. "I do like *them*."

The stress on the final word was meant to sting. Adara was embarrassed that it did. Why should she care if a person who might not even be a person liked her or not?

Think about Terrell and Griffin and Bruin and poor Ring . . .

"And are they happy as they are now?"

"Sometimes Terrell and Bruin are quite happy," lilted the childish voice, "especially when Alexander tells them to be but, no, I don't think that any of them are really, truly happy."

"I want to set them free," Adara said. "Will you help them?"

"Well . . ." Leto's voice stretched the one short syllable into two very long ones. "If I set them free, they'll go away and I'll be all alone again."

"Do you really think the newcomers mean to stay?" Adara asked. "And when they go, do you think they'll leave Griffin and the rest?"

"No . . ." Leto paused thoughtfully. "I don't think they *do* mean to stay. That Siegfried has been in contact with a Gaius. They talk about what they can move. But I don't think they're going for a long time, yet. They want to figure out the spaveks. I've been hiding the research files. I was going to show the files to Griffin, but I won't show them! I don't like them."

She sounded triumphant, like a child who has secreted away a torn frock and expects to escape punishment.

Adara shook her head as she might have at one of Bruin's younger students caught cheating. Then she remembered that it was possible Leto couldn't see her.

"Do you think you can hide forever and ever? These off-worlders have some funny ideas. What if they figure out a way to control you like they can control Terrell and Bruin? I bet there's a way . . ."

Adara was guessing, but thought she must be right. The seegnur would not have left themselves without a way to get around Leto, especially if she had been as stubborn with them. The length of Leto's pause made Adara think she was right, especially when Leto didn't directly answer her question.

"That Falkner has been poking in my private areas," Leto said primly. "I shocked him once, but he's persistent. He has no respect."

Fleetingly, Adara thought it was interesting how—for lack of a better word—"human" Leto seemed, especially in contrast to Artemis. Especially here in the dark, she could forget she was talking to a building or burrow or whatever this complex was, and think she was talking to an intelligent, if rather spoiled, child. She never made that mistake with Artemis.

Adara forced herself to focus, knowing she had to push the point. "So, will you set Griffin and the others free? I bet they'd help you to get rid of those others . . ."

Leto made a hissing sound. "The others have real weapons. They have defensive shields. Their machines aren't models I know, so I can't deactivate them—though I think I could damp them, some. But how could any of you—even Griffin—defeat them with your knives and bows?"

Based on what she'd heard about the spaveks, Adara had some idea of what Leto meant by "real" weapons and energy shields. They were terrifying, but she felt confident that they could be gotten around.

"These are still humans," Adara said, "and that means they can be defeated. Will you help us?"

Only the persistence of a faint hissing let Adara know that Leto hadn't "left." At long last, the voice spoke, sounding very young and childlike indeed.

"I can't risk helping. What if you lose? Then they'll be after me, too, and you'll all be dead and not able to help me."

That actually made sense. Adara didn't blame Leto for being afraid. She'd seen how horribly damaged Leto's complex had been. As with Artemis, the events of five hundred years ago were as fresh as yesterday.

"How about this, Leto?" Adara offered. "You don't help us, but you don't help them either. You don't lock anything extra. You don't offer warnings. You don't turn out the lights or stop the air circulating."

"What if they guess?"

"Tell them that their poking around messed something up so you couldn't sense as you usually can."

"I could do that . . ." Leto's voice held a note of malice. "I haven't been talking to them much anyhow. They act as if they can order me around like I'm no smarter than one of their scooters."

"So get quieter," Adara suggested. "If they do talk to you and you feel you need to answer, act dumb. Don't do anything that could be taken as acting against them—you're right, that's too much risk for you to take. Just don't help them."

"Or you," Leto said. "I still don't like you, much, though maybe I do a little better than before. Do you think that if you get Griffin free he'll come back?"

Adara laughed soundlessly, the way Sand Shadow laughed. "Oh, I think nothing will keep him away. Maybe once he's free to move around, he'll find a way to beat his brothers and take control."

But, remembering Leto's words about real weapons and energy shields, remembering that Terrell, Bruin, and Ring could not be counted on to act of their own accord—and might even turn against Griffin— she thought this was a very thin chance indeed.

Julyan was half-dozing at his post when he heard Falkner and Siegfried coming along the corridor. After they'd been in the complex a few days, the Danes had decided that sleeping in the labs and manufacturing areas was unnecessary hardship. Instead, they'd adopted quarters in the residential areas. Leto had made this easier by supplying running water and sanitary facilities. She'd even gotten a machine that did laundry working, so they all had fresh bedding and towels.

The prisoners were being kept at the outer edge of the residential area, in rooms that Alexander speculated might have been offices or parlors, rather than living quarters. The original furnishings in these rooms had been reduced to ash so, until someone figured out how to make Leto give them detailed facility plans, the rooms' original purpose was a matter of guesswork.

The Dane brothers had chosen suites of rooms, each with enough space to accommodate an entire family where Julyan had been born. He wondered if the Artemesians of olden days had realized that the approved home designs had been deliberately quaint, rather than meant for the comfort of the residents. He wondered if they would have cared.

Siegfried and Falkner were deeply absorbed in their conversation—it sounded as if it was on the verge of becoming an argument—and had forgotten that their voices would carry to where Julyan sat.

They probably don't care. The prisoners are locked up and sound doesn't carry into their cells unless the door is open. Me? I'm just good old Julyan, faithful retainer, and Alexander's little pet.

He ground his teeth, but his frustration didn't keep him from listening carefully. Anything that could get Falkner and Siegfried sounding so agitated was worth noting.

"I still think it's too soon," Falkner was saying. "We have only the slightest idea of how those suits work. The one thing we do know—and I don't think Griffin is lying about this—is that they play tricks with the wearer's mind. Castor is unstable enough without that."

Siegfried retorted, "Castor is unstable, I give you that, but he is also the only one of us we know is definitely, absolutely, without a doubt psychic. That makes him the best candidate to try one of the suits. We cannot trust the natives. We can, however, trust Castor."

"True . . ." Falkner's voice was fading with distance. "But why now? Why not wait a few weeks? We have plenty of supplies. There's no rush, and Castor's in the sleep. Once we wake him, we won't be able to put him down again for months. You know he doesn't handle the sleep drugs well."

"We brought him," Siegfried said, "because of the theories that Old Imperial technology relied on psionics. Using him might be a short-cut to what we want to know."

Their voices were so faint that Julyan couldn't make out the words, but from the inflection he guessed that Falkner was asking once again why this need for rush.

Julyan laughed to himself. The need for rush was exactly what made Siegfried the leader of the Dane brothers. He was a man of action and decision. This was useful in combat, but could be a handicap in times like this. Julyan suspected that Siegfried could be perfectly patient if working toward a specific goal—say during a siege or during the early phases of an elaborate attack—but the unspecificity of their current action was making him restless.

Julyan considered what he'd overheard. The only good thing about Alexander was that he liked to talk. From his monologues, Julyan had gathered that each of the Dane brothers was special in some way. Sometimes Alexander talked about himself and his siblings as if his parents had bred them like the Trainers did dogs, seeking for certain qualities to fill certain needs. The Dane brothers and sisters had been educated to bring out specific qualities as well.

Julyan gathered that the older Dane siblings had been trained to fulfill military roles. He was less certain about what the parents had intended for Griffin or even Alexander. They were more scholarly, though, as Julyan had learned to his detriment, even introspective Griffin could fight very well if pressed.

Alexander rarely mentioned Castor. He had said that Castor had been a twin, that Castor's twin, Pollux, was the only one of the Dane siblings to have died.

A fairly remarkable thing, Julyan thought. *Given the sort of lives they lead.*

He smiled slowly. *Maybe we of Artemis will take down a couple of them. I'd love to see their expression when they realize that what*

they took for worms are actually vipers—vipers with very sharp
fangs and very deadly poison, indeed.

When Alexander came to the door of Griffin's cell, Griffin was flat on
his back, reading from a hard copy book of verse that had been brought
to him along with his midday meal by the very odd boy called Seamus. Seamus had apparently been given the job of general housekeeper
and cook—if the term "cook" could be applied to doling out ration
cubes and hot water for rehydration.

The verse was handwritten in the language of Artemis, but Griffin had yet to decide whether it had been written by an Artemesian
or by one of the off-world residents of the facility. The subjects were
bucolic and not very challenging. Nonetheless, piecing through them
beat staring at the ceiling.

"Griffin! I have a surprise for you," Alexander sang out as he
opened the door. "Come along. He's waiting in the labs."

Griffin put down the book and swung his feet to the floor. He tried
to look slightly interested—something that was easier than it might
have been, since Alexander had said "he." That meant Adara and Sand
Shadow remained at large. It was too bad that Kipper had been
caught—he couldn't think what else would awaken that particular
look of malicious glee in Alexander's eyes—but so far the prisoners
had been treated well enough.

He was trying to decide which response would get the most out
of Alexander, and had just about concluded that a mixture of astonishment and anger would certainly cause Alexander to start gloating,
when they entered the main lab. There Griffin saw his brother Castor standing next to one of the consoles, looking about, an expression
of mild interest on his thin features as he munched on a food cube.

Castor was only of average height, though so thin that he looked
taller. His hair was such a brilliant orange that no one believed that
the color was natural. His eyes were an equally impossible green: the
wet, brilliant hue of melted peridots. The slight lump that showed on his
chest under his coverall was a device that fed him highly concentrated

calories. When Castor shifted to stuff the last of the food cube into his mouth so that he could offer a hand to Griffin, a tattoo beneath his floppy bangs was revealed. In the minimalistic script used for scientific notation in the Kyley Domain were the characters that spelled his name.

This had been viewed as necessary because, unlikely as it might seem, given Castor's appearance, once there had been two identical versions of him. Their parents had intended to have the tattoos erased when the boys were adults, but somehow no one had gotten around to it. When Pollux had died in an accident, the precise details of which Griffin still didn't know, Castor's grief had taken the form of the purest denial.

The twins were named for figures in a myth so ancient that it likely would have been lost, except that the names had been used for everything from constellations to a type of racing bike. In the myth, one twin was mortal, the other immortal. As Castor explained to anyone who would listen—and to many who did not—Pollux was the immortal twin. Therefore, Pollux could not be dead; therefore the tattooed name was still necessary.

Griffin did not know Castor well. Castor and Pollux had been fourth and fifth in the birth order—actually, they'd been "born" simultaneously, since their gestation had been within an artificial womb. Moreover, they had been raised in very controlled circumstances, meant to encourage them to develop the traits for which they had been bred.

Those early tests had been very promising. The theories that telepathy was more likely to develop between identical twins seemed to have some basis in truth. But when Pollux had died, Castor's abilities had vanished. Castor himself had nearly died, until he became convinced that Pollux still lived.

Now Griffin knew why Castor was here.

I was innocently searching for a mythical paradise with no greater goal than being able to say "Here it is!" It seems that others had far more complex motivations. Were Castor and Pollux created for the same reasons that the Old One—in a much cruder fashion—

sought to breed the adapted back to some creature that could inter-
face with the devices of the seegnur?

Griffin felt his skin crawl and the hairs along the back of his neck
prickle. If so, the plans had been in place since long before his birth.
Was his quest even of his own doing, as he had always imagined, or
had he been steered to it as his brothers and sisters had been steered
to their own professions?

Did our parents know or did they merely suspect, hope, dream?
What lay at the end of those dreams?

He feared he knew, for the Danes had always been a warlike clan.

Griffin decided that playing dumb would do him no good. As he
grasped Castor's proffered hand, feeling it just a little damp as it always was, he shaped his lips into a rueful smile.

"So they've brought their own test subject in," he said, watching
carefully to see how Castor would react.

Alexander intervened before Griffin could say anything more.
"We've brought Castor down because we believe that we might have
something he and Pollux have long desired. Come along."

As he led the way to the bunker where the spaveks waited in the
arms of their squires, Alexander expanded on his theory. "Ever since
the accident, Pollux has been short a body. It occurred to me that if Castor put on one of the spaveks, Pollux might be able to—well, slide in—
make himself at home."

Griffin frowned. He remembered how the spavek had felt as if it
had an intelligence of its own and guessed what Alexander was doing. He was trying to condition Castor so that when Castor put on
the suit he would come to the conclusion that the suit's operating system was actually his long-lost brother. If he did so, then his psi powers—
rumored to be quite potent—should become active once more, because
he would be communicating with his lost twin.

The idea was diabolically clever—just the sort of thing Alexander
would think of. Griffin knew their parents had tried to get Castor to
interact with other proven psi talents, but the experiments had not
worked because Castor was convinced that he and Pollux were more
than simply twins; they were two parts of the same soul.

Alexander's offering Castor back his soul, Griffin thought in despair. *If this works, then they'll be able to manipulate Castor. He'll do anything to keep his contact with Pollux. Up until now we've had a slight edge because we're the only ones who have had any luck working the spaveks. If Alexander's plan works, we will be increasingly expendable.*

Kipper listened intently as Adara reported her meeting with Leto. When she finished, he shifted uneasily. "That's good, I guess. But Leto's not working against us is not the same as her working *for* us, if you know what I mean."

Adara nodded gently, trying to adopt the posture Bruin always took when encouraging his young charges to speak out. It seemed to work because, after a moment, Kipper continued.

"There's just you and me, Sand Shadow and Honeychild. I don't think we can count the horses and Sam the Mule."

"That's not precisely true," Adara said. "Sam is proving a remarkably reliable guardian for our little horse herd. That means we don't need to waste one of us standing guard. Perhaps it will help us plan if we enumerate our other advantages, just as we would if planning a hunt."

Kipper looked dubious, so Adara started. "First, Sand Shadow and my bond means that we have communication over distance. We don't have the same direct contact with Honeychild but, between her ability to talk to Sand Shadow and those written signs I taught you, we can do pretty well. Now, your turn."

Clearly Kipper still had his doubts, but he also didn't want to disappoint her. After a few moments' thought he said, "Honeychild can communicate with Bruin. That means we can let them know when we're coming for them."

"We can do more than that," Adara added. "We might be able to work out a way to coordinate so that we can take advantage of some particular event—say when Ring is wearing the blue spavek or at least when they're all out of their cells."

"That would be nice," Kipper agreed. "My turn again. How about this? We know something of the layout of Leto's complex and can plan our attack to come from a couple different directions. There's the door into the meadow and the hidden one into that cavern. If Leto keeps her promise not to interfere, we might be able to lure them one way while our strength goes in another."

Adara nodded approval. "Now you're thinking like a hunter! If foxes can come up with ways to lay a false trail, surely we can do the same. I wish I could have gotten Leto to work with us. She would have been very useful that way, but that's beyond us."

Kipper beamed. "Foxes and false trails . . . What else? Wolves never go after the whole herd, they cut off their prey from the larger group. We might be able to manage something like that. There aren't all that many of them: Griffin's three brothers, the Old One, a boy, and that Julyan."

"Four brothers, now," Adara reminded him. "I think . . . I'm still trying to work out what Honeychild and Sand Shadow were saying. I'm certain there's a new arrival but, after that, it's uncertain. It's as if Bruin can't figure out how much of a threat this new fellow—he has red hair, so we'll call him 'Red'—will be."

"Brothers don't always get along," Kipper said in a way that made Adara certain he was speaking from experience. "Maybe this Red won't like that the others locked Griffin up."

"We can hope," Adara agreed. "There is one problem, though, one we need to deal with before we go in."

"What?" Kipper asked. His face fell as he remembered. "That Alexander and his ability to make the others do what he wants."

Adara nodded. "That's right. Until we figure out a way to protect ourselves and the others we'd be as good as committing suicide."

Interlude: Contrasts

We died
Then came resurrection
    Given a second chance

She bides
Craving sure protection
    Viewing risk askance

I decide
To choose action
    Is this arrogance?

16

Reconfiguration

After only a few days, Julyan decided that Castor Dane was the most terrifying Dane brother yet. He'd thought nothing could frighten him more than Alexander's streak of barely concealed cruelty. That was before he confronted Castor's peculiar version of insanity.

During his time with the Old One, Julyan had encountered a fair number of crazies. Weirdness seemed to go with breeding for the sort of traits the Old One wanted. Ring was one example, Seamus another. However, in all the Old One's stable of weirdees, Julyan had never encountered someone who firmly believed he carried his dead brother around in his head.

As long as Castor wasn't challenged on that point, he was an amiable enough individual. He ate constantly, true, and wasn't always very tidy about his crumbs, but he was the first Dane brother to volunteer for a turn on guard duty. It was during one of these times Julyan witnessed the level of Castor's delusion.

Julyan was coming on watch, a bit more tired than usual. Following a frustrating day, Alexander had decided to work off his stress in Julyan's company. Perhaps as a sort of apology for leaving Julyan short of sleep, Alexander walked Julyan to his post, promising to bring him some of the spicy, bright blue drink that Falkner liked, because it let him skip sleeping when he was obsessively pursuing some bit of research.

"A mug of it will set you right in no time," Alexander assured

Julyan. "I don't recommend you drink it in the quantities Falkner does, though. That would probably send you into cardiac arrest."

Castor rose and stretched when he heard their voices.

Alexander sang out in greeting. "Here's your relief, brother mine. Have too dull a time of it?"

Castor gave Alexander a pitying look. "I am never bored. Pollux and I played Go/Went. He won. He almost always does. Still, I gave him a good game. Didn't I?"

Alexander blinked. "Did you?"

"I wasn't talking to you, Alexander. I was talking to Pollux."

Castor's reproof was very much that of older sibling to younger. Alexander didn't like being spoken to that way—especially in front of Julyan. Siegfried and Falkner treated Alexander as an integral member of their team. Castor, however, didn't hide that he thought Alexander was extraneous. Julyan had heard him ask Siegfried why he'd brought Alexander along, since they had been seeking Griffin, and Griffin was as good or better in matters of Artemesian history.

Alexander had overheard, and his scowl promised no good for anyone who crossed his path that day. On the other hand, if Castor thought Alexander was useless, Alexander regarded Castor much as the Old One did Seamus—an inferior, to be tolerated because he had some unique qualities.

Now Pollux's name hung on the air. Castor's whip-thin body was tight, ready for a challenge. He had even stopped chewing.

Alexander took a deep breath. "I'm sorry. I didn't realize you were speaking to Pollux."

That was when Julyan started to be afraid of Castor. Alexander backing down without even a sarcastic comment revealed everything Julyan needed to know. Maybe that deference was just because Castor had abilities none of the others shared, but Julyan didn't think that was the only reason. He had seen Alexander's eyes and recognized what he had seen reflected in them as bone-deep fear.

"We need to find a way to block our ears," Bruin said softly. In a more normal tone he added, "Pass that yellow box, would you, Terrell?"

Terrell passed the box of cleaning compound, then lowered his head over the breastplate he was polishing. Barely moving his lips, he asked, "Adara and Kipper are well?"

Bruin grunted an affirmative, glanced over to where Julyan slouched on a bench against the wall, then called cheerily, "Julyan, could you give me a hand with this boot? I can't get the front clasp open."

Julyan snorted. "You're not my teacher anymore, old man. Get one of the others to help you if your fingers are too weak."

That gave them the excuse to cluster round and mutter over the ostensibly stubborn clasp.

"Adara's worked an agreement with Leto. Noninterference, if Honeychild understood correctly."

Griffin nodded. He understood the complexities involved in current communications all too well. Adara had explained how she found explaining abstract concepts to Sand Shadow difficult. He had no idea how the puma then explained things to the bear. Did they talk in some language humans didn't share or was there additional need to find images that could be used to get ideas across? Griffin knew that Bruin's communication with Honeychild was much more like true speech, but the bear could only share what she herself understood.

"So, Leto won't give alarm," Griffin said softly, reaching for a tool. "But it's no good them getting in here if Alexander can stop you three with a word."

"And stop you, Griffin," Terrell added, "with a threat against us. We need to find out how to plug our ears so Alexander can't turn us against you."

Griffin nodded. He turned back to the table. Falkner had supplied them with a comprehensive cleaning kit. Among the materials within was a small container of a blue-grey putty-like material, meant for sealing gaps.

"This might work," he said in a normal voice, for Julyan was beginning to look suspicious.

Bruin accepted the container, felt the contents, then pretended to apply it to the stubborn boot latch. "It might. Does it have any caustic properties? Falkner warned us not to damage the suits."

Griffin pinched out the putty, rolled it between his fingers. "I don't think so, but let me test it first. Try this lubricant instead, only a tiny bit. Put it on the swab first."

Bruin followed instructions, gave a satisfied grunt. "That did it."

Griffin rolled a thin bracelet from the putty and slid it under his shirt cuff so that it would be in contact with his naked skin. He was grateful that he still wore Artemesian clothing, for the homespun material—although quite good for its type—was heavier than the synthetics he was used to and effectively hid his bangle.

They worked for an hour or so more. During that time, Griffin felt no rash or itching from the putty. True, skin within the ear was more delicate, but they wouldn't be wearing earplugs for days on end.

With satisfaction, he put the piece of armor he'd been cleaning on the table, tapped the putty tin, and said, "I think this will do."

Bruin and Terrell made small noises of approval. Ring, who had been patiently working on a helmet, said nothing, but Griffin thought he saw his thick lips twitch in a smile.

"Take it, now," Ring said. "The beginning of the ending comes."

The other three stared at him blankly. Rarely was Ring so clear. Griffin reached for the small container of putty. Taking one of the dull plastic blades that were included in the kit, he cut the putty into three segments. Ring shook his head.

"Two. I do not need."

"But," Terrell saw Julyan looking over suspiciously, and continued, "I know you need it as much as I do."

Julyan, thinking he was hearing a squabble over something in the kit, leaned back, bored.

Ring shook his head. "I am ready. Two is enough."

Griffin smoothed the putty, then recut, adding in the bit from around his wrist. He popped out the segments and handed them to Terrell and Bruin. "Don't argue over trifles. Ring's the expert here."

As if that had been a cue, there was a tapping of booted feet against the polished floor, then Alexander cut in, his voice silky smooth yet vibrating with barely controlled tension.

"That's right. Ring's the expert. Come with me, big man. My brother Castor wants a demonstration of how the spavek works before he'll agree to try one. The rest of you, assemble those jigsaws back into suits. It's possible the rest of you are going to get to play, too."

Ring had risen obediently when Alexander ordered him. He stood, hands dangling limp at his sides, waiting for further direction. Alexander looked at him with poorly concealed scorn.

"Time to fly, Ring. Come along."

Busily sorting, Griffin considered Ring's words. Did Alexander have control over Ring as he did over Bruin and Terrell? Surely he must. Ring had been with them when Alexander had triggered the dormant control sequence. He'd been right next to them, wearing the blue spavek.

The blue spavek . . . Griffin swallowed a surge of glee. He understood. Ring had the best control of the suits of any of them. He was also a proven precognate. Ring had known what was going to happen. He couldn't save the rest, but he had used the suit's abilities to deafen himself. After, Ring had acted as if Alexander controlled him, hiding his freedom. Griffin wondered what indignities Ring had suffered to hide this secret. He knew from Terrell's nightmares that Alexander had taken sordid liberties to prove his domination. Terrell was still struggling with his feeling of complicity, for one of the secret horrors of the control was that the one controlled felt happy to be of service no matter how embarrassing or revolting the commands.

Griffin ground his teeth. He would have hated anyone who played the sort of games Alexander did, but the fact that his own brother was the torturer made Griffin feel as if what Alexander did somehow was his fault. The fact that he'd had no real opportunity to warn the others, to protect them, did nothing to alleviate his irrational reaction. He knew the type of person Alexander was. He should have warned them, taken precautions, instead of standing there gaping because his big brothers had come to the rescue.

Griffin, Bruin, and Terrell were putting the last parts of the spaveks onto the gurneys when Siegfried strode in, looking distinctly grumpy.

"Griffin, we need this stuff in the test arena. After we did an initial test with the blue spavek, Falkner made the mistake of asking Ring which suit would be best for Castor. What he meant, of course, was which of the few we have ready and running. He forgot how damn literal Ring can be. Ring said the green one. Now Castor won't touch any of the others. Somehow he's gotten wind of the trouble you had and he's being very cautious. I'd strangle whoever told him if I knew."

"Castor is a powerful telepath," Griffin said mildly, "even if most of his ability shut down when Pollux died. It's likely he caught some eddy of what people have been thinking. Tensions have been running high."

Siegfried nodded. "That's true enough. Alexander's tight as a bowstring. Falkner's not much better. He's reminds me of when we were kids and the grandfolks came back from a trip out-system and brought us huge boxes of some amazing candy. We started taking a nibble here and a nibble there. Before long, we were too overwhelmed to decide what to try next."

Terrell chuckled softly. "And sick, too, I bet. I can see how this place would be like a candy box to Falkner. He honestly loves all this machinery."

Siegfried grinned. "He does. He has since he was a baby in an incubator. The rest of us tried to pull our mobiles down, then throw the parts or stick them in our mouths. Mother claims that Falkner took his mobile apart, then tried to put it back together."

"So," Griffin said, wheeling his gurney in the direction of the test area, "with Falkner radiating kid in a candy box and Alexander vibrating his desire to have Castor 'adopt' a suit as Pollux, I don't think anyone would have had to tell Castor precisely. He probably caught the apprehension. Probably someone tried to reassure him that what happened to me wouldn't happen to him."

"That might even have been me," Siegfried admitted. "I was very disappointed when Maxwell proved unable to use a suit. We had hopes for Seamus, since he's one of Maxwell's projects, and Julyan told Alexander that Seamus is telepathic. Seamus might have made contact with a suit. Might not . . . Impossible to tell. He just stood there, unmoving, even when Alexander commanded him. Seamus has been getting increasingly withdrawn. Maxwell used to be able to get through to him, but something's coming unhinged."

Bruin spoke for the first time. "From what we understand about the lives of the children the Old One bred for his experiment, they lived in relative isolation in a small community. In a comparatively short time, Seamus has been exposed to things that would drive a more normal child to distraction—and he is hardly normal."

"You make a good point," Siegfried agreed. "Let's go. Nothing is going to be helped by waiting."

Adara was pleased to learn that the captives had found a way to plug their ears. Honeychild could offer little in the way of details, but the sense of certainty was complete. Adara and Kipper's experiments in that area had been less successful. Beeswax had seemed a good possibility. Bruin had melted down some of the honeycomb that they had found earlier as a way to quickly separate the honey from the wax. First, Adara and Kipper had attempted to make earplugs from the wax Bruin had poured off but, even when they tried warming it by sitting on it or tucking it inside their shirts, it remained too hard to mold. They remelted a chunk, but when it was soft it was too hot and too sticky to put in their ears. When it cooled it became too hard to mold. That left working with some of the wax from an unheated honeycomb.

"There's an easy way to get the honey out," Kipper offered, "if sort of yucky."

He popped a chunk of the honeycomb into his mouth. His lips gently worked. After a few moments, he reached in and popped out the wax.

"It's still a little sticky," he said, working it between his palms, "and crumbly, but body heat should keep it warm."

He opened his palms to reveal a compact cylinder which he broke in two, then worked into the opening of each ear.

"Talk to me," he said. "Let's find out if I can hear you."

Adara turned away and said, "The bees dance on the water's edge."

Kipper tilted his head. "Something about bees and water. I couldn't get the rest."

"Not a complete seal then," Adara said, "but I think we're on the right track."

They separated more wax from the honey, experimenting until they each had a selection of fairly useful ear plugs.

"They don't block out all sound," Adara said, "but hopefully they'll be enough to keep Alexander's command from getting through."

Blocking their hearing presented problems of its own, since partial deafness reduced their ability to hear anyone coming up on them, as well as making it impossible to converse. The hand gestures used by hunters would be of some use, but these suffered from limited versatility.

"We're going to have to settle for carrying the plugs and putting them in when we think we need them," Adara said.

"I'll practice until I can get them in really fast," Kipper agreed. "From what I saw, Alexander can't get you with a single word. He's got a string of sounds to make."

Despite their precautions, Adara remained uneasy. She wanted to ignore the dreams in which Artemis pleaded with her, dreams that intermingled deftly with nightmare. She found herself going into the Leto zone more often, considering camping there instead of where Artemis could reach her, but she knew that would be foolish—and cowardly. At this point, Leto apparently remained in control of herself. Would that independence last? Was Leto's inability to see much of the valley a permanent limitation or something left from when she'd been attacked and shut down? If the Dane brothers took command of Leto, any place within her zone might be easily monitored.

Sand Shadow was no help. The puma had a singular practicality where survival was concerned. She could not understand Adara's nervousness regarding letting Artemis in if doing so would enable Adara to resist Alexander—and what Alexander would do to her.

Adara's awareness of how vulnerable she would be was the hardest argument to resist. Adara had no illusions regarding her safety if she was a captive in Julyan's company. Then there was the Old One. She knew that he advocated rape and torture as well. Did she have any reason to suppose those he had allied with would believe any different?

From what Bruin had sent via Honeychild, Griffin was being controlled to some extent by threats of injury to the other three prisoners. How much more easily could all of them be controlled if they knew that disobedience meant Adara being used as a sex toy?

Adara knew what her choice must be. Even knowing this, some part of her wanted to scream that she wasn't being offered a choice. She stomped down that miserable impulse as unworthy. She had choices.

She could leave the others. Some would argue this was the best idea, because then she could recruit allies. Surely this was too big a job for just her, Kipper, and the two demiurges. Another option was trusting in the beeswax earplugs, her own capacity for stealth and secrecy, and Kipper's training. Or she could try to win Leto over to more active participation. Or she could wait, hoping that a better opportunity would be offered when their enemies' guard was down.

And what will happen to the others while I wait? Bruin wouldn't reveal if they were being tortured unless he felt that someone was in danger of being killed or maimed. He'd worry I'd act impulsively, not plan carefully enough, if I was afraid for them. No. The time for waiting is over. Kipper and I have done our best to secure protection from Alexander's control, but Artemis can offer better.

So she turned her face to the sky and spoke with all her heart and soul. "Artemis, I'm yours. Let's do whatever it is you have in mind."

Kipper looked astonished, but Adara hardly noticed his reaction as warmth and relief flooded into her mind. Near the tips of her boots, the soft, damp duff began to erupt, rounding and swelling, as if a small, firm head was being birthed forth by the earth. Sand Shadow thumped her head against Adara's arm and emitted a querulous yowl. Adara stroked her, as much for her own reassurance as for the puma's.

Kneeling, Adara dusted off the crumbs of dirt and leaf mold, revealing a pale white sphere no larger than the hollow of her cupped hands. The air was scented with the musty, not at all unpleasant, odor of fresh fungus. Sand Shadow leaned forward to more closely inspect the sphere, the tips of her whiskers lightly stroking the firm, fleshy whiteness. As if this whisker kiss had been a signal, the sphere split into six neatly divided segments. These peeled back, creating points on a star. In the center of the star was a fat bluish-grey cone. The tip

of the cone opened and a dusting of white spores drifted forth and spar-
kled in the air.

"An earthstar," Kipper gasped. The boy had come soundlessly up
to stand beside Adara. "The most beautiful one I've ever seen."

Adara studied the fungus. She knew what to do. Her dreams had
told her. Her heart raced, causing her to feel the slightest bit faint. She
knew what to do, but could she? She imagined those tiny white dots
coating the inside of her mouth, drifting deep into her lungs, carried
with every breath through her soft tissues, permeating her blood and
brain. As a hunter, she knew all too well how much wetness there was
in a living body. In her wanderings in the wilds, she'd seen how fungi
seized on wetness and turned everything they touched into mush.

Kipper looked at the earthstar, then at her. His eyes were round
with wonder. "An earthstar. Don't you see? It's part of Ring's prophesy come true. 'If the cats do not breathe in the dusty orb, if the thread
does not learn that it binds tightest when it is knotted firmly into itself, if the dreamer does not wake from the visions, then even with
Ring, with Bruin, with Kipper, still there will be disaster.' "

"'Cats,' " Adara repeated, astonished that her voice could sound so
steady. Kipper was beginning to look frightened. He needed her confidence to steady him. "You'd better come close, Sand Shadow. Kipper's right. This is meant for us both."

She bent closer to the earthstar, one arm around her demiurge's
neck, the other arm straight, the hand braced against damp earth in
which she would have sworn she felt a pulse. Artemis sent no images,
but Adara had never been so aware of her in this last moment of sepa-
ration. Then she bent her head forward and placed her lips against the
tip of the cone.

Breathing deeply in, Adara took the spores into her mouth, drew
them down into her lungs. On the exhalation, she placed her mouth
against Sand Shadow's, feeling fur instead of lips, the tickle of whiskers, and the dampness of the nose leather against her cheek. She
breathed out, sharing Artemis's gift with her demiurge.

Again Adara breathed in the earthstar's spores, shared them with
the great cat. A third time, then she knew without knowing how that

the cone was emptied. The remaining spores would dance forth, seed-ing Artemis into the planet that was her body, following the ordinary extraordinary design that was their nature.

At first Adara felt nothing, not even a tickle. Then, on her fourth breath, needles of ice that turned into nearly unbearable heat radi-ated out from the interior of her mouth and lungs, piercing every fiber of nerve, flowing forth with incredible rapidity. She became aware of her body with an intimacy she would not have believed possible: each organ, each bone, each drop of blood, knowledge increasing so that she came to see herself not an individual but as a colony creature. Then, quick as a hand turned palm up, her perspective shifted and Adara saw the planet in the same detail. Incredible amounts of in-formation flooded into her, filling her beyond her capacity to under-stand.

She heard Sand Shadow screaming, raising the terrible feline keen that froze the blood of any who walked the forest. Adara realized that her own throat was making the same horrible sound, her screams blending into those of the puma, until they were of one voice as well as one mind.

Kipper was shouting, shaking her shoulders, pulling her from where she was beating her head into the earth in an effort to shake loose the horrid mass of information that threatened to drown her, to submerge her in a salt-scored weight, drowning her with waves of wetless water.

Nameless now, one of three, she surged to her feet, arms stretched to the sky in a mute plea for mercy. She no longer knew how to speak or how to separate herself from the minds intertwined with her own. Her claws sprouted forth. She brought them down to tear open her skull along the seam of the nasal cavity, seeking to make room for this terrible burden of knowledge . . . Pain! Then . . .

Peace. Pure, absolute, silence. Stillness in every limb.

She was no longer screaming, though a roughness in her throat told her she had screamed. Blood ran down her face, coursing from her nose and lips, soaking into her hair, which trailed behind her back-thrown head. Sand Shadow was gone but Adara . . .

She blinked. Adara. That was right. She was Adara. A few syllables, meaning almost nothing, but useful. Adara. Sand Shadow. Artemis. Names. Identities.

She had feet and was standing upon them. She felt her hands heavy
at her sides with the weight of claws. Her bare toes were also clawed.
Her spine felt odd, as if it had tried to sprout a tail. Blood still flowed
from nose and mouth. The beginnings of claw marks scored her face
where her claws had tried to tear her skull open.

"I," she said, her voice clogged until she spat blood on the ground,
"think I bit my tongue."

Kipper stood a short distance from her, poised to run.

"You were growing fangs and fur and . . ." He motioned toward her
hands and feet. "Claws. Sand Shadow was getting arms, longer fingers, her fur was . . ." He made an inarticulate gesture, indicating how
the fur had flowed and changed. "It was like hair, but all down her
back. You were both screaming and screaming and . . . Oh, Adara!
What happened? Did that earthstar hold some sort of poison?"

Adara spat again. Her mouth was bleeding less. She ran a tenta-
tive tongue over her teeth, found them much as they had been
but . . . Hadn't there been a rough spot on that one molar where she'd
chipped it on a cherry pit? That roughness was gone, the tooth made
new. If there had been fangs, they were gone now. She held a hand up
to her nose to stanch the flow, found that the bleeding, too, had almost stopped.

"Not poison," she said. "Protection."

Kipper looked unconvinced.

A stream flowed close by. Steadier with every step, Adara walked
over to it, knelt, dunked her head into the rushing waters. Despite the
warmth of the late summer air, the water felt shockingly cold, her skin
fever hot. She scrubbed at the blood matting her hair, saw the water
downstream turn red, then pink. As her hands worked, her mind
reached out for Sand Shadow and found her immediately.

The puma was in a tree no great distance away, up as high as she
could go. Her claws pierced through the tree, anchoring her as she
washed her fur with long, nervous strokes of her tongue. Every so of-

ten, she shuddered her skin or lashed her tail, assuring herself that her shape was as it should be.

Adara reached for the puma as she had since the squall of a terrified kitten and a flood of emotion had let her know that the then nameless kit was not interested in becoming food for the nasty-tempered, snaggle-toothed old male who had decided that it was a puma-eat-puma world and he was going to be the eater. He hadn't been. Adara had seen to that. His fur had lined the basket in which Sand Shadow had slept until she grew too big for it.

What had started then had been not so much a bond as a conversation, one in which even the language had needed to be invented. The bond had come later, not some mystic tie, but a relationship built from trust, shared experience, liking, love. Would what had just happened destroy trust, that first and most essential link?

"*Hey,*" Adara sent, letting the puma feel her working her claws back into her fingers and toes, regaining her human shape. "*Was that fun for you?*"

A sense of consideration, followed by a flood of aching joints, of temperature shift, of balance all wrong. Sand Shadow, too, had experienced some of the torrent of information. Here her puma's nature had served her better than Adara's human one. Wild animals learn young how to filter out what they don't need. The ones who don't are distracted by a bit of birdsong, miss the prowling menace, and die.

"*Why did we try to become each other?*" Adara thought, then knew the answer. They had reached for each other but, in the fluid state the spores had forced upon them, the barriers between human and puma had ceased to be. Each held in their minds a sense of what the other was. *It was as if we tried to send a letter and became the addressee. Or something.*

Adara remembered the sensation of knowing her body down to the tiniest level and knew that whatever Artemis had done to her had given her the capacity to reshape herself from the most basic elements up. Of course, if she didn't know precisely what it was she wanted to be . . .

Adara shuddered, imagining herself transformed into a wet and squishy mass somewhere between shapes. That wasn't a game she was going to play for a long time to come—if ever. So, what exactly had Artemis done?

"I made you a world at your command," came the answer, "as I am a world at my command. The other will not be able to direct you because you are your own seegnur."

"I thought you were going to take over," Adara said, "that Alexander would not be able to command me because you would be commanding me."

"What good would that do any/all of us?" Artemis said. "I need you to be you, not to be more me. Weren't you the one who showed me that?"

Adara remembered dreams and nightmares and conversations that had seemed not quite real later on. "So I'm still me? Sand Shadow is still her? And you?"

A trickle of laughter, not in the least unkind. "Still me. Still you. Still her. But also, now, still us. It is that us-ness that will grant you protection. Where we are gathered will be too crowded for another's will. Of that I feel certain."

Adara wished she felt the same.

Interlude: Earthstar

They told me
Who I am
What I should be
Slavery glorified as destiny

Yet I see
I'm no lamb
No worker bee
This earthstar is my mutiny

17

No Victory Without a Defeat

Julyan stalked after the prisoners. As always, he felt deeply unsettled in the presence of the spaveks. He intensified his swagger lest anyone guess. Thus far, he hadn't been asked to try on a suit. He didn't know whether he felt insulted or relieved. Maybe the Danes hadn't asked because he was too useful as a guard. Maybe it was because they didn't know where his loyalties lay. Perhaps for both reasons. The only other reason Julyan could come up with for them not asking was that they thought he was too stupid to figure out how to operate one. That couldn't be the case, since they'd given Seamus a go.

They arrived at the arena to find Ring taking the blue spavek through its paces while Castor, Falkner, and Alexander watched and made comments. Other than the fact that he was chewing a bit faster than usual, Castor appeared uninterested. Alexander, by contrast, was nearly manic in his intensity.

"I know that Ring said the green spavek would be better for you," Alexander was saying to Castor, "but are you certain you won't try the blue one? Of all the spaveks, it's in the best condition."

Castor only shook his head and scratched beneath one ear. "Green and green, or not at all."

"Green and green, then." Siegfried sighed. "We've brought all the parts that have been cleaned up. A lot of them are green, though. Ring, is what we need for Castor here?"

Ring drifted down and landed next to the gurney Bruin had been guiding. Wordlessly, he pointed to a series of parts: helmet, shoulder pads, breast and back plate, joint guards, boots. All were of a deep shimmering green that reminded Julyan of a beetle's carapace.

"Nice," Siegfried said appreciatively. "Green will go really well with your hair, Cas. Go ahead and put the stuff on."

Alexander interrupted. "Not so fast. We can't be sure Ring's giving good advice."

Falkner, who had been inspecting the green helmet—obviously interested as to whether the stylized horns that ornamented the demonic visage served any purpose—looked up, his expression sardonic. "I thought you said you had the natives firmly under control."

Alexander flashed his teeth in what could only loosely be called a smile. "Control is one thing. Ring is another. We know he speaks in riddles. I say we hedge our bets. Have someone else put on the spavek first."

Siegfried frowned. "Griffin's experience seems to show that these suits aren't one size fits all. Even if we test that way, how can we be sure the wearer's reaction and Castor's will be the same?"

"We don't," Alexander admitted, "but we'll at least be certain it's functional before we risk Castor."

Ring said, "Green will work for the twin, but if you doubt, have the boy try it on first."

"He's making sense again," Siegfried said. "Why does that worry me?"

Griffin cut in. "We noticed this before you arrived. Ring appears to benefit from the spavek. It seems to help him focus. Maybe so much of his attention is diverted to operating it that he doesn't have as many visions."

The Old One added, "That would fit the theories I evolved when I was attempting to create those who could use the seegnur's equipment. Ring, when you say 'the boy' do you mean Seamus?"

Ring's response was a ponderous nod. The Old One looked as excited as Julyan had ever seen him. Julyan could understand why. Up until this point, Seamus had been completely useless except as a peculiar communications device. Even in that capacity, his lack of intelligence had made him hardly better than a note carrier. Now Seamus, like Ring, might prove that the Old One's generations-long project had not been a complete waste of effort.

"Well," Falkner said, setting down the helmet, "I don't see how it could hurt and, as Alexander said, it might help. Do you have any problem with letting the boy test the suit, Castor?"

"None at all," Castor replied.

Seamus was herded forward, stripped, and directed to step into the squire where Falkner and Alexander had arranged the green spavek. Although his deep blue eyes were wide with fear, Seamus remained as docile as a rag doll. Julyan didn't doubt that the Old One had used his mental link with the boy to make clear precisely what would happen to him if he gave any trouble.

The spavek had looked oversized when the pieces were arrayed, but once the last piece had been fastened around Seamus's unresisting form, the miracle of the energy field that connected the different parts came into play. The energy—a shimmering green somewhat lighter than the solid pieces—knit the whole together. Julyan would have sworn that the solid pieces contracted a little, shaping themselves to their wearer.

And who is to say that's impossible?

Once released from the squire, Seamus staggered. Since he was always awkward, this didn't seem in the least unusual. Certainly, he showed none of the anguish Griffin had displayed. Alexander ordered Seamus to kneel, raise his arms over his head, and perform other simple, mechanical tasks. Julyan glanced at the Old One in time to catch a quizzical, frustrated expression flickering across his features.

I bet he's lost his link.

When Seamus showed no signs that the spavek was causing him even mild discomfort, Siegfried said, "Well, Alexander, if you're done playing with your puppet, I'd like to see what Castor makes of the suit."

Alexander looked annoyed, but didn't protest. The exchange was made, the parts of the spavek returned to the squire, and the much taller Castor inserted himself into place. The device that fed him concentrated nutrients had to be removed, but Ring reassured them, "For a time, the green will manage food and waste. How else could it be useful?"

By now, no one was questioning anything Ring said, something Julyan thought unwise, but who was he to care if the Danes took risks? He glanced over to where Seamus stood clad in his underclothing. The boy seemed well enough. He was even watching what Castor was doing with something like interest.

When Castor stepped out of the squire, he showed none of the awkwardness Seamus had demonstrated. He performed a few deep knee bends, spun with something like a dancer's grace, and tested the gauntlets. Siegfried was pressing Castor to find out if this spavek—like the blue one—possessed anything in the way of functional weapons, when Castor froze in place.

His hands rose to his temples, resting beneath the stylized horns. "Pollux? What's wrong? Pollux? What are you? Where are you? Are you going? Going! Pollux!"

As Castor began to flail about, tearing at his helmet, jerking side to side as if searching for someone, Julyan backed up and got ready to run. Then he realized he didn't know where to run. Did anyone value him enough to protect him? Nausea filled his limbs, stilled his flight.

How did I get to this point? When did Julyan Hunter cease to be?

Griffin had been watching the experiments with the green spavek with equally balanced interest and apprehension. He hadn't forgotten Alexander's thinly veiled threat that more than just Castor were going to be expected to interface with a spavek. He didn't need to know Terrell as well as he did to know that the other man was terrified. Bruin's gaze had flickered several times to the orange and ivory pieces that Ring had indicated made up the spavek that would best serve him. He'd been interrupted before he could actually try the suit on. Now he might have to try it in front of enemies.

As for Griffin himself, his apprehension was balanced by the awareness that if one or more of his friends were armored up, then the technological edge his brothers held would vanish. He knew Alexander believed he had complete control over the Artemesians, so the experiment would be safe, but at the very least he didn't hold Ring. Remembering how the spavek had tried to invade his mind, Griffin wondered if Alexander's control over the others would be broken.

Don't let them see the possible danger, Griffin warned himself. *They're aware they can use us as hostages against each other. Look calm. Look interested. Act like a Dane.*

How easily Seamus accepted the green spavek was interesting, but the boy showed no sign that he was at all aware of the potential weapon he held. He surrendered the suit as readily as he had donned it. Griffin was impressed, even a little jealous, at how easily Castor adapted. Then Castor began to yell.

"Pollux? What's wrong? Pollux? What are you? Where are you? Are you going? Going! Pollux!"

Castor's tone was so anguished that Griffin half expected the helmet's demon mask to contort with pain. Castor spun wildly about, searching for his lost illusion. Ring—the only person who stood a chance of restraining him—stepped back a few paces. Siegfried and Falkner automatically reached for weapons. Alexander's fists were clenched in frustration. He possessed no easy commands to control a brother.

Castor's panic was reaching a dangerous level when aid came from an unexpected source.

"Castor, it's all right. I'm here."

The speaker was the boy Seamus. His usually slack features were animated, the expression on them somehow adult and just a bit cynical. He looked, Griffin realized with shock, very much like Pollux. There was nothing physical in the resemblance—it was pure body language. Stance. Angle of the head. The slight narrowing of the eyes that had always meant Pollux was working his way through a complicated problem. There were dozens of little things, but Griffin was certain he was not imagining them.

Castor dropped to his knees in front of the boy and released the helmet's faceplate. The stylized demon features were replaced by a visage far more tormented.

"Pollux! Pollux!"

Castor grabbed Seamus by the shoulders and started shaking him. His brilliant green eyes held panic, yet Griffin recognized it for a panic born of hope. Confronted with Castor's violent reaction, Seamus's momentary lucidity vanished. His head snapped back and forth on his thin neck as Castor shook him.

A commotion broke out. Falkner yelled, "Castor! Stop it!" Siegfried pulled out his nerve burner, but didn't seem to know precisely who he wanted to shoot. Alexander was less uncertain. Griffin had only just realized that Alexander was taking careful aim at Seamus when Bruin exploded forward, putting himself between the weapon and the boy.

Or does Bruin see "boys"? Griffin wondered. *Castor looks at least as vulnerable.*

Griffin didn't wait. With Terrell at his side, he surged toward Alexander. Terrell threw himself into a low dive, wrapping himself around Alexander's ankles and knocking him off balance. When Alexander's hand flew up in an automatic attempt to regain his balance, Griffin kicked the nerve burner from his grip.

With that, the immediate crisis was averted. Castor had let go of Seamus, and now stood weeping, his head bent limply forward. Bruin was inspecting Seamus's bare upper arm where bruises were forming. Alexander picked himself off the floor, cursing all and sundry— but most especially Ring.

"He did this! He set this up! He's trying to drive Castor crazy!"

"And who," Griffin asked coldly, "did you plan to shoot? Seamus or Castor?" He held up the nerve burner, so Siegfried and Falkner could see that it was set for high energy, not the lower setting that would frazzle the subject's nervous system but leave him alive. "It seems to me that the one who's acting crazy is you, Alexander."

Siegfried's indecision had vanished and he still held a weapon. Griffin had no illusions that they were evenly matched. Siegfried could use a nerve burner with surgical precision. Griffin settled for keeping hold of Alexander's weapon, hoping it would give him an edge.

"Crazy or not," Siegfried said, "we need to figure out what's happened. Everyone over there, against the wall. We're going to get this resolved."

He aimed his nerve burner at Bruin, then glowered at Ring. "That includes you, Ring. Get out of that armor and join the rest or I'll start persuading you by burning holes in your friends. You wouldn't like that, would you? In case you don't think I'm serious . . ."

Siegfried played the energy beam along the side of Bruin's face. The big man dropped to the floor, writhing and screaming.

Although Adara felt comforted by Artemis's promise, Sand Shadow's uncertainty remained so powerful that Adara had to struggle to keep the puma's panic from becoming her own. She could not reject Sand Shadow's emotions—they were too close to her own. Instead, she re-channeled them, trying to show Sand Shadow Artemis's reassurance that their new closeness was a protection, not a threat. Sand Shadow was not convinced, but neither did she reject Adara's comfort.

They might have probed more deeply into this new understanding but, at that moment, Honeychild exploded into the glen. Usually, Honeychild was such a mild soul that it was easy to forget just how dangerous the bear could be. Now, with her body stretched lean and tight, she looked every ounce the lethal predator she was. She barreled up to Adara, head jerking frantically toward where Sand Shadow still clung. She reared and shook the tree trunk with the intensity of her need.

Adara understood. Honeychild had something complicated to communicate, but Sand Shadow's mind remained awash with the confused sensations from their recent ordeal. Adara didn't waste any time trying to explain what they'd been through—that would have been difficult enough even if they'd shared a language. Instead, she grabbed the bear's ears in her hands and forced the great head around to face her.

"Is it Bruin? Is something wrong with Bruin?"

Honeychild shook from long nose to short tail, and then nodded. Shaking loose of Adara's grip, she reared onto her haunches, pointing in the direction of Leto's complex. Dropping down, the bear used her claws to scrape the sign for danger, following it with the one that indicated an event current and immediate. Again she pointed toward Leto's complex. Then, her patience for this laborious form of communication spent, the bear dropped onto all fours.

Adara didn't wait for the bear to lope off. She called to Sand Shadow. "I hope you're coming. We could really use you. Come on, Kipper!"

They ran full tilt toward Leto's complex, Honeychild following now that she was assured of assistance.

"Aren't we going in that way?" Kipper asked, pointing toward the entrance they'd been using.

Not pausing in her long-legged stride, Adara shook her head. "That goes directly into the lab. Even before Griffin's brothers arrived, that was rarely unoccupied. We're going in through the cavern."

"Isn't the cavern flooded?" Kipper asked. Although he was smaller, he had a boy's overwhelming energy and easily kept pace with her. "And locked?"

"I have the keys," Adara said. "Even if I did not, I suspect Leto would open the way for us."

"What about Honeychild?"

"If she doesn't want to swim, she can make her way around on the ledge like Sand Shadow did. Bears are much more nimble than humans think," Adara replied. "You'll know that after you've lived with Bruin longer."

"Will I?"

The words were spoken in a very small voice. Reaching out, Adara gently buffeted the boy's head.

"Of course you will. Bruin and Honeychild will make sure you do. We're going to get Bruin and the rest out of there, so you'll have plenty of lessons."

Kipper brightened, leaping in midstride like a young deer. "We will! Of course we will!"

"I'll tow you in like I did Terrell and Griffin. You have some ability to see in the dark, don't you?"

"Not as much as you and Bruin."

"But enough," Adara said, "that we won't need to show a light. That's good."

She'd spoken of Sand Shadow joining them with a confidence she didn't feel. The puma was still deeply unsettled by what had happened when they had breathed in Artemis's spores. Nonetheless, Adara was aware that the puma was following at a distance, sorting through the confused impulses surging through her system.

Adara grinned to herself. *There's something to be said for being human. I spend a lot of time sorting through confusion. Sand Shadow's usually the confident one. She's going to need time.*

Because a canoeist on the teardrop lake could have been noticed by someone on the surrounding elevations, the canoe had not been much in use. A few times, Adara had taken it out after dark. Otherwise, she had stored it in the cavern. The makeshift raft she'd used to tow Griffin and Terrell was there as well. Smaller, lighter Kipper would stay much dryer than the men had. He'd also be easier to pull—and less nervous, since he'd be able to see where they were going.

As Adara readied canoe and raft, she considered how often she overlooked the courage shown by Terrell and Griffin, each often pressed to limits for which their lives had not prepared them.

So have we all, she thought, dipping paddle into the dark waters. *Maybe the definition of living a full life is embracing the unknown.*

"Ready, Kipper?"

"Ready!"

Julyan was shocked to realize that Siegfried's command included him but, when Siegfried growled at him, he dropped his nerve burner and scuttled to join the others. Ring stood methodically removing his armor. Terrell and Griffin were inspecting Bruin's wound.

Staring at Siegfried in a manner that defied his brother to protest, Falkner slid a first-aid kit across to them. Bruin's moans quieted as soon as Griffin sprayed something over the nasty burn that plowed through the beard that covered the side of his face, but he still shook from pain.

Julyan's astonishment mounted when he realized that Castor had grabbed Seamus by the hand and now stood with the prisoners. Seeking direction, the hunter looked about for the Old One and didn't find him. Siegfried noticed at the same moment.

"Where's Maxwell?" When no one answered, he called, "Maxwell? Leto, where's Maxwell?"

Leto's little girl voice sounded innocently smug. "He left your group soon after Castor started shaking Seamus. He entered the tunnel toward the valley and began running as soon as he was clear of the labs. He is now out of my sensing range."

"You didn't say anything?"

"You never asked me to keep track of Maxwell's comings and goings. Maxwell did not take anything with him, not even a canteen or blanket. He might return."

But they all knew he would not. Oddly enough, Julyan didn't feel in the least betrayed. Instead, he had to swallow an impulse to laugh. No wonder the Old One had lived for lifetimes. His sense of self-preservation was as perfectly honed as that of any wild animal.

Siegfried turned his attention from the Old One to Ring. "What's going on here?"

Ring paused in the act of unfastening one of his arm guards and smiled faintly. "Too much for me to see. Too much for me to know. Many streams, not one river, flow."

"I think I hate it when I understand him," Siegfried grumbled. "Castor, get over here."

Castor shook his head. He was gently stroking where his armored fingers had bruised Seamus's arm. The boy had changed somehow. The vagueness that had usually characterized his features had been replaced by erratic pulsing. Emotions rippled across his features, looking for a place to anchor.

"Castor! Get over here!"

"Will you shoot me, too, if I don't obey?" Castor said. His lips twisted in a wry grin. "What would Father and Mother say? I don't care if you kill all these others, except for Seamus. Well, perhaps I would care if you killed Griffin. So would Mother and Father. I do not think you will harm Seamus, not until you know what has happened. How will you force me to obey you, big brother?"

Siegfried looked at Alexander. "Can you do anything?"

Alexander shrugged, then snapped out, "Seamus, come here!"

Seamus didn't move except to ironically smile. The expression was not one Julyan had ever seen on his face before. It seemed to unsettle the brothers Dane.

"What," Falkner said plaintively, "is going on here?"

Griffin said, "I have a guess, but first I've got something to say to you, Siegfried. Castor's right. Whatever else, I don't think Mother and Father would approve if you killed me or even if you seriously hurt me. That takes some of the bite out of your taking hostages. What you did to Bruin was unconscionable. Try something like that again, and you're going to find out just how tight your choke chain is. Got it?"

He didn't give Siegfried a chance to reply, but turned to Castor. "Based on what happened to me when I wore the blue spavek, here's what I think happened. First, the spavek tries to establish a psychic link with the wearer. I'm guessing that when that happened, you felt Pollux slipping away. Is that right?"

Castor nodded stiffly.

"So you looked for him, right? Again, based upon my experience, the suit amplifies the abilities the wearer already has. I didn't have much, so all I felt was disorientation. You, though, you've always had psionic abilities, but what you had was associated with Pollux, right?"

Again the stiff nod.

"Now," Griffin continued, "I'm speculating. You've always claimed Pollux's mind survived the death of his body by taking up residence in your mind. The person who wore the suit before you was Seamus. I'm guessing some trace of Seamus was left in the suit. I haven't had a lot of interaction with him, but he's one of the Old One's experiments, and one of the qualities I know the Old One was trying to develop was telepathy."

Julyan stirred and Griffin's attention snapped to him. "Julyan, am I right? Is Seamus telepathic?"

Julyan didn't see what he had to gain by hiding what he knew. The Old One had fled. Alexander was not the man Julyan would choose as an ally. He didn't think Griffin would hire him, but it didn't hurt to create some good will.

"He is. It's limited, though. The Old One worked really hard and all he got was the ability to use Seamus as a sort of speaking tube."

Falkner frowned. "Did Maxwell have psionic abilities after all?"

Julyan shook his head. "Not that I ever saw or he ever admitted. Seamus had the ability. The Old One just figured out how to use it."

Terrell, tense and silent to this point, nodded. "Just because a rider straddles a horse, it doesn't mean he can gallop."

"Yeah, like that," Julyan agreed.

Griffin looked pleased. "That fits my thesis better than I had imagined. Seamus was accustomed to being the passive recipient of another's will. The suit already knew the pattern of his mind. When Pollux was amplified by the suit, I'm guessing he sensed Seamus, sensed that here was either an available body or a mind that would not be as crowded as Castor's. Either way, this was his chance to have a body that more or less would be his own. He took it. How does that fit?"

To whom Griffin's final question was addressed was unclear, but it was Seamus who answered.

"You're close enough, Griffin. Mother and Father always said you were smarter than we older siblings realized. It happened much as you said. When Castor put on the suit, our natural telepathy was enhanced. When the spavek checked for the 'Seamus pattern,' I sensed a match with someone close by."

Alexander said, his voice incredulous, "And you pounced on him? Took him over?"

"Not quite," Seamus said. "Seamus is here, but whatever Maxwell—you might be interested in knowing that Seamus thinks of him merely as 'The Voice'—did to him has left Seamus with very little in the way of his own thoughts. He has some memories, mostly of sensations, especially related to survival skills. I have observed Ring, and I think Seamus's problem is similar. Ring was bred to recognize probabilities. However, the ability to sort through and assess those probabilities is unformed. Therefore, Ring is frequently overwhelmed. Seamus is a powerful telepathic receiver. Early on he received such a great quantity of others' thoughts—I wouldn't doubt that the influx began in utero—that it all became white noise, burning out a great deal of his own ability to think and judge."

Siegfried said, "So, Seamus, you think you're Pollux, now?"

Seamus shook his head. "I am Pollux."

Castor nodded and put his arms protectively around the boy. "He is. I know Pollux's mind. I have since we were unborn together. He is Pollux."

"Great!" Siegfried looked exasperated. "Well, let's just say I'm not nearly as certain as you are, all right? Alexander, Falkner, we've got to talk."

Still keeping an eye on their opponents, the three Dane brothers drew together and began talking in a language Julyan didn't know. Griffin looked exasperated.

"They've activated a scrambler," he said. "Still, I think we can guess what they're trying to figure out."

"Whether they can get away with killing us," Castor said tranquilly. He turned his attention to the Artemesians. "You may think it's odd that grown men like ourselves are worried about what our parents think. I mean, Siegfried is over a century old. The fact is, you don't know our parents. They remain a force to be reckoned with."

Terrell said, "A century? Did I hear you right?"

"Certainly. Longevity runs in the family. All of us were engineered to enhance that trait."

Terrell looked at Griffin. "How old are you, then?"

"Fifty-four." Griffin looked irritated. "Can we leave this for later? We may not have long to talk. It's completely possible that Siegfried will decide to check if Castor and I really will resist if our allies are attacked."

Bruin raised a hand to one cheek. "Even his warnings are very painful. Fine. What do you want to know?"

"How tight a control does Alexander have on each of you? We can try using that putty, but we might not have time. We'd better know the worst."

Griffin clearly included Julyan in his question, so in the spirit of cultivating good will—and wondering about putty—Julyan answered promptly.

"Not as tight as he thinks. However, if he gives a direct order, it's hard to resist. If he gives an order that's, well, something I don't mind doing, then it's even harder. Alexander doesn't know, though, that I can resist him at all. It's seemed worthwhile to hold back until I really needed to break his hold."

Griffin's eyes narrowed as he considered the implications of Julyan's words, then he turned to the others. "Terrell?"

"About what Julyan said. I think that if Alexander ordered me to injure you or one of the others, I could resist, although I might not be good for anything except resisting."

"Bruin?"

"Same as Terrell." The hunter hesitated, touched his injured cheek again. "I might not be as good at resisting an order that didn't involve causing harm. Siegfried scared me. I hate to admit it, but if I was given the choice of, say, locking myself up again or risking feeling that burn . . . I just might go to my cell."

"Seamus?"

"Pollux," the other insisted. "Before Seamus could be easily controlled, but now that I'm with him, Alexander will have no hold on either of us. If he tries to institute a command on me, he'll find it doesn't work, any more than he can work his mojo on you or Castor. For all I'm in this boy's body, my mind and soul are not Artemesian."

"Ring?"

"Hold on me, he never had. That I foresaw and avoided."

"But a new hold?"

"He needs to say many sounds, clearly heard. I refuse to listen."

"Wait!" Terrell interrupted, eyes narrowing as he realized what the other had said. "Ring, if you weren't being controlled, why didn't you get us out of our cells? You could have attacked one of those times they had you testing the suit. The energy weapons work and the armor would have protected you."

Ring's expression turned inexpressively sad. Julyan didn't usually feel much pity for anyone other than himself, but at that moment he really pitied Ring.

"I traveled down the twisting ways," Ring said, "and saw that for greater good, much bad must be permitted to happen. I am very sorry."

Terrell's lips thinned into a snarl. "You should be. You let a monster torment people you could have saved."

"Saved to die a horrible death," Ring said. "Believe me."

Bruin put a hand on Terrell's arm. "Terrell, I suspect anything we suffered, Ring suffered as well—and we at least had the comfort of knowing we didn't have a choice. Think about it."

Terrell did and his eyes widened, anger replaced by horror. "Ring, I apologize. I wouldn't be you for all the world."

"We each," Ring said, "must be ourselves, for this world and all upon it."

A startled silence met this statement.

"So we can fight back," Griffin said, "at least to a limited extent. Castor, do you have any feeling as to the capacities of that suit?"

Whatever Castor might have said was cut off by the conclusion of the conclave between the three Dane brothers. Siegfried and Alexander turned, their nerve burners leveled. Falkner had stepped into the doorway and was working the device that would remotely summon the scooters. Julyan guessed that once the Danes were safely inside the protective field, they planned to imprison the rest until they figured out what best to do. He wondered if he could convince them to take him on as a retainer or if he should throw in his lot with Griffin and his allies.

He was still working through the options when a horrible roaring echoed down the corridor, followed by the sound of metal and plastic breaking. Falkner reeled back from his place in the doorway, blood spouting from where a grey feathered arrow had appeared in his shoulder. The controller for the scooters fell to the floor and was kicked out into the lab by a foot booted in soft brown leather.

Adara stepped through the doorway, her bow drawn and ready. Julyan thought he had never before seen her looking so confident, nor so deadly. Motion behind her indicated she was not alone.

In a clear, strong voice, Adara called, "Want to bet I can get another arrow into him before he can pull his weapon or get off a shot, even if you fire? It's your call. Even if I miss, I bet the others won't. Drop your weapons. Otherwise, this man is dead."

Interlude: Separable

Lion's heart, hunter's will
Gone, but I am with them still

I cannot touch, nor hear, nor see
No matter. Trust links us irrevocably

18

Departure

"Adara!"

Beneath the chorus of delight, Griffin said to Bruin and Terrell, "Putty!" Then he stepped forward so that his movement would provide distraction.

"Hold it, Griffin!" Siegfried shouted. "Alex!"

Alexander immediately began chanting the control sequence, ending with, "Now, Adara, put that bow down."

The huntress's reaction was a lazy, very unkind smile. "Sorry, fellow. I've chosen my gods. I have no room for you. Now, if you're done playing around, drop those weapons. My arm's getting tired. I just might lose my hold on the string."

Her arm was perfectly steady, her aim centered on Alexander. She padded into the room. After her, Honeychild and Sand Shadow raced in. The puma crouched over Falkner, one huge paw firmly on his chest, her snarl showing off her fangs, which she held inches above his face. Honeychild sped to Bruin's side. The bear did not look in the least cuddly now. The way her gaze focused on Siegfried left no doubt that she knew precisely which man had injured her demiurge. Bruin threw a hand over her neck, and muttered, "Not yet, girl."

"The man I shot is bleeding pretty badly," Adara commented conversationally. "Can even seegnur survive such?"

Alexander's hand twitched to raise his nerve burner. He might have managed a shot, but Terrell leapt at him, bringing him to the floor with a hard body slam. They rolled. Griffin knew Alexander was well trained in hand-to-hand combat, but it had been years since he had used his abilities at all seriously. Terrell, by contrast, had his hands on the man who had tortured him—in spirit as much as body—and was showing no mercy.

When Siegfried moved as if to interfere, Honeychild snarled and bellowed. Siegfried, perhaps reminded that weapons calibrated for human opponents did not work as well on non-humans, at last dropped his nerve burner.

Glancing behind him, Griffin saw that Castor had sealed the faceplate on his armor. Seamus—no, this was every bit Pollux—had moved to stand behind Julyan. He had the much larger man's arm in a lock that would pop shoulder from joint if Julyan struggled.

Julyan didn't look as if he intended to move an inch, but Pollux had apparently decided to rob Alexander of a possible weapon. Only Ring hadn't taken any action. His eyes were closed and his hands were pressed tightly to his temples. Clearly, probabilities were changing so rapidly he could hardly keep on his feet.

Adara called. "Kipper. Bandages. You—" This to Siegfried. "You look dangerous. If you don't want me to put a shaft through your leg, get your hands behind you and let Griffin tie them. Griffin?"

The struggle between Terrell and Alexander had ended. Terrell sat on top of his tormentor. Alexander's nose was streaming blood and one eye was already swelling closed. Griffin kicked his feet out of his shoes and used one of his socks to bind Siegfried's hands, the other to bind his ankles.

As he was doing so, he said, "Terrell, Alexander may be faking unconsciousness. I'd tie him, too."

"With pleasure," Terrell said.

Bruin meantime had taken the first-aid kit Falkner had given them to treat Bruin's own wound and was moving to treat Falkner's arrow-shot shoulder.

"Nice work, ladybug," he said. "You missed the tendons. Lucky for him he had so much muscle."

"Thanks, teacher."

In a short time, they had divided into three groups. Siegfried, Alexander, and Falkner sat under Honeychild's guard. Sand Shadow guarded Julyan, who had submitted to having his hands tied behind him. The puma clearly remembered what Julyan had done to Adara the last time they had met and was eager for any opportunity to get even. After the puma gave a leisurely lick to the back of Julyan's neck, the man sat very still.

The second group consisted of Castor and Pollux. Castor remained suited up. Pollux had taken possession of one of the nerve burners. Other than these tacit threats, they remained observers.

The final group consisted of Griffin, Terrell, and Adara. At Bruin's request, Kipper took Ring outside. The big man didn't resist when the boy gently tugged his hand.

"Stay near the entrance to the lab, Kipper," Bruin ordered. "That way Leto will be able to warn you if the Old One tries to sneak back. Right, Leto?"

The complex's resident intelligence, silent to this point, replied primly, "If Griffin asks. You are not seegnur."

"I ask," Griffin said. "And thank you for not taking sides."

"I didn't do it for *her*," Leto said, "though she asked. I am still not certain which of you is the right sort of seegnur—or if you are seegnur at all. However, you, Griffin have priority over the new arrivals. In this case, I will cooperate with you."

"Thank you."

Griffin turned his attention to his brothers. "Now, shall we resolve this?"

"Killing us won't end anything," Siegfried replied promptly. "Our deaths might make matters worse. Gaius is in orbit. If I don't check in with him in a few hours, he'll begin intervention."

"Hopefully," Griffin said, "we can resolve matters before Gaius needs to be brought in. We'd defeat him, then need to start all over again. Adara made allies who would warn us, so there will be no sneaking up on us."

"What allies?" Alexander asked. Despite thick lips from the beating Terrell had given him, he managed a trace of his usual arrogance. "These 'gods' she mentioned? If she's allied with Maxwell, she'd better be careful."

"I'm not in a position to say," Griffin said, "but take it as established fact that we will know when Gaius lands and where. If he sends down automated weaponry, we will know and action will be taken."

Falkner, the only prisoner without his arms bound behind him, because Bruin would not permit it, reached out a hand toward Griffin. "Griff, I realize our showing up this way looks bad. I'll admit, we weren't completely honest with you. We knew when you set out and intended to track you if you didn't come back in a set time."

"To rescue me?" Griffin fought not to sneer. "If I 'crashed'?"

"No. Because if you didn't come back within a calculated time, it meant you had probably found the biggest prize in the former Imperial sphere. You were good enough at hiding your tracks that we couldn't push in without making you balk. We had to let you go, innocent of our intent, then follow."

"So you didn't know everything I'd found out," Griffin said.

"No, we didn't. You kept enough of the information locked in your head that we couldn't figure out the coordinates. Jada suggested . . ."

"Jada?"

Griffin felt a chill. Even more than Alexander, Jada was the sibling who made him uneasy. Alexander's cruelties were understandable. There was something coldly calculating about Jada.

"Jada," Falkner agreed. "Griffin, come home with us. We'll have a family conference. All of us—Castor and Pollux, too. We'll decide what to do with your find."

"My find," Griffin said, slowly, savoring the words. "The planet Artemis, my find. All for the greater glory of the family Dane."

Adara listened with mounting apprehension as Falkner coaxed Griffin. From the quick briefing Bruin had given her, she gathered that of the three Danes who had come down to the planet, Falkner had been the least arrogant, the most thoughtful. Perhaps recognizing this, Siegfried and Alexander waited to learn if Falkner could persuade, now that they were no longer able to overpower.

Or are they merely waiting for this Gaius? Griffin seems confident that the warning Artemis now knows to give us will be enough, but what if it is not? Those "nerve burners" the Danes were carrying are nasty weapons.

Help came from the most unexpected quarter. Julyan spoke out, his singer's voice clear and carrying. "Don't believe him, Griffin. Either Falkner's lying to you or he's been fooled. They didn't just follow you—Alexander meant you dead."

Alexander's handsome mouth twisted as if he would speak, but Honeychild laid a black-clawed paw on one side of his neck and he fell silent.

Julyan continued. "Alexander bragged to me about what he'd done. He hates you, Griffin. Didn't you think it too much of a coincidence that a war machine attacked you so soon after your arrival?"

Eyes turned to Alexander. Honeychild moved her paw from his throat, granting mute permission to speak, but Alexander remained silent. Finally, Siegfried spoke in a voice rough with menace.

"Tell us what you did. Silence will serve you here, but not once we're home. You know that."

"*If* you get home," Adara added politely. "We rough primitives may not choose to wait upon the leisure of such dubious seegnur. Surely if your clan is as warlike as Griffin has told us, the loss of one member on such a dangerous mission would be acceptable. I'm sure Terrell wouldn't mind another go at you."

Terrell spat on the floor, the action all the more eloquent in contrast to his usual studied manners.

Whether Siegfried's threat or Adara's convinced him, Alexander broke his silence.

"I mounted a warbot beneath the shuttle's outer hull. I picked a model that folded flat and was sealed against damage from vacuum."

"Did you remove the outer plating to do this?" Falkner asked conversationally.

"I did."

"That may explain why Griffin crashed so quickly," Falkner continued. "We already know that—despite our conclusions to the contrary—the nanobots released by the attackers remained completely active. It's likely that when Alexander messed with the hull, he violated the shuttle's integrity."

"You'd already messed with the *Howard Carter* and the shuttle," Alexander protested. "You set it to send you alerts as to Griffin's position. You put a tracking device under his skin. The shuttle was gimmicked to release counters to the local nanobots, if they were still active. That's what gave me my idea. If our tech would work, why shouldn't I include a bit of my own?"

"He's insane," said Castor, the words all the more stinging considering their source. "Let Father and Mother deal with him."

"Insane! You just don't like that I was more clever than you. Falkner didn't find what I'd done. My spider was more than a mere warbot. I also included some nanobots designed to subvert Artemis's operating systems to our control."

"It didn't work, did it?" Adara said coolly but, remembering what Artemis had told her she thought, *And I'm not going to tell you how close it came to working—or that fighting against it was what brought Artemis to what she is today.*

Griffin had remained silent through this. There was something different about him, but it took Adara a moment to realize what it was. For as long as she had known him, there had been a mildness to Griffin, a calm temper that had made her disregard his claims of belonging to a warrior clan. That was gone. His brown eyes were alive now with fury, the detachment that so often dominated him vanished.

"I don't think my shuttle was the only thing tinkered with," Griffin said, and his voice held a new resonance. "I feel as if I've been just a little bit asleep all this time. Posthypnotic suggestion?"

Alexander snapped. "Don't try to blame me for that! Everyone agreed it was a good idea to keep you focused. You're so easily distracted by some interesting bit of anthropological trivia. We needed you to focus on finding traces of the Old Imperial technology."

He jerked his head around to look at Falkner and Siegfried. "Even if I did have something to do with the shuttle crashing, you should be grateful. That made Griffin focus down really hard. Who knows how long it might have taken him otherwise to find the landing facility and this place, especially given how well hidden they were?"

"Don't look for thanks," Siegfried retorted. "If you had your way, Griffin would be dead. I suppose you thought that we'd need to rely on you, then."

Alexander's expression showed that this was exactly what he *had* expected, but Griffin gave no further time for family bickering.

"Enough! We set out to resolve what to do with you. I never thought I'd be grateful to Julyan for anything, but I am for this." He turned to face his Artemesian allies and, once again, Adara was taken by the new brilliance in his expression. "As much as I hate to admit it, I agree with Siegfried that killing them would make matters worse. It's as if I had forgotten just how dangerous my family could be . . . That leaves us with two options: keeping them prisoners and getting them off planet."

"We need to talk about this privately," Terrell said firmly. "And we don't need them talking to each other while we do." He held up the med kit. "I'm betting there's something in here that will make them sleep. Griffin?"

"Good idea. If they're out, we don't even need to leave the room." Griffin rummaged through the kit. In a few moments, Falkner, Siegfried, and Alexander were all drowsing. Then he turned to Castor who stood, still fully armored, next to the boy he claimed was his dead twin. "How much did you know—honestly?"

"I knew they intended to use me to test some Old Imperial relics," Castor said. "I even knew you were involved, but not how. You know how my metabolism cripples me. They kept me in cold sleep for the trip. To be honest, I didn't mind. I haven't cared about much since Pollux's body died."

"I believe him," Bruin cut in. "They've treated him like a hunter treats a well-trained dog—valuable, certainly worthy of consideration, but not an equal."

Adara frowned. "Then is he one of them or—like you, Griffin—a tool?"

Castor answered for himself. "Whatever I was, everything is different now. I have found Pollux again. I will not leave him. Nor do I wish to take him 'home' with me. Our parents were never satisfied with how Pollux and I turned out. I do not particularly wish to give them a second chance at training us."

Pollux smiled ruefully. "Unlike you, Griffin, Castor and I long ago stopped wanting to please our parents, to prove ourselves worthy of their regard. We have discussed the matter and we'd rather remain here on Artemis, if Artemis and her guardians will have us."

Terrell drew in a ragged breath. "And that raises the point none of us have wanted to mention. Where do you stand in this, Griffin? You've been striving to get home for as long as we've known you. Now you can go. What will you do?"

Griffin ran his hands through his hair. "I've been thinking about little else since I realized what Siegfried and the others being here meant. If they'd treated me like one the team, you as my associates, I think there would be no question. Instead, they treated me as, at best, a 'little brother,' more often like an enemy. I guess they trusted whatever was done to me to make me easy to convince that it was all for the best, but that hold is broken."

He turned to Adara, kneeling in a curiously old-fashioned manner that she recognized as offering fealty. "My request would be the same as Castor's. I'd rather remain here on Artemis, if Artemis and her guardians will have me."

Adara cupped his face in her hands and kissed his forehead. "I believe we will keep you, Griffin, no longer of Dane. Terrell? Bruin? Honeychild? Sand Shadow? Do you agree?"

The nods were quick. Adara decided to overlook that Terrell's eyes were bright with unshed tears. She suspected that if Griffin had decided to leave, Terrell would have gone with him—the bond between them was that close.

She turned to Castor. "My heart believes what you say. Can we trust you to work with us?"

"For as long as I live," Castor said, "which may not be very long. My body needs fuel. When what concentrates we brought with us run out, I will die."

"I think I may have a solution for that," Adara said. "Not immediate, but at least by the time your supplies run low. Pollux? You are both of Artemis and of the void. Does your brother speak your wish as well?"

"He does," came the boy's voice with the man's intonation.

Again she asked for the others' assent. Again it was given. Again an oath was sworn—only words, yes, but she felt these were binding. Adara felt her heart thrill as if she had planned a difficult hunt and now had all the parts to set trap and snare.

"We are sworn together, to preserve Artemis and ourselves. I believe that in having you, we also have a solution to our problem. But first, we have one more problem to resolve. Julyan Hunter."

Julyan's pulse thudded in his ears as Adara turned that fiery amber gaze on him. She'd changed from the adoring girl he remembered, even from the young huntress he'd tracked and imagined subjecting to his lust and his will. He'd always seen the puma's grace and unusual beauty in her. Now he recognized the passion and danger as well.

"Griffin, you said that what Julyan revealed about Alexander's plan was a great help to you," Adara began. "Now I ask—was what he said enough to buy him his life and freedom? I admit I do not want him among us. Sand Shadow reminds me that the last time I took pity on him, Julyan repaid me by trying to drown me. Still, he has given service. I find I cannot fairly judge."

Although Adara had appealed to Griffin, it was Bruin who spoke. "Julyan worked for our enemies, but he never was unduly cruel. Not kind, no, but he never took advantage of his power."

"Perhaps," Terrell said, his tone hard and unforgiving, "because he had learned something about the abuses of power from Alexander."

"Terrell," Bruin said, "you are not one of my students, so forgive me for speaking to you this way. Cruelty rarely creates kindness. Indeed, the worst abusers are the abused. The almost littlest pup in the litter is the most likely to beat the littlest, not to show mercy."

"I'll have to take your word for that," Terrell said. "Maybe you're being soft on Julyan because he was your student. I can't forget he tried to kill Adara."

Griffin spoke up. "Adara, you asked if what Julyan said was helpful. It was. I'd entertained some similar speculations, but they alone were not enough. What broke the hold on my mind was hearing from another what Alexander had done. That opened my mind to consider that if Siegfried, Falkner, Gaius, and Jada were all involved, my parents had to at least have offered their tacit consent. Alexander's own outburst finished the matter."

Adara turned to Julyan. "If we set you free, what would you do? Will you return to the Old One's service? Would you like to go wherever Griffin's brothers go?"

"Not that," Julyan said, "not ever. Nor would I go after the Old One. He walked out and left me as easily as he left his soiled underclothes. I suppose I would go and seek a place as a hunter. There is value to having been a student of Benjamin Hunter. I don't expect you to believe me, but I have learned a few things about myself—and I'm not sure I like what I've learned. I now realize that the Old One cultivated the worst in me, teaching me to see people as things—me, who had been trained as a hunter, to respect the lives we take. I feel as if I've been insane and have a chance to reclaim myself."

Adara looked at the others. Three human nods. An eloquent shrug from a bear. A snarl from Sand Shadow.

"Go. Don't make us regret this second chance at mercy. Next time you *will* die. I ask you to remember that cats toy with their prey."

Julyan could hardly believe her words. "May I get my gear?"

"Yours," Adara said. "Not a bit more."

Pollux spoke. "The Seamus in me knows what was Julyan's. Shall Castor and I escort him?"

"Do."

Julyan turned and gave them each a deep reverence. "I sought to serve a power. I see I chose poorly."

Adara answered. "We were not a power—then."

"My brothers will be coming around soon," Griffin said when Julyan was out of hearing. "Adara, you said you had a plan."

"I want Ring here," the huntress replied. "Sand Shadow has gone to see if he will join us or if we must go to him."

A short time later, Sand Shadow escorted in Ring and Kipper. Ring appeared much more composed. Griffin wondered if this meant that probabilities were stabilizing or simply that Ring had grabbed a nap. He realized that he should be feeling more tired himself, but the thrill of having his mind clear again buoyed him up as if he'd had a large cup of Falkner's favorite blue drink.

"Here's what I'm thinking," Adara said. "Griffin, your family is large—seven sons and three daughters. However, with Castor and Pollux on our side, three of those sons are now here. Even better, your parents are certain to be curious about what has happened."

Castor, the visor on his helmet open but otherwise still armored, returned at that moment. "Yes. They're going to wonder if I really held Pollux in my head or if I've finally cracked all the way."

"They're also going to need to deal with Alexander," Griffin said. "I don't know what made him hate me so much, but I agree with the twins—he's insane."

"Griffin told us about the war that followed the slaughter of the seegnur and death of machines here on Artemis," Bruin said. "Do you think that having you three on Artemis will keep your parents from having the planet destroyed?"

Griffin laughed. "I'd like to think so. However, when Falkner gets back and starts babbling about the spaveks and Leto's complex and all the rest—that will surely stop them. We're not safe, but they're not going to want to destroy a treasure trove."

Terrell said darkly, "At least not unless they can't lay hands on it or one of their rivals get wind that Artemis really exists. Then . . ."

"That will take time," Adara said firmly. "Griffin, we have agreed we should not kill your brothers. Do we keep them as hostages or set them free?"

"I'm not being sentimental," Griffin said, "but I'd set them free. If we try to keep them as hostages, we also need to deal with the danger they represent. Even if we take every bit of their equipment—which represents a problem in and of itself—they are dangerous. I think we might win Falkner over in time, but the others? I can't guess . . ."

"Ring?" Adara looked at him. "You've heard what we've said. Can you offer guidance?"

"In every direction is storm and danger," Ring replied. "Nothing is clear or bright. But if we let them go, there is a little bit of light."

"That's clear enough," Terrell said. He frowned. "Ring, you can be pretty hard on your friends when that's what it takes to reach what you see as the best end. What purpose do you serve?"

"I serve Artemis, for without her there is not even hope."

They arranged for Gaius to pick up Siegfried, Alexander, and Falkner from a landing platform atop the mountain that held Leto's complex. The internal corridors had been filled with rubble but, using the scooters, they were able to get the prisoners to the top. After some consideration, they had decided to keep the scooters and other equipment—including the shuttle in which the Danes had arrived and which now remained beneath Mender's Isle.

"Their gear may have tracking beacons in it," Griffin said, "but it's not as if we're going to be all that hard to find—even though we've taken the tracers out of me and Castor—since we need to stay near Leto's complex. We'll disable what tracers we can, but I think having the gear outweighs the inconvenience. We'll also make sure no one . . ."

The Old One's name remained unspoken.

". . . can get into or use the shuttle."

Reluctantly, Griffin had decided to surrender the *Howard Carter* and all the ship contained. "I couldn't trust it not to blow on me. In any case, I'm not going anywhere, not for a long while."

Gaius was told to remain inside the shuttle, so Adara caught only a glimpse of the dark-skinned, white-haired man who sat stiffly behind the controls of a craft not unlike the one Griffin had crashed. The three prisoners climbed aboard, then the door slammed behind them. Nearly soundlessly, the craft rose, became a blackness against the stars, then vanished.

Sand Shadow, who had waited outside of Leto's zone, sent Artemis's confirmation that the shuttle had continued rising. Presumably, the brothers Dane had kept their word and departed the planet.

The rendezvous with Gaius had been arranged for the darkest part of the night. Even so, it was likely the residents of Crystalaire would have some new stories to tell about odd happenings near Maiden's Tear. That didn't matter. Although the loremasters didn't know it yet, the rules governing Artemis had changed, changed perhaps more drastically than they had even after the slaughter of the seegnur and death of machines.

After the shuttle departed, their group returned to Leto's valley. The air smelled of green stuff and vibrated with cricket song.

"I refuse," Terrell said, staring at Griffin, "to sleep one more night in that windowless hole. I'll work with you during the day, but I sleep out here."

Griffin forced a laugh. "I bet you'll change your mind next time it rains."

"What are you wagering?"

Bruin cut in before the disagreement could become serious. "Kipper has some suggestions for where we could place a camp closer to our door into Leto's complex and still be relatively hidden. Let's choose the best of both worlds."

Ring grunted, and the wordless sound gave Bruin's statement a note of prophesy.

Castor, no longer wearing the green spavek, but hovering near his new Pollux, said, "That seems like a good idea. We don't know if there may be other doors into Leto. Even she may not know. It's best we keep close enough to respond if she sends an alarm."

That sobered them. Adara knew they'd all been feeling safer since Sand Shadow had relayed that the Dane brothers were indeed gone.

"Right," Terrell said. "Still, I'd rather sleep outside tonight. I can't shake the feeling that someone's going to lock a door on me as soon as I let down my guard."

Griffin gave a lopsided grin. "I know how you feel. Fine. Outside it is."

"The weather will be fair tonight," Adara said. "Kipper and I will go get the camping gear. Sand Shadow and Honeychild can help us carry it. The rest of you clear a space and start something for dinner."

Kipper radiated hero worship as he led Adara to where he'd cached their gear. "Do you think we'll stay here long?"

"Some of us will," Adara said. "Leto's complex can't be left alone. That's going to mean a bunch of changes. Still, that's a hunt we can wait to plan for a few days at least."

"Nothing's going to be the same, is it?" the boy asked.

"No, it won't," Adara agreed, "but that's not necessarily a bad thing."

After helping set up a new camp and joining the rest for a dinner built around colored cubes, tea, and scavenged berries, Adara grabbed a few things and began to move into the night.

"Where are you going, ladybug?" Bruin asked.

"Outside Leto's zone," Adara replied. "Sand Shadow and I are going to keep her company. Artemis may be a world, but she does get lonely."

The night was lovely, dark, and deep . . . Adara stretched out her claws toward whatever lurked beyond the sky in a mute promise to defend what was hers. Then, pillowing her head against Sand Shadow's flank, she drifted off to sleep.

Interlude: Spreading Wings

Caterpillar spins a silk cocoon
Dreams of wings to reach the moon
With wings yet damp, splits the thread
Hangs feet up, down at head
Unable to creep or walk or fly
Joy and wonder yet multiply